ISLE OF SIN

S. FIRECOX

This is a work of fiction. Names, characters, places, and incidents are either the product of the author's imagination or are used fictitiously, and any resemblance to actual persons, living or dead, business establishments, events, or locales is entirely coincidental.

Isle of Sin

Editing by: A.S. Grayson

Cover Design: Raven Designs

Cover Photography: CJC Photography

Models: Eric Guilmette & Lauren

ISBN: 978-1-68530-113-2

Published by: Ninja Newt Publishing, LLC

Imprint: Sin Cave Publishing

Print Edition

ISLE OF SIN

Isle of Sin

There are three rules on Sinners Isle.
Submit.
Obey.
Consent.

Adalyn Rose didn't consent.
And the one who brought her here paid the ultimate price.
Now she's mine to care for. Mine to train. Mine to protect.

A sweet little heiress with a heart of gold.
And a body built for sin.

She'll kneel for me because she wants to.
Then we'll explore her limits.

Assuming her past doesn't come for us first.
Because her world of wealth and sin is filled with dark secrets.
Including one that may just cost me my life.

Turns out my isle was meant to be a training ground.
For *her*.
I ruined the game by claiming her as mine.
This affair of seduction and intrigue just turned into a battle of survival.

But they made one crucial mistake.
They brought this fight to *my* island.

Welcome to Sinners Isle.
Where dark fantasies come alive.
Allow me to be your guide...

About The Sinful 8

Isle of Sin is part of The Sinful 8 Collection, which is a series of standalone novels featuring the eight children of Mr. Sinner, a wealthy businessman who enjoyed indulging in the darker pleasures of life. Upon his death, he left a significant inheritance behind for his children, as well as a collection of eight dungeons that he'd purchased throughout the world.

All with the sole purpose of passing on one location to each child.

He only had one stipulation: *Each location is designed to cater to the various kinks of the BDSM community and cannot be used for anything else. However, my children can run the location as he or she chooses.*

The eight Sinner siblings divided the locations accordingly, agreeing as a unit to fulfill their father's wishes.

This novel features Asher Sinner, Mr. Nicholas Sinner's seventh child. Asher took over *Sinners Isle,* located on a private island in Fiji. His location specializes in wealth, secrets, and decadent pleasures.

And his story entangles him in a whole different world of pleasure and pain.

One none of the other Sinner children know about.

The world of Sin Cave and the Elite.

Introduction

Sin Cave is a global organization owned by four influential families, each of whom takes responsibility for a single arm of the business.

Sin Cave Fantasies—A members-only club that meticulously designs sexual fantasies to their clients' specific requirements. You won't find evidence of their locations online, but they're there—in every major city in the world. Membership is strictly by invitation only.

Elite Brides—Future wives of the world's elite, these women are provided with the best education money can buy, including a warfare-style program on elegance and societal expectations. In later years, they receive extensive education on the sinful deeds husbands enjoy behind closed doors.

Elite Maidens—Trafficked virgins who are put through a series of tests by a member of the Sin Cave Elite, including their tolerance to pain and sexual deviancy. If they meet the stringent expectations, they join the "Elite," a club with enormous privileges, where they are matched with a small selection of men whom they serve. Those who fail the tests are sold into brothels, where they will remain for the rest of their lives.

Ecstasy—A high-end chain of nightclubs catering to the rich and famous. Those deemed worthy are invited to become members of Sin Cave Fantasies or, in rare cases, to the Elite.

Welcome to Sin Cave.
You are about to enter the Elite Bride Training Program.
Where every path is carved and cultivated to suit the future husband's needs.
Each journey is woven with darkness and depravity.

Consent is not an option.
You either bow.
Or you endure a fate worse than death.

This world is not kind.
It's cruel.
It's corrupt.
And it's deadly.

But Adalyn is about to find her light...
Assuming she survives.

A Note From Sin

This novel contains scenes of non-consent, sexual violence, torture, blood play, and suicidal thoughts. These scenes involve the antagonists of the world, not the hero. Because Asher Sinner believes in consent and safe play. And with those notions in mind, he helps our heroine thrive. For this story is about healing, growth, and learning to overcome a horrific past.

S. Firecox

PROLOGUE: ADALYN

STAY SILENT.

Submit.

Survive.

That mantra radiated through my mind as I bit my lip to keep from screaming. Everything hurt. Everything stung. Everything *vibrated*.

The male behind me grunted, his release throbbing between us as he finally found his happily-ever-after. I hated him. I hated them all.

But I despised Nate most of all.

My *trainer*.

The fucking devil incarnate.

He smiled at me now as though he knew exactly what I was thinking. How badly I wanted to kill him. How much I loathed every fucking thing he made me do.

This was his idea of a celebration.

The end of my college education.

The beginning of my real future.

He saw this as an introduction to what my future husband would require of me—*sharing*.

My so-called freedom had come to an end. Tomorrow, we would leave for Nate's version of a graduation ceremony.

In Fiji.

Most people would be ecstatic by the prospect of going somewhere so exotic as a "graduation gift." But I knew better. I knew exactly what would happen there.

Wealthy sadists from around the world were being invited to partake in open season on my body.

It served as the culmination of all my mandated training.

Nate considered it a bachelorette party of a sort since I was scheduled to be married in a month. My husband-to-be might even come join in on the fun. However, I doubted he would bother. The whole purpose was to train me so I knew exactly what to do on our wedding night.

To spend time with me beforehand would prove futile.

This was the world of the rich and powerful.

A world I had been born into without any say as to my future or whom I would end up with.

They'd called me an *Elite Bride* from the day of my birth. Fruitful arrangements had been made, and my training had begun.

There were no alternatives.

Nowhere to run.

Nowhere to hide.

Not when it came to this society of dominance and prestige.

To escape would result in a fate worse than death.

My father expected me to show up at that altar, trained and prepared to be a proper high-society wife. Nate was the one assigned to ensure that happened.

And he was *very* skilled at his job.

Except for one minor detail—he hadn't broken me yet.

It was a secret I harbored deep within, a secret he almost brought out to the surface tonight.

But I dropped my gaze with a forced grimace, submitting once more.

Stay silent. Submit. Survive.

I knew how to play this game. I'd mastered every angle.

And in Fiji, I would finally make my move.

CHAPTER ONE
ASHER

Is she there yet?

The text sprawled across my phone, disrupting my morning routine of reading current news reports from around the globe.

Yeah, I typed back. *Just going through a final security check at the gate.*

Bet she loves that was Tru's reply.

I expected your message to be another rant from her, I admitted, my lips twitching at the sides. *She's already sent three.*

Sounds like our baby sister. His words deepen my amusement. Darby hates when we rag on her for being the baby of the family. *Give her a hug for me*, Tru adds.

I'd invite you to join and give her one yourself, but I don't really want you on my island, I replied, smirking as I imagined my older brother's resulting expression from reading my message.

Worried I may run that isle of yours better than you, hmm? he taunted.

Worried you might try to turn it into a voyeuristic playground, I retorted.

Isn't that what it is already?

I snorted. *Only for those who want it.* Which wasn't many, considering the clientele I serviced at Sinners Isle.

All seven of my siblings had inherited a club after our father's death. I'd taken the one out in the middle of the Pacific Ocean. Mostly because I preferred isolation and had a knack for keeping secrets. The elite of the world frequented my club because they enjoyed the anonymity my isle offered them.

Which was also why Darby had chosen to come here for her belated honeymoon with Yon and their now one-year-old son.

I'd made nanny arrangements for them for the week to ensure they had some private time, too.

Private time that I didn't intend to be involved with whatsoever.

It was hard enough knowing my younger sister was into kink, just like the rest of us. I didn't need to know what type or how far that kink went.

Which probably made me a hypocrite because I didn't care at all about Truman's preferences. Which was how I knew about his penchant for voyeurism and exhibitionism.

Most of my other siblings were pretty open about their likes and dislikes, too.

I supposed that came with the territory of owning a string of dungeons and sensual clubs around the globe.

My phone dinged again, this time with a message about another incoming arrival—Nathan Spencer and his guest, Adalyn Rose.

I didn't typically greet my guests personally at the airport, but as I was already here to collect my sister, I opted to also make myself available for Mr. Spencer. His seven-year-old membership to Sinners Isle had placed him on a priority list, yet we'd never had the pleasure of meeting.

Mostly because Mr. Spencer had only visited twice during that period of time. Both times had occurred during one of my many trips to New York City to see Tru.

So this would be our first proper introduction.

I shot another text off to my brother with a promise to call him later, then slipped my phone into my pocket and stood.

There were only a few lingering employees at the private lounge inside the airport, all of them mine.

Because I owned this entire island.

It was arranged with water bungalows and huts along the shores, offering the privacy my clients craved.

With a variety of play areas set up throughout the island.

An erotic paradise that many celebrities and wealthy patrons fancied for their own lurid affairs. Discretion was the name of the game. And sex was our primary currency.

Our resort catered to every need and kink, and we took our security very seriously.

Hence the men outside scrutinizing the jet my sister had just flown in on.

You're going to be an old man by the time I get off this jet, Gramps, she told me in a new message now. *All gray and decrepit.*

Already halfway there, Kid, I sent back to her, chuckling at the nicknames we'd given each other years ago. I was the second youngest in our family of eight, with her being the baby.

She was almost twenty-eight now.

And I was only a few months shy of turning thirty.

Making us less than two years apart.

Yet *I* was the old man.

I shook my head, chuckling to myself. I supposed that made our oldest brother, Damiano, positively ancient in comparison.

"Yep, totally gray," my sister said as she burst through the loading door ahead of my personnel. They would be annoyed, but they wouldn't dare comment. The Sinner children were infamous and very much in charge.

And Darby was no different, even as the youngest.

"Can you see me from all the way over there?" she asked, squinting at me. "I hear old age impacts vision and all that."

"Maybe you should call Eli or Damiano and ask them about it," I suggested, starting toward her. "They're almost forty, right?"

"And you're almost thirty," she replied, visibly shuddering. "When did you and Tru get so old?"

I laughed and wrapped my arms around her in a hug while meeting the dark gaze of her husband over her head. "I have no idea how you put up with her full-time, Yon."

He chuckled in response, his hands busy guiding the stroller before him. "I'll have help soon once the little man starts growing up."

Darby rolled her big brown eyes as she released me. "Cute." The word seemed to be directed at both of us. At least until she added, "Let's see if you get laid later."

"Oh, I definitely will be," Yon replied, a hint of his dominance underlying those words as he glanced down at the collar around Darby's neck.

Her cheeks turned pink, her long eyelashes fanning downward as she gave him a demure look.

A look I really did not want or need to see on my sister's face right now.

I cleared my throat. "I know you're eager to start the honeymoon, but how about we wait until you reach your bungalow, yeah?"

Their son, Graham, chose that moment to coo, almost as though to say he agreed. Darby immediately turned toward him, fussing in a way our mom used to do over us as kids.

At least over me, Darby, and Tru.

We all shared the same biological mother and father, while our siblings had other mothers. Two, to be exact.

But it didn't stop us from being close.

And while our father had been married three times, he hadn't exactly been a bad dad or husband. He'd just liked variety and struggled with the concept of monogamy.

A trait some of us shared with him.

Others, like my sister, not so much.

However, we all enjoyed various levels of the lifestyle. Probably because of our father's influence and the clubs he'd gifted us upon his death.

"Mister Sinner?" David's voice came from behind me, causing me to turn toward him. "Your guests are deplaning."

I nodded. "Can you escort my sister and her family to the car? I'll join after I finish the introduction."

David dipped his chin. "Of course, sir."

Darby raised a brow at me. "Guests?"

My lips twitched. "Guests who prefer their anonymity, Kid. Follow David and I'll be right out."

She scoffed at that. "I'm part owner."

"An owner of the London location who is on her honeymoon and not working," I clarified for her. "Just let me handle this one thing, and I promise I'll give you a proper tour after."

Yon pressed his palm to her lower back, his opposite hand still on the stroller. "It'll take us a few minutes to get everything situated anyway."

Darby considered him for a moment and shrugged. "I'm on vacation."

"You're on vacation," he echoed, giving me a knowing look as Darby's focus shifted to little Graham again.

Thank you, I mouthed.

He dipped his chin slightly, then escorted my sister away from the airport lounge and through the exit with David leading the way.

I ran my fingers through my hair and fixed my tie, then blew out a long breath and waited for Mr. Spencer to arrive.

Unlike my sister, he didn't barge through the loading doors, instead allowing my security to enter first. He stepped through the threshold with a stern expression, his demeanor all dominant male as he moved.

This was the kind of guy used to being the alpha in the room.

I'd allow it.

Even if it wasn't accurate at all.

This island was mine, making me king of Sinners Isle. However, I could pretend to bow if it put my clients at ease. That ease made them easier to read.

And I prided myself on being able to understand the intentions of others.

It was what made me a good Dominant—the ability to understand body language and discern the less-than-obvious cues.

Cues like Mr. Spencer's astute gaze and the sharp look

he gave my security as he realized there were more of them in this room.

They were here to protect me, and Mr. Spencer knew it, too.

His focus turned to me as he openly debated my trustworthiness and evaluated my worth.

I didn't let the scrutiny bother me. I merely stood in the center of the room and waited for him to approach.

Because this wasn't a typical hotel operation. I had a general manager who oversaw the accommodations, while I maintained the entire operation.

That distinction provided me with a very different role in this relationship.

Because in my world, the customer was not always right.

I decided who maintained membership here and who did not.

Thus giving me an air of superiority in this situation.

However, I affected a casual front, allowing Mr. Spencer to feel like he owned the room. That lie caused his lips to curl a little, his overconfidence leaving a hint of distaste in my mouth.

A distaste that worsened as a female with dark hair stepped into view behind him.

She kept her eyes on the ground, exuding the picture of perfect submission.

Which would have been fine if we were in the club or in an open play area, not in the middle of an airport lobby. That posture alone told me a lot about Mr. Spencer's dynamic with Adalyn Rose—Master and slave.

Except she didn't wear a collar around her neck.

Nor did she appear to have any other markings on her that denoted her as *owned*.

Her heels clicked lightly against the tiles, her legs long and athletic like a dancer, moving gracefully with every step.

A gorgeous woman.

With a body built for sin.

Yet those lowered eyes grated at my instincts. Something felt wrong with her submission, almost as though it was forced rather than readily given.

A strange inkling, one that had me looking at Mr. Spencer again.

He'd caught my perusal—something that seemed to amuse him more than anger him.

He must be into sharing, I thought, recalling some of his requests for his visit. A private bungalow—a standard requirement. But with an open entertaining area.

Because he intended to have friends stop by to visit his sub.

How do you feel about that, little one? I wondered, glancing at her again. *Do you like to be shared?*

Her dark irises lifted as though she'd heard me, her cheeks darkening to a pretty ruby shade as she found me openly evaluating her.

A hint of defiance crossed her features, causing her nostrils to flare.

And then she was staring at the floor again.

Just as Mr. Spencer glanced back at her.

Almost like she'd known to expect his look.

An odd dynamic, I decided, making a mental note to keep an eye on Mr. Spencer and his activities.

There were very few rules at Sinners Isle, as I preferred to allow my patrons to set their own limits. But consent sat at the top of the list in terms of items I would not negotiate on.

Safewords were paramount. While the word "no" could often be heard from various areas of my island, it was always moaned in a way that actually meant "more." And that was absolutely tolerated, if not *expected,* here.

But consent still mattered.

"Mr. Sinner," Mr. Spencer said, holding out a hand. "It's a pleasure to finally meet you."

"My father was Mr. Sinner," I replied, accepting his palm. "Please call me Asher."

"Of course." He tightened his grip just a little, exerting his dominance. I didn't react, just shook his hand and released him.

"I don't often greet my guests, but I saw you were flying in today and thought it would be good to finally introduce myself," I told him, making sure he understood that this wasn't typical and that I'd given him special attention.

It served as an ego stroke.

And also a warning.

Because now that I'd seen his little sub, I would be watching him.

My senses told me something just wasn't right here, and I'd learned long ago to never ignore my instincts.

However, I hid that inclination now with a smile. "Your accommodations are ready, and your driver will take you directly to your bungalow. Then Cassandra will be by in an hour to discuss your meal preferences for the week." Each guest was given their own private chef, as well as a housekeeper, for their stay. Of course, my staff didn't reside in the bungalow with them. They had their own lavish apartments elsewhere.

And they were invited to play as the mood struck them.

An employee perk.

One I sometimes indulged in myself.

With females like Adalyn Rose, I thought, glancing at her again. *Beautiful brunette with curves in all the right places. Absolutely my type.*

Except for that hint of wrongness.

Hmm.

I refocused on Mr. Spencer. "I'll be around for the week as well. My private line is in your welcome materials. If you need anything at all, please let me know directly and I'll see to it personally."

"Thank you. I actually may need to take advantage of that offer sooner rather than later."

"Oh?" I raised a brow, genuinely intrigued. His concierge should have handled any and all preliminary requests. "Was something missed in your initial booking?"

"No, I've just had a few colleagues inform me that they are planning some spontaneous visits to the island this week. I'd like to organize a gathering, if possible."

"In a play area?" I guessed aloud while mentally making a note to check on these "colleagues" he was expecting this week. I had a list of all anticipated arrivals and their known associations. I would have to check them against Mr. Spencer's dossier.

He nodded. "Yes, and I will have a list of necessary instruments."

Adalyn flinched with the words, the movement barely perceptible but there. And it wasn't the kind of flinch that told me she was excited by the prospect of his request. "I see," I said, in reference to both her grimace and his statement. "I'll see what I can do."

And I'll absolutely be watching you, I added in my mind.

"I assume this will be a private affair for just you and your colleagues?" I guessed, still holding his gaze while observing Adalyn's reactions from the corner of my eye.

"Yes, but there may be others I'll invite along the way," he replied, his tone and expression suggesting that I might be on that list if I played my cards right.

However, his statement elicited another wince from Adalyn.

So you don't like to be shared, I thought at her. *Do you even want to be here, little one?*

I cleared my throat, my lips curling into a practiced grin. "If you provide me with your list, I'll oversee your arrangements personally." *Because something is very wrong here and I don't allow this type of fuckery on my island.*

"Excellent," Mr. Spencer replied. "I look forward to getting to know you better then, Asher."

"Likewise, Mr. Spencer," I said, meaning it.

"Nate," he corrected. "Since we're on a first-name basis now."

"Of course." I purposely used his term from earlier and gave him another smile. "Well, I'll show you to your transport, then, and perhaps we can arrange to have breakfast tomorrow morning."

"I would like that."

"Me, too," I said, glancing at Adalyn. "She's welcome to attend if you wish to bring her."

His smile turned lecherous, the look sending a chill down my spine. "I just may do that."

Her fingers curled into fists at her sides, then quickly relaxed.

But it was enough to tell me she very much did not want to join us for breakfast.

Which meant that if he brought her, she was absolutely not being looked after properly. Because a good Master would ensure his slave's comfort, even if he preferred sadism and darker games.

"This way." I gestured toward the exit, leading them both out while considering how to approach tomorrow morning's meeting.

I would need to have Clive and Bryant there for security purposes, just in case I chose to physically remove Nathan Spencer from my island.

Adalyn would be another matter entirely.

I nearly cursed because a broken sub was not what I wanted to deal with right now. But the task came with owning the territory. Fortunately, I'd just not had to deal with this sort of thing often. Most of my clients weren't stupid enough to show up here with a non-consenting partner.

Oscar, one of my drivers, stood just outside by one of the luxury cars, awaiting Nathan and Adalyn. I walked them both right to him and turned to shake Nathan's hand again. He didn't try to squeeze this time, likely because he'd already decided he was the bigger man in the room. Or perhaps he intended to use Adalyn to tame me, as he'd likely taken my frequent glances her way as sexual interest, not genuine concern.

"I'll have Cassandra provide you with details for breakfast," I told him.

"Or we can have breakfast in my bungalow," he offered, saying the words like he owned the property and not me.

I considered him for a moment, debating locations before glancing at Adalyn once more. "I think I would like that." Because it just proved that he didn't care at all about her comfort or he'd notice the way her shoulders tensed now at my acceptance of his insinuated proposition—breakfast with a side of fucking in his bungalow.

"Nine o'clock?" he asked.

“Sounds perfect,” I replied, releasing his hand before my instinct to rip his arm off took over.

Maybe I was reading Adalyn’s discomfort the wrong way.

But she certainly appeared ready to break right now with how rigidly she held her spine.

However, Nathan opened the door for her and gently helped her into the car, his soft touch belying the way he’d just put her body on offer.

I’d have to observe them a bit more to determine the truth of this situation.

Which I’d do over breakfast.

“Enjoy your afternoon and evening,” I told Nathan as he slid into the car.

“Oh, I intend to.” He wrapped his arm around Adalyn, but the door closed before I could see her reaction.

Oscar immediately moved around the car to take the driver’s seat. I only watched for a beat before turning toward the car waiting for me behind them.

Fortunately, Darby and Yon were already in the back seat. Otherwise, I suspected my sister would have a few questions. She knew me better than most people did, and she’d absolutely be able to pick up on my concern, even while I hid it behind a professional mask of indifference.

Thankfully, I intended to sit in the front passenger seat.

Which meant she wouldn’t be able to see my face for another ten minutes or so.

By the time we arrived at her bungalow, I’d have my emotions under control and she wouldn’t have a clue as to what nagged at me.

This wasn’t her Sinner location to manage; it was mine. And she deserved to enjoy this honeymoon. So I’d ensure she did while I handled the Nate and Adalyn situation quietly.

Just another day in the life of being a Sinner sibling.

By this time tomorrow, it'd be dealt with and done.

Until then, I'd relax. Show my sister and Yon around. Introduce them to their babysitter. And wish them well on their honeymoon.

CHAPTER TWO
ADALYN

Nate's palm landed on my ass, the slap leaving behind a stinging sensation that rivaled the other marks he'd just put on my body. None of them would leave a permanent mark. But that didn't make them any less painful.

"Up," he demanded, his voice cold. "Go shower and prepare yourself for dinner."

I eagerly accepted his reprieve, exhausted after being in his presence here all day.

He'd been... creative.

Playing with toys.

Knives.

Items meant to prolong my torment and enhance his pleasure alone.

I shivered, my body bruised and abused and bleeding.

Nate wouldn't care. He never did. But tonight marked a new experience between us, one defined by the single bed in this bungalow.

He intended for me to *sleep* beside him.

Or perhaps on the floor.

There wasn't a cage, which meant he didn't plan to lock

me up. And that provided the opportunity I'd been looking forward to on this trip.

He used to lock me up after fucking.

Because I'd often fought back.

But I'd eventually learned that obedience could earn rewards—like a taste of freedom.

One day, he hadn't locked me up, just left me in the basement dungeon.

A few weeks later—or maybe it was months; I wasn't sure—he'd given me a bedroom with windows.

When I hadn't run, he'd started leaving the door unlocked.

After that, I'd been allowed to roam the house he'd kept me in.

That had later escalated to being enrolled in university courses.

Then the ultimate test had come when he'd allowed me to move into an apartment with another girl. Not an Elite Bride like me, but an ordinary student.

Jenica Roberts.

She'd become my one and only friend.

Yet she didn't really know me at all.

Because I hadn't been allowed to tell her anything about me. Our whole living situation had served as the ultimate test, one I knew Nate heavily monitored.

So I'd played every move correctly, all the while pretending to be the perfect little slave.

I'd attended my university classes as expected.

I'd shown up for my requisite hours at Ecstasy—a sex club owned by the Sin Cave Elite—every single week.

I'd knelt for Nate every time he'd demanded it. Sucked whoever's cock he'd told me to suck. Fucked until I couldn't walk. Had done every sick and depraved thing he'd demanded of me without trying to fight him.

All to gain his trust.

To lead to this moment.

The one where he finally let his guard down because he thought his job was done.

I should be at some college graduation celebration right now, bonding with Jenica over our college accomplishments and reminding her how Logan Pierce didn't deserve her. If he wasn't going to man up and own his feelings in front of her brother, then Jenica needed to move on and find a new love. She needed to *live* and enjoy life. She deserved better than a man who wanted to keep everything a secret.

But I couldn't tell her any of that.

Because I was standing in this magnificent bathroom adorned with marble floors and stone walls with decorative gold fixtures. Too lost. Too unfeeling. Too busy staring at my body reflected in a mirror that spanned an entire wall.

Bruises. Bleeding cuts. Handprints and fingerprints. Rope burn. I truly resembled a broken woman.

Which was exactly what I desired.

Exactly what I *needed*.

Nate wouldn't second-guess me in this state. He'd relax and eat his food and either invite me into the bed or send me to the floor.

Regardless of where I ended up, it would be near him. Near where he slept. Near where he would finally be somewhat vulnerable in my presence.

Near where I could hurt him.

He knew I hated him.

But he also assumed I would never do anything to stop him. Because he'd drilled the consequences firmly into my head, telling me over and over again how much better my life would be as an Elite Bride.

I might have to fuck every male my husband brought home, but at least I'd be respected in society. A woman of worth. A wife to an Elite.

Fighting my future would remove any and all aspects of protection afforded to an Elite Bride.

Nate was convinced that I knew better than to test his theories.

But he failed to understand that I would prefer that fate to bending over and taking it for society's enjoyment.

There might not be any true escape.

There might not be any alternative.

However, I would hate myself if I didn't try to do something to fight this.

They might catch me and subject me to a life of misery. But if Nate had taught me anything, it was that my life would be miserable either way.

So why not take charge? Why not test my fate? Why not end this training game *my way*?

I smiled, the expression oddly cold in the mirror.

A haunting image that imprinted itself in my mind as I moved to take my shower.

That smile was still there even as I flinched from the water touching my fresh cuts. Even as I soaped myself up and grimaced from the resulting stings and tenderness. Even as the water washed all the soap and grime away. Even as I eventually dried off and found the mirror again.

My lips were no longer curling.

But they were inside my mind.

Because I had a plan. A lethal one. And tonight, I intended to act.

Just not yet.

I still had a submissive role to play.

I braided my damp hair the way Nate liked, the strands the color of midnight from the water glittering against the dark color. An appropriate look, one that matched the hardening of my eyes.

Yet I softened them almost immediately, aware of what Nate would expect to see in my features.

Perfect, I thought, ready to play my final role.

There were no alternatives to my plan. Nate had made it quite clear that he intended to start his sharing activities tomorrow with the owner of this fucked-up little island. And I just wasn't interested.

Well, no. That was a bit of a lie. I'd stolen a peek at the man in charge—*Asher Sinner*—and I hadn't been appalled by his features at all.

However, I knew what kind of man lurked beneath that flawless skin. He had *sadist* practically engraved into his nearly black eyes. And while I enjoyed a little pain with my pleasure, I knew he would go too far. They all did.

As a test.

To expand my limits.

To deaden me to the world.

Hence the fresh wounds on my body now. They would heal, and the ointment Nate had provided would help reduce any potential scarring.

My future husband wanted me perfect, after all.

Sexy. Confident. A well-cultured bride in public. A willing deviant in the bedroom.

That was what all Elite Brides represented—high-society blood with a penchant for masochism.

But it wasn't by choice. No, we were *trained.* Forced. Taken from our homes in our teens and given to men like Nate Spencer.

My jaw clenched, the action there and gone in a blink. My eyes took on a glassy appearance once more, my lips pouty, my expression utterly submissive.

Practiced.

Cultivated.

A mask I'd created and perfected to hide my every thought.

I'm ready, stepping away from the mirror and heading toward the door. No clothes. No towel. Just my freshly cleaned body and braided hair.

Nate would have told me if he expected me to wear anything at the table. But all he'd told me to do was shower and prepare myself. That meant he wanted me without clothes and on my knees.

I moved through the bedroom without looking up from the plush carpeted floor, into the hallway lined with marble tile. There was a living area with white furniture and more marble fixtures, framed by patio doors that opened to a staircase that led down into the ocean.

I'd momentarily contemplated jumping off them and swimming until I found new land or drowned.

But knowing I would be alone with Nate tonight had kept me secure and sane.

Just as it kept me steady as I continued through the living area to the dining room, just off the full kitchen.

A kitchen that has knives, I thought as I went to my knees beside the head of the table. I bowed my head, my face carefully blank, and waited.

This was another one of Nate's tests. A way to ensure my absolute submission.

Because he hadn't been in the bedroom, living area, or anywhere around the table when I'd entered. Which meant he'd stepped out for a moment. Probably to take a call. Or perhaps to wait outside to see if I deviated from his instructions.

I wouldn't give him a reason to punish me.

Not tonight.

Not when I was so close to my goal.

I counted to five hundred before Nate returned, his flip-flops flapping as he walked through the apartment-like bungalow. He said something to the chef about leaving early, saying he would handle serving the food.

She left without argument, probably eager to be out of his presence. He put on a good show, but she'd likely heard some of the acts from the bedroom while preparing food this afternoon.

I'd done my best to keep silent. But there were times when I couldn't hold back my scream.

Those were the times Nate loved best.

He usually came when I cried out in agony.

Sometimes I screamed just to end my suffering.

Other times, I kept quiet because I knew that was his desire. He wanted to work for it. Those were our worst sessions.

Today had fallen somewhere in between. I'd been so caught up in my endgame that I hadn't really felt it. However, I'd definitely screamed loud enough for Chef Cassandra to hear.

"You're such a good pet," Nate praised, patting my head as he stopped by the table. "Maybe I'll feed you more than my cock tonight, hmm?"

"Thank you, Master," I replied, the phrase one that he'd etched into my tongue years ago.

Yes, Master. As you wish, Master. Whatever pleases you, Master.

I'm going to kill you, Master.

That last line was for me.

One I'd vowed years ago.

A promise I would fulfill. *Tonight.*

Nate busied himself with fixing a single plate and some wine, then joined me at the table a handful of minutes later.

He didn't invite me to sit.

He expected me to stay on my knees.

It was a position I knew well.

Nate took his time eating his fill, forcing me to hear him chew and swallow and "Mmm" as he enjoyed his meal.

My stomach rumbled in response, my throat parched for a drink.

But I knew better than to ask.

When he finally finished, he set his mostly empty plate on the floor and told me to "lick it clean."

Which I did. Because it might be the only food he'd give me.

He fixed himself some sort of dessert while I licked up the steak juice and residual mashed potatoes from his dish. I made it spotless, knowing he would call me ungrateful and punish me if I left anything behind.

"That's my good little whore," he said, picking up the plate and replacing it with a smaller dish of cut-up meat. "I made you an extra treat. No hands."

"Thank you, Master." I bent to pick up a piece of grilled chicken with my teeth, aware that this was his way of rewarding my good behavior. Rejecting that gift would not end well.

I ate every bite while he indulged in his dessert.

That dish he didn't give me.

My diet consisted of lean meats, vegetables, and other

lower-fat foods that kept my body in prime shape for my future husband.

For all the food Nate consumed, he at least managed to maintain a decent physique. It wasn't like he had a six-pack, but he didn't have much of a gut either.

He was actually fairly decent-looking. Forty-two years old, blond hair, hazel eyes, a hint of a five o'clock shadow on his square jaw, over six feet tall, and athletically built.

When we'd first met, I'd found him attractive.

At least until he'd introduced me to his violent side.

But his looks added to his overall charm, which allowed him to enchant others rather easily. That was what made him such a good trainer—he knew exactly how to play the society game, whom to rub elbows with, and how to appease his benefactors.

While being an absolute sadist behind closed doors.

A monster, even.

He collected my dish from the floor and walked away. "Head back," he said as he returned.

I didn't look at him, but at the ceiling, as I knew he wouldn't appreciate direct eye contact.

He pressed a bottle of water to my lips. "Open."

I stole a quick breath, then did as he asked and started swallowing as he fed me the water.

He wouldn't stop until I choked.

So I took as much as I could, trying to make it last as long as possible, before eventually sputtering. He made me inhale a few drops before he finally took the bottle away, the bastard always finding subtle ways to assert his dominance.

I coughed a little, the sound forcibly quiet.

Then he repeated it twice more until the bottle was gone.

"I need to make some calls regarding your schedule this week. Wait for me in the bed."

"Yes, Master," I replied, forcing myself not to smile.

Because that meant I was right about his intentions for tonight.

He's going to let his guard down.

And he's just given me some freedom to properly prepare.

It's finally time.

CHAPTER THREE
ADALYN

Nate's snores filled the room, the repetitive sound making my heart race.

It's time.

He'd allowed me to sleep beside him in the bed, his big arm clamped around me as though he owned me. His words from before he fell asleep still rattled through my mind.

"We only have thirty more days together. I want to make them count."

He'd almost sounded sad. Like he was disappointed that he'd be losing the pet he'd just spent the last six years training.

Like we would be "breaking up."

Which would imply I'd been with him willingly from the beginning.

A preposterous notion.

I was just a project. A means to an end. A female for him to break for the benefit of another man—*Taylor Huntington*. My betrothed.

Not if I can help it, I thought, my pulse thrumming with anticipation.

Nate liked his knives. And he'd left several out in the room. All of them sharp and deadly. Just like the butcher's knife I'd hidden in the nightstand.

I'd positioned weapons all over, uncertain of which one would do the trick.

But he'd made this so easy by falling asleep next to me.

All I had to do was dislodge his arm and grab a knife.

I squirmed a little, inching out from beneath his grasp and freezing every time his breathing changed.

Slowly. Slowly. Slowly.

Almost there.

Just a little more...

If he wakes, I'll tell him I need to pee.

So close.

Just a few more in—

His snoring stopped.

I paused, holding my breath. *I just have to go to the bathroom,* I reminded myself. *If he wakes up, that's my excuse. He shouldn't care, right?*

My heart thudded loudly in my ears, drowning out all the sound.

Until he released another soft little snore. It wasn't as loud as the others, more of a reverberation that suggested he was falling back to sleep.

I waited for several beats, counting to two hundred before I started to move again.

The drumming in my ears made me dizzy, my exhales sounding too loud in the room. *Focus. Breathe. Calm down.*

But I couldn't seem to stop shaking, not even when I finally slipped free of his grasp. If anything, I trembled more.

Go to the bathroom, I told myself. *Just in case he wakes up.*

That way I would have an excuse for moving around.

Swallowing, I forced myself to move. My hands were clammy, my chest aching from my erratic breaths.

I closed the door of the bathroom and pretended to use the toilet. Then I splashed water over my face instead of washing my hands.

It helped a little, the cooling liquid grounding me in the present.

I took my time drying myself off, needing the moment to calm down.

You can do this, Adalyn, I said, meeting my gaze in the mirror. *You know where the knives are. Pick one and slit his throat.*

I counted several more beats, willing my heart to stop racing.

And slipped back into the room.

Nate hadn't moved, his snores still soft and even.

I crept across the carpet toward the nightstand, my focus on him, waiting for him to react. It would be just like him to set all this up as some sort of test.

Because everything with Nate was a test.

My throat worked, my mouth feeling dry, as I reached the drawer.

I gently pulled it out, careful not to make a sound, and slid my hand inside.

Only, I felt nothing.

No cold steel.

No handle.

Nothing at all.

My brow furrowed. *Did I accidentally push it to the back when closing it earlier?* I glanced down, the darkness of the room making it difficult to see.

Pulling the drawer out a little more, I bent to search for the knife.

It's not there.

How—

"Looking for something, Adalyn?" Nate's deep tone sent a chill down my spine. It wasn't laced with sleep at all. But very awake.

I gradually returned my gaze to where he lounged in the bed, his long body reminding me of a jungle cat. All lazy arrogance.

And in his hand was a blade.

"*Kneel.*" He uttered the word with all the force of his dominance, making my legs quake with the need to obey.

I almost did.

I almost fell to the ground in submission to beg for my life.

But I knew how much he would make this hurt.

Sadistic energy poured off him in waves, that knife appearing all the more dangerous in his hand.

He might not kill me. But he would injure me severely. Then invite his friends this week to prolong my agony, to torture my body and spirit until I finally broke.

I was already so close to that edge.

I refused to cross it. Refused to let him degrade me for another second.

I didn't want this life or the future his training had prepared me for.

I wanted freedom. Even if it was temporary. Even if it would worsen my fate that much more.

I craved his death. His blood. His *screams*.

That knife wasn't the only one in the room. He had a bag of toys only a few feet away.

I just had to lunge for it.

"What was one of our first rules together?" he asked silkily, sitting up in the bed. "Someone is always watching."

I took a step back as he continued to shift, his movements leisurely yet undeniably purposeful as he gestured around the room.

"There are cameras everywhere."

I swallowed. *Of course there are. Why wouldn't there be?*

This island was just a glorified hotel version of Ecstasy, something I should have known upon arrival. But I'd been so caught up in my hope and desire to kill Nate that I hadn't considered there being cameras in our room.

I'd thought he believed me to be broken, that he'd finally let his guard down.

I should have known better.

I should have been more discreet.

I should have thought this through.

But I'd been desperate to flee.

Desperate to *kill*.

"I know where you put every knife, Adalyn." One leg slid off the bed. "I watched your every move. Just as I always watch your every move."

Another chill kissed my lower neck, spreading down my back. My knees locked as I tried to move away from him, making me feel clumsy and wrong on my feet.

"I'm so glad you did this, baby," he murmured, standing now. "I've missed our early days. And you just gave me permission to return to those darker moments to break you all over again."

He smiled, his teeth flashing in the darkness in a way that resembled a true nightmare come to life.

"So thank you, Adalyn. This is the best gift you could have given me after our time together."

Oh God. If I hadn't known before that he planned to truly harm me, I did now.

I either fought for my life or finally succumbed to the pressure to indefinitely hide within my mind.

The latter wasn't acceptable.

Making this an obvious choice.

I fight.

But I had to be smart about it. Smarter than I was before.

"I-I'm sorry, Master," I whispered, allowing him to hear my fear. It would lull him into a state of triumph, help inflate that confidence just a little more.

"You're not," he countered. "But you will be soon."

I knelt beside his toy bag, attempting to show my subservience. However, my gaze didn't really go to the ground. It went to the unzipped leather bag beside me.

He might have seen me stash knives around the room, but I'd never once touched his toys.

Because I was already intimately familiar with them.

I knew what each tool did. How sharp they were. How they felt against my skin.

There were several I could use against Nate. I just needed him to be vulnerable first.

I peered down into the unzipped bag, searching for a glint of silver. But the dark room cast everything in shadows. I'd be going in blind, which wasn't going to work.

This has to be executed perfectly.

I'd already messed up once. I couldn't afford to do it again. He was amused right now. If I pushed him too far, he'd become enraged.

An enraged version of Nate was dangerous. Lethal, even.

He owned my life.

I might be a promised bride to an Elite member, but if I proved to be too difficult for the role, the society in charge would grant Nate full immunity for his actions. They would consider it my fault that I couldn't conform, not Nate's.

A fucked-up reality.

One I intended to end.

I just needed to play this right.

"Hmm," he hummed, stepping behind me to drag the sharp edge down my spine. Just hard enough for me to feel the threat without drawing blood.

I swallowed, my gaze begging for a light to be able to see the contents of his bag. They were all in a meticulous order. I should be able to do this blind.

But the stinging sensation against my skin distracted me, my heart racing for an entirely new reason now.

Especially as he met the crevice of my ass and drew downward.

He paused at the puckered hole.

Pressing in slightly, making me bite my lip to hold back my cry of pain as he inserted it enough to make me bleed.

Fuck...

He twisted it a little, scattering goose bumps down my arms. *He... he won't... right? He won't actually—*

The blade disappeared, drawing an unbidden sigh of relief from my lips. Only to cut off on a scream as he rammed the hilt inside me, tearing me open with the blunt end of the knife.

I couldn't hold back my violent shudder, the handle unexpected and *dry*.

"Do not fucking move," he snapped as I started to fall forward.

My abdomen clenched automatically, pulling myself upright as tears flooded my vision.

He's going to fuck me with that in my ass.

It'll drive in with each thrust.

Cutting me as the sharp edges enter from the wrong direction.

Oh God...

I shivered violently, earning me a bite on the shoulder as he moved around in front of me, his hard dick at eye level.

He wouldn't ask me to suck.

Not yet.

He'd tie me up first. Probably use a ring on my mouth as well, just to keep me from being able to bite.

I had to act before that happened.

I had to do *something* before he made it impossible for me to move.

He knelt to begin rifling through his bag, finally giving me the view I needed. He would assume I'd knelt here on purpose, familiar with his desire to have his tools nearby while he worked.

Which made it perfect.

As did having his balls right in front of me, his naked body making him just as vulnerable as me.

He went for the rope first, confirming what I already knew about his intentions. *Out of time,* I thought, panicked. *It's now or—*

The flash of metal caught my gaze as he finished pulling out the rope, his blades carefully packed against the side of his bag, only inches from my knee.

I didn't count.

I didn't second-guess it.

I reached for the knife and drove it upward, right between his groin.

He dropped the rope, the bindings temporarily blinding my vision as he jumped backward with a roar.

I wasn't even sure if I did enough damage. I couldn't see, the fury around me a cloud of movement that had me trying desperately to roll away from him.

Which lodged the blade higher in my—

"You fucking bitch!" he shouted.

I ignored him, my hands reaching around me to try to dislodge the weapon. He'd shoved it in so far... I... I couldn't grab the hilt... I had to... *fuck*.

He fell to his knees, his hands on his groin, giving me the moment I needed to make a flash decision about the knife.

I wrapped my fingers around the metal and yanked, a shriek parting my lips at the pain. But it was better than leaving it there. And it gave me a tool to use.

He'd yanked his own blade out, the dagger much smaller than the one I now held. Because it'd been the butcher knife handle he'd shoved up my ass.

His knife was the kind meant for sex. Small. Almost scalpel-like.

Mine was meant to *kill*. To *butcher*. To *maim*.

I started toward him, needing to use his distraction to my advantage. My insides rioted, but my determination outweighed the pain.

I just needed to stab him.

Slit his throat.

Do *something*.

His gaze was down, his focus on himself, not seeing me at all.

Or that was what I thought until his fist met my jaw, followed by a slur of fury as he pinned me to the floor beneath him. It happened too fast for me to comprehend, my knife flying out of my hand as his palm wrapped around my throat to lift my head up enough just to slam it back down against the marble floor.

Light danced around my vision before bleeding into waves of black.

Another hit to my head made stars appear.

Then my lungs started to beg for air, his hand clamped so tightly around me that I couldn't inhale. I grabbed his wrist, clawing at his hold while he spat hateful things at me above.

I couldn't see. I couldn't really think. I was blind, suffocating, and dizzy as hell.

I bucked upward, squirming, trying to dislodge him, causing him to hiss in pain as I pressed into his wounded groin. *Yes*. I did it again, his grip loosening enough for me to gasp in some air.

He slapped me, causing me to release his wrist to try to protect my face as I tilted my head toward the ground. A flash of silver glinted only a foot from me.

I wasn't sure how it had gotten there. Maybe I'd dropped my knife closer than I'd thought. Maybe it was a new one. But I reached for it without a second thought and brought it up to his torso on a surge of adrenaline. I wasn't sure where it'd come from. My will to survive? My need for revenge? My desire to be in charge for once in my life?

It didn't matter.

Because I connected with his stomach, lodging the blade deep enough to give him pause.

Then I yanked it out and sent it into his stomach again.

And again.

Until I went for his throat.

All while he straddled me.

All while his palm was against my own neck.

He wasn't squeezing now. He seemed to be in shock.

Or maybe I was the one in shock.

I couldn't stop stabbing him.

Each strike seemed to jolt along his body.

Until finally he fell off me.

And I still kept plunging the blade into him.

Someone was screaming.

Probably him.

Or a spectator.

I didn't care. I kept going.

And going.

And going.

Everything was painted in bright lights, blackness, and *blood*. I couldn't see straight. I could barely move. I just kept driving that knife in and out of his chest. His throat. His abdomen. While screams echoed. Murderous rage. *Fury*.

It went on for hours.

Or perhaps minutes.

I wasn't sure.

But I eventually collapsed on top of him, his blood warm and sticky and *wet*.

The world spun.

The universe shifting around me to depict a new reality.

Death.

My head pounded, my hands ached, and my body felt *tired*.

You need to run, some rational part of me whispered. *Get up and* run.

I rolled to my back instead, sucking in gulps of air as I stared at the ceiling.

Something slippery was beneath me. Something that reminded me of water, only thicker.

I almost looked.

But then the moon caught my gaze and the gentle ocean beneath it, rolling up onto the beach.

The image called to me, luring me toward the patio doors. *Wash it off*, that rational part instructed. *Jump in and wash it all off.*

It had to be close to midnight. Maybe after. I wasn't sure.

Yet as I gazed down at the blood on my hands, I realized that I *should* wash it all off. Wash *him* off. The sins of the past. My torment. My proverbial initiation into this fucked-up society.

More men would be here soon.

I needed to run.

To hide.

But where? On this island?

I shook my head slowly back and forth. I hadn't thought this all the way through, my desire to kill Nate outweighing every other rational consideration.

Does it matter? I thought, a huff of a laugh catching in my throat. *I'm going to die anyway.*

At least this was my choice.

And I took the monster down with me.

My hand slipped over the handle of the door, making it harder to open than I expected. But I finally made it slide.

The warm sea air felt damp against my skin.

Ocean, I thought, gazing out at the stairs only a few feet away. *Go into the ocean.*

Yes.

I followed the steps down.

Down.

Down.

Into the welcoming depths below.

So calm. So soothing. Such a beautiful place to die.

I pushed away from the stairs to float on my back, my gaze on the moon above.

I'll watch it as I drift.

Watch it as I find peace.

Watch it as I finally... *sleep*.

CHAPTER FOUR
ASHER

CHECKS complete on south side of the island.

Clive's report buzzed along my wrist. I sent him back a thumbs-up and continued my walk along the beach, enjoying the night air. I'd taken the north side of the island for tonight's security checks, mostly in an effort to avoid my sister and her husband. The last thing I wanted was to see them playing near their bungalow on the southern part of the isle.

With Graham safely tucked in with the nanny I'd hired for them, they were free to roam at will.

Although, I suspect Darby wouldn't go too far.

She was just like our own mother—protective and loving and incapable of staying away for too long.

Which made my life here in Fiji difficult for our mom to accept because she couldn't just hop over to say hello.

But I sent a jet for her whenever she wanted to visit.

Then I met her on the main islands rather than on the isle. Not because I was ashamed of my life here—she knew everything about the Sinner lifestyle and the clubs the family owned—but because I preferred to focus on her and not my work.

Like many of my siblings, club ownership was my life. I lived and breathed this job every day, which made it hard to take a break.

However, family always came first for me.

Especially my mother.

Sighing, I continued my trek toward the play area on this side of the island. I tended to make my presence known, as it improved customer satisfaction.

It also reinforced how seriously I took my rules.

Something I suspected one of my newest guests would need to be reminded of tomorrow at breakfast.

I'd spent most of the day thinking about Nathan Spencer and Adalyn Rose, my instincts flickering long after they'd departed for their bungalow.

All of my staff filed reports after spending time with guests.

Oscar's statement on their drive had been minimal, as the couple hadn't really spoken much.

Meanwhile, Cassandra's comments had been plentiful, her observations confirming the Master and slave preferences of the couple. However, she also included a note of concern regarding Adalyn Rose and whatever punishment she'd received.

It sounded painful, and her reactions weren't ones of enjoyment.

That wasn't necessarily uncommon. But something about it must have unsettled Cassandra enough for her to include it in her report.

Sharon, the housekeeper assigned to Mr. Spencer's villa, submitted similar notes to Cassandra.

And both staff members had been dismissed early.

That was the other reason I'd opted for a stroll along this side of the island tonight. Breakfast in the morning felt too far away. I wanted to see Mr. Spencer in action, review his tendencies, and evaluate him for myself.

Assuming he took Adalyn to the play area, of course.

His bungalow out on the water appeared dark, suggesting he might have done just that.

Or perhaps decided on an early night after their trip.

I considered wandering down the dock, just to listen outside, but that seemed too intrusive. Especially as I didn't have much proof beyond my instincts and a few notes.

Observing a scene would...

What is that? I wondered, my gaze narrowing as my original train of thought disappeared into the night. *Is that...?*

It looks like a woman.

Floating...

My eyes widened.

Dark hair. Pale skin. Naked.

Late-night skinny-dipping wasn't abnormal on this island.

But nothing about this seemed sexual.

"*Fuck.*" Sand sprayed around me as I took off at a dead sprint toward the water, my pulse racing as her lifeless body rolled in the waves.

It bobbed.

Went under for a second.

And popped back up again.

This time facedown.

No movement.

No signs of swimming or trying to reach the shore.

"Fuck!"

I ran faster, my dress shoes less than ideal for this

terrain. But I didn't care. I sprinted right into the water and started swimming, the distance between me and the girl seeming to expand with each passing second.

My arms moved forcefully through the ocean, taking command of the waves and propelling me forward.

Hours seemed to pass, my heart thudding loudly in my ears as I pushed my body forward.

Another wave rolled the woman to her back, her lips parting on a gasp as I arrived right beside her.

She didn't open her eyes, just sucked in the air as though greedy for it.

Adalyn Rose.

She must have gone for a swim.

But why?

And where is Nathan Spencer?

She was clearly conscious. Yet seemed to be... I wasn't sure. Letting the waves try to drown her?

She almost appeared to be asleep.

Yet she was crying.

No. Not crying. *Sobbing.*

My feet kicked beneath me, my shoes finding the ground. I had probably six inches of height on her. But she could easily stand here.

So why is she rolling around helplessly?

What the hell is she...?

Is that...?

My lips parted. *Blood.*

The liquid painted her torso in muddy ink beneath the moonlight.

It seemed to be swarming around her.

Oozing all over her.

"Where is the wound?" I asked, trying to figure out

where to touch her. "What happened? Where are you hurt?"

Big ebony eyes locked on mine, true fear etching itself into her angelic features as her lips parted on a scream.

A scream that was soundless.

A scream that came from a throat that could no longer form sound.

I knew that reaction well, had enjoyed bringing women to that state on countless occasions.

But something told me Adalyn's experience had varied significantly from my own.

Because she appeared to be in true agony, her terror palpable.

"Shh," I hushed, lifting my hands out of the water in a placative mood. "I'm not—"

Another wave took her for a spin.

"Shit."

I reached for her this time, pulling her to the surface. It was the absolute worst thing to do, especially if she had a neck or head injury, but she didn't appear capable of swimming and I wasn't going to let her dro—

Her fist slammed into my jaw, her body suddenly in full-on fight mode as she tried to force me to release her.

I did.

And she immediately went under the water, almost as though her legs weren't working.

"God damn it!"

I pulled her up again, this time wrapping my arms around her upper body to keep her from hitting me again.

"I'm not going to hurt you," I said against her ear, my voice taking on a low, commanding note. "Calm down. I just want to help."

She trembled violently against me, almost as though she were shaking with uncontrollable laughter.

My arms slipped, the blood coating her skin mingling with the salt water and creating a deadly lubricant.

I needed to get her out of the ocean for evaluation.

"We're going ashore," I told her, starting backward. "I'm not going to hurt you." It seemed like the right phrase to repeat with how badly she shook in response to my words. "You're going to be all right."

The same could not be said about Nathan Spencer.

Because he'd obviously done something to her.

I just had no idea what.

My wrist buzzed as I pulled her from the waves onto the shore, one of my security personnel checking in. I couldn't read it or respond, too focused on the vibrating female in my arms.

She was openly sobbing again, words spilling from her mouth that didn't make sense because she didn't have a voice. They were broken noises that only seemed to make her shake harder.

"Adalyn. It's okay. I'm not taking you back to him." My instincts told me that was the right thing to say.

And the way she froze against me suggested I'd been right, too.

Or maybe it was because I'd spoken her name.

I wasn't sure, but at least she wasn't fighting me anymore.

"I need to know where you're hurt." I tried for a more soothing tone this time, hoping it would help keep her calm.

She didn't react.

She barely even breathed.

She seemed to be in some sort of trance. Shock, perhaps.

I carefully released her, uncertain of whether or not she would attempt to hit me again. But she remained utterly frozen, resembling a marble statue beneath the moonlight.

A marble statue with smatters of bloody water all over her, I corrected, my gaze trailing over her torso in an attempt to find the source of the blood.

My wrist buzzed again.

Bryant checking in.

I replied to him this time with an SOS. It wouldn't take long for him to dispatch security to my area, my phone being a beacon for my location.

Fortunately, it was waterproof—something I'd paid a lot for, but seemed like a necessity with living on an island.

Tonight had proven that investment worthwhile.

"Can you point to where it hurts?" I asked Adalyn, still not seeing any wounds on her. Just a lot of bloody water.

Her eyes met mine, her dark irises resembling black pools of haunted memories.

Someone had hurt this girl.

Badly.

I opened my mouth, ready to tell her that I wanted to help.

When her fist connected with my jaw again.

Her feet started moving across the sand in a haphazard run that would have been comical if she hadn't just punched me in the face. *Again.*

I cursed, darting after her, and catching her easily by the hips.

Her knees buckled in the next instant, her body going completely limp beneath my hands.

I shifted quickly, my arm catching her back as the opposite went to her knees, to lift her into the air.

Her head hung backward, her eyes rolling with emotion.

"Jesus," I breathed, blinking down at her now unconscious form. "What the fuck happened to you?"

Her chest rose in an unsteady inhale, her exhale just as shaky.

I carefully lowered her to the sand, laying her down in a manner that would make CPR easier, just in case. I pulled my phone from my pocket, dialing Bryant.

"What's going on?" he asked before the first ring even ended.

"Adalyn Rose is unconscious in the sand. I need Dr. Zansky. Now."

"I'll alert him," Bryant replied.

"Send security over to Mr. Spencer's hut and detain him for questioning as well." I tolerated a lot. But this? This I did not tolerate.

"On it," Bryant promised. "I'm sending London and Mason your way."

"Good."

"I'm right behind them."

I nodded. Not that he could see. "Thanks, Bryant." I hung up before he could reply, my hands going to Adalyn's neck and the signs of bruising against her delicate skin. There were cut marks all over her chest as well, but nothing that could have caused the amount of blood in the water.

Her stomach and thighs displayed similar signs of knife play.

None of it looked sensual, more like torture—paper cuts meant to sting.

Her nipples were swollen as well, suggesting she'd been

put in clamps for too long. I suspected her clit would be the same.

My jaw clenched.

The bruises and superficial scars, all of which would heal, pointed at what I already knew—Nathan Spencer had severely damaged this woman.

To the point where she'd gone for a midnight swim and just let the waves take her.

"Were you trying to die?" I asked her softly, running my fingers through her tangled dark strands. My heart broke for her; this beautiful creature didn't deserve that sort of pain. No one did. "I don't know what he did to you, Adalyn. But I promise he'll never touch you again."

Because I would be removing him from my island.

Just as soon as he told me what the fuck he'd done to this darling girl.

My security arrived a handful of seconds later.

Followed by Dr. Zansky ten minutes after that.

Adalyn hadn't woken up at all, but her pulse was steady and she appeared to be breathing better now.

However, one look at Dr. Zansky's expression told me that didn't mean much. He ordered a stretcher to be brought for her. "I'll take her to the medical station."

I shook my head. "No. Take her to my villa. You can treat her in one of my guest rooms."

He blinked at me. "I need my equipment—"

"Bryant will make sure you have everything you need." I glanced at my security officer as he arrived. "Right?"

"Yes," he agreed without missing a beat. "Tell me what to bring over, and we'll get it done."

Dr. Zansky appeared ready to argue.

A raised eyebrow from me had him shaking his head and keeping his comments to himself.

Was it the right move on my part? Maybe not. But I'd just promised the girl I would keep Nathan away from her, and I'd meant it. She would be under my personal watch until this situation resolved itself.

Dr. Zansky started listing what he needed for Bryant as two of the other men carefully pulled Adalyn onto the stretcher.

Bryant cut him off mid-list with a "Hold on." He pressed his finger to his ear. "Say that again." His hazel eyes flew to mine as whoever reported to him spoke through his earpiece. He blinked, his lips parting. "You're sure?"

I frowned. "What's wrong?"

Bryant glanced down at Adalyn with a scrutinizing look before returning his startled gaze to me. "We need to go to the bungalow." He blinked and focused on his men, spouting orders about supplies and helping Dr. Zansky. "I want a guard on the girl, too," he finished, his demand deepening my frown.

But I waited until he was done issuing demands before I asked any questions. I'd hired him and Clive to lead my security team for a reason. I trusted them entirely.

However, the minute Bryant and I started walking toward the bungalow, I looked at him and demanded, "What the fuck is going on?"

He met my gaze without flinching. "Nathan Spencer is dead."

CHAPTER FIVE
ASHER

WELL, I knew where all the blood had come from now.

Nathan Spencer.

He'd been stabbed at least a dozen times, all over his torso and groin.

And it seemed fairly obvious that Adalyn Rose had wielded the blade.

"Poor bastard," Bryant had muttered upon seeing the scene.

It was a sentiment we didn't share. Because something told me Nathan Spencer had earned this death.

An instinctual response on my part. One I intended to prove.

Adalyn had been in shock. Perhaps as a result of the murder she'd just committed. But I suspected her reaction had resulted from something much deeper than that.

My wrist buzzed with an incoming update from Dr. Zansky. *The woman has a concussion, likely related to the bump forming on the back of her head. She's also severely dehydrated. I've started an IV, and I cleaned up the wound on her hand.*

There are also signs of sexual trauma outside the norm of consent.

I read the message out loud to Bryant.

"So some of the blood is hers, then," he translated.

"Yeah, from pulling a dagger out of her ass." Clive's dark tone came from across the room, his expression murderous as he met my gaze. "You're going to want to see this, boss."

He'd arrived about thirty minutes ago with some clothes for me to change into. Then he'd immediately gone to work on Nathan's phone.

Bryant handled security operations personnel.

Clive handled the tech.

They were both badasses in their own rights, marking them as perfect candidates for their enforcer-like roles on the island.

But they were so much more than that beneath their strong exteriors.

Bryant had a knack for analyzing people, reading situations, and managing expectations.

While Clive specialized in hacking.

Hence the reason he'd immediately taken over Nathan's phone and laptop.

We were the only ones in the room, my other staff having been temporarily dismissed with orders not to tell anyone about this. They'd obey because they were paid handsomely to do so.

I walked over to where Clive sat at the living area desk, a pair of glasses perched on his nose. He had the phone hooked up to his own devices, displaying files and videos on a larger screen beside him.

The one he had playing now was footage of the room. "He has live cameras set up everywhere." He started pointing to where they were throughout the villa. "It's all recording, but the feed doesn't appear to be going anywhere other than to a folder on his phone."

He clicked the one in question—the title of it reading *AR*. I assumed that stood for *Adalyn Rose.*

"There are hundreds of videos in here." Clive's deep green eyes met mine. "Training documentation."

I frowned. "Videotaping kink?" I guessed.

"Maybe. But some of these..." He trailed off. "I've only seen a few. But they're bad, boss."

My brow inched upward. For Clive to say something like that after all the shit he'd witnessed over his forty years, it must have been a lot worse than just "bad."

Bryant folded his arms across his chest. "So does it show her murdering him?"

Clive nodded. "Yeah. After he drove the hilt of a blade into her ass—*raw*—and started going through his little toy bag over there to pull out some rope. But there's also footage of her stashing knives around the room before that, which is what set him off. However, after their playtime earlier today, and some of these other videos..." His gaze met mine again. "The murder is justified."

He didn't elaborate any more than that, instead choosing to show us the footage of Nathan's death.

Then the earlier video of their time together in the villa—a video that had my hands fisting at my sides. It was sufficient proof of Adalyn's unwillingness, confirming all my instincts regarding her consent.

And then Clive started showing us images of previous events.

Adalyn crying.

Adalyn covered in bloody marks and cum, unconscious on the floor.

Adalyn being shared by multiple men while restrained.

Adalyn in a cage with a timestamp from six years ago.

Sixteen years old, I thought, my stomach twisting as I quickly computed her age at the time. *She wasn't even a consenting adult.* Because she was twenty-two now. At least according to her file. Nathan was nearly two decades older than her.

"Turn it off," I said, taking a step back before I hit something. "Turn that shit off right now."

I'd seen enough.

The murder was absolutely justified, just as Clive had said.

And the look on Bryant's face told me he wholeheartedly agreed. Because he'd probably done the math on her age, too.

Fuck.

I pinched the bridge of my nose, blowing out a long breath.

This was the kind of shit I hated in the world of sex and pleasure. The kind of thing some men thought made them dominant and powerful.

But that wasn't the purpose of my island at all.

Fetishes were explored here via safe and established means. I didn't condone slavery or trafficking or sensual servitude.

"Jesus," I breathed, stalking over to the kitchen for a much-needed drink. I didn't even care that there was a massacre in the other room.

Hell, I was *happy* about that savage scene.

Because it meant Nathan was dead.

Good. Fucking. Riddance.

I poured myself a healthy glass of brandy from the liquor cabinet. Every villa was stocked with the best of the best. But I barely tasted the liquid as it burned my throat.

Clive and Bryant spoke quietly, giving me my moment to think.

Not that I knew what to think about.

Adalyn was the daughter of Albert Rose, CEO and owner of Rose Royale—a renowned hotel brand famous for its opulence and five-star hospitality.

Nathan Spencer was the third son of a wealthy oil family. Was that how they'd met? Via the elite circles of the world?

But at sixteen years old?

Did her father approve of this? Did he have any idea?

My teeth ground together, the glass nearly breaking in my hand.

This was chaos. Insanity. A relationship born of the devil himself.

Those images...

I poured myself another drink. "This is a fucking nightmare." I downed the brandy in one gulp and slammed the glass onto the stone counter.

"Can you open that?" I overheard Bryant asking. "No, the graduation thing in her file."

Clive had turned off the videos like I'd asked, but he still had all the folders open. "Adalyn's Graduation Celebration?"

"Yeah, that one."

I started toward them as Clive opened an image on his screen. It resembled a golden key with a blood-red dot at the top that quickly morphed into a list of names and kinks.

I frowned. It almost looked like a blackmail directory, except there were dates and times listed next to each person.

Future dates and times.

For this week.

"What the fuck is this?" I whispered, more to myself than to my men. I recognized most of the names as men expected to arrive this week.

Many of them weren't Sinners Isle members but guests of influential investors of my property. Which meant I treated those guests as though they belonged here because they might become future patrons.

A trial period of sorts.

One meant to ensure they understood the rules.

And an opportunity for them to decide if they wanted to apply for membership.

"A training schedule," Bryant whispered, his eyes widening as though he'd just pieced something together. "Fuck. He brought her here for her final round of *training*." He looked at me. "Adalyn Rose. As in... Rose Royale?"

My brow furrowed. "Yeah. That's her. But what do you mean by 'training'?"

He muttered a curse and reached for Nathan's phone, unplugging it from Clive's monitor.

The color drained from Bryant's normally tan skin as he scrolled through the contact directory, his jaw clenching as he read a few of the names out loud.

They were all ones I recognized as running in high-society circles.

Not really a surprise, given Nathan's background and the clientele I typically catered to on this island.

Bryant wandered over to the body, kneeling to check the dead man's hand.

Then he dumped his bag of toys and cursed as a ruby-colored ring rolled across the carpet.

He pulled his own phone from his pocket, Nathan's device falling to the floor.

Clive jumped from his seat. "Hey—"

Bryant held up a hand, indicating he needed a minute.

I shared a look with Clive. He appeared as lost as I was.

Then Bryant started speaking. "Yeah. I know what time it is." He waited a beat, pinching the bridge of his nose. "Fine. But you owe me a favor. Several, actually." His lips twitched, though the action appeared strained. "Exactly." Another beat. "Yeah, tell me about Adalyn Rose."

My eyebrows lifted. "Who are—"

He flashed me a look, one that told me to keep quiet. I narrowed my gaze. Bryant Ferraro might have a lot of connections in this world, and an impressive background in security, but he still worked for me.

And I did not appreciate being left in the dark on my own fucking island.

"Taylor Huntington," he said, staring at me as he spoke the familiar name.

Is that who he's talking to? I wondered, confused as to why he'd call the notorious trust-fund playboy. He was another spare heir, similar to Nathan, only from an even more powerful family in the entertainment industry. His parents owned all the largest television networks. *What does he have to do with this?*

"I see." Bryant listened intently to whatever Taylor, or whomever he was speaking to, said. "I might. Nathan Spencer brought her to Sinners Isle for some training. It didn't go according to plan."

My jaw ticked at him for revealing that information without asking my permission.

"No. Mr. Sinner values consent. As you can imagine, it didn't take long for him to realize Adalyn's lack thereof."

I frowned. *What is going on? Who are you talking to?*

"Yeah." His attention shifted to the dead body near his feet. "I don't know. He wasn't informed—" Bryant's jaw tightened, his hazel eyes meeting mine. "He's inside with him now."

My frown deepened. *What?*

"This property isn't part of the Sin Cave network, Julian."

My eyebrows lifted. *Sin Cave network? What the fuck is that? And who the fuck is Julian?*

I looked at Clive. He appeared to share my confusion.

"He's rightly pissed," Bryant said, sounding tired. "I don't know. That's why I called." He ran a hand over his face and blew out a breath, humming at whatever *Julian* said back to him. "He's a good man, Julian. Better than you."

Bryant grunted at whatever his friend said in response.

"As I said, he values consent. And it's his island. If you wanted to conduct training here—" His jaw tightened. "Well, then Nathan has earned his fate."

He looked down at the body again.

"No. But it's likely," he muttered.

Another few beats passed, causing Bryant to nod.

"I would appreciate that, yes." Bryant appeared somewhat relieved. "Yeah. I'll see what I can do, but he's pissed." His shoulders went rigid at whatever Julian said next. "I'm not sure that's wise." His eyes rolled at whatever the man said back to him. "And you wonder why I left."

More listening.

Followed by a smirk.

"I'll call you back." He hung up the phone, his amusement dying as he took in Nathan's remains again.

"She's an Elite Bride in training." His voice was soft, his words making no sense to me.

"What?"

"She's an Elite Bride, Asher," he repeated. His expression held a note of severity to it that made my blood run cold even though I had no idea what that term meant. "She's part of the Sin Cave network. A bride in *training*. For Taylor Huntington."

I blinked at him. "What the fuck does that even mean?" And how the hell did he know any of this? "Who were you just talking to?"

"Julian Jovanni."

My jaw dropped. "*What*?"

"Like, Julian Jovanni of the Jovanni mafia? The Red Prince?" Clive asked, his expression and tone rivaling my own.

"He's an old friend," Bryant muttered. "His family also owns part of the Sin Cave network. Specifically, the Elite Brides. Which Adalyn's parents must have given her over to in exchange for an affluent connection with the Huntington family."

"An old friend," Clive echoed. "Yeah. Cool. That's not alarming at all."

Bryant gave him a look. "I had a life before this island, Clive. So did you."

Clive snorted. "My life didn't involve working for a renowned criminal empire."

"No, you were just a hacker for a private sector security firm that specialized in what again?"

"Nothing illegal. Kane wouldn't allow that shit."

"Hmm, and what about your employer before you met Kane?"

"That's not—"

"*Stop.*" I did not have time to sit through one of their infamous verbal sparring matches. One day, they'd fuck it out. Or kill a woman between them. Whatever the hell it was they needed to do. But that wasn't today.

Today, we were dealing with a much larger issue.

"What the hell is Sin Cave?" I demanded. "And what the fuck do you mean by Adalyn's parents gave her to an organization to train her to become an *Elite Bride*?"

CHAPTER SIX

ASHER

"Ecstasy."

My brow came down. "What?"

"You've heard of the Ecstacy chain," Bryant clarified, phrasing it not as a question but as a statement.

Because of course I'd heard of Ecstacy.

It was an elite dungeon circuit with clientele that rivaled my own. They weren't necessarily competition, though. Many of my members also belonged to Ecstacy. "You used to..." I trailed off.

Oh, fuck.

Bryant used to work for the New York City location.

That was the reference he'd given me seven years ago.

His affiliation with Ecstasy was what had qualified him for the job here.

Bryant must have seen the dots connect inside my mind because he said, "Sin Cave owns Ecstacy. It's one of their more legitimate businesses, meant to cater to their Elite members and give them a place to safely network with others. But Elite Brides often frequent those facilities. It's where many of them train."

"But Ecstacy believes in consent and safe practices." I'd been to a few of their locations as an invited guest of mutual clients. I'd witnessed their procedures firsthand. Fuck, I'd even played in a few of their rooms.

"Yes. Some of the brides consent. Others do not." He cleared his throat. "Most of them undergo rigorous training before they're taken to the clubs. This would have been Adalyn's final test to prove she could behave and submit in a more public setting. Outside of the Sin Cave owned establishments, I mean."

I glanced at Nathan's dead body. *Looks like that test went well.*

"Ecstasy is the legal part of the enterprise," he continued. "Not all members are affiliated with the network. But everyone within the network has access to the clubs. Which is why they're often used for final phases of training."

"Which is how you know about the Elite Brides," I inferred.

"There's a list. All members are familiar with who is on it. The women are considered untouchable unless the assigned trainer approves the scene."

"And no one sees anything wrong with that?" I asked. Because I sure as fuck did.

He gave me a long look. "You know as well as I do that money buys silence in every situation. These brides are the daughters of the world's wealthiest families. No one is going to fight that. And most of the women appear to be consensual."

"*Appear* being the operative term in that statement."

"I'm not saying I agree with it, Asher. Fuck, man. Why the hell do you think I came to work for you?" He shook his head, his expression shifting between shades of frustration and a glimmer of resolve.

Clive cleared his throat. “All right. So what now?”

“We make a decision,” Bryant replied, his eyes finding mine. “*You* make a decision.”

I arched a brow. “Something tells me I’m not going to like my options.”

“You’re not,” he agreed. “But Julian... owes me.”

“Do I want to know more about that?” I asked.

“Considering that it involves his own Elite Bride? Probably not.” He swallowed. “It’s also not my story to tell. But maybe he’ll share it with you when he comes to visit.”

“When he comes to visit?” I repeated.

“Yeah. That plays into your decision.” His shoulders straightened as he boldly met my stare again. “If this were any other situation, I’d suggest covering it all up and making it look like Spencer and Rose died somewhere else. But this is Sin Cave. They’re too resourceful not to investigate the death of a trainee and his Elite Bride.”

“We’re not killing Adalyn Rose.” The words came through clenched teeth, as I didn’t much care for his hypothetical scenario.

“I know. I’m saying it’s what I would have recommended if the network wasn’t involved. So you have two choices. You can tell them the truth about what happened. There’s video evidence. Share it. They’ll clean this up and handle Miss Rose.”

His tone told me I wouldn’t like how they would “handle” Adalyn at all.

“Or you can tell them that you killed Nathan for breaking your rules. He wasn’t here under Sin Cave authorization. Julian confirmed that Nathan chose this location for Adalyn's final test. That means the network won't fault you for responding accordingly. Because this island isn't under their jurisdiction."

I folded my arms across my chest. "And what happens to Adalyn in this scenario?"

"They take her, and she'll likely be married off to Taylor Huntington as expected." He shrugged. "It beats what they would do to her if they learned the truth."

"And if she spoke after the fact? Said she killed him and we covered it up?" Clive asked, bringing up a good point.

"It's a risk," Bryant replied, slipping his hands into the pockets of his dress pants. "It's also worth noting that regardless of what path you choose, you're now involved in Sin Cave business. Which I suspect has always been a potential future for you anyway."

I arched a brow. "A potential future?" No part of me would ever condone any of this shit. If Bryant didn't know that about me by now, then he didn't know me at all.

"They've invited you to their clubs countless times, Ash," he said, using my nickname as though to confirm how well he knew me. Sometimes I wondered if he possessed a weird superpower to hear thoughts. He was constantly in my head and the minds of everyone around him.

"They've been recruiting you," he continued. "I'm assuming that's why Nathan came here. Someone probably suggested it as another way to test your interest. But it obviously wasn't an official visit, or Julian would have known about it."

My jaw ticked. "Nathan did invite me over for breakfast tomorrow."

His hazel irises darkened. "I'm guessing he intended to offer you more than food."

I'd already suspected that prior to this entire mess unfolding. "So it would seem."

Silence fell, Bryant's attention shifting to the dead man on the floor. I followed his gaze as I considered everything he'd said.

He'd essentially implied that the network would allow me to kill Nathan Spencer for using my island for this bullshit.

But it would come with a cost of association, something Bryant had insinuated would happen regardless of my choice.

"If I claim I killed him for breaking my rules, wouldn't that imply that I don't agree with the network's methods?" I wondered aloud. "Wouldn't that mean I failed Nathan's supposed test?" It was all theoretical, but I could see Bryant's logic. I had been invited to Ecstacy numerous times.

But no one had ever mentioned the words *Sin Cave* to me.

"It depends on how you phrase it," Bryant said, his focus still on Nathan's dead body. "You could claim that you killed him for disrespecting your business. This is your territory. He attempted to abuse it for his own gain. That's an insult in the Sin Cave world."

"But you told Julian I value consent."

"Yes. And Nathan Spencer violated that rule, thus earning himself an appropriate punishment." Bryant lifted his gaze to mine, his greenish-brown irises glittering with intelligence. "You didn't consent to him using your island as a training playground."

I contemplated that for a moment. "But killing him puts me at a disadvantage. They'll tell me I owe them if they forgive the death."

"They're going to expect you to owe them regardless," he muttered. "You're too close now, Asher. Whether you want it or not, your fate is already decided. You'll either join the network willingly, or you'll create a very powerful enemy."

I arched a brow. "So you're still part of it, then?"

"I only worked for them. But yes, if they need something, I'm duty-bound to respond. However, I have a trump card." He paused for a beat, his expression giving nothing away. "Julian owes me. He won't let them drag me back in. That's why I was able to come here."

"And what about me?" Clive asked, finally speaking up. He'd been leaning against the wall, listening intently and not saying a word. "Are we going to pretend I wasn't here?"

"That's exactly what we'll do," Bryant replied. "You might have been part of the initial discussion in determining Nathan Spencer's true purpose here, but Asher excused you early on, choosing intelligently to question Nathan alone. Which is when he learned the truth about Adalyn Rose's purpose here."

"And then I killed him for not only breaking my rules but also conducting illicit business on my island without permission."

"We could even say that he didn't tell you everything, and you assumed it was a trafficking issue." Bryant shrugged. "There are a few ways to spin this."

"But regardless of what I do, I'm going to face the network," I said, returning us to the primary issue at hand. "And they'll be taking Adalyn back into that world."

"It's where she was always going to go," Bryant pointed out. "She knew that. Even while killing him, she knew there was no real escape. Because even if she succeeded in fleeing your island, they'd find her."

My jaw ached from clenching it so hard.

Nothing about this was right.

Adalyn Rose rightly killed Nathan Spencer. But it seemed her parents deserved a similar fate.

Who the fuck sent their daughter into a world like this?

Elite Brides.

More like well-educated, blue-blooded sex slaves.

"Fuck," I muttered, rubbing my hand over my face. One thing was certain—I wouldn't be letting these assholes punish Adalyn for what she'd done.

Which meant I'd be claiming that I'd killed the bastard.

Considering how badly I wished he was still alive so I could do just that, it wouldn't be a difficult lie.

But knowing they would just come and retrieve Adalyn afterward left me uneasy.

I didn't know her. I didn't owe her anything.

Yet I felt inclined to save her somehow.

Put her on a boat and sequester her away. Help her escape. *Hide* her. All impossible and irrational notions.

I just couldn't stand the idea that she would be sent back to that world, forced to endure a new trainer or be married off to a man who felt that this sort of treatment was acceptable.

"If I say I killed him, what happens next?" I asked, needing a distraction before I did something stupid like run back to my villa and take off with Adalyn.

Bryant remained quiet for a beat before saying, "Someone will come meet with you, perhaps offer an apology for the affront, and likely discuss the future. Which I imagine will be a conversation about what Sin Cave can offer you... and what you can offer them."

I could only imagine what that would be. "They'll want to use my island for training."

"Or perhaps as a place for their members to vacation with their Elite Maidens."

My eyebrows lifted. "Do I even want to know what that means?"

"Well-kept mistresses," he clarified. "Who also happen to be trained."

"Jesus," I whispered. "What fucking world is this?"

"A dark one."

No shit, I thought, running my hand along my face. "I feel like I've just been inserted into an alternate reality," I muttered, thinking through everything he'd just told me.

I was quite familiar with high society. I socialized with their key players all the time.

As did most of my family.

"Do any of my brothers know about the network?" I wondered aloud. If they did, I imagined they would be quiet about it, given everything Bryant had told me. "Does Kane know?" He owned a club in Baltimore, but he primarily worked in securities.

"No, I highly doubt it," Bryant replied. "And if he did, he wouldn't tell you."

I nodded. *As I thought.*

"But he might be a good person to bring in," Bryant hedged. "He has a lot of... contacts."

That he did. However... "No. I'm not going to involve my family in this. It's my mess to clean up."

Bryant gave me a look that suggested he wanted to argue. Clive did also, probably because he knew Kane well —he used to work for him, after all.

However, Bryant's phone started to ring before either of them could say a word. "It's Julian," Bryant said after glancing at the screen. "He's going to want an update."

I sighed. "Tell him I'm interrogating Mr. Spencer." I

glanced at Clive. "I gave strict instructions not to be interrupted."

Bryant nodded. "And what should my gut be telling me?"

"That Mr. Spencer likely won't live to see another sunrise," I growled, imagining all too well how it would feel to be in a room with a still-alive Nathan.

I wouldn't have let my emotions show.

But Bryant knew me well. He would have seen right through my calm façade to the fury burning beneath.

I listened as he answered the phone with a grim tone, telling Julian that Nathan Spencer's hours, perhaps even minutes, were likely numbered.

He met my gaze as he added a line about this being an insult to my business, setting up the justification for murder.

Because I'd already decided to own that burden.

What I needed to figure out now was what to do about Adalyn Rose.

Because I couldn't in good conscience allow her to be taken from my island.

She'd been strong enough to survive this long and had gone as far as to kill her own tormentor. That sort of spirit deserved to be worshipped, not punished.

So no, I would not be sending her back to that hell.

I would keep her here instead. Introduce her to a new life. And when the time came, I'd help her fly away.

Yes, I decided. *Adalyn isn't going anywhere.*

She was my responsibility now.

Since no one else clearly wanted the job, I'd take care of her myself.

I eyed her masterpiece on the floor, my lips threatening to curl. Such a beautiful work of art.

Yes, she absolutely deserved to be praised and adored.
I would see that it happened.
Welcome to my world, sweetheart.
You're about to find out what it means to be mine.

CHAPTER SEVEN
ADALYN

A SHARP SENSATION in my arm pierced through my mind, stirring me to awareness as a male voice said, "She's all yours, sir."

"Thank you, Dr. Zansky," a cultured tone replied. One I recognized but couldn't quite place.

Not Nate, I thought warily. *Whoever he'd left me with last night, maybe?*

I tried to think back through the events of yesterday evening, but everything was foggy. Dreamlike. Which was strange because I didn't often dream.

My life was a nightmare, not a fantasy.

A damp cloth wiped along my brow, the cool texture a welcome reprieve from the heat bathing my skin. I nearly sighed at the soothing sensation.

Whatever had happened last night, it'd clearly knocked me on my ass.

Nate must have invited several friends over to fuck me, I thought warily. *And now one of them is trying to wake me up.*

It would be so easy to feign sleep.

Except I knew that wouldn't stop Nate's friends. It

never did. They'd fuck me back to life even after trying to kill me.

It was all part of their sick and twisted games.

Which was exactly why I intended to kill—

Wait... An image of blood flashed through my mind. Of Nate on the floor. A blade moving in and out of his torso on repeat. Lifeless eyes. Lying in a pool of death.

My eyes flew open as I sat up abruptly.

Dream or reality? I wondered, looking around and freezing as I found a man staring down at me with piercing black eyes. They reminded me of obsidian gems, glittering with the night.

Set in a face crafted by God himself.

Handsome as sin.

A cruel jawline decorated with a neatly trimmed beard. Chiseled cheekbones. Thick dark-brown hair. Pale skin slightly tanned by the sun.

"Welcome back, Adalyn," he murmured, the cloth in his hand moving along my cheek. "How are you feeling?"

I swallowed, trying futilely to identify this man. I knew his face. I recognized his voice. But I couldn't think of his name. One of Nate's friends? An Elite borrowing me for a round of fun? The choices were endless.

"Who are you?" I asked, my voice hoarse as though I had been screaming for hours. Given the ache echoing through my head, I probably had been. *What the fuck did they do to me last night?*

Another vision of Nate's mutilated form crossed my mind, only to be cut off by the man's deep tones.

"Asher Sinner," he murmured. "I suppose we weren't properly introduced yesterday. But I'm the one who owns this isle."

"Isle?" I repeated, blinking.

"And the one who found you covered in blood last night," he added, his words sending a chill down my spine.

"Last night?" I felt like I couldn't process words properly, so I kept repeating them as though that would help.

"Here," he said, lifting a glass with a straw to my lips. "Drink."

I obeyed because I desperately wanted to soothe my throat. The chilled water had me closing my eyes, a dreamlike sensation of tranquility settling through me.

Until his words started to register in my mind.

Asher Sinner.

Isle.

Covered in blood.

Sinners Isle, I finally pieced together. *I'm in Fiji.*

And I'd killed Nathan Spencer.

My eyes flew open, water spewing from my mouth as my latest swallow failed.

Asher immediately switched his washcloth for a dry towel and dabbed at my chin, completely ignoring the water I'd just sprayed all over his dress shirt. "Shh," he hushed. "You're all right."

I gaped at him. *I'm what? All right?* "Are you fucking serious right now?" I was the opposite of all right. I'd killed Nathan Spencer.

And now...

Now I was...

Found.

"*And the one who found you covered in blood last night,*" he'd said.

He knows what I did. He knows I killed Nathan Spencer. And he was the one who had *found* me. Which meant I was his to punish. His to do whatever the fuck he wanted to.

And he owned this goddamn island.

Fuck!

I pressed my palms to my eyes, ignoring his touch as he finished wiping the water away from my neck and chest. "I'm very serious," he said calmly. "You're safe here."

I huffed a humorless laugh. "Okay." I was safe nowhere. Especially not here. Not with one of Nate's friends.

Especially after I'd killed Nate.

God, I couldn't remember what I'd done afterward. Fallen into the water? Tried to wash away the evidence? Floated for eternity?

It was all so fuzzy in my mind, my head aching with the source of my fogginess.

I'd sat up too quickly, as evidenced by the way I began to sway.

Asher caught my shoulder as he pushed me back to the bed.

Here it comes, I thought. *The part where my punishment begins.*

Except he just picked up the washcloth again and continued drawing it along my overheated skin. I waited for the touch to move downward, to become cruel.

But all he did was pull the sheets up over my breasts—which I'd apparently knocked down upon sitting up—and ran the cloth along my neck.

Soothing.

Gentle.

Caressing.

This had to be some weird form of punishment, a way to lull me into a state of peace and hopefulness before reminding me of my place in this world.

Nate had done that several times, pretending to be a friend only to destroy me in the next second.

He'd never been quite so skilled at faking aftercare, though.

Asher's strokes were coaxing in nature, urging me to relax with each brush against my skin. I listened as he dipped the cloth into what I assumed was the source of the coolness. Then he drew the refreshing texture along my forehead again.

Hours seemed to pass.

He said nothing.

When he sat on the bed beside me, I tensed, waiting for whatever came next.

But nothing changed, his touch resuming and never dropping below my shoulders.

I counted to a hundred.

Then a thousand.

Waiting. Waiting. Waiting.

Because this had to be a game. I just didn't understand it yet.

After what felt like a lifetime, I finally opened my eyes again to find him studying me intently. He'd obviously known I was awake, but he'd chosen to remain silent. To continue his torture with that fucking cloth.

"Just get on with it," I told him, impatient.

"Get on with what, sweetheart?" he asked, reaching over to dip the cloth into a bowl of ice water on the ebony-colored nightstand.

I glared at him as he brought the texture to my temple, his thumb massaging it into my skin and relieving an insane amount of tension at the same time. "Stop."

He stilled. "Does it hurt?"

"No." *It feels too good.*

He frowned but pulled the cloth away. "Dr. Zansky said this would help. Is it making it worse?"

Are we speaking the same language? Why would he want to *help*? "Just get on with it." I didn't want to feel good. I didn't want to crave something that didn't exist. I didn't do aftercare or beforecare or whatever the fuck he wanted to call this. "Just do whatever you came to do."

Or perhaps that was the purpose of this—to draw out my fate.

I knew killing Nate would have consequences.

I'd just hoped to enjoy his death for a little longer than a few hours.

Alas, it seemed my fate had been sealed all along.

Asher set the cloth down, his gaze surveying my face as though he were trying to solve a puzzle.

"What? Did Nate not share his notes?" I taunted.

He arched a brow. "There are notes?"

Who is this guy? I was almost intrigued. All the other games had become fairly mundane in their predictability. But this one... this one was new.

I took his measure again, noting the way he'd left the top button of his dress shirt open to expose just a hint of his masculine throat. He'd rolled the sleeves to his elbows as well, giving me a nice view of his muscular forearms.

Nice vein action, I thought before shifting my gaze to his torso and his tapered waist. *Definitely in good shape.*

Which meant he'd be a beast in the bedroom.

And given the dark flare in his eyes as I returned my attention to his face, I suspected he enjoyed doling out pain.

So this would hurt once he engaged in round one.

Maybe I could provoke him to start, help him over the finish line before he had a chance to truly kill me.

Or perhaps I should wait and ensure he did end me.

Death had to be better than going to the fantasy wing to be used in whatever way a man chose.

Except wasn't that my fate already? To become a personal plaything for Taylor Huntington? He would be the man choosing my fate, giving others permission to do as they pleased.

My hands curled into fists.

This was what had driven me to murder Nathan Spencer, this realization that the "fate worse than death" was already my future. It was already my *life*.

So why bother?

Why not fight back?

Why not *kill*?

Asher's gaze narrowed as though he could hear my thoughts. Maybe I wore my intentions on my face.

But I couldn't kill him right now. I didn't have any knives nearby or a plan. Just a few towels and water and sheets.

This is a really sparsely decorated room, I realized, glancing around at the modern fixtures. The curtains were gauzy and white, framing several floor-to-ceiling windows that appeared to also function as doors to reach the patio beyond.

Not bad for a jail cell, I decided.

Although, I suspected this was temporary.

Asher was probably the one in charge of me until someone else arrived to take me to wherever the fuck bad Elite Brides truly went.

Taylor would probably decide. We'd still be wed, the company given to him via the agreement with my parents, and he'd ship me off to be fucked by whomever, whenever, and however.

I'd probably die there.

Which would be convenient for my future husband, actually. Because then he could pick a new bride. A better-behaved one. A female who wouldn't try to stab him in the middle of the night.

"Adalyn?" Asher murmured, his voice drawing me back to him. "Can I get you anything?"

I blinked at him. "Why are you doing this?"

"Doing what?"

"Drawing it out?" I asked, sitting up again and purposely letting the sheet drop. His gaze flicked downward, his nostrils flaring. "I know you want to hurt me. So do it. Get it over with. Fuck me. Knock me out again. I don't fucking care. But I won't play this game. It's boring me." A lie. I was absolutely fascinated by his approach, my curiosity more than piqued. But I wouldn't dare admit that out loud.

"I don't want to hurt you, Adalyn."

I scoffed at that. "Yes, you do. You have *sadist* written all over you." I tilted my head, evaluating him. "I'm guessing breath play." I looked down at his full lips, taking in the way they tensed at my words. "You like control. Feeling a female helpless beneath your hands. Mmm, bondage, definitely."

I stared at his throat, watching as he swallowed, confirming my comment.

"Shibari takes too much time, and the focus is on the female. So you probably just use cuffs, maybe some thick rope if you want to make it chafe." Hmm, but he winced with those statements. *Interesting.* "So no rope, then?" *How... refreshing.* I met his gaze again. "Shibari?"

"It's not one of my skills, but I enjoy watching it." His gaze narrowed. "Why are you trying to provoke me, Adalyn?"

"To get the party started," I replied. "You can't put me at ease. It's impossible. So stop trying to mindfuck me."

"I'm not trying to *mindfuck* you."

I rolled my eyes. "Do you need me to act out? Is that it?" *Does he want me to try to fight him? To attempt to escape?*

Maybe that was the key to hastening this endgame.

I ripped the blankets away from me to roll off the bed, only for him to catch me with his arm around my torso.

"*Adalyn.*"

I grabbed his forearm and dug my nails into his skin, trying to rip his grip away from me. He cursed, removing his arm. I scrambled toward the edge of the bed. My feet touched the ground and I moved to run.

Except the room started to spin.

Violently.

I fell backward into a wall of steel and felt a pair of muscular bands wrap around my torso.

Everything turned upside down.

And somehow I found myself staring up at a pair of furious black eyes.

The wall of steel had moved to my front, my back pillowed by the soft mattress beneath me.

My hands were pressed into the pillows on either side of my head, and my hips were pinned by his. *Now we're getting somewhere,* I thought deliriously. "Do your worst," I slurred.

He grunted. "I prefer my women to be conscious and healthy, thank you."

I tried to shrug, but the motion felt stilted and sluggish. "Your loss." The words came out on a hiss, and I shut my eyes, the lids too heavy to keep open.

I must have fallen asleep because when I came back to

awareness, he was no longer on top of me, but sitting beside me again.

There was no more cloth this time.

Just him doing something on his phone. I ran my gaze over him again, noting the way he relaxed against the headboard, his long legs stretched out and crossed at the ankles. He appeared to be the epitome of relaxed grace. Elegant. Model-like.

His dark eyes drifted down to mine, perhaps feeling my focus on him. “Good. You’re awake,” he murmured. He went back to his phone for a moment before reaching over to set it on the nightstand.

I glanced around him to see that the sun had entered the sky, confirming that I’d fallen asleep. I had no idea for how long, but the exhaustion in his features suggested it’d been a while. Something told me he hadn’t slept last night. At all.

Because he’d been waiting for me to be awake enough to fuck?

That took dedication and admiration.

“We need to have a discussion about your situation,” he said, finally arriving at the point.

“Yes, let’s do that.” I meant the words to come out with a snarky lilt, but my voice was hoarse again.

He reached over for a glass—the same one as before, only it was full again—and brought the straw to my lips.

I sipped and swallowed the water because I wanted to.

He watched and waited for me to finish, the cool liquid just as refreshing as the first time. *Definitely a recently filled glass.* It made me wonder if he’d felt me waking up or if he’d continued to replenish it with ice while I slept.

“Nathan Spencer brought you here as a guest,” he stated as he returned the glass to the nightstand. “He then conducted business on my island without my approval. And he broke one of my primary rules—*consent*."

Um. "Okay?" That wasn't the summary I had anticipated, nor did I really understand it.

"This is *my* island," he continued as though I hadn't spoken. "And I don't tolerate trafficking or slavery of any kind."

A rich statement from a man of my world. But all right.

"It's an affront to my business to break the rules," he went on. "So I killed him for the offense."

I gaped at him. "Wait, what?"

"I killed him," he repeated.

"No, you didn't." Because we both knew that wasn't true. "*I* killed Nathan Spencer." I wasn't afraid to admit it. Hell, I was *proud* of myself for it. And I would kill this asshole as well, just as soon as he gave me the chance.

"No, Adalyn. You didn't kill him. I did. That's the story we're going to tell everyone. Which is why we need to discuss the details—so we're on the same page."

"But..."

"It's already decided. I've informed several others of his death and how *I* killed him. Not you." His dark eyes smoldered with dominance, yet his voice carried a velvety softness to it as he whispered, "I've already taken on this burden. There's no going back now."

CHAPTER EIGHT
ADALYN

"Wh-what? Why?" I stammered, trying to wrap my head around the words Asher had just spoken. "Why would you do that?"

"If I tell them you killed him, what will happen to you?" he asked, his dark eyes searching mine. "What will they do to you, Adalyn?"

My brow furrowed. "You know what they'll do."

"Maybe. But tell me anyway."

I swallowed.

Was he demanding this to remind me of my fate? To warn me? To hurt me with words?

Nathan used to do that to me often, constantly making me reiterate whatever threat he'd just laid at my feet. Reminding me of my potential future had been one of his favorite taunts because it'd forced me to behave.

"I'll still marry Taylor so he can take over the company, but it'll be in name only. I'll become a toy, likely used in the Sin Cave Fantasy circuit, or somewhere worse." My voice gave away my nerves, the hairs along my arms standing on end.

His eyebrows lifted. "Sin Cave Fantasy circuit? Is that part of Ecstasy?"

I blinked at him. What kind of question was that? "No. It's a different branch. Though, I guess some Ecstasy members have access to both." I frowned. "Aren't you part of both?"

He snorted. "I'm not part of any of it."

I searched his gaze, not understanding. "Not part of any of what?"

"The *network*." He spat out the word like it was a curse.

"I... I don't understand."

"I'm not a member of Ecstasy or the Fantasy circuit you mentioned. I'm not part of your Elite circle either. I just learned about Elite Brides last night." His gaze was intent. "But it seems I was on the recruitment list for potential membership, and now I have no choice in the matter."

I... I didn't know how to respond to that.

He had to be lying.

Another mindfuck. A trick. A way to provide false hope. However, I'd learned years ago that hope didn't exist in my world. Maybe for other people, but never for me.

I started to shake my head. "I'm not falling for this, Mr. Sinner. Try again."

"There's nothing to fall for, *Ms. Rose*. But I need your cooperation. I'm expecting several Elites to arrive on my island soon, which means our stories have to match one another. Otherwise, there will be more issues than I care to deal with."

"Our stories," I repeated. "You want me to lie about killing Nate. Say you did it instead." I snorted at the insanity of that ploy. "Let me guess—the purpose is to ensure the severity of my punishment? To make it worse than it already will be?"

I gave him a once-over.

"A sadist through and through," I mused, rolling my eyes. "I killed Nate. I own that. You don't need to play a game to fuck me. Unless that's how you get it up."

A taunt, one that I realized might be true.

I almost started to laugh, but his expression had me freezing in place.

I'd pushed a button.

Something to make the gentleman façade fade into the monster beneath.

Because he appeared ready to commit murder.

"A sadist, yes." His fingers caught my chin, giving it a little squeeze as he forced me to hold his burning gaze. "But I only play with willing masochists, Adalyn. Because I believe in *consent*." He released me and slid off the bed. "Stay there and don't move."

He didn't look back to see if I obeyed him, leaving me to wonder what the fuck he meant about being willing and consenting to whatever he had in mind.

I would never be willing.

Or consenting.

Those were two concepts that didn't exist in my world.

"Bryant!" he called from the doorway, making me jump.

"Yeah, boss?" a deep voice returned.

"I need your assistance." The words sounded angry.

Is he inviting someone to join us? To try to force my willingness? A game of normal sadist and worse sadist? A way to show me why I may prefer the sadist who hadn't raped me while unconscious, maybe?

"Did she claw you up again?" Bryant asked, a note of amusement in his tone as the sound of footsteps announced his arrival.

Asher glanced down at his forearms. I couldn't see them

from here but now wondered if I'd drawn blood earlier. "No. I need my laptop."

A male with brown hair appeared, the edges of it falling to his ears. It was the sort of style that almost looked as though he needed a trim, just like the light dusting of hair along his square jaw. I suspected that was the look he enjoyed—messy but purposeful.

Dangerous, I translated. *Rebellious.*

Yeah, this was definitely about to become a game of *Who can be the worst sadist?*

Great.

Just what I'd always wanted.

Of course, I'd known this would happen the moment I'd decided to kill Nate.

Sighing, I sat up on the bed, letting the sheet fall again. "Look—"

"I told you not to fucking move," Asher cut me off, his expression smoldering with fury. "Cover your damn breasts."

I arched a brow at him. "What? You don't like seeing Nate's handiwork on my skin? Does that turn you off? Because that may be a problem. He left knife marks all over my body." I held up my palm, recalling the moment I'd yanked one of those knives from my ass. The stitches on my hand were a new touch, giving me pause for a moment.

That gash must have been worse than normal. This may even leave a scar.

"Well, at least he didn't break her spirit," Bryant said softly.

"Laptop. Now." Asher slammed the door, causing me to jolt once more, my heart flying into a chaotic rhythm as he stalked toward the bed.

Shit. I always was a bratty sub, but only because most Doms enjoyed having a reason to punish me.

This one didn't appear all that enthused by my antics.

Actually, he appeared downright infuriated by them.

His dark gaze went to my breasts—I hadn't covered them up yet—and his jaw ticked.

He started unbuttoning his shirt, making my mouth go dry. *This is it. He's finally going to act.*

But as he began revealing his fit physique, I wasn't entirely sure this was a bad thing. Except, no, it was definitely a bad thing. Because a man in his shape could last for a long time. He could actually hurt me. Horribly, even. All those rippling muscles spoke of a stamina that might just rip me in half.

Fuck.

"Here," he grated, handing me his shirt. "Put this on."

I blinked. "What?"

"Put. It. On." Each word was enunciated slowly, his tone leaving no room for argument.

My instinct to rebel vanished behind a wave of necessary submission, my fingers shaking as I grabbed the cloth and quickly did what he commanded. A hint of minty aftershave touched my senses, swathing me in his masculine scent.

Warmth touched my skin, both from the residual heat embedded in the fabric and the shame that came with knowing I'd angered my superior.

I hated this feeling.

Hated how it belittled me.

I should be proud for standing up for myself, for pushing him, but some sick and twisted part of me didn't like disappointing the men in my life. It was a part of me that Nate had cultivated and groomed and exploited.

“Thank you,” Asher said, his tone softer now as he brushed the back of his knuckles against my cheek on his way down to grip my chin. His grasp wasn’t as hard as before, more of a gentle caress as he pulled my gaze up to his once more. “I’m not here to punish you, Adalyn. I’m not here as part of Sin Cave. And I’m going to prove it to you once I have my laptop.”

I frowned at him. “How?”

“By showing you the arrangements I’ve already made on your behalf.”

He drew his thumb along my jaw as he sat beside me, not against the headboard, but facing me with one leg pulled up on the mattress and the other hanging off the side of the bed.

“You have no reason to trust me, Adalyn. And I know you’ve been through hell. But I don’t have a lot of time to convince you of my intentions.” He slowly lowered his touch to the shirt, his opposite hand joining it as he began fastening the buttons around me. “I had no idea what Nathan was going to do to you on this island. But I suspected something was wrong the moment I saw you. I already had Nathan on my watch list when you killed him.”

“W-watch list?” I repeated as he fastened a button near my lower belly.

“There are rules on my island. Rules I take very seriously. And if I feel someone may be breaking those rules, they’re put on the observation list for my men. The breakfast I requested with Nathan was meant to be an evaluation. Obviously, it didn’t come soon enough.”

A knock sounded, interrupting whatever reply I would have made to that—not that I really had one. I was still trying to process his statements and the warmth his touch spread through my body as he *dressed* me. It was the opposite of what every man before him had done. They'd never wanted me to cover up; they'd wanted me to strip.

"Come in," Asher instructed, his focus on me and not the door.

Bryant entered, carrying a laptop, his brown-green irises taking in the scene with a quick sweep of his gaze. The action, coupled with the way he carried himself, suggested he was some sort of bodyguard.

And definitely a Dominant, too.

Men with a superiority streak carried themselves in a manner that I recognized instantly, usually with just a glance at their shoulders—straight, imposing, and almost regal in nature. They also wore their preferences in their eyes, via that penetrating stare that demanded submission. Like an alpha wolf on the prowl, commanding everyone in his path.

I glanced down now, knowing better than to challenge two Doms.

"Do you want me to arrange a wardrobe for her?" Bryant asked as he set the laptop on the nightstand. "Her suitcase only has lace in it."

I almost grunted at that.

Because Nate packed it for me, I thought.

I only had the one outfit I wore on the jet to appear professional. And a second dress to wear home. Everything else was revealing and meant to be worn for a week of constant sex.

Asher nodded, his fingers returning to my chin as he guided my focus away from my lap and up to his gaze once more. "What do you like to wear, Adalyn?"

I blinked at him—an action that seemed to be happening a lot this morning. "Whatever I'm told to wear."

He arched a brow. "That's not what I asked."

I stared at him.

He stared back, waiting me out.

I swallowed. "I, uh..." I wasn't sure how to answer this question. "For you? Or... when I'm... not training?" It came out almost incoherent, making me want to kick myself. But this male was all sorts of confusing.

Absolutely Dominant.

Primal, too.

Yet he wasn't touching me in the way I'd anticipated, and he seemed hell-bent on trying to provoke emotions from me. Emotions like *hope*. And I sort of hated him for that.

Well, no, I *did* hate him.

I hated all of them.

Every man. Every Elite member. Every fucking male who looked at me.

Some women, too.

"What do you like to wear at home when you're alone?" he rephrased.

"Jeans. Yoga pants. Tank tops." I shrugged. "Sometimes nothing at all. The cuts sometimes sting when..." I trailed off, not wanting to finish that statement because he would probably make me wear something that chafed just to ensure I felt those injuries with every movement.

His gaze went to the shirt covering my skin before his attention shifted to the male standing beside the bed. "Summer dresses. Yoga pants. Tank tops. I imagine she at least had some undergarments in that suitcase?"

"Crotchless ones," Bryant replied.

Asher's grip tightened on my jaw, making me wince. He released me, his hand falling to his lap. "Get her everything she needs. Comfort over sexy."

Bryant nodded. "On it. Clive is downstairs in case you

need more ointment or anything." His lips quirked as he glanced at Asher's arms.

I followed his look, my lips parting upon seeing the scratch marks I'd left on his skin. *Shit.* If I'd done that to Nate, he would have strangled me.

Yet Asher... Asher had barely touched me.

He'd forced me to wear a shirt instead.

I considered him for a moment as his friend left, my mind struggling to compute his motives. Emotional torture wasn't outside the realm of possibility, especially if the Elite wanted to break me irrevocably to guarantee I never acted out again.

However, other than grip my chin, he hadn't really exuded much dominance over me. Not even when he'd pinned me to the bed earlier.

"Fuck both of you," Asher muttered as his friend stepped away from the bed.

His friend chuckled in response, the door softly closing behind him as he left.

CHAPTER NINE

ADALYN

Asher blew out a breath and shook his head, then he reached over for his laptop.

He said nothing as he opened the lid and started typing, his fingers flying over the keyboard as he worked.

I slid backward a little to lean against the headboard, causing his gaze to flick upward and his hands to still.

I froze.

When he didn't chastise me, I slowly continued until my back met the cushioned surface.

He moved to join me, his long legs bending as he made an angled table for his laptop. It gave me a view of his screen, which I noticed was an email inbox.

"This is the notice I sent to guests and clients Nathan Spencer invited to your *graduation ceremony* this week," Asher informed me, his voice darkening as he said "graduation ceremony."

An email appeared on the screen, the words short and to the point.

Nathan Spencer has been removed from my island. Your

invitation to join him at Sinners Isle has been revoked. If you have any questions, please follow up with me directly.

Best,
Asher Sinner

He started showing me some of the replies asking for clarification, or an updated location for the "party," all of which he'd responded to in the same way.

The "celebration" has been canceled. And your presence here is not welcome.

Best,
Asher Sinner

There were a few follow-up questions that essentially read, *Do you have any idea who I am?* He started replying to them while I watched.

Yes. I am aware of who you are, Mr. Strider. However, these antics have proven that your network *is unaware of who* I *am. And I do not tolerate disrespect of this nature on* my *island.*

Best,
Asher Sinner

He copied that language for two other emails, only changing out the name of whom he addressed in the reply, and hit Send.

He then pulled up an email from Julian Jovanni and hit Reply, causing my stomach to churn.

Julian Jovanni.

Heir to the Jovanni family empire.

His family owned the Elite Bride program. Yet Asher claimed not to have anything to do with Sin Cave. This proved that everything he'd said was a lie.

Except that the subject was entitled *Meeting Request.*

Good morning, Julian,

Your meeting terms are acceptable.

However, I need twelve days.

My sister and her family are on my island right now. I cannot entertain your organization while she is here, and I can't send her home without raising unwanted questions.

Please inform Mr. Rose and Mr. Huntington that Adalyn is under my care. I'm denying their shipment request. This is my island. I will handle things as I see fit.

Including the removal of Nathan Spencer from my island.

Best,
Asher Sinner

He hit Send without batting an eye, then looked at me. "Bryant has spoken to Julian three times already regarding the Nathan Spencer incident. He's confirmed with Julian that I killed him for his disrespectful behavior on my island."

Asher scrolled up to show me Julian's original message requesting a meeting to discuss recent events. And a note regarding *shipping* the cargo back to the mainland.

Apparently, I was that cargo.

Or that was what I gathered from Asher's response.

"This organization underestimated how seriously I take my business. Now they know I won't tolerate having my resources taken advantage of, or being lied to about the purpose of a visit." He skimmed a few more emails while I watched, then slowly closed his laptop. "I'm showing you these so you can see that I'm not lying to you—I'm not part of the network. Nor do I wish to join the network. But it seems Nathan has forced my hand in the matter."

He set his laptop on the nightstand before shifting his gaze to me.

"I don't agree with what has been done to you, Adalyn," he said softly. "I'm not here to punish you. But I do need our stories to match one another. They cannot know the truth about how Nathan died. I've already taken the blame. His body has been disposed of. The villa you were in is nearly clean. And all the video evidence has been erased."

"But why?" I whispered. "Why are you covering up what I did?"

"To protect you," he replied, shrugging. "To make a statement. I'm not really sure. But my instincts say it's the right move, so it's what I've chosen to do. I'm also going to demand that you be allowed to remain here. Indefinitely."

I gaped at him. "Wait, what? My parents are never going to allow that."

He shrugged as though unbothered by the statement. "I don't intend to give them a choice."

I shook my head. "You don't understand. They have an agreement with the Huntingtons. They won't go against it."

"As I said, I won't be giving them a choice." His intense expression told me he meant that. But he didn't know these people like I did.

Especially if he wasn't even a Sin Cave member.

"You don't know how this game is played," I whispered. *Assuming he's telling me the truth.*

But on the off chance he meant it...

On the off chance this was truly real...

Then he needed to understand... "There are no rules in this world. They'll kill you for getting in their way."

"They may try," he agreed. "But this is my island. And I'll remind them that there's a reason they have me on their recruitment list. Perhaps I'll agree to join if they give me you."

I wanted to argue that I wasn't a possession to be given to anyone.

But I knew that wasn't true.

I'd been born as a possession. A woman without value beyond my name and status. Hence the need for all my training and the marriage arranged for me while just a child.

My college degree meant nothing.

I hadn't even taken it all that seriously because even if I were able to escape, I wouldn't be able to use it, as I'd have to change my name and identity.

I also had no work experience.

Which meant my only skills were centered around how to properly please men with dark fetishes.

And how to endure pain.

"I'm not like them," Asher continued softly. "I meant what I said about consent, Adalyn. It's the primary rule of my isle, something all my clients are aware of. It's something Nathan Spencer attempted to take for granted, and his death will prove to everyone how serious I am about my rules."

"They'll kill you," I repeated in a whisper, needing him to understand that. "You realize that, right?"

"I realize that they may want to kill me, but I don't think they will. Nathan was here without their approval, thereby acting within his own realm of incompetence. His death is warranted by their standards. And I'm within my rights to demand recompense. As I have no use for money, I'll demand something of higher worth. I'll demand that they give me *you*."

I narrowed my gaze. "For someone who claims not to be part of the Elite network, you certainly seem pretty confident in your expectations." And he'd very clearly decided on keeping me as a prize. His very own mostly trained Elite Bride.

He relaxed beside me on the bed, his long legs stretching out to cross at the ankles. "I'm not naïve, Adalyn. I know this world is dark and dangerous, that I can't save many from their fates within it. But for whatever reason, I've been provided with an opportunity to save you. So I will."

"But why?"

"Because I can," he replied with a soft smile. "I have twelve days to convince you to play along. Twelve days to prove my intentions. Consider this day one." He placed his palm on my thigh over the blankets and gave it a gentle squeeze. "Rest. Shower. Explore the house. But be careful. Dr. Zansky says you have a concussion."

He removed his touch to grab my wrist, flipping my hand over to reveal the stitches on my palm.

"Be careful with these, too. No strenuous exercise. No overexerting yourself." His dark eyes captured mine. "Perhaps go easy on the knives for a few days as well, hmm?" He almost seemed amused. "My room is next to yours. If you need anything, knock. Otherwise, I'm going to go have a much-needed nap. And tomorrow, I'll give you a proper tour of the island."

He released my wrist and slid out of the bed.

"This agreement is rather simple," he added as he picked up his laptop. "You help me succeed; I'll help you live again."

My brow furrowed. *"Help you live again." And that meant what, exactly?* I wondered.

"I have no use for a slave," he went on. "Nor do I want a woman in my bed who doesn't desire being there. I'll never force you. But I do need you to work with me, at least for the next twelve days. After that, I'll do whatever I can to give you freedom. Even if it's just on this island. Unless you want to marry Taylor Huntington, in which case..." He trailed off, his eyebrow rising.

I swallowed, unable to speak. Because I wasn't sure what to say.

No, I did not want to marry Taylor Huntington.

But everything else... it felt... too unreal to consider. *Freedom? Live on this island? Paradise? Not as a slave, but as a... a* what, *exactly?*

"Take the day. Think about it. Tomorrow morning, I'll take you to breakfast. You can ask me anything while we eat. Until then, Caylin, my personal chef, will bring up some food for you. And Bryant will drop off clothes after he's done acquiring them." He used his laptop to point to the wall opposite the windows. "As I said, I'll be in my room. Just knock if you need something."

He didn't wait for me to reply.

He merely left.

Almost silently, too. Because he wasn't wearing shoes.

And all he had on were those dress pants that hugged his ass.

Not that I noticed.

Just like I didn't notice the way his back muscles flexed as he moved.

Well, there could be worse men to be enslaved to. That much was clear, anyway.

Unless this all turned out to be an emotional mindfuck, in which case he'd just become the most dangerous Master of all.

Because part of me believed him.

Part of me *hoped* he meant every word.

Part of me had secretly wished for a man like him to save me.

Which made me hate him more than anyone I'd ever met. Because he was either a dream that would soon become my worst nightmare. Or a dream that had taken far too long to appear in my life.

So what are you, Mr. Sinner? A hero? Or the most immoral villain of them all?

CHAPTER TEN
ASHER

Adalyn remained silent all day and night, making me check on her more than once. Each time, I found her in the same place I'd left her—in the bed—still wearing my shirt.

She'd tensed every time I'd entered, almost as though she'd anticipated me charging her.

I'd kept my distance on purpose, demonstrating through action that I wasn't a threat.

But as I entered her room now, I realized it hadn't helped at all.

She was still in the bed, hair rumpled, eyes wary.

Sighing, I leaned against her door frame and folded my arms across my freshly pressed dress shirt. "Having trouble sleeping, darling?" I asked casually.

Her nostrils flared. "I'm not used to big fluffy beds."

"Would you prefer a cage?" I wondered aloud. "I can find one."

I wouldn't actually put her in one unless she really needed it.

Dr. Zansky had commented that she might struggle with the concept of freedom, given what she'd probably been through. She was used to having someone tell her what to do, and while she clearly possessed a defiant streak, she required that hint of dominance to ground her.

Which he'd continued on to say was something I would need to provide for her, if I wanted to help her heal.

It seemed counterproductive to her situation, but his logic held merit.

And I'd seen proof of it yesterday when I'd demanded that she put on my shirt.

She'd immediately moved to comply, even after taunting me just seconds before.

It'd almost broken my heart.

Just like the conflict in her expression now.

"Tell me what you need, Adalyn," I said, pushing off the door frame to start toward her.

She was sitting up again, her body tensing as I approached.

I moved slowly and purposefully toward the bed, then sat close enough to touch her without actually encroaching on her space. "Would it be easier if I told you what I want?" I gentled my voice, very aware of the chaos darkening her gaze.

Maybe giving her this big room had been a mistake. But had I closed her off in a smaller one, she still would have fretted over whatever came next.

So I'd give her a normal day today.

Show her what life on my island could be like.

"Yes," she whispered. "Tell me what you plan to do. What you want from me. Please."

Poor darling sounded so broken.

She'd obviously been up all night worrying herself to death.

Because she didn't trust me.

And I couldn't blame her at all for that.

What she needed from me now was patience with a subtle hint of dominance, both of which I could give.

I reached out to cup her cheek, my touch purposefully gentle. "I want you to take a shower while I select an outfit for you. Then I would like you to go to breakfast with me. Okay?"

She nibbled her lower lip, her brow furrowing. "And then?"

"And then, I need to do some work. But you can wander the house, maybe even take a walk on the beach. Nothing too strenuous, as Dr. Zansky says you need to rest. We'll plan to have dinner here, perhaps a bit early since it seems you didn't sleep much." I let my hand fall. "If this bed is too soft, then I'll find you something else, all right?"

"Like a cage?" It almost sounded like a retort, but it lacked heat.

"If that's what you need, but it wouldn't be my preference."

Her dark eyelashes fanned out across her pale cheekbones before lifting to reveal big, beautiful eyes. "What's your preference?"

"For you to be comfortable." I drew my thumb along the hollow beneath her eye. "Let's go eat. Then we'll discuss more, okay?"

She swallowed but nodded a little.

"Go shower," I commanded, my voice gentle yet firm. "I'll find something for you to wear." Bryant had put all the clothes in the closet, per my request.

"Okay." She slid out from beneath the sheets, pulling my shirt down along the way, and swayed a little as she stood.

I moved to my feet and walked around the foot of the

bed toward her as she started forward. Her knees nearly buckled, but she caught her balance and blew out a breath.

"Did you eat anything yesterday?" I asked.

She shook her head. "I learned a long time ago not to eat much before a session."

"Because you expected me to come back for you last night."

"At some point," she corrected, gritting her teeth. "Yes."

I nodded. "Well, I'm here now. But not to fuck you." Crass words, but they were the ones this situation required of me.

She eyed me warily. "I don't want to believe you."

"I know." I pressed my palm to her lower back. "How about I prove it?"

This would not be easy, but at least it would give her an idea of my control.

Her lips turned down as we walked, her fear mounting with each step. "I'm not going to fuck you, Adalyn," I told her as we entered the bathroom. "But I am going to bathe you."

She gaped at me in the mirror. "You're going to... to what?"

"Hands on the counter, sweetheart," I commanded.

She obeyed beautifully, her body seeming to respond before her mind even caught up. I left her there and went to the shower to turn on the water. Then I stripped down to my boxers—which I would have to change after this—and returned to stand behind her.

She kept her head bowed in submission, her need to supplicate radiating between us.

Perhaps she'd given me every ounce of her fight yesterday, and today, she couldn't stand the thought of rebelling. Regardless of her reasoning, I knew how to handle her in this state.

I moved her hair away from her neck, pulling it over one shoulder, and ran my finger along her spine over her shirt. "I need to undress you," I informed her softly. "Then I'm going to guide you backward into the shower and wash your hair. Do you understand?"

She nodded slowly, her throat working to swallow. "Yes, Sir."

I bent to press a kiss to her neck. "Good girl, Adalyn."

She shivered in response, her nails seeming to bite into the counter. It made me wonder if anyone had ever praised her before. I made a mental note to do it again later.

I reached around her slowly to unbutton her shirt, my gaze observing the motion in the mirror to ensure I didn't touch her inappropriately. Her breathing escalated, her back brushing my chest with the motion, her head still angled downward.

She had her lip clenched between her teeth, her eyes closed as though anticipating the worst. I pressed another kiss to her throat, my lips skimming her ear as I whispered, "It's okay, sweetheart. Breathe for me. That's it." I reached the final button, my gaze tracking the movement. "I'm going to pull my shirt off your shoulders now, okay?"

She started to nod but froze when my mouth brushed her skin. "Yes, Sir." It sounded like an ingrained response, words she'd been taught to utter on repeat all her life.

I wouldn't deny the beauty of hearing them on her lips.

Or the very real arousal I felt spiraling inside me at the mere act of undressing her.

But I knew how to temper my urges. I knew how to properly care for a submissive. Perhaps not one as broken as

Adalyn, though. However, I would do my best and learn her cues along the way.

Her rosy nipples beaded as I exposed them to the air, her body seeming to react on instinct alone.

She'd clearly been trained to respond to a man's touch, even when she didn't desire it. That would make her harder to read, but not impossible.

I ran my fingers down her arms with the fabric. "Stand up straight," I told her.

She obeyed.

I removed the shirt from her wrists and set it aside. Then I took hold of her hips and slowly rotated her to face me. She didn't meet my gaze, her submissive pose seeming to be the only thing holding her upright.

"Eyes on me," I whispered.

She swallowed, then obeyed, her watery gaze breaking my heart a little. She was trying not to show her fear, trying not to allow me to see what this was doing to her. And it killed a part of me to even think about what had driven her to look at a man in this manner.

Accusations and hatred poured from her beautiful eyes.

Followed by pain.

And a hint of panic.

I drew a little circle against her hip with my thumb, then took a step backward toward the stone-walled shower. It was a walk-in style meant to accommodate two or three people with a waterfall fixture overhead that provided a nice touch to the already exotic ambience.

My own shower was actually partially inside and outside, my rooms overlooking the ocean below.

It allowed for a taste of exhibitionism as well.

Which was what made this shower better suited for Adalyn—it was enclosed by glass on two sides and stone walls on the others, making it private and for her alone. If I'd invited her into mine, she'd be entirely exposed. And I suspected that would do more harm than good.

I moved her into the center beneath the falling water, then turned on some of the wall sprays as well, ensuring she received the full experience.

A violent tremble worked its way through her, causing her knees to bend. But I caught her before she could fall. Her hands grabbed my forearms, her eyes blowing wide open with a mixture of confusion and alarm.

I frowned at her. "Were you going to kneel?"

"Y-yes," she whispered.

"Sweetheart, if I want you to kneel, I'll tell you. Right now, all I want is for you to stand here and let me take care of you, okay?"

Another shudder worked through her as her body and mind seemed to argue about how to proceed.

"Do as I tell you." I infused a hint of dominance in my tone, sensing that she needed it. "Stand here in the center. Close your eyes. And let me take care of you."

Her throat moved, another shiver seeming to consume her. But then her legs locked and her eyes fell closed, just like I'd commanded. "Very good, Adalyn," I told her softly, one of my hands leaving her hip to move up to her face. I brushed my knuckles against her cheek, noting the way she leaned into my touch rather than away from it. "You're very beautiful, sweet girl." I meant it. Because she was quite possibly one of the most stunning women I'd ever met, and it wasn't merely because she stood naked before me now.

There was just something unique about her.

Not only in looks, but inside her, too.

A fighting spirit, I thought. However, it was more than

that. Even a wounded animal would fight against perceived threats.

No, Adalyn struck me as calculative.

She read people and their motives, something she'd proven last night when she'd called me a sadist. When she'd called out my kinks as though I'd written them down for her.

Except for the rope fetish.

I would never bind a woman to the point of pain.

Shibari? Yes, I enjoyed watching that.

But nothing extreme. Nothing that made something hurt for the sake of hurting. That wasn't what I enjoyed. A little pain made me hard because I knew I would be the one to make her feel better, to chase that sting away with my hands and with my tongue.

So I was somewhat of a sadist as a result. But nothing hard-core. Not like other men I knew.

Adalyn remained perfectly still as the water dampened her black hair, the long strands reminding me of sensual ink trailing over her slender shoulders and touching the tips of her perfect breasts.

I could see why someone might want to enslave her.

If she were mine, I wouldn't get anything done. I'd be too busy fucking her all day and night.

An inappropriate assessment, maybe. But I couldn't bring myself to take it back.

Instead, I busied myself with caring for her the way I'd said I would.

Every touch was meant to help her heal. Every stroke was my way of promising not to push her too far. Every caress was meant to apologize for all those who'd come before me.

I shampooed her hair.

Then rinsed it.

Careful of her eyes, which she kept closed the whole time.

Then I coated my hands with conditioner and combed my fingers through her hair. She seemed to fall into a trance by the time I finished, her breathing slow and steady and her face almost relaxed.

I took advantage of her calm state and knelt to thoroughly soap up her calves and thighs, my eyes on the various scrapes and bruises marring her otherwise perfect skin.

A true sadist understood how to turn pain into pleasure.

It seemed Nathan had only played at the role, assuming her pain had equaled his own pleasure. And maybe it had. But that made him a psychopath, not a sadist.

I carefully cleansed her inner thighs, my gaze drifting up to her face as I did.

She'd stiffened a little, her eyes having opened to watch me.

Not with contentment.

But with fear and a hint of something darker. Something expectant.

Damn. I'd lulled her into a state of comfort, and something I'd done had disturbed the peace. She appeared to be on the edge of a reaction.

I just wasn't sure if she meant to scream, cry, rage, or try to kill me.

Perhaps all of the above.

Well, shit.

CHAPTER ELEVEN
ASHER

"Are you all right?" I questioned softly, aware of how close my mouth was to her shaved pussy. Was that what had her on edge now? Or was it something else?

"I..." She cleared her throat, her voice sounding hoarse.

"Do you have a safeword, Adalyn?" I asked her, realizing I should have addressed that from the beginning. But we weren't exactly in a scene, even though I'd used my dominance to lull her into one.

I stood and washed the soap from my hands, then took hold of her hips.

"Have you ever been given a safeword?" I rephrased. "One you could actually use?"

She blinked up at me as though I spoke a foreign language. But this beautiful girl had to know what I meant.

Alas, she shook her head.

"My limits are infinite," she informed me. "I have no need for a safeword."

My eyebrows lifted. "Is that what that jackass told you? That you have no need for a safeword?" God, I would kill him if he were still alive. The only thing that kept me from raging was knowing that she'd stabbed him a good ten times before he'd died.

"My limits are infinite," she repeated, tears entering her eyes. "I don't need a safeword."

"Oh, beautiful girl," I said, wrapping my arms around her in a hug and holding her as she started to break against me. Those words were programmed into her, that repetitive statement clearly one she'd been trained to say.

I lifted her off the ground to cradle her in my arms as I moved to sit against the stone bench.

She fully broke then, sobs racking her body as she fought for her steadfast control, fought to hide beneath whatever veneer she'd crafted over the years.

"Everyone has a safeword," I told her softly. "Because everyone has limits. And it's a Dom's responsibility to ensure you're never taken to a point where you feel you need to use your safeword." Which I'd suspected was near when I'd knelt before her. Something about my soaping up her legs had awakened her from her cocoon of bliss, and that look on her face had bordered on wrongness.

That wasn't the sort of expression a woman should give a man when he was busy taking care of her.

And this reaction now proved all my instincts right.

"Wh-what do you want from me?" she sobbed. "I... I don't know... I don't know how to play..."

"This isn't a game, Adalyn. I'm not part of Sin Cave. I'm not trying to hurt you. I'm trying to take care of you."

"Why?" she demanded. "*Why* are you doing this?"

"Because someone needs to," I said, at a loss for a better explanation. What was I going to do? Tell her that one look at her at the airport the other morning had me wanting to yank her away from Nathan Spencer and hide her from everyone and everything that wanted to hurt her? It sounded insane to my ears. I didn't know her. This shouldn't be my problem at all.

But Nathan had chosen *my* island.

He'd sealed all our fates.

And now I was determined to make this right with Adalyn. To help her. To fix her. To *soothe* her.

To save her.

A dangerous notion.

However, I'd already set myself down that path.

Julian had responded to my last email, asking me how I intended to "handle" the package. I'd responded, stating I would provide my own style of training.

Needless to say, it had intrigued him.

And he'd provided the "okay" for Adalyn to remain here.

Bryant had later read the email and warned me that I'd just entered a dangerous game.

He wasn't wrong.

Adalyn continued to cry and ask me what I wanted from her. I told her I didn't want anything other than to heal her.

She accused me of lying.

I promised her I wasn't.

At one point, she tried to slap me.

I merely caught her wrist and gently held it against my chest.

She vibrated with fury. Shook with fear. Screamed with pain. Cried with a sadness I felt to my very soul.

I held her through it all, until she was so exhausted that all she did was lie there limply against my shoulder. Only then did I finish bathing her by pulling one of the showerheads off the wall.

She didn't fight me. She didn't say a word, just let me

rinse the remaining soap from her skin and the conditioner from her hair.

I moved her onto the bench, grabbed the soap, and did the best I could with her torso and back. It was like trying to wash a life-size doll. Somehow, I managed it.

Then I turned off the water and wrapped her up in a giant fluffy towel.

She shook, her expectations becoming clear as I carried her to the bed.

"We'll do breakfast together tomorrow," I told her as I laid her down on the comforter. "For today, we'll stay here. I'll work. You relax. But tomorrow, we have to be seen together. If Sin Cave is going to believe that I've claimed you as mine, then we'll need people to see us together."

Her big eyes met mine. "I don't understand you."

"I know." I went back to the bathroom for a second towel that I spread out along the pillow for her hair. "Just lie down for a bit. I'll arrange breakfast. Then you're going to eat."

Her nostrils flared like she wanted to refuse.

"You're going to eat," I reiterated, ensuring she could hear my command. "I'll hand-feed you if I have to."

She flinched, my phrase obviously bothering her.

Which was when I recalled the video of Nathan treating her like a dog.

Fucking prick.

Rather than elaborate or correct the assessment, I merely guided her back into the pillow with the towel on it and kissed the top of her head. "Be a good girl for me, Adalyn. And I promise to reward you."

That had her eyes meeting mine. "How will you reward me?"

I wondered if she meant that as a sarcastic retort.

But something in her gaze told me she'd meant the question.

Perhaps Nathan had worked on some sort of fucked-up reward system.

"What kind of reward would you like?" I asked carefully, searching her gaze.

"I... I would like a week of no sharing, please."

My eyebrows lifted, shocked by her request.

"A-a day," she quickly amended. "Just twenty-four hours to recover. P-please."

Jesus, that's her idea of a reward? I shook my head, and her expression fell. "Oh, sweet girl." I knelt on the bed and cupped her cheek with my palm. "I'll give you more than a week. I'll give you a lifetime, if that's what you want."

Her lower lip quivered. "I-I'm sorry, Sir."

"Don't ever apologize to me, Adalyn," I told her sternly. "And I'm not punishing you. I'll give you whatever you ask, just be good for me, okay?"

She started to cry again, breaking my heart. Rather than speak, I merely lay down beside her—still soaked from our shower—and held her again.

I'd have to change the sheets later, or maybe give her a different room. But it was worth holding her for now. Worth giving her my strength when she'd clearly expelled what was left of her own.

My wrist buzzed some time later with a message from Clive saying my sister was looking for me.

I clicked the microphone icon and replied, "Tell her I'm busy. I'll call her later."

Adalyn stiffened against me, almost as though she'd forgotten my presence.

"My sister," I whispered against her ear. "She's pestering my men about my location." Which only further complicated everything at present, but I'd deal with it in time. "Are you ready to try to eat something, Adalyn?" I asked softly.

"Your sister?" she repeated.

"Hmm," I hummed, chuckling a little. "She's persistent." As evidenced by Clive's reply of *She says she wants to meet you for lunch.* I clicked the microphone again, "Tell her I have plans for lunch."

Adalyn stiffened.

"Not those kinds of plans, Adalyn," I said, aware of where her mind was going. "I'm going to feed you. Then I need to work."

My wrist buzzed again. *She's on her way to your villa, sir.*

"Fuck," I muttered. "I need to go handle my errant sister." The last thing I wanted was for her to meet Adalyn and get the wrong idea in her head.

Another message came through, this one from my brother. *What are you doing that makes you too busy for our dear sister?*

I growled, rolling out of the bed, and went to find my clothes. At least my boxers were mostly dry now. But I yanked them off in the bathroom to pull on the dress pants because, knowing my sister, I didn't have a lot of time. I buttoned up my dress shirt, then took my phone from the pocket of my slacks and dialed Tru.

I had no idea what time it was over there, but he was obviously awake, thanks to our sister.

"Did that little brat actually call to complain to you?" I asked when he answered.

"Of course she did," he drawled. "I'm her favorite brother, after all."

I snorted. "Right. I have work to do."

"As do we all, but when the baby wants something, she gets it."

"You realize that's why she thinks she's the center of all our worlds, right? Because we let her do this?" I stepped into the bedroom to find Adalyn watching me.

"Life would be very boring without her."

"A fact she enjoys reminding us of every day," I replied, smiling despite my mood. "Next time she wants to tattle on me, tell her to try Beckett or Damiano. I like talking to them more than you."

Tru snorted. "You've always been a terrible liar, little bro."

I nearly asked if I could put him on speaker to repeat that out loud for Adalyn, but I didn't want to have to explain her presence yet. "I'll handle our darling little brat of a sister. But I'm sending her to you on her way back to London."

"I'm not sure if that's a threat or a gift..." He trailed off.

"A mixture of both," I promised, hanging up the phone and looking at Adalyn. "I'll be back with breakfast. There are clothes in the closet if you want them."

I started to leave when another thought struck me, sending me back into the bathroom.

"Or you can wear this," I said as I returned to the bed with a robe in my hand. I set it beside her. "Whatever makes you the most comfortable. But put on something, Adalyn. Not just the towel, okay?"

"Yes, Sir," she replied, her voice soft.

"Good girl." I leaned down to kiss her cheek. "I'll be back."

And I would try to explain to her what I meant by "reward." Because clearly she needed a lesson in appropriate gratification.

CHAPTER TWELVE

ADALYN

A HIGH-PITCHED SQUEAL from downstairs caused me to sit upright, my heart in my throat. *What was that?*

I'd been debating what to wear since Asher had left the room, my brain struggling to understand this strange reality.

He'd held me while I'd cried.

I'd... I'd only started to tear up because I'd thought that was what he'd needed to fuck me. And then it'd morphed into a true sob, into terror and horror and pain and a myriad of other emotions I couldn't name. I'd felt lost and utterly destroyed.

Yet he'd been there the whole time.

Soothing me.

Caressing me.

Handling me with a care I didn't understand. No one had ever touched me so tenderly. No one had ever praised me, either.

Then he'd offered me a reward.

And I'd spoken without thinking it through.

He'd been shocked.

I'd tried to take it back, but he'd just *hugged* me again. Which had only made me cry harder.

I felt utterly destroyed. Shattered beyond recognition. Almost as though years of torment had unfolded all at once into a session of agonized pain that I could no longer control.

Why did he hold me?

Why is he being so kind to me?

It was almost cruel. Because I knew it wouldn't last. Yet a part of me prayed it would. A part of me prayed this was real and not some twisted dream.

The squeal sounded again, making me jump.

It... it almost sounded like a child?

My eyes widened. *Oh, no...* Did he have a child here? To... to...? My throat started to close, my lungs refusing to work. *Is that why he hasn't needed me?*

That... that would be a new fetish. One I'd heard about but had never seen. *Oh God...* That had better not be what was happening here!

I couldn't allow that. I... I had to stop it from happening. Offer myself. Something. *Anything. Fuck, maybe this is the pain he wished to inflict upon me?*

That... that would be the worst kind of pain.

But the squeal didn't sound pained, did it?

As it rang through the walls a third time, I frowned. *No, it sounds happy.*

My brow furrowed. *Does he have a kid?*

Why hadn't I heard it before?

I picked up the robe he'd left on the bed and slipped from the sheets to put it on. Every part of me ached as though I'd just run a marathon, but I forced myself to my feet and headed toward the door.

It wasn't locked—something that surprised me. I

hadn't bothered trying last night, as I'd assumed I wasn't really allowed to leave.

But the door appeared normal with the lock on my side, not the hallway.

So perhaps... perhaps I was allowed to leave? To truly wander? Had he mentioned that yesterday? I couldn't remember. Everything felt so foggy. So unreal. So... *unexpected.*

I crept down the hallway, noting the other rooms along the way. Two more bedrooms, both of which were similar to the one I'd spent the last however many hours in. *Had it been a day? Two days? A week?*

No. Not that long.

He'd said we had twelve days until members from Sin Cave arrived.

It felt like a year had passed since killing Nathan, but it was more realistically only a day or two at most.

"You work too much," a feminine voice accused, giving me pause near the top of the stairs. It was one of those open-railed spiral designs that circled down to the first level. Which gave me a view of the foyer from up here, and a peek at the living area beside it.

"I could say the same to you," Asher replied, his voice holding a touch of humor to it.

Another squeal sounded, the high-pitched noise making me wince once more. But this time I heard the laugh that followed, the child clearly happy.

A male chuckled as well. A male that sounded like Asher. "I think he likes me, Kid."

"Of course he does, Gramps. You're letting him yank on your hair," the female replied.

"Well, he can't yank on Yon's hair."

"Hilarious," a male voice deadpanned. *Not Asher. And definitely unamused, too.*

"Not a joke if it's true," Asher returned, a note of teasing in his tone. "Your son is— *Ow.*"

"I stand corrected. That was hilarious," the other man said. "Do it again, Graham. Pull on Uncle Asher's hair."

"Let's not teach our child to abuse..." The female, who I assumed was Asher's sister now, trailed off. "No, yeah, actually, do it again, Graham."

"I'm starting to regret inviting you to my isle," Asher muttered. "Aren't you two supposed to be on your honeymoon? Why are you in my villa?"

"Because we didn't see you for breakfast. *Again.*" Yeah, that definitely sounded like a sisterly tone. I'd witnessed my old roommate, Jen, give her older brother that tone on numerous occasions. Usually when discussing her age and being an adult, though. He had a knack for seeing her as a kid, which was a problem because she was not-so-secretly in love with his best friend... who also saw her as a kid sister. At least until recently.

A night at Ecstasy had changed all that.

Sort of, anyway.

I frowned, wondering if anything had changed at graduation. She'd been planning to confront him for a final time. But I'd been on a plane to Fiji, and there hadn't been an opportunity to follow up with her.

There likely never would be.

My chest gave a pang at the thought of never speaking to Jen again. She'd been my only friend. The only sense of family I'd ever really known.

And now...

Now that felt like a lifetime ago.

"If I promise to make an appearance at breakfast tomorrow, will you let me get back to work?" Asher asked.

"Hmm, maybe," his sister replied. "But only if you agree to have dinner with us one night this week."

"I don't think she understands the point of a honeymoon, Yon," he said conversationally. "Maybe you need to give her a tutorial?"

"Trust me, I'm trying. But she has this weird obsession with her older brothers."

"I do not!" she exclaimed, eliciting a giggle from her son.

The giggle almost made my lips curl. It was such an innocent, happy sound. *Did I ever sound like that as a child?* I wondered, taking a step back from the railing. I'd intruded enough on their conversation, and I wasn't brave enough to go down dressed in a robe.

Besides, I doubted Asher wanted to explain my presence to his sister.

So I crept back to my room, only to pause at the entryway and eye the closed door at the end of the hall. *Asher's room,* I recalled, thinking of how he'd pointed toward his wall yesterday.

I kept going on instinct, curious to see what kind of room a man like Asher called his own. Would there be a cage under the bed? Beside it? Bars along the wall? A cross?

His door was unlocked, making it easy to enter.

But my breath caught in my throat at what existed on the other side.

Windows.

So. Many. Windows.

He had a balcony that circled two-thirds of his room, his ceilings over two stories tall and lined with skylights. And his bed—a huge four-post ordeal with gauzy white curtains decorating the poles—was against one of the room's only walls.

No cage.

No bars.

No kink of any kind, really.

But absolutely masculine in a way I couldn't define.

It certainly suited the island ambience with the dark wood furniture and decorative stone floor. The white linen added to the effect and matched the billowing curtains along the glass walls. Two doors were open, allowing for a calm breeze to flow through the room, bringing with it the scent of salt and ocean. I inhaled deeply, moving toward it, desiring more of the calming reprieve.

When I stepped through the glass doors, I quickly realized that the balcony spanned more than his bedroom; it actually continued along the one I'd been put in as well.

That meant he could sneak into my room from the balcony.

Not that it mattered.

He could use the hallway door, too.

And he hadn't exactly tried to bother me much, just kept checking on me.

Then bathed me today.

I ran my fingers through my knotted hair, realizing I probably should have picked up a comb or a brush. *Oh well.*

With the view of the endless ocean water and soft sand beach below, my hair felt inconsequential.

This view... was heaven.

His home wasn't like the villa I'd been in that first night. He wasn't on the actual water here. He had a beach front instead, and a dock that led to a yacht.

There didn't appear to be another property in sight, suggesting he owned this small section of the island.

Well, no, he owned the whole thing.

But this was his residence.

And he didn't put guests near his home.

Not even his sister and her family.

Interesting, I thought, inhaling once more and releasing a calming breath.

So beautiful. So mesmerizing. So perfect.

I could stay here forever.

Which… hadn't that been part of Asher's offer? To let me live here?

Of course, that would require me to *believe* him. A concept that was becoming a bit too feasible for me. Especially after overhearing him with his sister.

She… she sounded happy. Because she'd been arranged with someone she actually liked? Or… or because she wasn't an Elite Bride at all?

Most women with brothers in the network were all sent to the Elite Bride program because it meant they were within the network and likely came from families that would profit from arranged marriages.

Such as my own. As the sole heir to Rose Royale, my father needed a good candidate to take over his business.

But he wanted one he could control.

Hence, he'd chosen Taylor Huntington.

And it'd become my job to meet all of Taylor's commands for a wife. No matter what.

I gripped the balcony railing, my gaze on the sea. I'd considered suicide a number of times, especially in the early days of my training. But something had always held me back.

Some sort of pride.

A need not to give in to the darkness, I supposed.

But as the wedding neared, I kept considering it more and more.

Killing Nate was the first step.

I'd never really had a second step other than to survive. Then Asher Sinner had... *found* me. I vaguely recalled our moments on the beach, his face a bleak memory overshadowed by darkness.

Who are you really? I wondered, glancing around the beach before taking in his balcony and turning to eye his villa. *What do—*

My knees nearly buckled as I found him leaning against his sliding door, hands tucked casually in his pockets, gaze on me.

Shit! I pressed my palm to my chest, my heart beating a mile a minute at him startling me.

He pushed off the door to saunter toward me. "Taking in the view?" he asked, his voice pitched low.

"Y-yes," I stammered, swallowing.

His expression suggested he didn't quite believe me. But then he glanced around as well, nodding. "Would you like to eat breakfast out here?"

I glanced down at the stone patio floor, my lips twisting. "Um." If I told him I did, he'd probably make me kneel here to eat. If I told him I didn't, he'd also probably make me kneel. So there wasn't really an option.

"Adalyn?" He caught my chin with his fingers, pulling my gaze upward.

"I..." I cleared my throat. "Whatever you desire, Sir."

He gave me a look that said I'd disappointed him. Then he pulled his phone out from his pocket and lifted it to his ear. "We're going to eat out on my balcony." He held my gaze while he spoke. "Cushions would be great, thank you."

Cushions? I thought, my brow furrowing.

But he grabbed my hips and spun me back out toward the ocean, walking me to the edge, distracting me from my thoughts. "This is how things are going to go," he said against my ear as he reached for my hands and placed them on the balcony.

I shuddered, waiting for him to remove my robe or pull it up to my waist.

However, all he did was gently lay his hands over mine, caging me between the railing and his muscular body.

I hated how good his chest felt against my back.

How warmth seemed to bleed from him into me.

How my heart skipped a beat as his lips grazed my neck before returning to my ear. "When I ask you something, I want you to tell me truthfully how you feel. Anything that you fear. Anything that makes you uncomfortable. Such as just now, you didn't want to kneel on the stone. Had you admitted that, I would have explained what I meant by my question regarding eating out here or elsewhere."

The air seemed to shift as someone stepped out onto the balcony behind us. Interesting that I sensed that disturbance but hadn't noticed Asher's arrival. Perhaps because the minty scent had already been abundant out here, the wind having carried it from his room to mingle with the salty air around me.

And now, there was something else.

Someone else.

I started to turn toward the intruder, but Asher reached up to clasp my neck, forcing me to continue staring out at the sea while his mouth remained by my ear. "I would have told you that I have furniture specifically for that purpose. Furniture that is now being brought up here for us to sit on while we eat. Because I don't treat women like pets, Adalyn. I treat them like equals."

He nuzzled my throat, causing my pulse to skyrocket.

Because he was touching me.

Holding me.

Telling me things I longed to hear. Words I worried would be ripped from my chest in the next second. A dream I feared I would one day wake from.

"I want you to choose a safeword, Adalyn. Something that you can say if you're pushed too far. Something to tell me that you're uncomfortable with a situation. A word you can use at any time without repercussion." His thumb drew a line down the opposite side of my neck, making me feel utterly trapped. Yet oddly secure.

Like he was holding my balance in his palm.

Maintaining my being with that simple touch alone.

What is this man doing to me?

"A safeword," I repeated, almost drunk on his presence. It was on the tip of my tongue to tell him I didn't need one, that my limits were undefined. But the phrases I knew so well didn't come. It was almost as though his hand choked me, refusing to let me utter the statements that weren't truly mine to say.

Yet I could breathe just fine.

Which meant he wasn't choking me at all.

"Yes, Adalyn. That is today's reward for being so good. I'm giving you a verbal token that you can use to escape a situation of your choosing, anytime you need it."

My eyelids lifted. I wasn't sure when they'd closed, my mind lost to the male at my back, but they were open again now.

A reward.

A one-time-use safeword.

"Any situation?" I asked on a breath.

"Any situation," he repeated back to me. "Any time you

feel uncomfortable, you can use the word. And if you're really good and eat all your breakfast, I'll reward you by adding a second-time use of that word."

So two times that I could use a safeword to escape a situation not of my liking.

My heart skipped several beats.

Nate had never offered me anything of the sort.

But I found myself yearning for it now—proverbial escape cards, a way to say *no*. A way to *choose*. "Yes," I whispered. "Yes, please."

His hands went to my hips, his motions gradual as he gently rotated me to face him. "What word would you like to use? What word will you use to stop a scene and express your discomfort?"

I considered him for a long moment.

"It should be something you would never normally say. A word you either despise or something you would never think of in a sexual situation."

I knew what a safeword was, but I didn't tell him that. Mostly because I preferred his definition over the one Nathan had once provided when I'd asked him to explain the concept after overhearing the term at a club.

"It's something bad subs use when they can't handle the pressure anymore. It's a word you don't need because you have no limits. You'll do whatever I want, however I want, wherever I want. And no word will ever save you from me."

I shuddered with the memory of what he'd done next. He'd proven his point by taking me to a new height, one that had my knees buckling now just from the thought of it.

Asher caught me, my name leaving his lips.

My legs shook as I fought to stand upright, my hands on his biceps to hold myself in place.

He gave me a moment, let me breathe in the refreshing

air, allowed me to wrap myself up in the salty air tinged with his minty essence.

Safe, a small voice whispered. *Finally safe.*

It was a lie, of course.

A dream.

A figment of my imagination.

But I allowed myself to believe it for the moment, to give myself the strength I needed to collect my thoughts.

He wanted a safeword.

Something I would never say during sex.

There were so many things I didn't want to say during sex that I'd been forced to say. *Bleed me. Hurt me. Strangle me.*

None of those were things I ever desired or wanted to voice aloud.

I could so easily list those phrases now, but they wouldn't work. It had to be something I shouldn't say, or wouldn't be required to say, anyway. Otherwise, I'd waste my safeword. Because I could handle bleeding and pain and breath play.

No, it had to be a word I wouldn't typically voice.

Something I hid deep inside.

A fear, perhaps.

One I wouldn't want to ever reveal in that situation unless I absolutely needed the escape.

"Dreams," I whispered.

He blinked down at me. "What?"

"Dreams," I repeated, meeting his smoldering gaze once more. "My safeword is *dreams*."

Because dreams didn't exist in my world.

To be allowed to leave a scene would be a *dream* for me.

Which made it the perfect word to use.

Dreams were an escape. Dreams were make-believe. Dreams were fantasies that didn't exist.

Just like a safeword.

There was no such thing as a limit for me. No such thing as denial.

And to believe that he would ever actually allow me to use a safeword was just another silly dream.

However, I'd use it to amuse him.

See if it actually worked.

Because maybe, for once in my life, my fantasy would come true. And I'd be given the right to *dream*.

CHAPTER THIRTEEN
ASHER

Dreams.

Adalyn's safeword had haunted me all day and night. As had her behavior at breakfast—which had really been more like a brunch by the time we ate—and dinner.

She'd been perfectly behaved.

Elegant.

Poised.

Beautiful.

Acting as though nothing was wrong.

So I'd rewarded her with two more instances where she could use her safeword. My intention had been to give her an *infinite* number, as that was the purpose of a safeword—to give the sub control.

But clearly, that concept had been ripped away from her long ago. Which meant defining her limits would be difficult.

And I didn't just mean sexually, but emotionally as well.

Consequently, her perfect behavior irked me. She was hiding behind a façade of contentment, behaving as though everything in her life was perfectly fine. Yet I knew it was anything but fine. I'd witnessed her meltdown *twice*.

However, she was standing before me now in a pretty light blue dress with her hair pulled back into a bun and her hands clasped demurely in front of her.

She had on little white sandals, perfect for a stroll on the beach.

Absolutely stunning.

And staring at me expectantly.

It was as though she desired an opportunity to test out her safeword, to see if I would actually allow her to use it.

Which told me she didn't understand the concept at all.

And she didn't trust me in the slightest to keep my word.

That was the crux of our problem—neither of us trusted the other. This would prove to be dangerous when the Elite members began to arrive in ten days.

Because I had no faith in her staying quiet about Nathan's death.

She still believed me to be like them.

And unless I convinced her otherwise in this very short period of time, we would likely both suffer the consequences.

"How are you feeling today?" I asked.

"Fine, Sir."

I narrowed my gaze. "Did you sleep last night?" Because the hollows beneath her eyes suggested she hadn't.

"Yes, Sir."

I nodded. "I see. So we're going to continue lying to one another today, then?" She'd done that yesterday on the balcony when she'd refused to tell me her concerns about eating outside.

The moment she'd glanced at the patio floor, I'd known her concern was me making her kneel there while I fed her. It was what Nathan would have done—something I'd witnessed on the video feed from his phone.

But she hadn't voiced the concern.

Just like she hadn't told me what she'd wanted for dinner. *"Whatever you want, Sir."*

When I'd asked where she'd wanted to eat, she'd said, *"Wherever you want, Sir."*

And something told me breakfast today would be a repetition of the *"Whatever you want, Sir"* phrase.

"Adalyn, we have ten days to get to know each other." I stepped forward, purposely encroaching on her space and forcing her to look up at me. Only she stared at my chest instead. "Eyes up."

She swallowed but slowly obeyed, her subservient act nearly flawless apart from the minute flicker of fire in her dark eyes.

"You need to tell me what you want, Adalyn. You need to express your fears. You need to start telling me some of your limits."

I held up my hand when her lips parted.

"Do not spout that shit about having no limits again. *Everyone* has limits. I need to understand yours so we can face the Elite members as a team. You're the one with network knowledge, not me. You're the one trained to exist among them, not me. I am relying on you to guide me here."

Her lashes fell as she blinked her big dark eyes at me. "You... you want me to teach you?"

"I want you to talk to me," I corrected her. "I want you to open your eyes and realize I'm not like them, that I may be your best opportunity right now. Help me help you, Adalyn. I can't do this on my own."

I sounded desperate, but I didn't know how else to get through to her.

She considered me for a long moment, her shrewd gaze telling me she was analyzing every scenario, every potential play, every chess move.

This beautiful girl was brilliant. Spirited. A survivor.

My fucking kryptonite.

Except she was utterly broken as well. A puzzle I longed to solve. If I wasn't careful, this woman could become an addiction.

I wanted to save her, but she had to allow it first. She had to want to be saved, to believe she could be saved.

And we were nowhere near that point yet.

However, she nodded a little. "I feel tired today. No, I did not sleep well. I kept waiting for you or someone else to come test my safeword."

Several truthful answers.

I accepted it as an olive branch, a sign that she intended to try to be more forthcoming.

"The purpose of a safeword isn't to test it. A good Dom never pushes his sub to the point where she needs to use it. But as it's clear your limits have not been properly established, I need you to use that term to help me learn more about your comfort levels."

She just stared at me, my explanation clearly not registering.

Oh, she understood me just fine.

She merely didn't trust a word I'd said.

That was fine. I'd prove it through actions.

"Are you hungry?" I asked, changing the subject.

"I am, yes."

"Do you feel up for a walk?" I'd told Darby she would see me at breakfast today, and I didn't plan on letting her down.

I also needed to be seen with Adalyn, as it would lend credence to the whirlwind romance story I intended to craft for the Sin Cave members.

Your organization did too good a job. I've fallen for her. And now I am going to keep her.

Not really, because I didn't want to own her.

But she would stay on my island and remain under my protection.

"I would like a walk." Her gaze actually brightened with the words.

"How about a walk to breakfast, followed by a tour?" I offered, having mentioned the concept the other day, but our plans had been derailed. However, we were back on track.

I still needed her decision—which would be difficult to acquire, given what little trust existed between us.

So perhaps I'd take another day to prove myself to her.

And ask again tomorrow.

Because we had to provide a united front or none of this would work.

"What will the tour include?" she asked cautiously.

"Whatever you want to see." I shrugged. "We can start with breakfast. You can express your desires from there."

She gave me another of those shrewd gazes, telling me she intended to test me.

What was the phrase she'd used the other day?

Ah, yes. *Do your worst, darling.*

She smiled as though she could hear my thoughts. Then she said, "Breakfast sounds lovely."

A fake statement, but I let it slide. "Follow me."

I led her down the hall to my staircase and paused at the bottom by the foyer table.

Glancing at her, I made a quick assessment and handed her a pair of smaller sunglasses.

Then I grabbed my own and stepped outside to put them on. She followed suit, the shades a little too big for her slender nose. But they did their job of protecting her eyes.

"Did you bring any sunglasses with you?" I asked her as we walked.

"I'm not sure. Nate packed my suitcase."

I hummed in response, hating the bastard all over again. Fortunately, I was here now to take care of her properly.

Assuming she let me.

I moved alongside her, setting a slow and leisurely pace. It allowed her to take in the scenery while also guaranteeing that she wouldn't overdo it. She still had a concussion, after all.

Her eyes danced along the greenery before moving to the ocean on her right. She took it all in, her lips curling just a little to confirm that the view pleased her.

"These flowers are beautiful," she said after several minutes of silence.

I followed her gaze to the pink hibiscus trees along the stone path. "They're an island favorite." I reached for one as I said, "Hold on a minute."

Adalyn paused midstep, her shoulders immediately tensing. I hated that a simple command could ruin the moment for her, but I intended to make it better.

With the pink blossom in my hand, I stepped around her. "You don't have any plant allergies, do you?"

"No, Sir," she whispered, falling instantly into her role.

"Asher," I corrected her. "I only scene when in the bedroom or a play area." I gently tucked her hair behind her ear, then slid the stem into place.

She held her breath, not moving a fraction while I worked.

Once the flower was secure, I released her with a smile. "Beautiful."

She waited, clearly expecting something else to happen.

"We're almost there." I pressed my palm to her lower back and gently coaxed her onto our path. Her shoulders remained stiff, but she moved gracefully alongside me. It made me wonder if she'd been a dancer in a previous life, or if she would have become one in this world had her parents allowed it.

Did she have any hobbies? Had she even been granted the opportunity to explore any?

It angered me that so much had been taken from this girl. So much life. So much freedom. So much *free will.*

I took a calming breath, needing to cool down before I said or did something that would frighten her. My blood boiled every time I considered everything she'd been through. But I soothed myself with promises for the future.

I couldn't save everyone.

But I would save her.

I drew my touch up her spine to the back of her nape, giving it a little reassuring squeeze as we approached the breakfast area on the island. It was all open air and decorated in palms, the fans overhead keeping the atmosphere cool while filling the dining area with a refreshing sea breeze.

There weren't many guests here yet, Adalyn and I

having chosen an early breakfast since she hadn't been sleeping anyway. But the few who were already here all glanced up at me with satisfied looks, many of them smiling with gratitude.

Good.

That was what I wanted to see on my island.

There were no submissives kneeling, everyone eating calmly at their respective tables. Although, Matthias Bronson appeared to be hand-feeding his wife. The way she licked his fingers after each bite confirmed it was a sensual game, one I wouldn't mind replicating with the woman beside me.

But that would have to wait.

I wasn't sure we would ever truly play, given our circumstances.

However, that didn't mean I was opposed to it. Someday.

"I typically sit over there," I told her softly, gesturing to the table closest to the kitchens with a view of the entire room. "But how would you feel being closer to the beach?"

She glanced at my usual seat, then back out at the sea, her throat working.

I slid behind her, my hands on her hips as I pressed my lips to her ear. "Tell me your preference, beautiful. Tell me where you want to sit."

"Don't you mean kneel?" A hint of derision underlined her tone.

"This isn't a scene, Adalyn. This is just breakfast."

She started to turn her head toward me, but I wrapped my palm around her throat, forcing her to continue surveying the room.

"Close your eyes," I whispered, willing her to ignore everyone and everything around us. Including my head waiter, a short and stocky man who had started toward us the moment he'd seen me enter. I gave him a look now, telling him not to intrude.

He nodded, backing away from us as Adalyn's long lashes fanned across her cheekbones, her eyes closing just as I'd requested.

"I want you to pretend you're alone on this island," I breathed against her ear. "You've escaped the horrors of your past. No one can touch you here. No one can hurt you. Every decision is your own. This is a new day. Your *first* day. And you get to choose where you eat. What you eat. What you drink."

She shivered against me.

"Think about what you desire," I continued, my lips brushing her neck. "And when you're ready, I want you to open your eyes and pick a table."

Adalyn inhaled slowly, her pulse beating heartily against my thumb. And then, ever so gradually, she opened her eyes. "There." Her gaze went to the table for four nearest the water with a fan directly overhead.

"Good choice, sweetheart," I murmured, giving her a little squeeze before releasing her.

Taking her hand, I pulled her toward the table and to the seat with the best view of the water.

She frowned as I pulled the chair out for her. "I... I can get it."

"You could," I agreed. "But you're not going to. Now sit down and tell me what you want to eat."

Her jaw ticked a little in response, a hint of fiery defiance shimmering in her dark eyes.

There she is, the survivor beneath the façade.

Come play with me, sweetheart.

It's you I want to know, not this docile creature you hide behind.

I placed my hand on the wicker backing of her chair and my other on the table in front of her. It was a purposeful move, caging her between me and her seat. "What do you want to eat, Adalyn?"

CHAPTER FOURTEEN
ASHER

ADALYN'S NOSTRILS FLARED, her gaze boldly meeting mine. "What do I want to eat?"

"Yes. That's what I asked. Tell me right now what you're craving."

Make a choice.

Tell me what you *really want.*

"Fine. I want eggs." She considered for a moment. "Actually, no. *Waffles.* And pancakes. French toast. Lots of syrup. Sugar. And did I mention syrup? I want one of those metal boats of it. Maybe some fruit, too. Bacon. Sausage. Any chocolate you have. And some ice cream as well."

I arched a brow. "Are we eating breakfast or dessert?"

"Why not both?" she countered.

"I see." She was trying to press my buttons, to see what I would allow and not allow. Probably because her trainer had controlled her diet previously. Which would explain the pet-like scene Clive had shown me from her dinner with Nathan.

Well, I wasn't Nathan Spencer.

Something she would learn, if it was the last thing I taught her.

"I'll see what my chef can do," I told her, stepping away from the table.

If she wanted to test the limits of my patience, I'd show her just how infinite that boundary could be.

And I wouldn't make her kneel on the floor while I did it, either.

I recalled every detail of what she'd requested as I met with Mitch. His eyebrows were in his hairline by the time I finished. "You think you can do that?" I asked him.

He pondered my request for a few seconds before slowly nodding. "I'll have to send Jaz out to grab some supplies from another kitchen, but yeah, it's doable."

"Thanks," I replied. "I appreciate it."

Then I met with my head waiter, Herald, on my way back to the table. "Anything to drink, sir?" he asked me.

I glanced at Adalyn. She was sitting in her chair, looking out at the sea, her shoulders tense again. She probably thought she'd pushed me too far.

I'd prove to her now that she wasn't even close to pissing me off.

If anything, she'd thrilled me with her little show of defiance.

"Two waters, some coffee, and the most decadent hot chocolate Albert can make," I said, referring to the bartender assigned to this location. "No alcohol, just a lot of chocolate and sweetness."

Herald gave me an amused look. "Whipped cream, sir?"

"Yes." What kind of hot chocolate would it be without whipped cream? "Can you also bring over a flight of juices? I don't know what Ms. Rose prefers most, so we'll give her all the options to choose from."

He nodded. "Of course, sir." He gave me a weird little smile before allowing me to resume my path toward Adalyn. He was probably amused by the sight of me having a woman at breakfast. I always dined here alone, as this entire island served as one giant office. Sometimes I played, but never here at Sinners Isle.

These were my clients.

Except for Adalyn Rose.

She was now my personal guest.

I settled into the chair across from her and noticed her wince as she shifted toward me. My lips curled down. "Are you all right?" She'd done that yesterday as well, suggesting a hint of pain in her lower body. *Probably from the blade.*

Typically, I enjoyed watching a woman squirm after a good spanking.

But this was different.

This situation made me want to break something.

"I'm fine," she told me, causing my eyebrow to inch upward.

"And we were doing so well with truths," I murmured, relaxing into my chair.

"Would you rather me tell you that my ass is sore?"

"Yes, Adalyn. I would."

"And that my head is throbbing? That my hand feels a bit numb?" she continued, challenging me with her words.

I frowned at the hand in question. "Let me see it."

"What?"

"Your hand." I held my own out for her. "Let me see your hand."

She appeared ready to argue, but one look from me had her obeying. I hated that I had to dominate her to force her to comply. However, I also understood the necessity of it. She'd been commanded her whole life. While her instinct was to rebel, she continued to do it in a way that hurt herself more. And I couldn't allow that.

Her small hand fisted as she laid it in my palm. I gently pried her fingers apart to look at the stitches. The skin was a bit pink, but it didn't appear to be infected at all.

"I'll ask Dr. Zansky to stop by later today for an evaluation," I told her. "Your hand shouldn't be numb." I drew my thumb along the puckered skin, softly caressing the injury before releasing her. "As for your head, that's to be expected. Napping this afternoon would help. And your ass..." I trailed off. "The pain meds should help."

She glanced down, making my eyes narrow.

"You've been taking the pain meds, right?" I'd left them in her room with instructions from Dr. Zansky. But one look at her now told me she'd ignored those directions. I sighed and shook my head. "Adalyn, those meds are there to help you."

"They make me feel groggy."

"Yes, which is why you should take them and sleep."

"But then you..." She trailed off, her focus going to the water.

"If I wanted to fuck you while unconscious, I would have already," I told her in a low tone. "And if I wanted to make you hurt, I would have done that already, too."

"You're just waiting."

"For what?" I asked her. "What am I waiting for? I've had you in my house for two days now. Two days at my mercy. Two days where I could have done whatever the fuck I wanted to you. I realize that's a small span of time, that trust is going to take us a lot longer to build, but ask yourself *why* I would wait."

"To destroy me emotionally," she whispered, her words so soft I almost didn't hear them. But her eyes cleared as she met my gaze. "You're playing a mind game with me as the ultimate form of punishment."

"For killing Nathan?" I asked her, keeping my voice low. "I've already shown you the emails, Adalyn."

"Emails can be faked."

I blew out a breath. She wasn't wrong.

"I'm not sure how else to prove this to you, Adalyn," I admitted after a beat. "What you've been through... I can't even begin to understand it. But I'm trying. And I understand why you expect me to hurt you in some way. All I can do is continue to try to show you who I am."

She studied me as silence fell between us, her gaze seeming to take in my every feature.

I gave her that moment, allowing her to think through everything that had occurred between us, while quietly willing her to believe in me. At least a little bit.

Herald eventually interrupted us with a tray, bringing over every drink I'd requested.

Adalyn's gaze grew wider and wider with each glass he set on the table. "It's a good thing you chose a table for four," I said, amused by the number of cups we now had between us.

"And a black coffee for you, sir." Herald set my drink down last with a grin, then walked away, leaving us to our liquid meal.

"I wasn't sure what juice you like," I told her, gesturing to the sampler flight. "So I ordered one of each. You also appeared to be in a sweet mood, so I requested a hot chocolate from Albert—one of the best bartenders on the island. It's nonalcoholic, though. And water, in case you want to chase all that sugar down with something cleansing."

She gaped at me. "You... you ordered all this for me?"

"I did." I picked up my coffee and blew on it. "If you need anything else, let me know and I'll order it, too."

"Oh, look, he does leave his villa!" a familiar voice said from behind me, making me wince.

I'd almost forgotten about Darby and Yon. Setting my coffee back down, I leaned forward. "Try to behave," I said under my breath to Adalyn as I stood to hug my baby sister.

She flounced up to me in a bright-colored summer dress that seemed to match her personality. Yon strolled along behind her in a pair of jeans and a floral-patterned shirt, his eyes smiling as he watched Darby embrace me.

"Is the nanny working out, then?" I asked him.

He nodded. "She's great, yeah."

"Good." Childcare was a service I wanted to start offering on the island, and I intended for Lauren to potentially come on full-time to lead the program. This week was an audition of sorts.

"And who is this?" Darby asked.

It didn't take a genius to know whom she meant.

I rotated toward the dark-haired beauty at the table. She hadn't stood, but she appeared perfectly poised in her chair, the picture of stunning elegance.

"His mistress for the week," Adalyn replied in a tone that matched her exterior, her added smile almost meeting her eyes.

"Perhaps for more than the week," I corrected her before refocusing on my sister. "How has your week been going?" I asked, wanting to change the subject before my sister could drill Adalyn about being my supposed *mistress*.

Something told me that was a line Adalyn often used in situations such as this.

Girlfriend. Mistress. Date.

My teeth nearly ground together with each term.

Pull it together, Asher.

"Is everything to your satisfaction?" I added, my brain automatically forcing the words from my mouth, as they were common ones I said to my clients.

Darby's cheeks blossomed with twin pink shades, her dark eyes flitting to Yon before she replied, "Yes. Very satisfied."

Yeah. Wrong choice of words. "The accommodations are acceptable?" I rephrased, my voice a bit tight. Because yeah, I did not want to know how *satisfied* my sister was by her husband's antics.

And I still wasn't over Adalyn referring to herself as my *mistress.*

It sounded wrong.

Dirty.

Inappropriate.

Because part of me wished it were true.

Another part of me... wanted her to be more. Which was why the *more than a week* comment had left me without much thought.

Of course, that was the plan—to provide her with a cover here on the island as my own personal pet. So perhaps I was just falling into my role naturally.

"It's a gorgeous island and the rooms are very accommodating," Yon answered, bringing me back to the discussion. His tone wasn't at all apologetic about his wife's blushing state. He actually kissed her on the cheek as though to praise her for her response.

Jesus fuck, this was a bad idea, I told myself. *Why did I offer up my island for her honeymoon, again? Ugh.*

I looked away from them and down at where Adalyn still sat, her dark gaze filled with an emotion I couldn't exactly define. She almost appeared curious. But somehow closed off at the same time.

Darby cleared her throat and took the chair beside Adalyn. “What are we eating for breakfast?” she asked.

“Whatever Mr. Sinner ordered,” Adalyn replied without missing a beat.

I gave her a look. “I ordered exactly what you requested, sweetheart.” I glanced down at the abundance of drinks, telling her I meant it.

She blinked as though surprised, her full lips parting.

But my sister spoke before Adalyn could deliver any sort of response. “Which was...?” she prompted.

“None of our business,” Yon interjected, his palm sliding around the back of her neck. “I believe they were just enjoying a private breakfast, something we should consider doing as well.”

Darby scoffed at that, pulling a napkin into her lap. “And give up an opportunity to learn more about my brother’s *mistress*? No, thank you.”

“It wasn’t a request, baby.”

“Then consider me in a bratty mood,” she replied.

Yon gave me an apologetic look, then leaned down to whisper something in her ear. Whatever that something was had her lips parting and her gaze flashing up to his.

He righted himself in the next moment, his eyebrow arched in a way that said, *Your move, love.*

Darby cleared her throat and slowly set her napkin back on the plate. “Right. I forgot we had plans for breakfast.” She slowly pushed away from the table, her gaze meeting mine. “Sorry.”

“No apologies needed,” I assured her, as well as Yon. I wasn’t about to be the cause of whatever kinky punishment he intended to deliver.

Darby whispered a polite goodbye to Adalyn, saying she hoped they could speak more later.

And then Yon escorted my now squirming sister to the opposite end of the room.

I sighed, shaking my head. "I shouldn't have offered my island for their honeymoon." It was a thought that had already rolled through my mind, one I felt compelled to say out loud.

Adalyn glanced around me, watching whatever Yon and Darby were doing behind me, her expression pensive. "She seems... content."

"Oh, she's more than content. She's positively spoiled," I muttered, taking my seat—which, thankfully, faced away from my sister and her husband's table. "Yon is head over heels for her. Which is probably a good thing, or he'd be answering to seven very protective older brothers."

"Seven?" Adalyn repeated.

I nodded. "My dad had eight kids. I'm number seven. She's number eight."

Her lips parted. "Oh."

I shrugged. "Sounds like a lot, but he had three different wives. Darby, Tru—who is number six in the Sinner family—and I all share a mom. The others are split between the first two wives." Which wasn't how I usually referred to my father's exes, but it was easier than explaining their names and associations.

"I see. And was he...?"

"An Elite member?" I finished for her, the question giving me an idea. "What would happen to an Elite Bride after a divorce?"

She blinked at me. "Divorce doesn't exist in our circle."

"Ever?" I pressed, my idea sharpening.

She considered it for a long moment and slowly shook

her head. "Not that I've ever heard of. Elite Brides... can... disappear." She swallowed. "But they're presumed dead." Her gaze darkened. "They might actually be dead. Or they might be somewhere worse."

That was the fate she feared—the something worse.

However, she'd just provided me with another way to prove I wasn't part of the network.

"And I assume fathers and sons in your circle both take Elite Brides."

"Yes." She gave me a strange look, like she couldn't figure out why I had all these questions—questions an Elite member would know the answers to.

"And your mother?" I pressed. "Was she an Elite Bride?"

She dipped her chin just enough to confirm it.

"I see." Well, at least that explained how a mother could do something like this to her daughter—she didn't have a choice. "My father married and *divorced* three times. All three women are very much alive." I pulled my phone from my pocket to find a photo of my own mom. "This was taken a few months ago when she came to visit."

"Without your father?"

"My father's no longer with us," I told her. "Seven years ago. He left all his kids a Sinners club." I smiled. "I picked this one."

She studied my phone. "So your mom is free of him."

I snorted. "My mom isn't free of anything or anyone. She married my father for love; it just didn't last. They divorced well before he died."

I pulled my phone away from her and slid it back into my pocket.

"My father enjoyed his playmates, and he's always been into the lifestyle," I explained softly. "Hence his gifting of the clubs. The only rule he had was that each location had to be used for BDSM in some way, not for anything else. So I turned my island into a fetish resort for those who require secrecy."

She glanced around. "It's certainly secluded."

"Yes. And it obviously made me a target for the Elite of your world." I picked up my coffee to take a sip, my eyes holding hers. "I'm not part of the network, Adalyn."

Her gaze left mine to focus on something behind me, her lips flattening. "I'm starting to believe you, Asher."

I couldn't tell if she was saying that to try to expedite whatever game she thought we were playing or if she actually believed it. But I suspected it was my sister she had her eyes on.

There was no denying how happy Yon made her.

That sort of act couldn't be faked.

So I gave Adalyn her quiet moment and just enjoyed the sea breeze.

Suddenly, her eyes widened, making me frown. "Adalyn?"

I glanced over my shoulder, trying to figure out what had her so shocked.

"Oh." I grinned at the parade of dishes making their way to our table. "Breakfast time."

Adalyn's jaw was on the ground as I faced her again.

My smile grew.

Her expression alone was worth every calorie we were about to consume. "Bon appétit, sweetheart."

CHAPTER FIFTEEN
ADALYN

Oh my God.

I felt like a penguin, waddling around Asher's villa, searching for some way to burn off the insane amount of food I'd eaten for breakfast today.

He'd taken me on a partial tour of the island, but it hadn't been enough to help me feel better about our gluttonous activities this morning.

No one had ever allowed me to eat like that.

Ever.

Not my parents. Not my instructors in school. Not Nathan or any of the men he'd sent me out with.

It was my duty in life to remain petite and curvy in only the right places. But Asher hadn't said a word as I'd shoveled bite after bite into my mouth.

I'd kept waiting for him to react.

All he'd done was smile and join me in the unhealthy feast.

Then he'd walked around with me, holding my hand like I was his date, and brought me back here to meet with Dr. Zansky and his nursing assistant, Miranda.

I suspected he'd brought her along to help me feel more comfortable with his visit.

It hadn't worked.

Anything involving a physician usually equated to pain.

However, all he'd done was check my hand and the back of my head. He'd asked about everything else without demanding I show him and had said I was healing appropriately. But he wanted me to keep an eye on my hand and the numbness I'd reported to Asher.

I'd been surprised to hear that he'd actually passed that information along.

"Asher also tells me you're not taking your medication," he'd added. "Are they making you feel sick, or do you have an aversion to them?"

"I prefer not to take them," I'd admitted, not trusting him or the pills he'd given me.

Rather than fight me on it, he'd nodded. "Well, they're there if you need them. Or if you prefer another brand, then let Asher know and we'll order whatever you need."

I still couldn't believe he'd just accepted my refusal. I'd expected him to go straight to Asher to voice his disapproval, but he hadn't.

Instead, he'd met with Asher in front of me, saying that I was recovering as expected and to continue limiting my activity.

Asher had nodded, thanked him, and then said, "Feel free to take a nap, Adalyn. I have some work I need to catch up on."

Then he'd disappeared into his office—which I now knew was on the first floor near the back of his property with windows that overlooked the beach—and hadn't said a word to me since.

I'd stood just outside his door, wondering what I should do.

Then I'd taken myself on a tour of his downstairs.

Living area with two couches.

Huge kitchen with a breakfast nook framed by windows, just like his office.

A dining room.

Another seating area, but smaller—this was the one I'd been able to see from the stairs.

And a darkened room in the opposite corner of his home from his office, the windows here all covered in black shades. It had given me chills until I realized the chairs were all facing a screen.

A theater.

I wasn't sure what he liked to watch.

I wasn't sure I wanted to know.

Lie, some part of me had whispered. *You very much want to know.*

Which was what had led me to finding his closet full of movies.

Action flicks.

My brow had furrowed and I'd left, confused once again by Asher Sinner and his intentions.

I'd wandered back upstairs and tried to nap, yet couldn't.

And now I was waddling through his house again.

He hadn't left his office, so I decided to give myself a tour of the outside.

I stepped through the sliding doors at the back of his living area and took in the massive pool patio resting between me and the beach.

I could go for a run, but the wave of dizziness hitting my skull told me that probably wasn't a good idea.

However, I needed to do something to help expel some of this guilt from overeating.

It was a horrible sensation, one I hadn't anticipated while taunting him with my food. Perhaps that was why he'd allowed me to continue stuffing my face.

Although, I suspected that wasn't the case at all.

He'd been trying to make a point these last few days to prove that he wasn't like the men I knew. Meeting his sister was proof enough of that. She'd been... happy. An emotion I recognized because I'd seen it on Jen's features several times throughout our college years.

Especially when she spoke about Pierce.

At least until recently.

I twisted my mouth to the side, wondering if I could find a phone to call her.

But I didn't want to risk anyone picking up on the conversation.

I knew our old apartment was bugged—it was the only reason Nate had allowed me to live there. A test to ensure I didn't say anything to anyone outside the inner circle.

That test had come to a head a few months ago after I'd taken Jen to Ecstasy with me. We'd run into her older brother and his best friend, also known as the love of Jen's life. The two men had seen me with my trainer, which had resulted in a few questions from Jen.

But I'd handled them.

Something Nate had rewarded me for by giving me a weekend off from testing my limits.

Definitely not the same kind of rewards Asher kept giving me.

Dreams, I thought. *A safeword.*

I was starting to believe that he meant it, that he meant *everything* he'd said to me.

Hence the reason he'd given me the liberty to eat whatever the fuck I wanted today.

"Ugh," I muttered, pressing my palm to my stomach. I didn't actually feel much different, telling me the sensation was more mental than physical. But I'd eaten a lot.

My gaze fell to his pool, assessing the length of it.

Maybe I could swim some laps.

That wouldn't be too vigorous. It kept me nearby—something I suspected he wanted—and it wouldn't be nearly as high impact as running.

Of course, now would be the time to try to escape, I thought, glancing out at the waves. *But where would I go?*

And if I were being completely honest with myself... I kind of wanted to stay.

Which was obviously insane and likely a desire created by my head injury.

It had nothing to do with how Asher made me feel every time he touched me. Or how my stomach fluttered each time he whispered in my ear.

Such a unique sensation. When Nate spoke to me in that manner, I usually felt sick inside.

But Asher's words and tone warmed me instead. He left me feeling light. Airy. *Breathless.*

I wanted to lean into him, not away from him.

A dangerous desire. One that suggested I was beginning to trust him more than I should.

I needed something to distract myself. And a way to feel better about this morning's feast.

A swim. Definitely a swim.

I didn't have a suit. But I doubted they were required on this island, let alone in a private pool.

I kicked off my sandals and pulled my dress over my

head. Then I shimmied out of my thong before unclasping my bra.

Nudity had never bothered me. Perhaps because of my training. But I'd always been confident in my body, even in my teen years.

That confidence had bled into my sexuality as an adult. While there were certain activities I despised, there were just as many that I enjoyed.

Such as submitting.

And being tied up.

Both actions typically turned me on.

Unless I was being bound for cruel purposes—something Nate had liked to do for punishment. That I did not appreciate. Which he'd known, of course. Hence the reason he'd used that pleasure against me.

I don't want to think about him now, I decided, taking a deep breath of fresh air. *He'll never tie me up again. Because he's dead.*

"Good riddance," I muttered as I jumped into the pool.

I was never the type to slowly slip into the water. I preferred to rip the bandage off and go for it.

The cool liquid swallowed me whole, causing goose bumps to pebble along my arms. I smiled, loving the buoyant sensation as I broke the surface.

Swimming calmed me.

I wasn't very good at it, but I loved the way it felt to command the water with my fingertips and toes. Floating made me feel free. Like I could conquer anything in this weightless state.

My eyes closed, the sun warming my face as I kicked my feet to propel me slowly to one end. I turned and started back toward the other side, only for a shadow to disturb my serenity.

A chill swept along my spine as I realized a man stood at the edge with his hands on his hips, his posture disapproving.

The place he stood made it hard to see his features, the sun blinding me and lending him a figment-like appearance.

"What the fuck are you doing?" he demanded, making me blink.

Asher.

The ice dancing along my spine melted beneath a wave of warmth, my toes curling as I moved to tread water in the deeper end of his pool. "I'm swimming."

"Is that considered a restful activity, Adalyn?"

"Yes," I replied. "Very restful."

I couldn't see his expression, but I suspected it held a touch of disapproval because his posture appeared rigid. "Get out of the water, Adalyn."

My brow furrowed. "Why?"

"Because I said so." The dominance in his tone almost had me obeying on instinct.

But I rather liked my tranquil state.

And I didn't feel like leaving it.

"No," I told him, resuming my floating position.

"No?" he echoed, the word rippling against my ears beneath the water. "*Adalyn*."

I ignored him.

Maybe this was the push he needed to act.

I probably shouldn't test that with a stomach full of food. There was a reason I'd tended to eat very little around Nate and his friends—they'd often done things to me that had left me feeling sick, or worse.

However, I'd indulged this morning mostly to see how far Asher would let me go.

As far as I wanted, apparently.

So why not test him again by allowing my bratty side to come out to play?

He'd wanted the real Adalyn, right? To know how I felt. To know what I desired.

Well, right now, I desired a swim.

"Adalyn," he repeated, sounding closer this time.

"I'm busy swimming right now, Mr. Sinner," I informed him with a happy sigh. "Come back later."

It was a dangerous statement.

A taunt.

An invitation, I realized, grinning inside.

He kept playing these games, refusing to show me his dark side. But I felt it humming beneath the skin. I wanted to provoke him into showing me his true colors, to make him react and prove that my suspicions were right about him.

Because if he didn't do that soon, I would start to consider the unthinkable—that all this was true.

That he really did want to help me.

Heal me.

Save me.

Heroes don't exist in my world. Only villains.

CHAPTER SIXTEEN
ASHER

This woman is going to be the death of me.

Perhaps literally.

I kicked off my shoes and started unbuttoning my shirt. "You have ten seconds before I come in after you, Adalyn," I warned her.

"Mmm, well the water is quite nice," she hummed in response.

I narrowed my gaze.

This little deviant was playing with fire. Trying to push my buttons and see how I would react.

She'd done the same thing over breakfast, stuffing herself beyond the point of comfort just to test me. If she wanted to devour an entire buffet, I wouldn't stop her.

Because I knew she would pay for that choice later.

I also didn't own her. She could do whatever the hell she wanted.

But I drew a line at putting herself at risk—like she was doing now.

Dr. Zansky was clear about her needing to rest,

something she'd clearly not done since he'd only left ninety minutes ago.

When I'd heard the splashing outside, I'd come running, worrying that she'd fallen in. After our interaction on the beach the other night, I wasn't sure she knew how to swim.

However, she'd been kicking across the pool just fine when I'd arrived.

Then she'd flipped to continue her journey back the other way.

Flipped.

At the fucking wall.

Spinning in a circle.

Something I was certain couldn't be good for a concussion.

And now she was about to do it again at the opposite side, her long legs having fluttered across the pool after ignoring my demand for her to get out.

I unfastened my final button and pulled the shirt off to fold on a nearby chair. I'd given her more than ten seconds to react to my command. She was clearly disobeying me.

Brat, I thought, pulling off my socks.

My pants were next, leaving me clad in a pair of boxers.

Another pair to soak through at this female's expense. It was becoming a ritual between us.

I walked around to the stairs and entered the water as she started her journey across the pool again. I swam over to the wall and waited for her with my arms sprawled out along the edge. It was deep on this side, the water well over my head when I stood at the bottom.

She continued her fluttering, humming to herself, evidently pleased with her decision.

Until she bent her head back to search for the wall and found me waiting for her.

She froze.

Then jackknifed upward on a gasp when her body began to sink.

I reached for her with one arm, wrapping it easily around her waist to pull her back against me. It was a careful movement, one meant to protect her head, but she floundered anyway as though trying to escape me. I tightened my grip. "Stop," I said against her ear.

She grabbed my forearm, much like she had the other day, but she didn't dig her claws in this time. Instead, she stilled and sucked in a breath.

I gave her a moment to calm down, aware that any amount of panic wouldn't be good for her condition.

"If you're intent on swimming, then we'll swim together." That way I could control her movements and ensure she didn't overdo it.

Or drown.

Like she almost had the other night.

"This isn't swimming." Her tone held a note of challenge in it.

"Then what is it?"

She moved her head back to my shoulder and tilted her face up to see me better. "Resting at the wall."

I cocked a brow. "That suits your condition better, doesn't it? *Resting*?"

She scoffed at that, righting herself again and gripping my arm a little harder. "I don't need rest, Asher. It's a head injury. I've had worse."

My arm flexed around her, making it clear that I would not be releasing her. Not even if she dug her nails into me again. "You have a concussion, Adalyn. And you're under my care. That means I make the rules." Since she obviously couldn't be trusted to look after herself.

"What if I don't want to follow your rules?" she asked, those sharp talons of hers starting to dig into my skin. "What if I want to make up my own rules?"

Her stomach flexed beneath my arm, her throat working as she fought to swallow.

She was pushing.

Testing the limits of my patience.

Determining how far she could go before I reacted. Before I did something to punish her. Something to put her in her place.

"I know what you're doing, Adalyn," I said, my thumb brushing her side as I relaxed my arm in a show of restraint.

She stilled. "What am I doing?"

"Testing the limits of my patience," I whispered against her ear. "Attempting to draw my Dominant side out to play." I nibbled her earlobe, my teeth biting down hard enough to sting without actually hurting her. "Trying to top from the bottom."

A typical bratty sub.

Something I would find alluring on an average day. Tempting, even.

But there was nothing *average* about our situation.

She shivered against me, her lower half squirming in a way that confirmed my every word. "Let me go."

"No." I pressed my lips to her neck, loving the way her pulse sang against my touch. "I have limits, Adalyn. You attempting to hurt yourself is one of them."

She stilled again. "I'm not trying to hurt myself."

"You're being reckless and careless with your head injury, sweetheart. That counts as trying to harm yourself."

Her nails sank into my flesh as she tried to rip my arm

away. "I am *not* trying to hurt myself," she repeated, her voice holding an edge to it this time. "A head injury is nothing compared to what I've been through. *Nothing*, Asher. Let me go!"

She started fighting me in earnest now, her lethal little claws drawing blood as she attempted to dislodge herself from my hold.

Her legs kicked backward into mine, her head flying back toward my shoulder, her movements all wild, terrified female.

Shit.

"Adalyn!" I let go of her, only to grab her hips and pull us both under the water, trying to cool her off. Because this was dangerous. *This* would hurt her, thus proving all my concerns right.

She kicked out, trying to escape me, but I pulled her with me to the shallower part of the water where I could stand. Her screams were waterlogged, her hair a web of darkness that swallowed her face.

I quickly stood, guiding her up with me, and grabbed her flailing fists. I wrenched them behind her back to secure her wrists with one of my palms against her lower spine, then grabbed her throat with my free hand.

It wasn't my first time restraining a woman.

And it likely wouldn't be my last time, especially if Adalyn Rose stayed in my life.

She was at a disadvantage, her shorter height leaving her without a way to touch the ground, my strength dwarfing hers easily in this position.

"Calm down," I demanded.

Her nostrils flared, her pupils blown wide.

Not with fear.

But with *lust*.

Fuck. She'd done this to provoke me again. To see what I would do. To force me to show her the side of me that I'd kept carefully restrained these last few days.

She wanted to know what kind of Dom I truly was.

To learn my intentions. To learn my preferences. To figure out what kind of game we were playing. Because that was all this continued to be for her—a scheme that would end in her pain.

She still thought I was here to discipline her for what she'd done to Nathan Spencer.

And rather than wait, she'd decided to push me, to force me to show my cards.

Deep down, this woman was terrified of what I would do to her. Terrified of the punishment her former world had in store for her.

Until she overcame that fear, she would never believe my intentions. Never believe that I truly wanted to help her.

And that would be detrimental to the meeting being planned for next week.

We had less than ten days to sort this out between us, to figure out how to assist each other rather than hurt each other.

"All right, Adalyn," I said, staring down into her beautiful eyes. "You want to see what kind of man I am? I'll show you."

I leaned down, forcing her back and hair into the water as I bent over her, my lips nearing hers with the intent to kiss her.

But her entire body went rigid.

Some of the lust bled from her expression, leaving a ghostly pale glow against her cheeks in its wake.

I frowned.

It was like she went from hot and bothered to terrified in a blink.

I straightened, giving her space.

But that only seemed to upset her more.

She trembled, her eyes falling shut as though to escape to somewhere else.

I pulled her back up until her breasts met my chest. She gasped as though she'd just been underwater. Then she held her breath, her upper torso stiff.

"Adalyn?" I gentled my voice, my lips near hers. "What are you thinking about right now?"

She didn't answer, too busy holding her breath and squeezing her eyes closed.

I released her throat to palm the back of her neck. "Adalyn?" I whispered, still speaking close to her mouth.

She trembled.

I gave her back the use of her arms, and she immediately grabbed my shoulders. But she didn't try to push me away. She clung to me instead. Her legs went around my waist as well.

And suddenly we were hugging.

Or she was hugging me, anyway.

I gently wrapped an arm around her lower back, my opposite hand remaining against her nape.

"Where did your mind go?" I asked, my lips against her ear again. "What did you think I was going to do?"

"Waterboarding." The word was a soft whisper of sound, one I almost didn't catch.

I frowned. "I wasn't going to waterboard you, sweetheart." I wasn't into breath play like that. A little asphyxiation to demonstrate dominance? Sure. Waterboarding or evoking true terror in my sub? Absolutely not.

However, I noted that limit for her.

She'd claimed not to have any, but her body had just revealed it as one for her.

Something told me these cues had been ignored in the past, or perhaps exploited.

I ran my palm up and down her back, offering her comfort. "I was going to kiss you," I told her softly, then demonstrated against her neck. Her legs tightened around my hips in response, suddenly drawing my attention to just how close we were.

The thin fabric of my boxers wasn't doing much to hide my reaction to having a gorgeous woman wrapped around me.

If anything, it was *accentuating* that reaction because of how constrained I felt below. The fabric rubbed along my dick as she pressed herself more firmly against me.

Fuck.

I could feel how hot she was despite the cool water around us.

Just like I could feel her nipples beading against my chest.

She was no longer stiff, but relaxing more and more with each breath.

I swallowed, the feel of her far too perfect in my arms. This wasn't what I'd planned to do. I'd merely intended to give her a demonstration with my mouth.

Now other parts of my body wanted to play, too.

Adalyn pressed against me again, her hot little cunt a sensual kiss to my senses that had my palm flexing against her lower back.

A moan slipped from her mouth, one that had my muscles tightening in response.

"Kiss me," she whispered, repeating my words.

Or I thought she was repeating them.

Until I realized she'd meant it as a request.

To *kiss* her.

Just like I'd said I was going to do.

But now I wasn't sure if I should.

She didn't trust me.

Because she doesn't know me, I thought. *But I could help her get to know me.*

By kissing her.

By showing her what it meant to be with a man who cared about her pleasure more than his own.

By demonstrating to her how a Dom should act.

By rewriting her history with my own instructional touch.

Yes, I decided. *Yes, that's what I should do.*

CHAPTER SEVENTEEN
ASHER

ADALYN'S LIPS skated along my jaw. "Kiss me, Sir," she requested again. "Please kiss me."

She sounded desperate, her voice a seductive beacon that called to my very soul. I should tell her no. I should pull her from the water, carry her upstairs, and demand that she rest.

But I couldn't seem to find my control.

It left me feeling inadequate. Off-balance. *Wrong*.

A soft, needy noise from her grounded me in the next moment, forcing me to react. To possess her. To *soothe* her.

I slid my fingers into her wet hair, fisted the slick strands, and angled her head toward me. Her pupils were wider than before, begging me to take her, dominate her, *save* her.

It provided me with the flicker of consent that I needed to find my authority once more.

And *claim*.

Just a kiss, I promised myself. *Just a kiss with a lot of tongue.*

Because fuck, the moment our lips met, I needed more.

I wanted to taste her. Devour her. Memorize every goddamn inch of her.

She felt too perfect against me. Too ready. Too *mine*.

Her muscles clenched, her thighs seeming to agree with the possession of my mouth, her beckoning heat rubbing against me once more as she searched for the friction she desired.

And found it with my pulsating cock.

Her responding groan went straight to my gut, the sound a caress that tightened my groin and provoked an immense craving inside me.

Fuck, this female was undoing years of experience and rewriting them with her tongue. She kissed me as though I were the air she needed to breathe. Just as she clung to me as if I were the lifeline keeping her from drowning.

It made me feel powerful.

Desired.

Needed.

The embrace resembled an intoxicating drug that made me feel invincible. On top of the world. *Dominant.*

She was flawless, her touch potent, her being more desirable than anyone else I'd ever met.

I walked her toward the side of the pool where water drizzled down the tiled wall to keep the contents fresh and moving all day. Almost like a waterfall, but softer. Less intimidating.

Yet the wall provided the balance I needed, giving me somewhere to hold her in place while my hands roamed her exquisite form.

She shivered as her spine met the wall, her arms tightening around me, only for her head to fall back on a moan as my palms skimmed up her sides.

I watched her squirm, ensured she was still safe and

with me, and palmed her breasts. She arched into me in response, her plump lips parting on a beautiful sound that had me flicking her rosy tips with my thumbs.

"Yes," she breathed, her eyes drowsy as she met my gaze. Her dark irises possessed no sign of hesitation or pain. Just blatant *need*.

"Gorgeous," I praised. "It almost makes me want to demand that you beg for more."

But I wouldn't do that to her here.

Not when she'd so beautifully given me control.

It was a small act of trust, perhaps one ingrained in her mind that forced her to react. But I wouldn't take advantage of it now.

No, I'd give her what she wanted.

Reward her for being so open.

Thank her for allowing me this gift.

Submission should be commended, not taken for granted.

And I intended to show her that now, not with words, but by creating a memory to help overshadow her past.

This is who I am, I whispered against her throat with a kiss. I didn't dare speak the words out loud, not wanting to distract from the moment. Instead, I licked a path down to her breast and nibbled her tender peak. Not harshly, but enough to give her a little bite of pain with her pleasure.

She grasped my shoulders and bowed off the wall with a groan, confirming my instincts about her preferences.

I chased the ache away with my tongue, then took her abused nipple into my mouth.

"More, Sir," she whispered. "Please."

Ah, so she was listening to my comment about begging. "Such a good girl," I murmured, switching to her other tit.

Her thighs clamped down around my waist again, her pussy demanding *more,* just like her mouth had.

My palms grazed her sides to grasp her hips, pulling her into a position against my throbbing shaft where she could find that friction she clearly craved.

Her nails dug into my skin in response, not to hurt me or to push me away this time, but in another nonvocal request for me to continue. For me to give her everything. For me to help drive her over the cliff she was obviously already climbing.

I wasn't sure what had worked her into this state so quickly, but I didn't mind it.

I loved a hot and needy woman.

And Adalyn didn't disappoint.

She panted as I kissed a path back up to her mouth, her eyes twin pools of dark need. If I asked her to fuck me right now, she would. She'd give me anything I desired to take her over that edge.

Because in this moment, she was mine to possess. Mine to own. Mine to claim.

And I did so with my mouth, punctuating my presence here with my tongue and demanding that she acknowledge who commanded her body now.

She shuddered, her body putty beneath my hands.

So perfect, I thought, expressing my admiration for her with my tongue instead of my words.

It wasn't enough.

She needed to know just how special I found her. Just how much I respected her. Just how much I wanted to help her *fly*. With me, she would never crawl. Not unless she desired it.

With me, she would always be pleasured.

Always scream my name in orgasmic bliss, not painful torment.

I believed in using sensual agony to enhance the experience for both of us, not just myself.

That wasn't how this game was played. Not in my bedroom, anyway.

Like right now. She was burning. Aching. Needing so much more.

But I prolonged her gratification by applying only subtle pressure against that hot apex between her thighs. I allowed her to feel my arousal, my own heat, my *need*. Just through the boxers, not bare. A tease meant to bring tears to her eyes. A subtle torture meant to heighten the expectation.

A cruel sadist would leave her in that state and never satisfy her.

I wasn't cruel.

I merely enjoyed delayed satisfaction. Just as I preferred games of sensual play and sensory deprivation.

She'd learn that in time. This was meant to be an introduction, a way to show her my intentions, to *prove* to her that I wouldn't hurt her. Not like the men of her past.

I would take care of her.

Just like right now.

Give her what *she* needed and ignore my own cravings.

Because this was about her, not me. This was about grounding her, helping her find her own footing, and giving her a piece of herself back.

Her own sense of control.

Her own pleasure.

Her own reason to *breathe*.

I captured her mouth again, worshipping her with my tongue as I slid one hand between us to palm her between the thighs. She whimpered against me, her desire a palpable presence that I stroked with two of my fingers.

Her resulting quake vibrated me to my very being, her pussy so fucking needy that I easily slid both fingers inside her. My thumb found her clit, the swollen little nub practically pulsating and begging to be touched.

It made me wonder if anyone had ever granted her orgasms during their scenes.

Because she was reaching her peak so much faster than I'd expected, her whimpers turning into cries as I brought her closer and closer to the realm of no return.

"That's it," I told her. "You're going to come for me, aren't you, little one?"

"Please," she begged. "Please... Please let me come. *Please*."

I wasn't sure if her previous trainer had required her to beg before pleasing her, or if she needed permission to let go, or if she was begging me not to stop because other men would.

But I strove to give her exactly what she yearned for.

"I want you to come all over my hand, Adalyn." I bit down on her lower lip, ensuring she understood the demand in my voice. "I want you to scream and tell the world how good it feels." I laved the hurt away. "Don't hold anything back, sweetheart," I continued, my lips going to her ear. "This orgasm is for you, and you're going to take every ounce of pleasure that it gives you."

She shook so violently against me that I worried she might lose consciousness, but her resulting scream told me she was very much aware and alive.

And *ecstatic*.

She clenched around my fingers, her pleasure rippling up my arm and going straight to my heart as she let herself go entirely, giving herself over to the hedonistic waves that racked every inch of her luscious form.

It was a sight to behold.

A sound I would fantasize about for years to come.

Utter. Erotic. Perfection.

Her full lips were parted on her cries of pleasure, her back arching as though to present her beautiful tits to my mouth, as she squeezed the hell out of my fingers.

I even felt her clit pulsate against my thumb.

If pleasure had a form, it was Adalyn.

Delicious.

Intoxicating.

Addicting.

The only way to make this moment better would be if I had my mouth between her legs instead of my hand.

"So fucking beautiful," I whispered as her head went to my shoulder on a sob of exhaustion.

She'd worked hard for that moment of magnificence.

And now she was feeling the aftermath of her lack of sleep.

I slowly made my way back through the pool, one arm around her lower back and the other around her shoulders.

She jolted a little as I started up the stairs, her legs tensing.

I hushed her and took her inside the house, ignoring the damp path we left in our wake.

Adalyn needed to rest.

I pressed my lips to her temple as I started up the stairs, careful not to slip on the wood planks. Then took her down the hallway and into the guest room I'd given her. As much as I'd love to put her in my bed, we were nowhere near that point yet. We might never be there.

But I bypassed her bed for the bathroom, needing a towel.

I grabbed the nearest one, swathed her in it, and brought her over to the mattress. She was barely awake by the time I laid her in the center, her eyelids drooping.

My lips twitched. *So the best way to make Adalyn rest is with a mind-blowing orgasm. Noted.*

I kissed her forehead and tucked her in, then backed away.

I glanced back at her as I reached the doorway, taking in the soft rise and fall of her chest. She was already asleep.

However, I felt the need to say, "This is who I am, sweetheart."

Someone you can trust.

Someone who will protect you.

But only if you let me...

CHAPTER EIGHTEEN
ADALYN

Mmm. Something smells good.

I stretched, my limbs more relaxed than they'd been in a long time. Everything felt warm and refreshed, like I'd just spent a year in bed.

Maybe I had.

No, I thought, peeking at the sun streaming through my windows. *Still daylight.*

I yawned and stretched again, rolling toward my other side to find the scent of deliciousness that had woken me up.

And froze when I found Asher sitting beside me with a tray on his lap.

"You missed dinner and breakfast, so I brought you lunch," he said conversationally. "Sit up and eat with me, and I'll reward you."

I blinked at him. "Dinner and...?" I trailed off, my throat reminding me of a cotton ball.

He lifted a drink off his tray and pressed the straw to my lips. "Suck."

That single word went straight to my heart, causing it

to skip several beats as I obeyed. My thighs clenched, the sensuality in that term matching the look in his eyes while he watched me swallow.

"Good girl," he murmured, smiling. "I squeezed those oranges this morning for you, since you seemed to favor that drink yesterday. But then you never came down to eat. So I chilled the glass to go with lunch."

My eyebrows rose as I took another pull from the straw, the liquid heaven along my tongue. But I didn't want to rush it. I wanted to savor it. So I stopped drinking and shuffled to sit next to him against the headboard.

He studied me as I studied him, the events from the pool playing through my mind.

The pleasure.

His hands.

His mouth.

That *kiss.*

I'd been so tired afterward that I'd fallen asleep without pleasuring him in return. But he hadn't demanded it. He hadn't woken me up or shoved his cock into me.

He'd just let me sleep.

For nearly a day, apparently.

"How do you feel?" he asked softly, setting the glass back on his tray.

"Well rested," I admitted, still staring at him. "Why...?"

He arched a brow. "Why what, darling?"

"I..." I wasn't sure how to phrase my question.

But then something he'd said yesterday swam through my thoughts. *"You want to see what kind of man I am? I'll show you."*

He'd whispered something about that before leaving, too.

Something I'd barely heard, the words chasing me into my dreamless state.

"This is who I am, sweetheart."

I sat there and marveled at him, at a loss for words.

His brow inched up higher, clearly expecting me to say something.

But I had nothing to say.

I'd tried to provoke him in the pool by blatantly rejecting his command and essentially disrespecting his authority.

And he'd responded by giving me the best orgasm of my life.

Perhaps because it was the first one that hadn't felt *forced.*

He'd pleasured me for me, not for himself. And it had created a sensation unlike any I'd ever experienced.

I'd felt *safe.* Warm. Well cared for. *Adored.*

So much so that I'd fallen into a deep sleep for hours, something I couldn't recall happening in several years.

"I think I like it here, Mr. Sinner," I admitted softly. The words tasted foreign on my tongue, almost as though each one had been underlined by *hope.*

Such a forbidden concept in my world.

But this man didn't appear to be from my world at all.

He was the white knight I'd refused to fantasize about every night.

The hero I swore didn't exist.

He could still be lying. This could all be some elaborate ruse to hurt me worse than anyone ever had.

However, a naïve part of me chose to consider the reality of this situation. Chose to believe, just a little bit, that Asher Sinner might just be a dream come true.

His dark eyes held mine for a beat, his lips curling a

little at the sides. "I like it here, too," he replied, his voice just as quiet as mine. A tender exchange of words that resembled a secret that existed only between us.

A secret of *trust*.

He cleared his throat, his focus returning to his tray. "I made grilled cheese and heated up some soup from Caylin."

"You made grilled cheese?"

"And the juice," he reminded me, arching a brow. "You look surprised."

"I am."

"Because I made a sandwich and squeezed some oranges?"

"Yes," I admitted.

He smiled. "Then I'll have to give Caylin the night off so I can properly impress you in the kitchen."

I stared at him. "You've already impressed me, Asher." Apparently, I woke up today and decided to be truthful. But given everything that had occurred between us, it felt needed.

"Have I?" His lips curled into a slightly arrogant grin, his gaze darkening with a hint of satisfaction. "Well, then I'll endeavor to impress you more."

He picked up the plate and handed it to me.

"We'll start with this. It's my own special creation."

I gave him a look. "A grilled cheese."

"Just try it," he murmured.

I shrugged. *Why not?* I was hungry again, my stomach having finally finished processing the monstrous breakfast from yesterday.

The sandwich was fortunately not very bready.

But it was greasy.

And cheesy.

So, so cheesy.

"Oh God," I said after a few bites. "How?"

He grinned. "It's my own special blend of cheese. All French and very melty."

"And rich." It was so decadent, to the point of almost being overpowering. Except a hint of something calmed the potent flavor. "Cranberries?"

"A cranberry jam." His eyes captured mine. "Impressed?"

I wanted to say no, just to knock that growing expression of arrogance from his features. But I couldn't lie. "Yes."

His resulting smile was one I would forever remember. All masculine pride set in a face destined to grace the covers of high-fashion magazines.

With his physique, he could easily start a new career in modeling.

I reached for the juice, needing something to wash down the grease.

Then I finished my sandwich.

Asher gestured to the soup, but I shook my head. "I really want to freshen up first. I also ate way too much yesterday."

His gaze ran over my breasts and down to my stomach, reminding me that I was very much naked. I hadn't even really noticed, so used to being without clothes that I hadn't even considered my nude state.

But I noticed now.

Especially when I caught the hint of smoldering heat in his irises as he met my gaze again. "Your figure is no worse for wear, Adalyn. I think you're allowed a few more cheat days."

I scoffed at that. "It's not about my figure but how all that food made me feel."

He gave me a knowing look. "Maybe next time you can focus on what you want rather than try to test my reactions, hmm?"

I so badly wanted to deny that or come up with a retort. But I couldn't. Because he was right—I'd wanted to see what he would do.

Just like in the pool yesterday.

I kept testing him. Waiting for him to show me his evil side.

But he didn't seem to have one.

I leaned in to kiss his cheek. "I'll be good at dinner tonight, Sir," I promised him. "I'm going to shower now."

Then afterward, maybe we would talk.

Because I wanted to better understand him and his intentions regarding Sin Cave.

Learn more about how he intended to take credit for Nate's murder.

And ask him bluntly what he truly wanted from me. He might be a good man. But taking on this challenge far surpassed typical decency.

He'd want something in return.

After my shower, I'd find out what that something was, and we'd go from there.

CHAPTER NINETEEN
ADALYN

Asher wasn't in the bedroom when I finished my shower.

I combed my hair, leaving it down to dry, and pulled on a dress without bothering with undergarments.

Then I wandered downstairs toward his study.

"Yes, that's acceptable," I heard him saying. "I'll make arrangements for them as well."

I paused in the doorway, and he glanced up at me from his desk as a male voice replied, "Mr. Rose will appreciate that."

My limbs locked into place, my breath stilling at the mention of my father.

"He may wish to bring Mr. Huntington as well," the voice added.

Asher leaned back in his chair, his focus returning to his screen. "I may not have a villa available for Mr. Huntington."

Silence followed.

"That may not be acceptable," the male eventually replied.

Asher lifted a shoulder as though he couldn't be

bothered to care. "I didn't find Nathan Spencer's actions acceptable either. And I associate those actions with Taylor Huntington and your organization, Mr. Jovanni."

"Actions our organization has confirmed we knew nothing about."

"Hence the reason I'm allowing you to visit my island next week, but that invitation is limited in number."

Another beat passed before the male said, "I see."

Movement behind me had my heart kick-starting in my ribs.

Asher's gaze lifted again, not to me but to the presence at my back. He nodded once.

I frowned, not understanding.

A hand went to my hip, causing me to jump, ready to fight, but all he did was gently move me to the side as he entered the office.

"Are you giving Julian a hard time?" he asked conversationally.

"Hardly." Asher smiled, but it wasn't anything like the one he'd displayed earlier. "Just providing information regarding the accommodations here on the isle."

"He doesn't seem keen on allowing Mr. Huntington to join our party," Julian added as the other man stepped up to Asher's side.

"I can't imagine you're too disappointed about that," the dark-haired male drawled, his easy candor suggesting he knew the man on the phone—who I assumed was on the screen facing Asher.

"No, I can't say that I am," Julian admitted. "But Mr. Rose will be."

"Then he should have considered that before he authorized this training expedition on my island," Asher interjected.

"I'll pass on that message," Julian conceded. "But be prepared for his response."

Asher smiled again, the expression almost chilling. "I'm prepared."

"You're not," Julian replied. "But Bryant will ensure you are."

"He'll be ready," the other man said in a sobering tone, his gaze intent on the screen. "Is there anyone else joining the party?"

"Is that your sly way of asking after my wife?"

"I do prefer her to you," the newcomer replied, a hint of teasing in his voice now. "I'll handle her entertainment if you bring her."

"More like she'll handle yours," Julian returned, leaving no error for interpretation of their conversation.

I knew who Julian Jovanni was and what his family did. They owned the Elite Bride program.

And Julian's wife definitely came from my world.

The fact that this newcomer knew her said he knew about that life.

And he'd probably tasted it, too.

Which contradicted everything Asher had said to me thus far about not being part of this world.

Unless this newcomer was here as some sort of facilitator?

A trainer?

My blood went cold. *My new trainer.*

Asher's brow furrowed as he looked at me. "I need to see to Adalyn, Mr. Jovanni. Is there anything else you need from me?"

The newcomer followed Asher's gaze to me, his own smile disappearing at whatever he saw on my face.

"Is she there?" Julian asked, his tone taking on a strange note that I couldn't define.

"She just stepped in, yes," the newcomer replied.

Oh God. Part of me wanted to run before they could say anything else. But years of training held me stationary at the door, awaiting the next directive.

I already knew what the directive would be.

"May I see her?" Julian asked.

And there it was.

I shivered, my hands lifting to my shoulders in preparation to remove my dress. Because that was what he meant by *see*.

I wasn't ready for this with my damp hair and lack of makeup, but I didn't have time to prepare.

"Adalyn." Asher's demanding tone held me captive, my fingers frozen against the straps of my sundress. "Leave your dress on and come here."

I swallowed, his words wrapping around me and forcing my feet into motion.

My head bowed as I neared him and the one who I suspected would become my new trainer. My knees bent when I reached Asher's side, my need to resume a requisite position overpowering my every move.

But Asher's arm snagged me around the waist before I could kneel. I jolted a little as my ass met his lap, not from pain but from shock.

His arm tightened around me as his opposite hand went to my chin. He pulled my gaze to his, his eyes searching mine.

Silence fell, everything seeming to disappear around us. All that mattered was Asher and his intense gaze. His beautiful face. The way his thumb caressed my jaw.

"I'm starting to understand why Mr. Huntington may not be welcome on your isle," Julian said from the screen.

"When a man values something, he doesn't leave it in a place where others can take it," Asher replied, still looking at me. "That's how you lose valuable possessions."

He leaned forward to brush his lips against mine, the touch so beautifully tender that it brought tears to my eyes.

This man made me feel special.

Cherished.

Owned in the best way.

But why is the new trainer here? I wondered.

Asher cupped my cheek and pulled my head to his shoulder, holding me in his lap as he faced the screen again. "Is there anything else to discuss, Mr. Jovanni?"

I closed my eyes, allowing Asher to surround me with his strength. *Safe,* I thought. *I'm safe.*

"Not right now. I'll follow up with Mr. Rose regarding the accommodations," Julian said. "I'll also comment on the value of possessions as well. Perhaps there is a valuable item you wish to require for your official entrance into our organization."

Asher moved his hand to the back of my head. "Perhaps there is."

"I'll be sure to mention it," Julian said. "Thank you for your time, Mr. Sinner."

"Thank you for your time as well, Mr. Jovanni," Asher replied.

"Bryant," Julian added.

"Julian," the male beside us replied. "Send my love to Bria."

"Hmm," the other man hummed. "I see you miss our sparring days. Perhaps I'll arrange one during my visit to Sinners Isle."

The male—who I now realized was Bryant—chuckled in response.

I opened my eyes as he moved to do something with the computer. "Sorry, Ash. If I'd known he was calling, I would have been over here sooner."

"I suspect that was the purpose of his unannounced video chat," Asher replied. "He wanted to meet me without your influence." He ran his fingers through my damp hair, his focus shifting to me. "Are you all right, Adalyn?"

"Yes, Sir," I replied softly.

"We're not scening, darling. It's 'Asher' here." He kissed my temple. "Do you mind giving us a moment?"

"Yep." He'd already started walking toward the door. "I'll just be in the kitchen harassing Caylin."

"I'm not paying for damages if she stabs you," Asher called after him.

Bryant chuckled in response and disappeared into the hallway, the door closing behind him.

Asher continued running his fingers through my hair for a moment, his opposite arm still supporting my back as he held me on his lap. "You were fine until Bryant mentioned Julian's wife," he finally said after a beat. "Was she an Elite Bride?"

I blinked up at him. "I imagine so, yes."

He nodded. "I imagine so, too," he echoed. "But from what Bryant has told me, Julian and his wife have a good marriage. So are some Elite Brides treated well in the program?"

This type of question only proved how little Asher knew about Sin Cave. If he was playing a game with me, he might be able to make a few of these moves believable. But to consistently ask these types of things while also acting the way he did? That couldn't be faked.

And if it was somehow not real, if he was somehow just that good at this game, then he deserved to win at this point.

"Adalyn?" he prompted when I didn't reply.

I pulled back a little to look at him. *Really* look at him. That handsome face. Those perfect cheekbones. His sinfully dark eyes.

Such a beautiful man.

Strong. Dominant. Currently arching a brow at me in expectation.

My lips curled at that look, the defiant part of me wanting to push him to play a little.

But this was too serious a discussion for me to provoke him now.

He needed to understand this world. It was the only way he would survive it.

"Arrangements are made between the families," I told him softly. "And all the power is given to the male heir. So in my situation, Taylor said what he wanted, and the program molded me appropriately to suit those needs."

"And what was it that he wanted? A slave?"

I considered that and nodded a little. "He wanted someone willing to be shared. A masochist, specifically. From what I understand, that's a pretty typical request. But there are those who prefer to train their own wives. And not all requirements are the same."

"But what if the arranged bride isn't a masochist? She's just forced to become one?" A touch of incredulity underlined his tone.

"Yes. That's what the training does." I couldn't feel pleasure without pain now. I wasn't sure if that had been my preference all along or if Nate was the cause of my kinks.

Regardless, it didn't matter.

There was nothing I could do about my past or who he'd made me.

I am who I am, I thought, unapologetic about it.

"I don't know much about the other Elite Brides, as I was kept away from them. But I did meet a few of them early on, and I remember some of them were excited about their matches. I don't know if they maintained that excitement, though. Because everyone went down their own paths. Mine led me to Nate, and..." I trailed off because Asher could guess the rest.

"I see." His fingers slipped beneath my hair as his palm curled around my nape. "Would it help you to learn my preferences? Rather than guess at them?"

"You're a sadist," I whispered, fully aware of his preference for pain.

"To an extent, yes. I like giving pain to intensify the results."

"The results being your pleasure?" I guessed.

"Not exactly." He considered me, his midnight gaze assessing. "It's all about edging for me, knowing that I'm in control of when the woman falls apart. I can fuck with her senses, drive her to a point of agony, only to soothe her torment with the most intense orgasm of her life. That's true power. That's what I enjoy."

Yes, I could feel the evidence of that enjoyment growing against my ass. "Oh," I whispered, my own body reacting to his words. I'd experienced a little of that with him yesterday in the pool, but it'd mostly been about pleasure.

What would he be like in full Dom mode? I wondered.

"What about you, Adalyn? Is sharing one of your kinks?"

My lips curled down. "I... I do whatever I'm told."

"That's not what I asked."

"I know... I just... I don't know." I wasn't sure how to answer him. "I don't mind submitting—"

"But do you like it?" he interjected. "Do you like giving a man control? Letting him bind you? Tell you what to do? Dictate when you come and how hard you climax?"

My cheeks heated, his words igniting a flame within me. "Yes," I whispered. "Yes, please."

He arched a brow. "Which part?"

"All of it."

"Yet you reacted to me binding you yesterday in the pool. Was that only because you thought I intended to waterboard you?"

I dipped my chin a little. "I... I don't like water play."

"What about breath play?" His palm went to my throat, giving it a little squeeze. "Do you like that?"

I swallowed, my heart picking up a little in my chest. "With you? I think so, yes."

"But not with others?" he pressed.

"Not with others," I admitted. "I..."

I'd never been allowed to say this.

I'd never been allowed to question anything regarding my needs, to voice my desires, to utter comments about what I truly wanted.

But Asher was giving me the opportunity to do so now. And something told me he might actually *respect* my preferences.

"I don't like being shared," I confided in the softest voice I could muster. "I would prefer you not to share me, Sir."

My gaze fell, my heart suddenly in my throat.

Because I'd just admitted the one way he could break me—by doing the opposite of what I'd just requested.

"I'll never share you unless you tell me otherwise," he promised, causing me to freeze. "It's not one of my kinks. I enjoy exhibitionism and letting others watch, but once a woman is mine, I won't let anyone else have her unless she asks for it."

I blinked. "I'll never ask for it." I'd been forced to do that too many times in my life, always expressing desire for the men Nate had chosen for me to please.

But I'd never wanted any of them.

The only man I'd ever actually wanted, the only one I'd ever somewhat *chosen*, was this man. *Asher Sinner.*

"Then no one will ever touch you without your permission again," he vowed.

I frowned. Because that couldn't be true. I might be his for the next week, but beyond that... "You shouldn't make promises you can't keep, Asher."

He studied me for a moment, his gaze hardening. "You don't know me very well, Adalyn, so I'm going to let that insult against my character slide. But when I vow something, I mean it. And in this case, it is a promise I *will* keep. Because I intend to tell the Elite members that you're *mine*."

His grip on my throat tightened again as though to punctuate his statement.

I stared at him. "Yours?"

"I told you that was my intention, Adalyn. They owe me recompense for what happened on my isle, and you are the payment I intend to accept for their slight against my business."

My eyes widened. He had indicated his plans before, just as I'd picked up on the subtlety between him and Julian during the call. *I* was the valuable possession he'd mentioned—the one that had been left on this island for another man to find.

And he was that man.

"I told them I would pick up your training," he continued. "And that intrigued them enough for you to stay. It's all part of my plan to offer you freedom. But I need your help, Adalyn. You know this world better than I do. Likely even better than Bryant does. If you help me, I can help you."

My brow furrowed. "Bryant's a trainer. He knows the world as well as I do, maybe even better."

"A trainer?" he repeated, his lips curling down as he released my throat. "You know Bryant from the program?"

Uh... "No. No, I just met him today. But he's here to train, right?"

Asher blinked and then he smiled. "No, Adalyn. Bryant is the head of my security on the island. But he worked for Julian before coming here. And I've gathered he knows his wife well, but not as a trainer."

"Oh." My nose scrunched. "So he's not here to train me?"

"The only one who is going to *train* you is me, darling." He tucked my hair behind my ear and palmed the back of my head. "And you're going to train me, too. On your world and what the Elite will expect from me. Because I need to play my part convincingly to be believed. And in return, I'll give you safe passage on my island."

Safe passage? I thought. "Safe passage to do what?"

"To live in peace." His palm left my head to settle on my hip. "And if there comes a time when you can safely leave, I'll help you then, too."

I considered that for a moment. "But there's nowhere for me to go." And there likely never would be.

"That's something you obviously knew when you killed Nathan Spencer."

"Yes," I admitted. "But I just didn't care. I wanted out. I wanted away from him. I didn't want this week to happen."

"And you won, Adalyn," he told me. "But that was only an initial battle. Help me win the war, and I'll let you stay here. Unharmed. Untouched. To live however you want."

CHAPTER TWENTY

ASHER

ADALYN STARED at me with those big, beautiful eyes, displaying so much emotion that my heart hurt for her.

But she was finally where I needed her.

At a point of acceptance. The realization that I wasn't here to hurt her, but to help her.

Either she allowed it, or she rejected it.

I would have to respect her decision either way, as I couldn't force her to let me try to save her. She had to want to save herself first and foremost.

She searched my face, her dark irises flickering with a myriad of thoughts.

Until finally she said, "Not all Elites like to share. Nate actually had a list of men that I wasn't allowed to interact with at each Ecstasy location. He said they were too possessive, and as I was already spoken for, he didn't feel it was the right fit for my training."

It wasn't a blunt *I accept*.

However, I accepted her comments as a permission to move forward.

Because she was analyzing her world and letting me in on that thought process.

My eyebrow arched upward. "Was he worried they might claim you for themselves, thereby hurting the deal your parents had with Taylor?"

She shrugged. "I don't know, but maybe. There's a hierarchy to everything within the Elite. My family ranks somewhere in the middle. Taylor's family is higher, but he's not the heir; he's a spare. That technically places him at a lower level."

"And I'm guessing some of those possessive men on the list rank higher."

"Yes. Some of them are near the top." She listed a few examples, each name one I recognized. A few of them were even clients of mine. Something I might be able to use later, if I needed to do some convincing.

"I assume Nate and Taylor were friends, then. And he wanted to protect his friend's investment by not allowing you to potentially appeal to someone of higher rank."

She contemplated that for a moment. "It's possible, yes. But given that some of those men prefer not to share, your idea to feign a possessive front may work."

"I wouldn't be *feigning* anything," I clarified. "I don't share, Adalyn. As I said, the only exception is if my sub requests it."

Her eyes told me she would never request it.

Which just made her that much more perfect.

Because I preferred a female who only wanted me. I took it as a challenge to keep her satisfied. Unfortunately, most of my playmates only lasted a few weeks or months, so I'd never been fully satisfied with my challenge.

Maybe Adalyn would give me a chance to try it long-term.

"Okay, then you wanting me to yourself could be believable. But my parents and Taylor will still be a problem. If..." She trailed off, swallowing. "*Since* you're not part of the world, you have no rank."

I nearly smiled.

That little correction proved so much about how far we'd come in such a small period of time.

I would have kissed her to show my gratitude, but we had more important things to discuss first. *Then* I would kiss her.

"Do you want your father's company?" I wondered aloud, thinking about what she'd just said in regard to her parents. "Is that something you desire to own?"

She shook her head. "The only thing I've ever desired is my freedom."

"Then perhaps they'll agree to you signing it away," I suggested. It wasn't the best solution, but it would remove the *heiress* part of her future, thus removing the draw to marry her off.

She shook her head. "That's not how it works. I'm their only heir."

"All right, then why can't they just hire Taylor and eventually name him as the new owner? That's essentially what they're doing anyway, right? Just giving him the job of being your husband, then allowing him to take over?" I asked.

"No. They would still maintain partial ownership through me," she replied. "Or, well, my father would, anyway." Her lips twisted. "He wants to keep the company in the Rose family, and the only way to do that is to pass it on through me. But I'm a woman..."

"And what year is it?" I countered, my eyebrows rising. "Why the fuck does it matter if you're a woman?"

"The Elite is run by men," she answered simply. "It always has been. It always will be."

I scoffed at that. "A ridiculous notion." Women were just as capable as men at running businesses. Oftentimes even more capable.

"It's the Elite," she told me as though that explained it. "They have a certain way of doing things. Ways that go back centuries. And that includes arranged marriages and modern-day-style dowries."

Jesus, I thought, my hand threatening to tighten on her hip. "This is some archaic bullshit."

She lifted a shoulder. "You asked me to teach you."

"I know." That didn't mean I was going to enjoy the lessons. "Hold on." If we were going to do this, then I wanted to be more comfortable.

I shuffled her in my arms, stood, and carried her over to the recliner chairs in my den—the ones Bryant and Clive favored whenever they visited.

Rather than set her in one of her own, I sat and settled her on my lap again. I'd done this for show in front of Julian. Now I did this for me.

Because I liked touching her.

And given her reactions to me, she liked me touching her as well.

Perhaps because she'd been trained to accept it.

But there was something between us. Something hot. Something I intended to embrace.

Once we survived the Sin Cave meeting.

"All right, Adalyn. Continue."

Her lips pinched to the side, her gaze thoughtful. "Well." She fell silent for a moment. "I've always known I would have an arranged marriage. It's something my mother explained to me as a child. I thought it was normal." Her brow furrowed. "I thought everything was normal. Until college."

She went back to her early years, telling me how she had a private tutor for much of that time, then attended private school after that with other girls from the Elite circle. She made a few friends, but no one she still spoke to now.

Not since she was sixteen.

Her age when she'd first met Nathan Spencer.

I already knew that because of the videos and information on his phone, but I let her share her own details, telling me how he'd taken her to begin her training. She was given a private tutor to finish her high school courses while he took over her evening training.

My stomach twisted with each word.

But she spoke as though this was entirely normal, just as she'd said.

"Then Mason University changed everything for me," she told me.

And continued by telling me about those four years of society training.

Apparently, the whole purpose of her attending college had been to test her ability to be around other people without sharing Elite secrets, such as her arranged marriage and her nightly training—which had eventually turned into weekends.

Except for the summers.

Each summer she'd spent with Nathan.

"I *hate* summer," she added, trembling.

My heart broke for her, but she didn't stop talking. It was almost as though it felt good for her to purge it all. She told me about her friend, Jen, who was also her roommate.

"She doesn't know anything about my life," Adalyn

whispered. "Not really. Although, she almost found out a few months ago. Because I did something stupid." Her big eyes met mine. "I took her to Ecstasy for a guest night."

"I've been to a few of those with clients," I admitted. "But I've not seen anything to imply a lack of consent."

"You wouldn't," she agreed. "Because Elite Brides are well trained before they're allowed to enter the clubs." She cleared her throat. "But Jen's older brother saw me with Nate. And he told his best friend, Pierce, about it. Who then told Jen." Her gaze fell. "She had a lot of questions for me. I... I lied. Because I knew Nate was listening."

"She won't blame you for that, sweetheart," I told her softly. "You know that, right?"

She nodded a little. "I just hate that I had to lie. I hate that I had to *leave*. I don't even know if she sorted things out with Pierce or not."

"Her brother's best friend?" I asked, making sure I followed.

"Yeah." Her eyes lifted to mine again, a soft smile lurking in them. "Jen's been in love with him for years. And they finally hooked up at the club, but then he pushed her away again." She shook her head, sighing. "If I were them, I wouldn't let such a mundane thing as a brother get in the way of love. But, of course, I'm not them."

No, she wasn't. But that didn't mean she couldn't experience love, too.

"You're not them," I concurred softly. "You're Adalyn. You're a warrior. You're strong. You're beautiful. You're worthy of life and love and feeling and happiness. Don't let your past dictate your future." I ran my knuckles down her cheek, my opposite arm resting along her lower back. "You're free here, Adalyn. You're free here with me."

She stared at me.

I stared back, waiting for her to say more.

Although, I wasn't sure what else she could say.

She'd provided enough details of her past to paint a dark picture of her life. The only light appeared to revolve around her friend, Jen. They were roommates. Which meant she was probably worried about Adalyn right now.

Unless she thought she was just off on another summer vacation—which Adalyn had said was how she typically described her absence.

Holidays and school breaks were given a similar false title—*family vacations.*

All as some sick and twisted test to ensure she could be the high-society little wife Taylor Huntington desired, while also performing sexual tricks in the bedroom.

I found myself wanting to know more about the possessive men of her world. Were they just as twisted? Or were they possessive to protect their wives?

What category did Julian Jovanni fall into? Bryant's statement on the infamous Red Prince suggested the latter, but his reputation certainly qualified him for the former.

I'd have to evaluate him myself when I met him.

Adalyn's gaze fell to my mouth, then lifted to my eyes again. She seemed to be trying to decide something.

I didn't speak, letting her think, giving her space to make whatever decision she contemplated.

"I ate my food earlier," she whispered.

"You did. Are you hungry again?" I asked, recalling how she hadn't touched the soup.

She shook her head. "No. But you said I would get a reward." Her focus went to my mouth again. "And I don't want another instance for my safeword."

"Your safeword has infinite uses," I promised her,

hoping she believed me now. “But tell me what you want as your reward, and I’ll give it to you.”

“Anything?” she asked, a glimmer of optimism in her gaze.

My lips curled, intrigued by this side of her. “Tell me what it is, and I’ll do my best to give it to you.”

“I...” She swallowed, her nostrils flaring as determination settled across her features and she started to move.

I leaned back to give her room, rather pleased by her decision to straddle me. Especially in that short dress. It caused the fabric to ride up her pretty thighs, almost allowing me to discover whatever panties she wore beneath.

“I like where this is going,” I told her, my hands going to her hips as soon as she finished settling on my lap. “What do you want as your reward, sweet Adalyn?”

She grabbed my wrists and moved them down her legs, then she lifted and pulled her dress up.

And over her head.

Leaving her naked on top of me.

Because she wasn’t wearing *anything* under that dress.

Holy fuck.

“Pleasure, Sir,” she said. “I would like an orgasm, please.”

CHAPTER TWENTY-ONE
ADALYN

My pulse raced against my neck, the repetitive thud music in my ears.

I felt bold. In control. *Alive*.

God, Nate would beat me for this. For even thinking to ask such a question. Unless, of course, the man I was meant to serve had a gratification kink.

But I'd requested this reward for *me*.

I used to joke with Jen about wanting cock, mostly as a way to hide my reason for going to Ecstasy every weekend.

However, right now?

Right now, I meant it.

I wanted *Asher's* cock.

I wanted his tongue. His hands. *Him*.

"You're Adalyn. You're a warrior. You're strong. You're beautiful. You're worthy of life and love and feeling and happiness."

His words had cracked open my heart and made it beat so wildly that I couldn't think straight. I'd led with instinct instead of my mind.

And it'd brought me to this moment.

To the one where I boldly asked this man for pleasure.

The way he looked at me now told me it'd been the right move. His obsidian gaze glowed like dark flames, flickering with intrigue.

"An orgasm?" His black irises slid down over my body, the heat radiating from his stare resembling fire against my exposed skin. "Hmm..."

His hands went to my hips, and suddenly we were rolling in the chair with my butt bouncing on the seat as he went to his knees between my now sprawled thighs.

All the breath left my lungs, his abrupt movement making me light-headed. Yet I'd felt his hand in my hair, guiding me through the movement.

Always gentle.

Always guarding me.

Even when making me fly around him in a chair.

That left me even more breathless. Asher Sinner was unlike any man I'd ever met.

And now he was kneeling *for me.*

"Yes, Adalyn." He pressed a kiss to my knee. "I would be happy to reward you." He spoke the words against my thigh as he trailed a damp path upward. "With my tongue."

Oh God...

His mouth settled over my clit, sending a shock wave of heat through my body and eliciting a groan from my chest.

"Asher," I breathed, my orgasm already palpable. It was like he'd been teasing me for hours, yet we'd just started.

Maybe it was my emotions. His words. The fact that I hadn't been properly pleasured... ever?

I'd climaxed before.

But nothing compared to this. To Asher's tongue. And oh, his *touch.*

He skimmed his palms up my inner thighs, his hands sensual brands against my skin.

No man had ever touched me like this. Licked me like this. Or looked at me like *that*.

He was staring up at me with dark intensity, evaluating my reactions and testing different movements.

He sucked my tender nub.

Then nibbled.

And eventually *laved*.

Before inserting a finger into me. Followed by a second that he scissored against the first.

I writhed, feeling wanton and lost to his touch. His name kept rolling off my tongue, part plea, part benediction.

Oh, but his eyes.

Fuck.

I was utterly captivated by those twin dark orbs. Hypnotic and intense. Owning me entirely. "Asher," I whispered again, arching up toward his mouth. "I'm so close."

It seemed impossible to be this high-strung, this ready so damn quickly.

But he seemed to have lit a fuse inside me with his words. Then his hands and mouth only stoked the flames to burn that much hotter.

Like an inferno.

Pulsating. Throbbing. Licking sweet heat through my veins.

"Such a good girl waiting to come," Asher praised, each word spoken directly against my aching center. "Is this the reward you—"

A knock interrupted him, sending a jolt of need through my body. There was something undeniably erotic about being caught in the act. Like we were in the middle of an illicit affair that no one should know about.

Asher's gaze captured mine, a question in their depths. He'd admitted to exhibitionism being one of his kinks. I enjoyed it as well.

"Yes," I hissed, bowing off the chair and seeking his mouth. I was giving him permission to answer. Permission to control the scene.

Not that he required it. He was a Dom. It was my job to submit. However, I hadn't exactly been doing the greatest job of that lately.

Or maybe I had.

I really didn't know.

Fortunately, the slight curl of his lips told me he was pleased by my response. And that was all I cared about right now.

That and his tongue.

"Come in," he called, not bothering to glance over his shoulder. Instead, he licked me long and deep as the door opened.

Bryant entered, his hazel eyes going to the desk before finding us in the chair. His lips parted as though he intended to say something.

But whatever it was never came out, his mouth gaping for an entirely different reason upon finding Asher kneeling between my thighs. "Who is it, darling?" His voice vibrated my slick flesh, stirring even more yearning inside me.

"Bryant," I told him on a pant.

"Hmm," Asher hummed. "Tell him I'm busy. I'll be with him just as soon as I'm done making you come." He punctuated his statement by sealing his lips around my bundle of nerves again and sucking me deep into his mouth.

My nipples tightened painfully in response, my body strung tight and ready to explode.

"Tell him what I said, Adalyn."

Shit... I was barely able to breathe, let alone speak. I couldn't even remember what he'd said. Something about... about being busy... making me come.

Yes, that's it.

"Mr. Sinner is..." I bit off a moan as Asher nipped my swollen clit. "*Asher* is busy." I swallowed, my mouth dry. "Busy pleasing me."

Was that what he'd wanted me to say?

No. Something about coming.

"He'll..." I trailed off as Asher curled his fingers inside me to stroke that place deep within. *Fuck.* "He'll be with you... soon... *very* soon." Because I was so close. "As soon as... as I come."

"Such a good girl," Asher whispered, his neatly trimmed beard rubbing against me with his praise. He followed it with a deep lick of his tongue, his fingers still working my insides.

I tried and failed to swallow, my throat too constricted for the motion. My entire body felt tight yet swollen. Burning from the inside out.

"Is he watching us, sweetheart?" Asher's deep voice rumbled across me, making me quake.

It took effort to stop watching him and glance at the male by the door. "Yes." The confirmation left me on a hiss, my focus going hazy as Asher did something with his tongue.

"Where are his eyes right now?" Asher asked.

I moaned, his vocal vibrations coupled with his fingers driving me to the brink of madness. "My breasts."

"Mmm." Asher's own gaze went to my chest. "Look at

those needy nipples. Pinch them for us, sweetheart. Give them the attention they deserve and put on a show for Bryant."

God, his words were undoing me.

Yet a hint of fear spiked in the back of my mind at the same time. A fear surrounding the tentative trust we'd established. I'd told him I didn't like to be shared.

Us sounded like the beginning of a potential scene where—

"Tell Bryant I said that he can't touch you," Asher demanded, drawing my focus immediately back to the man between my thighs. His fingers had stopped, as had his mouth. "Tell him I don't share."

I shivered at the command in his voice. "Asher says you can't touch me." It came out raspy. "Because he doesn't share."

"Understood," Bryant replied, finally speaking. He'd stayed by the entry the entire time, his shoulder braced against the door frame as he admired the view.

"He says he understands," I told Asher, playing this game of erotic telephone with him. It wasn't something I'd ever done before, but I rather liked the sensation of power it gave me. He was still the one in charge, telling me what to say but allowing me to be an extension of his strength.

"Thank you, Adalyn." He licked me again. "You're so beautiful like this, sweetheart. Let's give Bryant a show, make him wish he was me, hmm?"

He didn't wait for my permission, just resumed his motions below, causing me to cry out from the sensations. They were even hotter now, provoked by that stroke of fear to my senses and heightened by the sheer domineering presence that was Asher.

I felt protected.

Safe.

Truly owned.

Not in a sinister way, but in a pleasing way.

Because he cared about me and my pleasure. I could feel the proof of it with every lick and nibble, his gaze intently watching me the whole time as he scissored his fingers and curled them and scissored them again.

"Asher," I breathed, my hands palming my breasts the way he'd requested, my fingers pinching my nipples. I wanted to put on a show, just like he'd said.

But it was for him.

And for me.

For *us*.

I could feel his friend's eyes on me, his desire a beacon that heightened my own reactions. "I'm so close," I told Asher, needing him to know. "Please, Sir. Please."

He circled my clit with his tongue, taking away from the pressure I craved and bringing tears to my eyes.

Oh God. "Please."

I needed him to let me explode, to force me over that final boundary into the world of nonexistence. To give me that sensation again like yesterday.

But he continued his torment, delaying the peak, edging me toward the end without allowing me to fall over the cliff.

I started to weep, my body so damn hot that I felt as though I might melt. "Please," I tried again.

"She begs beautifully," Bryant commented conversationally.

Asher grinned against my damp flesh. "She does." He licked me again. "Ask Bryant if he wants to see you come."

My insides resembled a strange sort of brittle material, bordering on the edge of shattering entirely.

But somehow I found my voice, my duty to obey overriding every nerve.

"W-would you like...?" I forced a swallow, my veins throbbing with fire. "Would you like to see me come, Sir?"

"I would," Bryant replied. "Very much so."

"He says yes," I whispered. "Please, Asher. Please?"

The stark hunger reflected in Asher's dark orbs had me clenching my thighs around him. He clamped down on my sensitive nub and sucked so hard that I saw stars. But it wasn't the permission I needed. It was just an invitation to disobey.

Fuck. His mouth was killing me. This was starting to feel like a punishment more than a reward.

Pain with pleasure, I thought, recalling his comments from earlier about his preferences. He'd said something about how he liked to edge a woman and control her climax.

He was demonstrating that now.

Drawing me to the point of agony, making me beg, ensuring every part of me burned...

I couldn't take much more. He was destroying me. All I wanted—

"Come for me, Adalyn. Don't hold anything back." His fingers curled inside me, demanding I respond.

And then he licked me in a way I couldn't ignore. A perfect swirl, practiced and skilled and pushing me right over the cliff into an erotic free fall.

I screamed.

Cried.

Writhed.

Too much sensation. Too hot. Too extraordinary. Too *powerful*.

A shock wave started at my core and pulsated through

every inch of my being. Destroying me. Captivating me. *Drowning* me.

I couldn't breathe. I couldn't see. I was utterly annihilated by the climax Asher had just unleashed upon me.

So much more powerful than yesterday. More intense than ever before.

I was panting. Clawing for the surface. Searching for my way out of the dark.

Only to be swarmed by his minty aftershave. Bathed in his masculine heat.

He held me against him. His strong arms clasped around my back as he rocked me in his lap.

Soothing me.

Bringing me back to Earth and allowing me to float in the aftermath of that detonation.

It was so undeniably beautiful. So powerful. So hypnotic and overwhelming.

I yawned and nuzzled into him, lost from the insanity he'd just inflicted upon me.

His voice rumbled beneath my ear, words leaving him that I didn't understand. Not right away. He was speaking to Bryant. Something about his sister.

"A warning would have been appreciated," he said, his words clearing in my mind.

"I attempted to provide that twenty minutes ago, but you were otherwise engaged," his friend replied.

Asher hummed, his lips touching my head. "Make her wait in the living room."

"I will," Bryant replied. "And don't forget to call Kane back. I think he knows something is up."

"Of course he does," Asher grumbled. "He's too aware for his own good."

"All you Sinner kids have your quirks. I'll leave you to yours now and deal with the other one when she gets here."

I vaguely heard the door closing.

Then Asher's lips were against my ear. "You taste so amazing, Adalyn. Even better when you come, too." He kissed my temple and ran his fingers through my hair. "I would do it again, but my sister should be here any second. So I'll give you another reward later."

My lips tried to curl. "A reward for what?" My voice sounded hoarse.

"A reward for trusting me," he replied, his voice filled with satisfaction. "Thank you, Adalyn. Thank you for letting me please you."

My heart skipped a beat. Men never thanked me, let alone for something that had been done in *my* favor. "I should be thanking you."

He chuckled. "You coming for me will always be a gift, darling." He caught my chin in his fingers and pulled my gaze up to his. "How do you feel?"

"Well used," I admitted.

"Good." He pressed his lips to mine. "But that's only the beginning."

My insides tingled. "I like the idea of more." The firm bulge beneath my bottom told me he did, too.

As did his smile. "Later. My sister will be here any minute, and if I don't go tame her, she'll barge in here."

"She's very confident."

"Because all her brothers never say no," he murmured, his voice holding a touch of fondness to it. "Do you want to come with me to see her or relax in here?"

"I'll come with you."

"She's going to question the hell out of you."

"Then it's a good thing I'm trained for that," I replied.

He frowned. "I hate having you lie to her, but she can't know about Sin Cave."

I cupped his cheek. "That's why I lie. It's never to protect the Elite, but to protect those who could be harmed by them."

That was how I'd justified lying to Jen for years. She was the closest person I had to a best friend, and she knew nothing about me because it was the only way to keep her alive.

"That makes for a lonely existence," he said softly.

He must have read that cue from my expression, or perhaps realized that truth from my words.

Regardless, he was right.

"It's how I've lived my entire life."

"Not anymore," he whispered, the words a vow against my mouth. "Because now you have me."

He kissed me as though to seal some unspoken promise. A pledge to always be with me.

I wanted to tell him not to make promises he might not be able to keep. But the hope he inspired within me overshadowed the worry.

For today, I decided to believe.

For today, I *indulged* in the now.

And returned his kiss.

CHAPTER TWENTY-TWO

ASHER

My sister had insisted on staying for dinner.

Which meant my intended meal for two had turned into one for four.

Graham was with the nanny, something I considered to be a blessing because it meant my sister would have to leave soon after dinner; she wouldn't want to be away from her son for too long.

Unfortunately, it still granted her ample time to question my *mistress*.

Something she was doing right now in the kitchen while Adalyn helped me chop up vegetables. I'd offered her the task with the hopes of pulling her away from Darby.

Alas, my inquisitive sister had followed us.

So far she'd only really asked for the basics, such as my mistress's name and how we'd met.

"Adalyn" and "On the island" had been the responses.

Then Adalyn had asked Darby about how she'd met Yon, and she'd continued her own line of questioning that had my sister spilling every detail about her life.

I suspected that natural flow of conversation had

something to do with Adalyn's "training" in the art of deflecting questions.

It'd worked for a while.

But my sister was persistent.

She perched herself on the barstool at my kitchen counter and sipped the cocktail I'd made her. Yon sat beside her with a beer, his gaze flicking to mine briefly.

We both knew the inquisition was coming. I could see the calculations forming in her dark eyes as her tongue played with her straw.

Adalyn ignored her, focusing on the vegetables. Her hair possessed a wild note to it since she'd let it dry naturally, the long, dark strands flirting with her upper back. She'd slid her dress back over her head in my office before running her fingers through her tangles. No other preps. And I found I very much appreciated this somewhat casual state.

Knowing she still wore nothing under that dress had my blood heating.

Primarily because I kept thinking about picking her up and devouring her on the counter.

Something I absolutely would have done if my sister hadn't intruded on my evening plans.

Caylin had helped a little by procuring more supplies for me, but I'd still dismissed her early. I'd promised her the night off, and I wasn't about to change that because of my sister.

I could handle a meal for four.

Especially with Adalyn helping me.

"Do you want me to boil these?" she asked, gesturing to the stack of potatoes I'd washed before starting to prep the meat.

I shook my head. “No, I’m making scalloped potatoes. Do you want to slice them?”

She considered her knife. “Um, yes. How thin?”

“You’ll want to use the mandoline slicer,” Darby told her before I could. “It’ll help make them even.”

I washed my hands before opening a cupboard to pull out the tool in question. She picked it up, her brow furrowing. “Okay.” She turned it over, causing the top to fall off of it. “Um, right.” She cleared her throat, picked up the top, and set the whole device flat on the counter.

That alone told me she’d never seen one of these before. “Want me to show you how to use it?” I asked her.

She glanced at me, her lower lip caught between her teeth. “Yes, please.”

I smiled. “First, it goes like this.” I kicked out the little stand on one side. “And you have to set the slicer width here.” I pointed to the dial, then moved it to the appropriate setting for her while she observed. “I’d also recommend a paper towel under it because the slices will come out here.”

She grabbed a paper towel and rearranged it. “And this?” she asked, holding up the part that had fallen off.

“That’s the part you jab into the potato to hold it in place.” I stepped up behind her. “Pick it up.” She did. “Grab the potato.” She selected one with her opposite hand. “Good.”

I reached around her to take hold of her hands. She felt good against me with her back pressed to my chest, almost making me want to cook like this every night.

“Now we’re going to press this button,” I said, my lips near her ear as I guided her finger to the button in question. “That causes the prongs to descend.”

“Okay,” she whispered, focused on the tool in her hand. “Should I stab the potato?”

"Yes." *Similar to how you stabbed Nathan Spencer, I imagine*, I thought. But I didn't voice that out loud for obvious reasons. Instead, I focused on gently holding her as she moved.

The sharp little blades bit into the potato, securing it.

"Perfect," I murmured, pulling one of her hands away to the slicer on the counter. "Press down here to hold it in place. Then place the potato here and slice it downward." I demonstrated once by leading her movement and providing just enough pressure to cut a piece off the potato.

"Oh. It's like a deli slicer." She glanced back at me. "This is useful."

"Yes, it is," I said, grazing her cheek with my lips. "Think you can make a pile for me?"

"And you want the skin?"

"It's my favorite part, so yes."

She nodded. "I've got this."

I kissed her on the cheek again before whispering, "Thank you, sweetheart," into her ear.

My sister was gaping at me when I released Adalyn, a myriad of questions filling her expression.

I warned her with a look not to voice them.

But of course she ignored me. "You met on the island," she said slowly. "How long ago?"

"Recently," Adalyn replied, her brow furrowing as she focused on her task.

"Let Adalyn breathe for a minute, Kid," I said before Darby could speak again.

"How about we go for a walk before dinner and let them work?" Yon suggested, picking up on my vibe.

"But I—"

Yon leaned in to whisper something in her ear, similar to breakfast the other morning.

And just like that occasion, her cheeks reddened. "Oh, okay," she whispered, clearing her throat. "We're going for a walk."

"Dinner should be ready in forty minutes," I told them. "We'll set the table for you."

I didn't want to know what Yon planned to do to distract my sister. I was just thankful he'd given me some space again.

"She's persistent," Adalyn mused after my sister and Yon disappeared through the sliding doors.

"That's one way to put it," I muttered, returning to the meat again.

"It's like she hasn't seen you with a woman before." Adalyn pressed down on the slicer, her focus on the potato and not on me. "She keeps staring at me with wonder in her eyes."

"Because she's never met any of my girlfriends," I told her. "And I've never had a *mistress* before, either."

Adalyn paused. "Never?"

"Other than the occasional date in high school? No, never." I shrugged. "I tend to keep my dating life private. Which is why she's so enamored with you. She had no idea you would be here, so now she thinks you're this big secret I've been keeping from everyone. She's in her digging phase now. Then she'll open up the sibling group chat and let them all know."

Big dark eyes met mine. "Will that be a problem?"

I shrugged. "Only if you dislike random visits from family members. They'll all want to meet you."

Which reminded me—I needed to call Kane back. He'd texted me an hour ago with a message that read, *Don't avoid me, brother. We need to talk about your flower problem.*

I assumed *flower* was a play on Adalyn's last name.

So either someone had mentioned her presence on my island to him.

Or he'd learned something about the events of this week.

Either way, I obviously owed him a phone call.

If I didn't react quickly enough, he'd probably put his ass on a plane and come harass me in person. And I really didn't want to deal with another sibling on my isle right now.

"Why will they want to meet me?" Adalyn asked quietly, her hands still frozen on the slicer.

I set the meat down again and washed my hands once more. "Because..." I stepped behind her and reached around to take hold of her frozen limbs. "They're going to want to meet the woman I've claimed as mine." I pressed my lips to her pulse before guiding her movements against the potatoes again.

"Claimed as yours," she echoed.

"That's the plan, isn't it?" I helped her finish the current potato before picking up another. "I'm possessive. You're mine. I don't share. Sin Cave owes me recompense. *You* are the valuable item I desire."

She shivered. "And then?"

"And then you stay here with me. Or in your own villa, if that's your preference. But you'll be safe and able to make your own decisions here." I considered for a moment. "You could even invite Jen for a visit. You said she's into the lifestyle, right?" She'd mentioned they'd gone to Ecstasy together.

"She has submissive tendencies. Her older brother is a Dom. So is his best friend."

"You could invite them all. I'd arrange a villa for them, free of charge."

"Assuming Pierce has come to his senses," she muttered, sounding slightly miffed. "I don't even know if they're together." Her jaw clenched. "I... I didn't expect to see her again."

I couldn't imagine that sort of pain, making a friend—someone who barely knew the real you—and knowing you'd never see her again.

Something told me Adalyn had kept her at a safe distance to ensure her protection. And that she likely considered a clean break to be the safest option for them both.

However... "You don't have to hide here, Adalyn," I told her. "We just have to convince the Elite that you're mine. Then, if you want to keep in touch with Jen, you can."

"But am I yours?" she asked, her hands still moving with mine as we sliced through the potatoes together.

"Do you want to be?" I countered.

She frowned. "That's not how it works."

"That's exactly how it works, sweetheart." I finished off the potato, then grabbed her hips and spun her toward me, wanting to see her eyes. "I realize your world is all about being told who to submit to. But I want a willing submissive, not a slave." I leaned into her. "So if you stay with me—*really* stay with me—it'll be because it's what we both want. Not because of some network mandate."

"But if they found out—"

"They wouldn't," I interjected. "Because we will play our roles. And I will protect you."

"Until you find a better submissive."

I arched a brow. "Darling, I don't think that's possible. You're absolutely perfect."

"I think you mean broken."

"I mean *perfect*," I reiterated, cupping her cheek. "You

have a past, yes. But don't let that define your future, Adalyn."

"Our history is what makes us who we are. It's the building blocks of our personalities and actions. And my initial foundation is flawed," she argued. "You have to see how unstable I would be."

I considered her for a long moment. "What I see is a strong woman who has survived hell and is still fighting for her future. A woman who stood up against her abuser and had the last word. A warrior who is going to stand beside me next week and *survive*."

I searched her face, willing her to understand.

She swallowed in response, her gaze still wary.

"Adalyn, you are the most stunning woman I've ever met," I told her. "Am I concerned about our roles? A little, yes. But I'm ready to be the stability you need to create a new layer in your foundation. A cement one that can't be broken or touched by anything or anyone."

It wouldn't be easy.

And I was probably insane for taking this on.

But there was just something about her that I couldn't turn away from. I wanted more, not less. A future, not just the present.

This girl was special.

And if I had to tell her that for the rest of her life in order for her to believe me, then I would. Every damn day.

"We're only just beginning," I promised her. "And maybe it won't work. Maybe you'll find someone else. Maybe you'll decide you want to leave. But right now, all we can do is take it one day at a time. And for the purpose of protecting my family, I will be claiming you as mine. Just like I will be staking that claim with Sin Cave. It's the only way to guarantee your safety and mine."

"At the expense of potentially your own happiness," she whispered back to me. "What if *you* find someone else?"

I sighed. "You asked me why my sister is so enamored with you. I told you—it's because she hasn't met a woman in my life before. As I said, I tend to keep my dating life private. But the reason for that privacy is because I haven't met anyone worthy of introducing to my family."

"And you only introduced me because of our current situation."

"Perhaps," I conceded. "But that doesn't undermine the fact that it felt right to introduce you to my sister. Which is why your *mistress* term is irking me. You're more to me than a mistress. You're... Adalyn."

She frowned. "Mistress is a more appropriate title since we just met."

"Perhaps. However, it's not who you are to me." I slid my palm to the back of her neck, giving it a squeeze. "This is all new. But give me a chance before you throw up your walls. Our circumstances may not be ideal, but I'd accept them again and again if they meant meeting you." I pressed my lips to hers, sealing my truth with a kiss.

Because I meant every word.

I had no idea what was happening between us or why I'd chosen this woman to save.

But it felt right.

And I wasn't going to turn my back on fate.

"Now, I need two more potatoes sliced, please. Then I'm going to make the sauce for them." I released her neck. "Help me and I'll reward you again later."

Her eyes instantly heated. "A reward of my choosing?"

"Always," I promised her.

She licked her lips. "Okay."

I smiled. *And you say you're not a perfect submissive,* I

thought, amused. This woman had no idea how special she was.

But I'd ensure she knew with time.

I'd heal every bruise, both physical and mental.

And if she wanted me, I'd claim her.

Again and again and again.

CHAPTER TWENTY-THREE
ADALYN

ASHER SINNER WAS A MASTER CHEF.

Hmm, he's a master lover, too, I thought, rolling onto my side.

He really could just be a master of anything, seduction included.

As evidenced by the pretty pink flower on the pillow beside me.

The last few nights had been all about rewards, typically provided with his tongue between my thighs.

I'd tried to repay the favor a few times, starting with the night he'd introduced me to his cooking skills. But he'd said something about needing to speak to his brother, and I'd fallen asleep while waiting for him to return. Then I'd woken up to a flower—similar to the one staring back at me now.

The following evening, he'd merely held me and hushed me when I'd tried to touch him. "My reward is hearing you come, Adalyn," he'd said. "I don't need anything else."

Need wasn't the same as *want*, something I'd almost told him then.

But I'd been too tired to argue.

And then the last two nights, he'd knocked me out with a series of such explosive climaxes that I hadn't been able to voice any desires beyond a yawn.

I picked up the flower on my pillow and inhaled the sweet scent. "Good morning," I murmured, thinking of Asher. He wasn't here, just like every other morning this week.

However, today he'd left me a note by the flower.

I stretched my arms over my head as I sat up, then plucked the white card off the pillow. His elegant scrawl made my lips curl. Somehow it just suited him.

Good morning, beautiful,
You looked so sweet in your sleep that I didn't want to wake you.
There's breakfast waiting for you downstairs under the heat lamp on top of the stove.
I needed to run to the airport to see my sister off, but I'll be back around lunchtime.
—A

I frowned. His sister was leaving today? Why hadn't he told me? I would have liked to say goodbye. I hadn't really gotten to know her well, but she'd come over a few times after our dinner. She seemed like someone I could be friends with someday.

Maybe Asher didn't want us to be friends because of all the Sin Cave business.

I set his card down, my mood falling with it.

That was probably exactly why he hadn't invited me along to say goodbye—he didn't want me associated with Darby.

I couldn't exactly blame him. My world was dark and

depraved. Darby's was all sunshine and happiness, just like Jen's life back in Oregon.

My chest rose and fell on a sigh. Holding people at arm's length was what kept them alive. I knew that better than anyone.

There was no use in brooding over it. Worrying never solved anything.

I rolled out of the bed and distracted myself by showering and getting dressed for the day.

Another sundress.

No underwear.

And combed, wet hair.

My trademark wardrobe for the week.

Although, today's dress was stark white, making me appear almost virginal. I studied it for a second in the mirror, debating whether or not I wanted to change it. I was down to my last three—this one, a dark purple dress, and a black one.

Hmm, if Asher is going to be gone all morning, then I need something to do.

Maybe I'll eat breakfast and go for a walk on the beach.

I hadn't explored much, choosing to stay close to his villa. But I'd been craving a date with the ocean. A white dress would suit being in the sun more than purple or black.

Stop overthinking and go eat breakfast, Adalyn.

Rather than stick around and argue with myself, I went downstairs and found a plate of French toast and eggs waiting for me beneath the warmer.

I carefully retrieved it and took it to the table, where Asher had left another note.

There is a little ceramic "boat of syrup" for you in the fridge. Put it in the microwave for thirty seconds.
—A

My lips curled at the quotations in his note. He was quoting me from the other day.

A third note waited for me on the fridge handle.

The orange juice pitcher inside is all for you, sweetheart. Enjoy.
—A

"You certainly have a way of sweetening me up," I told him. Not that he could hear me. But his notes improved my mood almost immediately.

As did the refreshing taste of all the food.

Definitely a master chef, I mused, finishing almost everything on my plate. It was a perfect portion of food, unlike the time I'd asked for the original boat of syrup.

I cleaned up after I finished eating, then found the sunglasses he'd let me borrow the other day and slipped them on. It was only midmorning, which meant I had a good hour or two to explore on my own.

He'd made it clear that I was free here.

At least until the Sin Cave members arrived. We hadn't reviewed who exactly would be showing up yet, but I knew my parents and Julian Jovanni were on the list.

The sun warmed my skin the moment I slipped out through the back doors of his villa. I bypassed the pool this time and stepped off the patio onto the beach. The sand burned against my feet, making me hurry toward the ocean shore.

"Ahh," I hummed as the water cooled the temporary burn. "Definitely a hot day."

A perfect one for a swim, actually.

But I didn't want to play in the ocean. It felt a little too out in the open. Maybe I'd take a dip in his pool on my way back in.

Or maybe I'd wait for Asher there whilst naked.

My lips curled at that thought.

Except he'd probably just please me again with his mouth and hands. Which I enjoyed. But I really wanted more. I wanted *him*.

He spoke about deriving pleasure from making me climax. I felt the same about the notion of bringing him over the edge. There was something so powerful about bringing a man to his knees, weakening his guard, watching him lose his senses for just a few split seconds in time.

Asher was so controlled.

So *dominant*.

I wanted to see him in those vulnerable moments and know that I'd pushed him there. Maybe even go over that cliff together.

With him inside me.

Pulsing.

Coming.

My thighs clenched. I wanted him to go bare. No barriers. No formalities. Just a Dom taking his sub.

Just Asher taking me.

My fingers curled as I fought the urge to lie here on the beach, spread my legs, and daydream about Asher's cock.

I hadn't seen it yet.

Just the rigid outline in his black boxers.

He was long and thick. I knew that much. He would fill me up entirely, maybe even stretch me a bit. *A perfect sensation*, I marveled, sighing as I closed my eyes and imagined him pumping into me.

Those burning eyes staring down at me.

His strong hands gripping my hips just a little too tightly.

Muscles contracting and flexing as he gave me all his power, driving us both toward—

"Adalyn?"

A chill swept down my spine, chasing away the heat in my veins. I swallowed, my eyes slowly opening to take in the scene around me. I'd been walking blindly down the beach, hugging the water's edge to protect my feet.

I wasn't sure how far I'd wandered from Asher's villa. Maybe half a mile at most?

But I'd clearly entered an area closer to the resort villas.

Yes. There are several right there, I realized, noting the eerily familiar docks that led to three discrete huts, each one evenly spaced to provide a semblance of privacy.

I'd stayed in one just like that.

With Nate.

Was that only a week ago? A little more? I wasn't really sure. Time had been irrelevant to me here, Asher's home having allowed me a false sense of safety. Being with him served as an alternate reality of sorts. An *escape*.

But that dream had just ended.

Because I now stood a mere ten feet away from one of my prior nightmares.

"It is you," the man said, a sly smile forming over his lips. I couldn't remember his name, my mind blocking it from my memory. But I knew *him*. I knew his desires. I knew his kinks. His proclivities. His penchant for making me cry.

"Wandering the beach alone? How daring." He stepped

forward, causing me to shuffle backward on instinct. "Or are you misbehaving?"

I swallowed. "I... Um." *Think, Adalyn.* "My Master said I could take a walk." I took another step back as he continued toward me. "I... I was just about to head back to him."

"Were you?" His salt-and-pepper hair flashed beneath the sun, his dark eyes resembling Satan's as he took in my dress. "Seems to me you're out here being a tease."

I shook my head. "N-no, my Master said I could go for a walk."

"In a see-through dress?" He tsked. "I think not, little slut."

My brow furrowed. *See-through dress?* It was light-colored, so maybe in the sunlight—

I jumped backward as he neared me. "My Master doesn't like to share."

He arched a brow. "And now you're lying?" His resulting chuckle was deep and menacing. "Oh, you really are inviting punishment, aren't you?"

He lunged for me and I skipped backward. "No!"

His smile turned into a scowl. "You know I'm not into chasing. Kneel before I beat your ass, Adalyn."

My knees threatened to obey, my heart skipping wildly in my chest.

Run! Some part of me yelled. *Run before he grabs you!*

I started stumbling backward, faster, picking up my pace, only for my ankle to hit a rock, twisting it and sending me down.

"Fucking brat," the man snarled.

Brevington, some dull part of my mind whispered. *Mitchell Brevington.*

That was his name.

In his late forties. Married. Enjoys flogging. The facts just kept rolling in my mind, distracting me from trying to scramble away from him.

My need to obey was overriding my desire to flee.

Because I knew better than to fight. Bad things happened when I fought.

Except, I killed Nate...

Oh, he must not know yet.

Unless... Did Asher...?

No. No, he wouldn't do that.

What if he did? a dark part of me whispered. *What if this was all a game to lull me into a state of contentment? Just for Mr. Brevington—*

He grabbed hold of my hair and yanked me out of the ocean, making me scream.

"Now you're just trying to make me hard," he accused, tossing me onto the beach. The sand stuck to my skin, making me feel as though I were sinking into it as he stood over me. "*Kneel.*"

My pulse raced, my throat working to swallow, to speak, to *scream*. I wasn't sure. I didn't know if anyone would come.

Maybe this was all a lie.

Why else would this monster be here?

Asher had shown me the emails. He'd told them all not to come.

But maybe... maybe it had been a lie. A ruse. A way to trick me into a trusting state.

My vision began to swim, my insides twisting. *No. I... I believed him. I... I trusted him.*

Yet I'd known from the beginning that it was all some dark form of torture, the worst punishment I'd ever receive.

Because I'd killed Nate.

I'd done the one thing that would sentence me to a lifetime of torment.

Asher had almost convinced me that he was my savior, that I could stay here, be *safe.*

However, Mr. Brevington's presence proved it all to be a fucked-up game. A way to finally break me. To crush what little spirit I had left.

To make me have feelings...

Just...

Just to rip them all away.

It wasn't true. None of it was true.

Mr. Brevington's foot met my side as he kicked me hard enough to leave a bruise. "*Kneel, bitch.*" He followed it up with another slamming sensation against my ribs. His foot? His fist? I wasn't sure. I couldn't seem to see straight. Everything was blurring. Turning dark. My world tunneling as I fought to hold on to my strength.

But I could feel it slipping.

Disappearing.

Shattering.

None of it was real, I whispered to myself, curling into a ball as Mr. Brevington hit me again. *Asher lied to me. He tricked me. He invited this vile man here to break me.*

Water stung my eyes.

The ocean.

No, tears.

Maybe both.

I couldn't process the dampness or the agony shooting up my side. None of it compared to my heart fracturing in my chest.

Ice followed, freezing me, numbing me from the sensations unfolding around me.

I closed my eyes.

I stopped listening.

I willed myself not to breathe.

What did it matter? I'd experienced bliss for such a short period of time. A vacation from my hellacious existence.

Dreams to last a lifetime, I thought, the word sticking in my mind.

My safeword.

Would it work? Would Asher stop this madness if I spoke the word aloud? Was this a test? To convince me to believe in him?

Or some wicked trial meant to make me suffer all that much more?

My lips parted.

That word was all I had.

If it would end this torment... If it would bring him to me... It was worth my pride to try.

"Dreams," I breathed, wincing as I felt hands grasping my wrists and shoving them into the sand.

Someone snarled in response.

Mr. Brevington.

"Dreams," I repeated, hanging on to that word as though it was my sole lifeline. "Dreams!"

"Shut the fuck up!" he shouted, his fist slamming into my jaw so hard I saw stars.

But I couldn't stop saying my word. "Dreams." It was my anchor. The only lifeline that I knew existed. "*Dreams.*" Asher had to hear me. He had to save me. He'd promised... *vowed*... not to share me. "*Dreams!*"

Mr. Brevington's palm covered my mouth, shoving sand over my tongue and making me gag.

I bit him in response, my teeth sinking into his skin as my limbs filled with the need to *fight*. To *hurt*. To *react*.

"Dreams!" It came out garbled, the sand choking me and making me hack as I tried to remove this man from my body.

My knees angled upward, catching his thighs.

He shouted profanities, trying to shut me up, telling me to stop fighting, *hitting* me.

I slapped him back.

Only to have my wrists caught again.

"Dreams!"

Asher had to hear me. He had to stop this. He'd promised me. He'd said that was my word. That it would make it all stop.

I couldn't see beyond the tears or hear beyond the roar of the ocean.

I couldn't *breathe*.

Mr. Brevington's hands were around my throat, strangling me.

But my hands were free again.

I grabbed his wrists, digging my nails into his skin, demanding freedom, begging for air!

His vicious laugh pierced my mind, his grip tightening.

I'm going to die.

Asher ignored my safeword.

Asher lied.

It was all... it was all...

My mental voice broke off on a sob, my insides shrieking with the need to breathe.

I tried to knee him again, but I couldn't reach him the way I needed to. My nails weren't making him stop despite the blood pooling beneath my fingertips.

My hand curled into a fist as I tried to hit him.

Narrowly skimming his jaw. No, his shoulder.

I couldn't tell.

Some bone.

Some... something...

Oh God...

Everything was turning black. Sensation... was... cooling. No, heating. Heating and cooling.

Dreams.

What a perfect safeword.

An amazing trick.

I'd always known dreams didn't exist. And neither, it seemed, did the safety Asher had promised me.

The... the vows...

Lies.

Dreams... are...

"Adalyn!"

I didn't recognize the voice. Just another male. Probably joining in on the fun with Mr. Brevington.

That would explain the loss of his weight. The other guy probably told him to move to take his turn with me.

My eyes remained unseeing, my ears flooding with rhythmic waves. It also seemed cruel to be taken by something so tranquil.

But everything else in my life had been ruined by the desires of men.

So why not destroy the beach for me, too?

"Adalyn?" that voice repeated, something warm touching my cheek. "*Fuck.* Get me Dr. Zansky! And throw that asshole in holding. Asher's going to want a word."

"He's going to want a hell of a lot more than that," someone else said.

I recognized one of them.

I couldn't figure out which one it was, though.

My mind wasn't working properly. All I could whisper was "Dreams." The word resembled cement against my tongue, my hope dying a little more with each time I said it.

Until there was nothing left inside me.

Only darkness.

And a strong desire to sleep.

Without dreams.

Because dreams don't exist.

Not for a woman like me.

CHAPTER TWENTY-FOUR
ASHER

My wrist buzzed with Bryant's name, making me frown. It was the third time he'd tried to call me in the last five minutes.

"He obviously needs something important," Darby said, following my gaze. "Just give me a hug. We're getting on the jet now anyway."

I gave her a tight smile. "Family is always first." It was an unspoken rule among us, a vow that we would always be there for each other. No matter what.

Another vibration came through, this one a text.

Darby gave me a knowing look. "Come here, Gramps." She wrapped her arms around my shoulders, distracting me from reading the message. Not that I'd really tried. But it was a bit troublesome that Bryant seemed so hell-bent on contacting me. He knew I was seeing my sister off today.

Yon met my gaze over Darby's shoulder, his dark eyes holding a question.

I shook my head. *It's fine*, I told him.

However, something in my gut didn't feel fine.

Probably because my world was about to be turned

upside down by Sin Cave assholes. They were scheduled to arrive in a few days.

And my brother Kane was coming tomorrow.

Because Clive had let him know about the situation. Something I was pissed at him for.

"You work for me," I'd reminded him. "Not my brother."

"Which is precisely why I called him," Clive had returned. "I protect you, even when you refuse to protect yourself."

Bryant had stayed out of the conversation, but his silence had told me he'd agreed.

I was in over my head.

It would behoove me to have backup, just in case.

The only reason I'd agreed was for Adalyn. If something happened to me, I needed someone well connected enough to help her disappear. And that someone was Kane Sinner.

Like all my siblings, he'd inherited a club. But his true passion revolved around private security, of which he owned his own firm.

And that firm had a lot of government and military connections.

Sin Cave might be powerful.

But so was Kane.

So am I, I thought, releasing my sister.

Yon's expression suggested he'd seen something in my face, some sort of hint of trouble. I didn't give him a chance to comment on it, or rather, my *phone* didn't give him a chance.

I sighed as I saw Bryant's name again.

"We're good," Darby told me, giving me a soft smile. "Thank you for the honeymoon."

"You're welcome back anytime," I told her, my voice matching her quiet tone. "I'll miss you, Kid."

"I'll miss you, too, Gramps," she replied. "Come visit me soon."

"I will," I promised.

"Tru, too," she added.

I rolled my eyes. "We'll see."

"I'm going to tell him you said that," she warned.

"Please do." My phone again started buzzing. "Jesus. I really need to take this, Darby." It wasn't like Bryant to keep calling. "You all be safe, okay?" I said, looking at Yon first because the words were mostly for him. *Take care of my sister,* I was telling him.

"Always," he promised, his smile growing with fondness as he glanced at my sister, his palm curling around her neck as his thumb stroked her collar. "Let's go, baby."

I knew what that meant.

I knew what it all meant.

But I ignored it because I really didn't want to picture the things Yon did to my sister as a result of that collar around her neck.

Her eyes glittered like stars as she looked back at him, the two of them so utterly in love it almost hurt.

Yon pulled her into a kiss before bending to retrieve their son from his stroller.

Darby gave me a little wave, her gaze a bit misty.

I smiled at her. "See you soon," I promised.

"Thank you," she repeated in a whisper.

I winked at her.

Then pulled out my phone as it started going off again. "Give me a minute," I said to Bryant, waving to my sister as she started up the stairs to the jet. I'd followed them onto the tarmac, wanting to say goodbye near the doors, mostly to ensure they were actually leaving.

I needed to know my sister and her family were safe.

And I needed her gone before Kane arrived, or that would raise a shit ton of questions I couldn't answer.

Which had also been my reason for leaving Adalyn at home. She'd handled my sister beautifully all week. But I knew Darby. It would be just like her to lay into Adalyn at the airport, just because she'd feel her time for answers was running out.

My suspicions had been proven correct when Darby had expressed her disappointment at my not bringing Adalyn with me.

Yon had distracted her by suggesting that I might bring Adalyn home for the holidays or something else in the future.

I'd nodded along.

Because yes, I would absolutely do that.

If Adalyn wanted to go.

Darby gave me one last wave.

Then disappeared inside.

And the aircraft crew began the process of closing everything up.

I gave the jet one more look and turned away, heading toward the building doors. "Okay. What is so urgent that you've called me seven times?"

"Nine," he corrected. "And it's Adalyn."

I paused midstep. "Adalyn?"

"Mitch Brevington fucking attacked her on the beach."

"*What*?!" I picked up my pace again, starting to walk faster toward the doors. I hoped like hell my sister couldn't see me right now. If she thought for even a second that something might be wrong, she'd demand to be let off that jet. "What the fuck happened?"

"I don't know. Someone heard her screaming about dreams on the beach and notified security."

My heart panged painfully in my ribs. *Oh, Adalyn...* "That's her safeword."

"*Shit.*"

"Where is she?"

"About half a mile from your place on the beach. Dr. Zansky just got here. She's..." He trails off. "She just keeps saying *dreams*, Asher."

"Did he hurt her?"

"I don't know yet. She's wet and covered in sand, but I didn't see any blood."

That didn't mean much. Injuries could be internal.

Or worse.

Mental.

"Clive took Mitch to holding," Bryant continued. "I called you as soon as we had the scene secured. My men have blocked access to the beach."

"Good." I reached the door and glanced back at the jet, checking to ensure Darby hadn't tried to come after me.

But everything appeared calm and normal. I raised my hand, hoping like hell it looked like an average wave, and disappeared inside.

"Give me three minutes," I told Bryant. Then I hung up, pocketed the phone, and sprinted through the airport.

Which was, fortunately, not that big.

And directly to my car waiting outside.

Oscar stood out there waiting for our next arrival, his eyebrows lifting. "Everything okay, boss?" he asked.

"Yep," I lied, then dove into the driver's seat, started the car, and did my best not to hit anyone on my way out.

More than three minutes had passed since hanging up on Bryant.

However, I couldn't seem to call him back. Not yet.

I needed to get my head back on straight.

Because fuck, this was a mess.

Mitch Brevington? Why the fuck would he attack Adalyn?

She used her safeword.

Did that mean she thought it was a scene? One I was orchestrating?

My stomach churned at the notion.

I'd told her I didn't share. I'd promised her that no one else would touch her. Why the fuck would she think I'd craft a scene with *Mitch Brevington?*

I knew the answer deep down.

She still didn't trust me.

But the fact that she'd tried to use her safeword showed on some level that she *wanted* to trust me. Because she'd believed that would save her.

Fuck.

Fuck.

Fuck!

I slammed my hand against the steering wheel, my mind going a million miles a minute. Then my phone started to ring again.

Bryant.

I hit the Answer button. "I'm in the car. Only a few minutes away from my place." Because I was driving eighty miles per hour on my island, which was really fucking dangerous. But I needed to reach Adalyn. I needed to make sure she was okay.

"Doc just gave her a sedative," he said softly. "She tried to hit him while screaming her safeword."

My throat went dry. "What the fuck did Brevington do to her?"

"I don't know, but I can find out."

I considered the offer. But I shook my head. "No. I want to talk to him. After I see Adalyn. Where exactly are you on the beach?"

He told me the villa number he was closest to.

"I should have guessed that," I muttered. "That's where Brevington's staying with his mistress."

The bastard enjoyed escaping to my isle to play with her because of the exclusivity on the island. The media couldn't find him here.

And neither could his wife.

But I suspected she knew all about his little pet.

"Is he part of Sin Cave?" I asked.

"I don't know," Bryant replied. "But I can ask Julian."

"Do that. And have Clive look at Nate's files, see if he can find anything on Brevington."

"On it," Bryant replied.

I couldn't bring myself to thank him, not with my control hanging on by a thread. That made me a bad friend. But he'd understand. He'd forgive me, too. "I'll be there in a minute."

I hung up again and cursed, my insides burning with the desire to *murder*.

That fucker had put his hands on Adalyn.

My Adalyn.

I might be claiming her for show, to protect her from a worse fate, but some part of me had begun to truly consider her mine.

Time didn't matter.

Our circumstances did.

Fate did.

The way Adalyn looked at me. The way she trusted me, at least partially. The way she came for me. The way she relaxed beside me. The way she asked for pleasure. The way she turned to me for guidance.

The way she felt against me.

The way she kissed me.

The way she existed with me.

That all mattered so much more than a simple clock.

This female was under my skin. She meant something to me.

It was almost as though she'd been made for me. Crafted into the perfect sub with a sprinkle of defiance on top. A remarkable spirit. Intelligent. Beautiful.

I swallowed. Everything about her screamed *mine*. I wanted her. I wanted to *keep* her.

And that bastard had touched her.

Made her scream her safeword.

"I'll fucking kill him," I vowed. I'd promised her that no one would touch her again.

A now broken promise.

Because Mitch Brevington had turned me into a liar.

That was unacceptable.

He'd tarnished my reputation with Adalyn.

Fuck everything else. Fuck him. Fuck this damn situation.

Adalyn mattered most.

And he'd had the audacity to tarnish her opinion of me. Ruin our tender foundation. Shatter what little trust I'd managed to instill in her.

My jaw clenched as I pulled my car over to the side of the road.

The door slammed in my wake, my body moving faster than I could anticipate as I sprinted down the beach, not caring at all that my shoes weren't meant for sand.

Bryant's men parted instantly, not bothering to speak as I plowed through their perimeter.

Dr. Zansky knelt near the water.

Bryant stood beside him, his expression grim as he saw me running toward them.

"Tell me she's okay," I demanded as I reached them. "Fucking tell me she's okay."

"She's fine," Dr. Zansky said, his voice calm. "At least physically."

He was doing something to her side, making me kneel on the other side of her. "What are you doing?"

"Brevington either hit her or kicked her." Dr. Zansky gestured to her reddening skin, only then making me realize she was naked.

A heap of white fabric rested a few feet away from her. "Did he...? Did he penetrate...?" I couldn't finish the questions, my fury mounting and cutting off my ability to speak.

"No, it doesn't appear that he was able to get that far. She fought back." Dr. Zansky showed me her hands and the blood beneath her nails. "Other than a few bruises, I think she'll be okay. Physically."

That was the second time he'd used that word. "What about mentally?"

His lips twisted to the side, his gaze finally meeting mine. "She was quite upset when I arrived, Asher. I'm concerned."

I nodded, expecting as much. "I'm going to fucking kill him." But I needed to ensure Adalyn was safe first. Not lying here exposed and unconscious on the beach. "Is it safe to move her?"

Dr. Zansky did a few more checks before nodding. "Carefully, but yes. She'll have some bruises and may cough up a little sand, but she seems to be all right otherwise. I'd like to keep an eye on her for a few hours, though."

"Yes, I would like that, too," I admitted. "Can I carry her back to my house?"

He dipped his chin. "Just don't jostle her too much. I don't know if she hit her head again or not."

I glanced at Bryant. "Will you help me lift her?"

"Yeah." He knelt on Dr. Zansky's other side.

"I just need you to keep her head and neck stable while I situate her. Then you can guide her head to my shoulder." I slid my arm under her knees and the other under her shoulders. "Ready?"

He made a noise of confirmation, and together we slowly stood. She didn't weigh much. I just wanted to ensure she remained steady, per Dr. Zansky's orders.

He observed our movements, his expression telling me we'd succeeded. When her head was nestled against my shoulder, I started walking.

Bryant followed. Dr. Zansky said he'd meet us there, heading toward his parked car.

I considered going to mine, but I didn't want to bother with the bucket seat. I also felt the need to hold her. To carry her. To literally shoulder the burden of her situation.

This was my fault.

I'd promised her safety on my island. And I'd failed her.

Never again, I vowed. *Your safeword will always be respected.*

Fuck, it still killed me that she'd used it. Only to be hurt anyway.

It hadn't gone too far, from what Dr. Zansky had said. But even a slight touch over her limits was unacceptable.

"Yeah?" Bryant said from beside me, his phone at his

ear. "Yeah," he repeated, this time not as a question but in confirmation of something. "I see."

He had one hand in his pocket, the epitome of relaxed elegance. Yet I caught the tension in his jaw.

"He'll want to have a conversation about this," he continued, his hazel eyes flicking my way. "No, his hands are full at the moment."

Another pause.

Then he pulled his phone away and angled it at me.

I frowned until I realized he'd turned his camera on. "Hands are literally full," he repeated.

"Shit." Julian's voice came through the speaker, making me narrow my gaze at the screen.

Bryant took him off speaker and put the phone back to his ear. "As I said, he'll want to have a conversation about this."

I didn't say anything.

I'd wait until he hung up.

"I'll let him know," Bryant replied. Several more beats passed, causing him to sigh. "Yes, I imagine he will."

Then he hung up the phone.

"Mr. Brevington is a high-ranking Elite member." He uttered the words without looking at me. "You can't kill him."

I grunted. In my current mood? "No promises."

"Asher, he owns the biggest financial corporation in the world. He's not a spare heir."

"I know who he is," I replied through my teeth. That didn't make me want to kill him any less.

Fortunately, I was carrying Adalyn right now. Otherwise, I'd likely be in the holding area, beating the ever-loving shit out of Mitch Brevington.

Which I knew would have severe consequences.

I'd have to calm down before I spoke to him.

"Do we know if he has a history with Adalyn?" I asked, needing more information.

"Clive is still going through the records he pulled from Nathan's phone. There are a lot of videos."

There were. Adalyn had said they were for documentation purposes. However, Clive had mentioned that none of them were in the cloud. Which he'd thought was strange because all the files were solely saved to Nathan's personal device.

"If they were meant for Taylor, wouldn't they be in a shared folder?" he'd asked the other day.

"Maybe they were meant to be a wedding gift?" Bryant had replied.

That hadn't seemed right to me. If Taylor wanted Adalyn trained for him, wouldn't he want proof of that training prior to their wedding?

Something wasn't adding up there.

None of this felt right.

Bryant moved ahead to grab the door for me, saying nothing as I stepped through with Adalyn still pressed to my chest.

I took her straight upstairs, but rather than head to the guest room, I carried her to mine.

Bryant didn't comment, just helped hold her head as we laid her down.

"I'll let the doc know where you are when he arrives," he told me, giving me a much-needed moment alone with Adalyn.

She was covered in sand.

Her hair tangled.

Her throat darkening with a bruise.

So fragile and wounded.

It hurt my heart.

But I forced myself to look at her, to face the failure in my protection. "Never again," I promised her. "I'll never let anyone touch you again."

Because this woman was mine. Even if she no longer wanted me after this, I'd still ensure her safety. Claim her from afar. Do everything in my power to make certain that no one ever hurt her again.

I leaned down to brush my lips against her cheek.

Then I wandered into my bathroom to grab some towels.

It would take a while to clean her up in this state, but I'd vowed to take care of her.

"I'm sorry, Adalyn," I whispered, running the cloth along her neck. "So fucking sorry."

CHAPTER TWENTY-FIVE
ASHER

MITCHELL BREVINGTON SAT at a plain white table in the holding room, wearing a ripped shirt and sandy pants. His wrists were cuffed on the tabletop, allowing me to see the dried blood crawling up his forearms. There were a few specks on his neck as well.

All of it was his own.

Because Adalyn had fought him.

I rather approved of her handiwork. I only wished she'd had access to a blade to finish the job.

Alas, that wouldn't have ended well for any of us.

"He wasn't a regular with Adalyn," Clive informed me. We were standing beside each other on the hallway side of the one-way mirror, observing Brevington as one would a caged animal at the zoo. "But he's been with her at least once."

"How brutal?" I asked.

"He's into shame kink. Degradation. Enjoys exerting power and making his subs cry. Adalyn wasn't easy for him to break. So he resorted to harsher methods." He cleared his throat. "Slapped her a bit in sensitive areas. Used clamps. Ensured all she felt was pain while he took her."

Given some of the other videos he'd shown me, that wasn't the worst she'd endured.

But that didn't make me any more likely to forgive this bastard.

"He likes when a woman fights him," Clive continued. "My guess is that he thought she was role-playing, something his mistress confirmed that he's into."

I grunted. "A good Dom knows when his sub is playing."

"He's not a good Dom," Clive returned. "He's not a Dom at all. Just a rich bastard who enjoys getting off on power plays."

I'd met enough of those types in my twenty-nine years of life—men who fancied themselves as into the lifestyle without truly knowing what it meant.

"What do you want to do with him?" Clive asked.

"I want to kill him," I said, not bothering to lie. "But I can't." Because of his status. It would bring about far too many problems. And Julian had brought up a good point during our call an hour ago.

"Showing leniency here may sway a powerful Elite member to your side," he'd told me. "Someone who may be able to apply certain pressures in regard to revised marital arrangements. He controls a lot of investments, after all. Which affords him some not-so-subtle influence in a variety of situations."

In other words, I had an opportunity here to potentially use Brevington as an ally.

Which was fucked up.

But it could lead to a guarantee for Adalyn's freedom.

Hence the reason I hadn't yet sauntered into that room and killed the son of a bitch sitting before me.

Oh, I still wanted to. *Badly*. However, I knew better than to let my emotions destroy an opportunity.

"He doesn't know why he's in there," Clive told me softly. "He kept asking why his scene was interrupted when we cuffed him. Then he demanded that we talk to Nathan, saying he would confirm the scene."

I frowned. "Brevington wasn't on that graduation list."

"No. But we only had the list of those who had accepted the invitation. Not the list of all those invited."

I considered that for a moment. "Mr. Brevington just made his reservation the other day."

"So he probably didn't know the party was canceled," Clive added. "And I'm guessing word of Nathan's death has been kept quiet while the network decides how to proceed."

"Yes," I agreed, my brow furrowing as I contemplated the notion of an unconfirmed participant list. "How many other last-minute guests are on the island right now?" I wondered aloud, running through all the villas in my head.

Clive wouldn't know the answer; it was more of a rhetorical question meant for me.

Something he understood, because he remained quiet while I mentally reviewed our current client list.

"Kingston." He'd made his reservation two days ago, then arrived the same day. "Parks." He'd also made a last-minute request. "And Mavens."

"I'll send their names to Bryant and ask him to check on them," Clive said, already drafting his text.

Silence fell as he slid his phone back into his pocket, both of us staring at the man behind the glass.

Brevington appeared to be tired, his shoulders sagging.

This was a man not used to feeling vulnerable. A man

who enjoyed being on top. A man who was absolutely going to lash out the moment I walked into that room.

I needed to be ready for it.

Or I'd react by hitting him.

And that wouldn't play into the leverage that Julian had mentioned.

Of course, I'd be well within my rights to hurt this man. He'd touched my Adalyn. A mistake he was about to learn had certain consequences.

There were rules on my island.

He knew those rules.

And he'd broken the one I cared about most.

Just like Nathan Spencer had.

"That's two slights against me on my island," I'd told Julian earlier. "Two cases of disrespect. How many more must I endure before I'm taken seriously?"

"I take you very seriously, Asher," Julian had replied quietly, his use of my first name giving the conversation a more personal tone.

"Then you'll understand me when I say Adalyn Rose is mine," I'd said.

"Yes," he'd agreed. "So let's discuss that more."

Which had eventually led to his commentary about showing Brevington some leniency.

Julian Jovanni's moniker, *Red Prince*, seemed inaccurate. *Strategic King* seemed more appropriate after our last few conversations. He struck me as someone constantly playing all sides of the board in a thirty-way chess match.

I cleared my throat. "All right." There wasn't much left to say. I had calmed down as much as I could in this situation. And I didn't want to stand here all night. I didn't want Bryant and Dr. Zansky to be the only ones there when Adalyn woke up.

She was mine.

And I'd remind her of that the moment she opened her pretty eyes.

Which meant I needed to finish this shit with Brevington right fucking now.

My hands curled into fists, then relaxed.

And I stepped toward the door.

Brevington's head came up the moment I crossed the threshold, his brown gaze sparking with fury.

"Mr. Brevington," I greeted in a bored tone.

"It's about goddamn time, Sinner," he spat at me as I forced myself to take the chair across from him. "I've been in here for hours. And I've got to say, I'm less than impressed with your hospitality."

I steepled my fingers on the table, my gaze meeting and holding his. "Well, I'm less than impressed with your behavior, so I assume that makes us even."

"What the fuck are you talking about?" he demanded, his tone reminiscent of a man used to running an empire. *Everyone bows to me,* that voice said. *I am king.*

Not on my island, I thought. "Adalyn Rose."

He arched a brow and tried to lift his arms. "I'm familiar with her."

"Yes." The word came out through a clenched jaw. "Nathan had a video of that *familiarity* on his laptop. What I don't think you're familiar with is the recent change in her status."

"Video?" he echoed, brow furrowing. "What video?"

"The video Nathan captured during one of his many training exercises. One that very much features *you,*" I informed him, his response intriguing me. Because it implied he hadn't realized he was being filmed.

But Adalyn had clearly known.

I'd have to ask her what exactly Nathan had said to her about it later.

"There's a video?" Brevington sounded uncertain.

"Is it not normal for your network to videotape Elite Bride training?" I asked him.

His eyes widened a little, the first real sign of discomfort showing in his features. "Elite Bride training?"

Ah, so he's just playing dumb, then. Which only irritated me more. "I'm very familiar with Sin Cave, Mr. Brevington. Don't insult me by denying your high-ranking status. I'm still quite angry about your last slight against my integrity. It would not suit you well to add another."

He considered me for a long moment. "I know you've been on the recruitment list. I wasn't aware that you knew about it."

"A lot has happened in the last week," I informed him. "As I believe you're aware, Nathan Spencer brought Adalyn Rose here for a graduation celebration of a sort. However, he only told me that she was his guest. Then he proceeded to conduct unauthorized business on *my* island. Breaking *my* rules regarding consent. He's now dead."

Brevington's eyes widened.

But I wasn't done speaking.

"Which is how Adalyn Rose became mine," I added. "I don't think anyone can blame me for seizing the opportunity of claiming such a well-trained submissive."

I hated those words.

Hated the way they made me feel.

Alas, I had a role to play. *For her.*

"Unfortunately for you, Mr. Brevington, I do not share. Therefore, you not only broke my rules regarding consent, but you also touched someone who doesn't belong to you."

I paused, giving him a moment to process everything I'd just said.

"I... I wasn't aware of the change in her ownership," he stated slowly.

"Yes. As I said, it's recent. Which is why it's been recommended that I give you leniency in this situation. Leniency that I did not provide to Nathan Spencer."

Mr. Brevington studied me, his eyes showcasing an intelligence I would have found admirable had he not tried to rape Adalyn. "I see. And who have you been talking to?"

Yes. I'd anticipated this part of the conversation arising, as had Julian. Which was why I'd brought my phone in here with me.

I pulled it out now and dialed the requisite number. Then put it on speaker.

"Mr. Sinner," Julian greeted, aware of why I was calling, as we'd discussed this potential need.

But he didn't know if I was calling to say I'd killed Brevington.

Or if I still had him in custody.

I waited a beat before saying, "You're on speakerphone, Mr. Jovanni. I believe Mr. Brevington would like some reassurances regarding my current recruitment position."

"Of course," Julian replied, his tone giving nothing away. However, I suspected he was relieved to learn that I hadn't yet killed the proverbial finance king. "Mr. Brevington, can I assume that you're being taken care of?"

"I'm currently handcuffed to a table, Julian. So it depends on your definition of *care*."

"It's better than the care you displayed toward my submissive," I informed him coldly. "Yes?"

He cleared his throat. "I wasn't aware of the change of ownership," he echoed.

"Yes, Mr. Sinner was kind enough to take on Ms. Rose's training in Nathan's absence," Julian interjected. "However, it seems he's become a bit enamored with our asset. So much so that he's requesting permanent ownership. I'll be flying out with Mr. Rose in a few days to discuss a revised agreement."

A saccharine summary of the situation. "It's not a request, Mr. Jovanni," I reminded him. "She's mine."

He chuckled, the sound grating on my nerves. "As you can see, Mr. Brevington, Asher is quite possessive of his new toy. Which is unfortunate, as I've heard Adalyn is quite well liked. But we're hoping to bring Mr. Sinner into the fold, and if this is his price, I think it's one we should consider paying."

Mr. Brevington stared at me.

I stared back, not bothering to hide my fury from him.

He swallowed, obviously sensing that I would kill him. Easily. Without an ounce of remorse. And it helped that he assumed I'd killed Nathan Spencer already.

This was my island.

I didn't allow outside security here because I had my fleet of deadly personnel, all led by Bryant and Clive. The men weren't obvious, their ability to blend in with their surroundings one of the key reasons they'd been hired for my isle.

And Mr. Brevington had met several of them today.

Which made his position here rather clear—outnumbered, outmanned, outmaneuvered.

He might own a financial empire, but that didn't guarantee a damn thing here.

Just because I sat here politely, resembling a casual businessman in my button-down shirt and slacks, did not mean I wouldn't beat the shit out of him in the next breath.

All facts I ensured he understood without words, merely by communicating through my eyes alone.

He cleared his throat after a beat. "Yes, it's a price we should definitely consider," he agreed, holding my gaze. "Is Mr. Rose amenable to a new arrangement?"

"It's an ongoing discussion. Perhaps you'd be willing to assist?" Julian asked.

"I would, yes," Mitch replied, still staring at me. "Assuming Mr. Sinner accepts my sincerest apologies and allows me to leave his island."

My jaw clenched. They weren't leaving me with much of a choice. "What assurances do I have that you'll assist me with the negotiations?" I questioned. "You can imagine why your word won't be enough for me in this situation, yes?"

It was an insult, one Mitch took in stride. Which was good because he'd more than insulted me; it was only fair that I returned the favor. "Julian, were you aware of the videos Nathan Spencer kept of his training sessions?" Mitch asked, his focus on me even while shifting the conversation.

"Videos?" Julian echoed.

"Yes. Mr. Sinner commented about a video he saw of me with Adalyn. It's not something I would like to have... *shared*."

Ah. All these men were rather clever in their word games, proving they'd been playing with each other for a very long time. "Yes, it would be most unfortunate for you," I agreed. "The video displays you as rather violent." Not much of a stretch, considering what Bryant had told me about it.

"I wasn't aware of any videos," Julian said, sounding a bit taken aback by that.

"There's a laptop full of them," I told him, realizing I might have even more leverage in this situation than I'd originally realized. This might explain why Nathan hadn't put them on a cloud. They'd either been for Taylor to potentially use in the future or for Nathan's own private purposes.

Blackmail, perhaps? I thought.

Well, I wasn't one to spoil an opportunity.

"Perhaps I'll share them with you when you visit, Mr. Jovanni." But I would be keeping a copy for myself for insurance purposes. I would never share them, as it would damage Adalyn more than the men involved. But these Elite jackasses didn't need to know that.

"And in the interim, you'll keep them safe," Mitch stressed. "While we work on these negotiations."

"Of course," I replied. "That sounds amenable." Because he was giving me my leverage over him—my guarantee that he would help me sort out the marriage arrangement issue.

Unfortunately, it only further cemented my involvement with Sin Cave.

But that part had been inevitable anyway.

"I do have one more requirement," I added.

"Name it," Julian said.

"Mr. Brevington's Sinners Isle membership has come to a permanent end." I ensured both men heard the finality of my statement. "The same applies to any and all men who participated in Adalyn's training. While I understand she has a past that groomed her for her present, her future is with me. And I do not share, not even with her memories. I will erase all of them from her mind, including today's incident."

It was an extreme statement.

One I knew they would understand as that of a possessive man.

But I also meant every word. I intended to erase all their touches, all their influences, and replace them with my own. By helping her *heal.* By being the salve she needed to recover from the wounds these assholes had created.

It would take years.

Maybe even decades.

And she might never accept me as hers.

That was fine. As long as she survived, I could handle whatever part of her she willingly gave me.

But I would chase away her monsters. I would help her *dream* again.

"Do you understand?" I asked, holding Mitch's gaze while making certain Julian heard the threat lingering in my tone.

"It sounds reasonable to me," Julian replied.

"Yes," Mitch echoed. "I'll miss your island, but I understand why this is necessary. And again, my apologies for this misunderstanding. I would never have touched Adalyn had I known she was yours."

Misunderstanding was an understatement. And if I stayed in this room for any longer, I'd be forced to demonstrate just how big a *misunderstanding* this was between us.

"Now you know. And I expect you and Julian to ensure that word spreads." I finally looked at my phone. "Julian, perhaps Mitch can also help you explain to Taylor Huntington why I suggest he stop insisting on visiting my isle."

I stood.

And Mitch sat back in his chair, swallowing.

“Yeah, I can do that, too,” Mitch said, clearly seeing the desire to *hurt* him vibrating down my arms.

“Excellent,” I replied through my teeth. “Anything else, Mr. Jovanni?”

“No, I think that covers it, Mr. Sinner. We’ll speak again soon.”

“Yes,” I agreed. “We will.” I snatched my phone from the table and hit the End key. “To be clear, Mr. Brevington, you’re very lucky to be alive. If you want to remain that way, you will get the fuck off my isle in the next sixty minutes.”

With that, I left the room.

“Uncuff him and escort him to a jet. I don’t care which one you put him on; just make sure he’s gone before I change my mind and kill him.” I raised my voice loud enough to ensure Mitch heard me through the still-open door.

Then I stalked out of the building, leaving Clive to handle the billionaire asshole.

I had a female to comfort.

My Adalyn.

Mine.

CHAPTER TWENTY-SIX
ADALYN

UGH.

What the...?

Everything felt fuzzy. Wrong. *Heavy.*

Like I was weighed down by mud.

Where am I? I wondered, my eyes refusing to open. It left me in an inky pool of darkness, my thoughts murky as I fought to recall whatever had put me in this state.

Did Jen and I go out drinking?

Fuck, I hope not. Nate will kill—

Wait...

Nate's dead.

An image of his body flooded my thoughts.

Followed by ones of Asher Sinner.

His villa. His guest room. French toast. A walk on the beach...

Dreams.

Oh God.

"Dreams," I breathed, my eyes finally working.

Black sheets. Bedposts. A balcony overlooking the ocean.

"Adalyn." The deep voice came from my left. "It's okay, sweetheart. You're safe."

Safe? Panic held me captive, stealing the breath from my lungs. *I'm not fucking safe!*

Everything had been a lie.

Safety didn't exist.

Safewords meant nothing.

Safe wasn't *real.*

"Adalyn," the voice said again, a strong hand cupping my jaw. His thumb traced my cheek.

And all I could think about were what his hands had done to me before I'd passed out.

My throat. Strangling me. Killing me.

I couldn't remember what had happened next.

Did he fuck me? Did Asher join him?

My brow furrowed. *Asher.*

That was his voice now.

So maybe he had joined him. But hadn't he said he preferred his women to be conscious?

Oh, but he'd also promised me a safeword.

Which hadn't been true at all.

"I'm sorry," he whispered, his touch going to my throat. "I'm sorry he touched you, Adalyn. I'm sorry I wasn't there. I'm sorry for letting you down. I'm sorry for everything."

My heart slowed, my breathing beginning to steady. "*I'm sorry I wasn't there.*"

He... he wasn't there?

"You did so good using your safeword, sweetheart," he continued softly. "Someone alerted my security team. But I should have been there. I shouldn't have let that bastard on my island. I promise it won't happen again."

He ran his fingers through my hair while I tried to process his words, my mind struggling to comprehend.

My... my safeword worked?

Or is this another lie?

"Clive is going through Nathan's files and making a list of those who have touched you. I've already told Julian none of them are welcome here. And Brevington's gone now, too. He left the island, and he's not allowed to return. I'll be issuing a ban to everyone else, just as soon as I have the list from Clive."

He gently took hold of my chin to drag my focus up to his dark, intense gaze.

"I failed you. It won't happen again. No one will touch you without permission, Adalyn." He traced my jaw with his thumb. "You're mine to protect. I know I bruised that faith. And I'm sorry. I'll prove my worth again, sweetheart. I promise."

I searched his features, confused. *Is this another game? Another way to hurt me? Emotional torture?*

What happened after Mr. Brevington choked me? I wondered, trying to recall what had come next.

I... I didn't feel *sore*. Just bruised along my sides. My throat felt raw, too. But nothing else really ached. At least not in the way it typically did after a harsh fuck.

"Throw that asshole in holding."

The deep voice echoed in my mind, followed by something about a doctor. Or had that been before the demand? I couldn't remember the order or what had really happened.

But I recalled feeling hands on me.

Someone hushing me.

Telling me it was all right. That Asher would be there soon.

However, I'd kept repeating my safeword, *dreams,* the

only phrase I seemed to know. It almost left my lips again now.

Because I felt broken. Shattered. *Used.*

Yet whole.

And...

And *safe.*

Which made no sense. That notion didn't exist. It was a lie. *Everything is a lie.*

Except some part of me—a naïve part, maybe—believed in Asher.

Or rather, that part *wanted* to trust him. Although, he kept holding back. He focused on me instead of himself, always in control, never allowing me to see his darker side.

"This is who I am," he'd said the other night.

But then what was that scene with Mr. Brevington? A fluke? A test? A twisted punishment?

I... I didn't understand any of this.

I didn't understand Asher's words or his desires or his intentions or any of his reasons. Everything was just so confusing in my head. Warped and wrong and wicked.

And fractured.

He'd engaged me in this torture, making promises I longed for him to keep. Then reality had spoiled each vow, tarnishing the edges of this fantasy world and grounding me in my former existence.

I felt as though I were drowning. Swirling. *Dying.*

Nothing made sense. Nothing seemed right. My world was up and then down and turned and then sideways.

"Adalyn," he breathed, his dark gaze holding a note of concern. "Talk to me, sweetheart. Tell me what you need."

Something real, I thought. *Something... something right. Something to ground me. Something to make the world stop spinning!*

I grabbed my head, hating how everything was spiraling. Hating how utterly wrong I felt. Hating the muddled thoughts and murky past. I wanted to... to feel normal.

To know Asher.

Truly understand him.

Feel him.

Be trained in his expectations. To understand the extent of his control.

I... I needed him to dominate me.

Anchor me.

Bring me back.

Help me.

His hands were suddenly on my cheeks, his body hovering over mine, his face swimming above me. I felt myself spiraling downward, sinking into a hole without an escape, the earth closing around me, suffocating me, making me—

"Tell me your safeword, Adalyn," Asher demanded. His voice wrapped around me like a noose, dragging me to the surface and forcing me to see him. To focus on him. To be here *with* him.

Yes, yes.

More.

I... I need... I can't define... I just... I...

"Tell me your safeword, Adalyn," he repeated, his tone harsher now, his hand going to my throat. "Tell me right now."

"D-dreams," I stammered, frowning. "But it doesn't... It's a lie." *Right?* Wasn't it a lie? A falsehood? A game?

"You say *dreams* when you want the scene to stop," he told me. "One word, Adalyn. That's all you need. What Mitch Brevington did wasn't a scene. It was attempted rape. You're mine to protect. Mine to please. Mine to take care of. When you say *dreams* with me, everything ends and we talk about limits. We talk about how to move forward. Brevington has nothing to do with us. He's gone. We're in the present now, and *dreams* is your safeword. Now say it again so I know you understand."

But I didn't understand.

I didn't understand at all.

"Asher, I—"

"*Sir*," he corrected. "We're about to begin a scene. You call me 'Sir.' Or 'Mr. Sinner.' Whatever you prefer. Now tell me your safeword, Adalyn. Say it with confidence. *Know* that you can use it. You're the one in control here. You're the one with all the power. It's my job not to push you too far. It's my job to *ground* you. But I need your consent. And you'll give it by reminding me of your safeword."

"Dreams," I whispered.

He shook his head. "Not confident enough, darling. That's your word that makes everything stop. It's your power. Don't let that asshole steal it from you. Don't let your past belittle it. You're here now. You're mine. And you have a safeword. One I will obey. One I will ensure you never have to use. Now say it again."

I shivered, the sheer dominance in his voice making me melt beneath him.

It was exactly what my body needed.

Exactly what my mind *required*.

An escape. An outlet. A way to turn everything off. To not think about anything other than this moment. Anything other than *him*.

Asher Sinner.

My Sir.

My Master.

"Yes." I stared into his eyes, everything else falling away around us. "Dreams."

"One more time for me, sweetheart," he said, his palm still around my throat. It didn't hurt. It felt reassuring. Like he was erasing the touch of those who'd come before him.

Such as Mr. Brevington.

Asher was replacing him in my mind.

Creating a new scene.

A new experience.

One that would overshadow everything and everyone else.

A scene I desired.

Perhaps for all the wrong reasons. But this... this felt right. It allowed me to breathe, granting me renewed life with a refreshing air of the present.

No more past.

No more thinking.

Just him. Just Asher. Just us.

"What's your safeword, Adalyn?"

"Dreams," I answered automatically. "My safeword is *dreams*."

"Good girl," he praised, his lips brushing mine. "And who am I?"

"My Sir."

"Very good, sweetheart." He gave me another kiss. "Now tell me what you need."

I blinked up at him. *What do I need?* "I need you." I needed his voice. His commands. His touch. His praise. His control. "I need to understand you." This game. This world. This reality. This *present*. "Everything feels so chaotic, Sir. Please fix it."

I wasn't exactly sure what I needed.

But some base part of me trusted that he knew what I

desired. Perhaps I'd lost my mind. Maybe I was actually dreaming right now.

Did it really even matter?

I wanted Asher.

I wanted him to prove that there could be more in this life. To show me what it meant to be his. To stop this insanity and just let me exist in the now. "Please," I repeated in a whisper, my gaze searching his. "Please, Sir."

He pressed his lips to mine, hushing me with a soft "Shh" against my mouth. Then he kissed a path to my ear. "I'll give you what you need, sweetheart." He nibbled the lobe before nuzzling my neck, his touch eliciting goose bumps along my arms. "Grab the headboard." His words were soft but underlined with command.

I obeyed.

"Such a good little sub," he whispered, kissing his way down my neck. He seemed to be tracing a path along some of the bruising, as the touch of his lips hurt yet soothed at the same time.

His tongue followed, licking a trail up my throat in a manner that left me trembling beneath him.

"If anyone other than me ever strokes this beautiful skin again, you safeword them, Adalyn," he said softly. "Scream it. Someone will come running. And I'll kill whoever it is that dared to touch you without permission."

I swallowed, uncertain.

He must have sensed it because he lifted up onto his elbows on either side of my head, his hands stroking my arms as I clutched the headboard above me.

"My security staff is well acquainted with your safeword now, Adalyn. You so much as whisper it and they'll come running. Because no one touches you except for me. Not unless *you* decide otherwise." He arched a dark brow. "Understood?"

I licked my lips. "Yes, Sir."

"Only me," he added. "I'm the only one who touches you. Ever. Unless you desire another. Then we'll revisit those limits. But until that moment, it's you and me. Always." His palm circled my throat again. "I'm your Dom now. Do you understand?"

"Always?" I echoed.

"For as long as you want me," he clarified.

My brow furrowed. "Will you always want me?"

His gaze darkened. "Yes, Adalyn. I will."

"How do you know?"

"Because I've never craved a woman as much as I crave you." He lowered his head to run his nose against mine, the touch so gentle I nearly began to weep from it. No one had ever handled me with this sort of care. Yet every move was underscored by his dominance, his control, his sheer force of nature.

It left me dizzy.

Unable to concentrate.

Something about his words had felt unbelievable. Curious, even.

But when he touched me like this, I couldn't question him.

It just felt too powerful, too *real*, too all-consuming, to ignore. "Okay," I breathed, consenting to something I didn't fully understand.

His lips captured mine in a searing kiss, sealing some sort of vow between us.

I didn't ask for clarification. I just fell headfirst into it, succumbing to every stroke of his tongue against mine.

His thumbs drew little circles against my inner elbows, his body so completely mastering mine.

Yet he wore clothes.

A cotton shirt and gray sweatpants.

I wanted them gone. I wanted him as naked as me. I wanted him *inside* me.

He'd asked me what I needed.

I understood now what that was.

"Sir," I breathed against his mouth. "I know what I need."

"Tell me, sweetheart." His words tasted minty on my tongue, his peppermint essence a seductive kiss to my senses that left me warm and ready beneath him.

"I need you inside me," I told him. "I want to feel you come. I need to be the one to bring you to that point. I need to *know* you. To *please* you." I opened my eyes, unsure of when they'd even closed, and stared directly up at him. "Please, Sir. I need more. I need *you*."

Maybe I was having a moment of impulsiveness.

Maybe I had a bad case of hero worship.

Maybe I'd just lost my fucking mind.

But life was short, I wanted him, and there was a chance that I might never be given this opportunity again. Everything focused on the *now*—our present. Because our future was undecided.

And I no longer wanted to exist in the past.

"I want you," I continued. "I want to know what it's like to be with a man who... who respects me. Who... who won't hurt me just to make himself feel superior."

I wasn't sure where the words were coming from or how I was able to string them all together, but hearing them aloud made me realize how true they were.

"All my life, every touch has been commanded by

someone else. Dictated by other men. I want this for me. I... I want my right to *choose*."

I swallowed, unable to say much else.

Because this was driven by so much more than physical need.

This was driven by an emotional wound that had bled inside me for far too long. A wound I needed to treat. A wound I wanted to start *healing*.

"Please." The word fell from my lips as a tear escaped my eye. I suddenly felt even more broken than when I'd awoken. Like something inside me had just ruptured. *Shattered*. Utterly destroyed. Perhaps because I'd just admitted something aloud I hadn't even admitted to myself.

My lungs deflated, my heart racing in my chest.

Because I had no idea what he would say next. How he would react. I was the sub. He was the Dom. I shouldn't be dictating to him.

But he'd asked what I needed.

And what I needed was the right to *choose*.

And I'd chosen him.

CHAPTER TWENTY-SEVEN
ASHER

Fuck.

Adalyn's words wrapped around my heart and squeezed so tightly that my chest ached.

She was asking for the ability to choose, to restore some of her power in this dynamic. To be what a submissive should be—*in charge*.

As her Dom, it was my responsibility to see to her every desire and earn her faith and trust. It was my job to read her cues, determine her needs, and correct her where appropriate.

Such as a few minutes ago when she'd begun to spiral into a dark state. I'd recognized the signs of her despair almost immediately, that haunted look in her gaze one that told me I was about to lose her to her thoughts.

My instinct to command her had flourished to the forefront, my Dominant side instantly taking control of the situation.

It had worked.

And now she was asking me to reinstate her power, to allow her to *choose* our path this morning.

I'd intended to go down on her again, bring her pleasure, and carry her downstairs for breakfast. But my sweet Adalyn needed more than that.

She needed to please me.

Not because of some ingrained desire to put my pleasure first, but to experience my version of rapture for herself. To *know* me. Because all I'd done was focus on her physical satisfaction, not her emotional *need.*

She required a connection. A link between our bodies. A thorough introduction into what it meant to truly be mine.

I understood that now.

Because she'd told me what she needed.

"Thank you, Adalyn." I pressed my lips to hers. "Thank you for being honest with me."

That was the key to a healthy bond—honest communication. I needed to be able to trust her to tell me her feelings, to know when to safeword.

Just as she needed to trust me never to take her too far.

We were finally on the precipice of that bond.

A beautiful moment. An emotional one, too.

I kissed her again, telling her with my tongue how much I appreciated her putting her faith in me. It might be minimal, and she might also still harbor reservations regarding my intentions, but I would use this experience to introduce her to our future.

Because she was mine now. For as long as she would have me.

I ran my palms down her arms, loving the way goose bumps pebbled in the wake of my touch. "Tell me who is kissing you right now, Adalyn."

"My Sir," she whispered automatically.

"Good girl." I licked a path to her ear. "Tell me how you want me to fuck you."

"However you like, Sir."

"Hmm." I nuzzled her pulse. "I want you to come so hard around my cock that I feel you for days, darling. I want to erase everyone who has ever touched you from your mind and leave only my imprint behind. So tell me how to do that, sweetheart. Tell me what you need so I can make you fall apart for me."

She shuddered in response, her thighs clenching on either side of my legs. "*Sir...*"

"Tell me, Adalyn. *Choose* what we do and how we do it." I wanted her to take back her power, to feel in control even while I dominated her.

It wasn't an easy task to take on.

But for her, I would do it.

For her, I would do anything.

"I... I want you naked," she replied softly. "I want to taste you, Sir."

I nibbled her earlobe, my voice low as I hummed, "But I thought you wanted me to fuck you, darling. That sounds like you want to suck me off instead."

She arched into me, her body producing a delicious friction between our lower halves. "I want both, Sir. Please."

"So needy," I whispered, loving the sound of her soft requests. I doubted I could ever deny her. Especially not now, not when she was trying to voice her yearning.

She wanted so much more than a rough fuck.

She needed a connection.

She needed to feel in control. She needed to experience *choice*.

So I would forfeit some of my dominance to her. Just enough to give her the upper hand I knew she needed while still exuding my power in a way that made her feel safe and secure.

"All right, Adalyn," I said, lifting to brush my mouth across hers. Then I went to my knees between her sprawled legs.

Her eyes instantly widened, her fear a whip across my senses.

I reached for her hand over her head and quickly brought it to my face as I hovered over her again, my opposite palm going to the mattress beside her to hold myself steady. "I want you to undress me. Now sit up and take my shirt off." I studied her eyes, noted the dilation of her pupils, and went back to my knees.

She responded well to commands.

Especially ones she wanted to obey.

And it seemed this one was a powerful enough demand to pull her away from her thoughts because she followed me upward, her breasts swaying alluringly with the movement. "Yes, Sir," she said, her fingers at the hem of my shirt.

I lifted my arms for her, allowing her to take control of the motions as she undressed my upper half.

Her eyes danced across my chest and down my abdomen, her appreciative expression causing my lips to curl. "You want to touch me, little one?"

"Yes, Sir," she breathed.

"Touch me," I said, inviting her to satisfy her desires.

Her throat worked as she swallowed, her cheeks blossoming with an alluring shade of pink.

"Now, sweetheart," I demanded, providing the edge I knew she needed to indulge herself.

Her palms immediately went to my chest, her nostrils flaring as she traced her thumbs across my pecs.

It was always nice to be admired by a woman. But to be admired by this female made me feel like a king.

Because she was a fucking goddess. And to know she found me attractive? Yeah, that was a heady sensation.

She drew her nails downward to my abdomen, tracing the ridges and worshipping me with her touch.

I let her take her time, giving her this gift of choice and control, and waited until she reached my pants.

"May I, Sir?" she asked.

"Only if you promise to properly kiss my cock after you're done," I told her, providing her with another command that met her needs.

I would be lying if I said the demand didn't also satisfy my own needs, too.

But that was part of the dance—mutual gratification.

Knowing she desired this, knowing she *chose* this, just intensified the experience.

She licked her lips. "Yes, Mr. Sinner." Her fingers slid beneath the fabric of my pants and pulled them down. I shifted to help her get it around my knees and to my calves. She bent with the movement and pressed her mouth to my dick as she reached around me to push the fabric away from my legs.

I grabbed the back of her head to hold her in place as I kicked my pants the rest of the way off, my fingers gliding through her long, silky hair. "Kiss me," I said, repeating the command. "Show me how much you want me, Adalyn."

She opened her mouth and swallowed me down, her lack of a gag reflex causing my balls to tighten.

Because *fuck*. This was a woman who knew how to suck cock. And I did not want to think about how she'd developed this skill.

She grabbed my hips to balance herself, her body shuffling back a little as I remained on my knees.

God, it was an erotic sight with her ass in the air behind her as she balanced on her own knees and her grip on my hips to hold herself steady.

But it was her eyes that undid me.

Because she was watching me, checking my expression, ensuring I liked her exploration. “You’re very good at that, little one,” I told her. “Are you satisfied with your taste, or do you want more?”

“More,” she hummed around me.

“Then start sucking, sweetheart. Take whatever you want. Touch me however you want. And don’t stop until you’ve had your fill.”

Her eyes took on a dreamy quality that made me feel weak. She liked being in this position with me. She liked having my dick in her mouth. And she liked me telling her what to do.

Fucking perfect.

But if she kept this up, she would make me come.

And I refused to give her that.

Not when she’d asked me to fuck her. I would save my load for her slick cunt.

“Are you wet for me, Adalyn?”

She mumbled an affirmative around my shaft, causing it to throb even more.

“Prove it, Adalyn.” I slowly sat back on my heels while pulling her with me, bringing her body closer to the bed. “Put one hand on the mattress to balance yourself. And use the other to reach between your legs.”

She groaned around me as she obeyed my command, her gorgeous eyes maintaining that dreamy glimmer the whole time.

"You're so fucking beautiful," I told her. "I could stare at you like this for hours, Adalyn." Although, I would not be able to keep myself from coming for that long. Especially not with the way her throat worked around me in time with her tongue.

Definitely a goddess.

"Show me your fingers, little one. Show me how wet you are."

Adalyn's pupils nearly engulfed her dark irises as she complied, her skin glistening beneath the low lighting streaming in through my windows.

I released her hair to grab her wrist and pulled her hand up to my mouth.

Her throat worked around me as I sucked each finger clean, her cheeks a glorious shade of crimson. "I want you soaking wet," I said as I finished. "Are you done tasting me yet? Because I want to lick you now. *Thoroughly.*"

She quivered, all traces of her earlier terror gone.

All I had before me now was a goddess who needed to be worshipped.

She released my cock from her plump lips and gave it a final stroke with her palm, stirring a rumble of approval from my chest. "I'm going to fucking devour your cunt, Adalyn. Now lie down."

Her skin darkened even more as she quickly moved to obey me.

"Wider," I told her, wanting to see every inch of her damp pussy.

She followed my command beautifully, displaying her pretty pink flesh and allowing me to see how much sucking me off turned her on.

Maybe I'd let her lick me clean later.

And come again down her throat.

I would just have to be careful with her neck, as I was moments ago, because I didn't want to risk hurting her. She was mostly just bruised, but her mental state was very fragile.

Something I kept in mind as I bent to lick her delicious heat.

I wanted her so focused on *us* that she couldn't even think about *them*.

No more past. No other men. Just me and my tongue between her trembling thighs. "Say my name, Adalyn. Tell me who is licking you right now."

"My Sir," she breathed, bowing up off the bed into my mouth.

"Good girl," I praised, spearing her with my tongue.

She quivered beautifully, her tits flushed with desire, her nipples tiny beacons of *need*.

I would pay them some attention in a moment.

Just as soon as I made her come against my mouth.

I slid two fingers into her, scissoring, feeling, testing her tightness. She mewled in response, her fingers grabbing the bedding as her hands curled into fists. "*Sir*," she hissed, her head thrashing as I went after her clit.

"Don't hurt yourself," I said, my voice sharp. "Stay calm. Breathe with me. Enjoy the moment."

She panted in reply, her head stilling. "I'm... I'm close..."

I know, I thought, laving her swollen nub. "Tasting me really turned you on, didn't it, little one?"

"Yes," she admitted. "Yes, Sir. I want to make you come with my mouth."

"Not yet, sweetheart," I told her. "First, you're going to fall apart against my tongue. Then I'm going to fuck you. And if you're a good girl for me, I'll let you suck me clean after we're done."

"*Ohhh...*" She practically vibrated in response, her thighs clenching on either side of my shoulders.

I pressed my palm to her abdomen to keep her on the bed as she tried to thrust upward, her inhibitions utterly lost to my tongue against her clit.

"Are you going to come for me, darling?" I asked against her damp flesh. "Make that pussy nice and tight for my cock?"

"Yes, Sir. Yes." She tried again to lift her hips, but I didn't let her, holding her captive beneath my touch as I drove her over the edge into an orgasm that rendered her useless on the bed.

She screamed, the sound one I'd heard a few times now, and yet I wanted to hear it a million times more from her sweet lips.

Her legs shook, her knuckles almost white from clutching the bedding so hard, and her inner walls clamped down around my fingers, telling me she was ready.

I gave her throbbing center a long, languid kiss, then left her to grab some protection from my nightstand. She didn't react to my lack of touch this time, too lost to her residual quakes to notice.

Beautiful, I thought, admiring the view of her trembling form as I rolled the condom onto my hard length. I wanted to take her bare. But that required trust, and we weren't quite there yet.

She needed to really know me first.

And I needed her to be able to voice her desires openly and completely.

We would work up to that.

Her lashes fluttered as I crawled over her again, her legs still as wide as I'd left them before. Missionary wasn't my usual style, but for her, it felt appropriate. She needed this emotional connection more than the pleasure derived by fucking.

I intended to give her both.

To ground her.

Make her realize what it meant to be mine.

Show her what control really felt like. Inspire her faith. And leave her begging me for more.

"How do you feel, sweet girl?" I asked, lowering my hips to hers and letting her feel my cock against her entrance. "Are you ready for me?"

"Yes," she whispered, her arms coming around my neck. "Please fuck me, Sir."

CHAPTER TWENTY-EIGHT
ASHER

NORMALLY, I would tell a sub to hold the headboard while I destroyed her with my hands and my mouth. I'd even consider some breath play.

But not with Adalyn.

She deserved to be cherished. So I slid inside her instead, allowing her to feel me, to embrace me, to *know* me.

Her legs automatically wrapped around my waist, her ankles clasping behind my back, her body hugging mine entirely.

Because this was the tenderness she required right now.

She wanted to know what it was like to be respected and cared for in the bedroom, not used.

So I showed her with my hips, my mouth, and my tongue. I cupped her cheek, my opposite hand going to her breast, where my thumb stroked her nipple.

Her inner walls clamped down around me as she lifted her hips to meet mine, our pace slow, erotic, *intense*, and so tenderly thorough.

Something about it felt even more powerful than a fierce fuck.

Perhaps because I could feel every inch of her, sense her heartbeat, and hear her soft sighs.

Slow seemed to work for us. At least while she acclimated to my length and size.

But it soon turned more heated. *Passionate*. Her arms loosened, her fingers threading through my hair to tighten her hold against me as her opposite hand went to my nape.

Her nails bit into my skin as she *squeezed*.

"You want more, darling?" I asked against her mouth.

"Yes," she breathed. "Fuck me, Mr. Sinner."

"How hard?" I thrust into her, giving her an introduction to my power. "This hard?" I inquired. Then I pulled out all the way to the tip and slammed into her, drawing a scream from her throat. "Or that hard?"

"That hard," she said on a pant. "Oh, definitely *that*."

So it seemed she wanted a little pain.

The darkness inside me pulsated, approving of the request.

"All right, sweetheart. You know your safeword. Tell me if I need to slow down."

She shook her head, then nodded. "Yes. Harder. Harder, Sir. Please, harder."

I lowered my hand away from her breast to grab her hip. Then I angled her up on the bed where I wanted her and drove into her.

Another of those beautiful sounds left her. "Keep screaming for me, sweetheart," I said, wanting her to drown me in her cries of pleasure.

Her nails bit into my neck again, causing me to release her cheek and grab her wrist. I pulled it over her head, then caught her other hand to gather them both beneath my palm, and restrained her against the bed.

Her lashes parted, her dark eyes immediately finding mine.

A small note of panic flared.

"Who is inside you right now, Adalyn?" I demanded. "Tell me who is fucking you."

"My Sir," she said, some of that panic disappearing.

"And you want me to fuck you hard, right?"

"Hard, yes," she whispered. "*Harder*."

"Good girl." I drew my nose against hers. "Now scream again for me, darling. Scream so everyone knows I'm fucking you."

She didn't disappoint, her voice going hoarse as she gave me everything.

I would owe her all the water and aftercare in the world after this, and fuck, I couldn't wait. I wanted to hold her. Cherish her. Kiss her until she passed out.

Only to wake her with an orgasm between her thighs.

Just thinking about it had me nearly there, my need for her an overwhelming addiction that threatened my control.

But I needed her to come again.

To fall apart.

To lose herself entirely.

I pivoted my hips in a way that stroked her clit, my eyes on hers as she started to shake. She was no longer screaming, but mouthing "Sir" on repeat.

"That's it, Adalyn," I encouraged her. "Tumble into oblivion for me, sweetheart. And take me over that cliff with you." I pressed my mouth to hers, soothing her tongue with my own as I continued to fuck her into the bed.

She quivered harshly in response, her legs tightening around me as though she needed to hold on.

"Come for me," I told her. "Clench my cock with your pussy, force me to follow you."

She moaned, the sound more of a vibration than a noise. Poor darling had screamed herself into a hoarse state.

I adored her for it.

Because she'd obeyed me. She'd submitted. And yet she'd chosen me for this task, too.

She desired *me*.

I thanked her with a kiss, pouring all my gratitude into her without words as I continued to give her what she desired. Her legs froze against mine, her hands tensing beneath my palm.

And then she shattered so wonderfully, so *completely*, that I couldn't stop myself from chasing her into that orgasmic state.

"*Fuck*, Adalyn," I groaned, her pussy squeezing me so damn tightly I could barely move.

Next time, I had to go bare.

Because *Jesus*.

She felt so damn good. So perfect. So *incredible*.

It left me shaking above her, my body nowhere near satisfied. I wanted more. I wanted to fuck her again. Right now.

Which was insane.

I could prolong a scene, enjoy two climaxes throughout the session, but Adalyn... she made me feel like I could come again right fucking now.

I buried my head in her neck as I tried to gather my self-control, to pull myself from the seductive haven between her thighs. *Fuck*.

"Can I taste you now?" Adalyn asked, her voice a whisper that sounded almost pained. "Please?"

I pulled away from her throat to find her staring up at me with stars in her eyes.

She wasn't lost to her sub state yet, but still in the scene, still wanting to *please*.

The woman is a goddamn deity.

Which I already knew. She was a goddess. An Aphrodite in my bed with a stamina that shouldn't be possible.

Yet she'd been trained for this.

A fact I really did not want to consider right now, not with her looking up at me like that.

"Is that what you want?" I asked her, trying to ensure that this was what she truly desired and not just some post-sex ritual she'd been taught to perform.

"Yes, Sir," she said, her voice a rasp of sound. "I want to taste you like you tasted me."

My dick throbbed, ready to come again from her words alone. And from the delicious fluttering sensations of her cunt.

"I need you to drink some water first," I told her. "Drink all of it for me, and I'll let you suck my cock."

She swallowed, her resulting flinch telling me my demand was necessary.

She needed hydration. She needed aftercare. While I could push her limits, I wouldn't do it like this. Not after everything she'd been through.

"Okay," she finally replied.

I praised her with a kiss, then slowly slid out of her. She watched as I moved, her gaze going to my groin, her tongue tracing her lower lip.

Any other day, and I would consider unloading the contents of the condom right into that thirsty mouth.

But she needed affection.

She needed to *heal*.

So I disposed of the condom in the bathroom and filled up a glass of chilled water for her.

Her expression held that note of fear in it again when I returned, her gaze running over my naked body as I approached the bed. She shifted slowly to sit up, her movements betraying another wince.

"What hurts?" I asked as I sat next to her with the glass of water.

She took it from me to begin swallowing before replying, "My side."

I gently ran my knuckles along her rib cage. "Here?"

Her throat bobbed as she nodded. "He... he kicked me."

I leaned down to run my lips along the bruises of the side closest to me before moving up to her neck. She remained utterly still while I kissed her, the water frozen in her hand. "I'm sorry, sweetheart," I said against her ear. "I'm sorry I wasn't there."

Her dark eyes met mine as I settled once more beside her. "You weren't there?" she echoed.

"I was at the airport with my sister," I reminded her. "Bryant called me to tell me what had happened. I came straight to you and carried you back here. Then the doctor watched over you while I handled Brevington. He's gone."

It seemed important to reiterate that fact, to ensure she understood what it meant.

You're safe, I was telling her. *You're safe with me.*

But I'd broken her faith.

I'd failed her.

And it was going to take time to restore that trust.

"My safeword... worked?"

Her question suggested she was finally processing and believing what I'd told her.

"Yeah, sweetheart. My security team handled the issue. I only wish they'd been faster."

"Did he...?" She glanced down, swallowing.

"He choked you," I told her. "From what Doctor Zansky said, your throat and ribs are your only injuries. Nothing is broken. And Brevington didn't fuck you."

She nodded. "Okay."

"Okay?" I repeated. "It's not okay, Adalyn. What he did is the opposite of *okay*. But I'm going to do everything in my power to make sure that never happens again."

Her dark orbs flickered with uncertainty, but rather than reply, she finished her water.

"Do you want more?" I asked her.

She dipped her chin a little. "Yes, please."

I gave her a kiss. "Thank you for being honest, Adalyn."

I went to the bathroom and refilled the glass and found her yawning when I returned.

Our scene hadn't been as intense as a normal one would be. But it'd clearly added to her already exhausted state.

I gave her the water and sat beside her again while she drank it in silence.

When she finished, she sighed. "I... I'm not sure..." She trailed off, her nostrils flaring.

This was what we needed to work on.

Her body was done for the day. She needed a break. But her mind was telling her to push through, to break her limits.

And that would not do between us.

I caught her chin and pulled her eyes to mine. "Darling, I only want your mouth around my cock if you're certain you want it." And her hesitation now told me she wasn't certain at all. "So how about a bath instead, hmm? Let me worship you a little with my hands, massage your sore muscles, wash your hair, and just hold you."

She blinked. "You... you want that?"

"I want you," I replied as I took the glass from her and set it on the nightstand. "And I want to show you what that means. Will you let me, sweetheart? Will you let me take care of you the way a Dom should take care of a sub?" Not just a Dom, but a man, too. All men should treat their women this way, regardless of their lifestyle choices.

"I..." Her lashes fluttered, her expression holding a note of wonder to it. "I think I would like that."

"Good," I said, drawing my touch along her jaw to her neck. I was careful not to squeeze, just to assert my dominance via a gentle touch. "Then give me five minutes to prepare, and we'll begin."

Because I hadn't intended to fuck her tonight.

And I rarely had women here. Actually, I'd *never* taken a woman in my room. I only had the condoms in the nightstand as a practical measure.

So I needed a bit to prepare my bathroom for Adalyn.

Fortunately, I had a lot of the luxuries in there that we needed, mostly because I enjoyed a good bath every now and then. Who didn't?

I kissed her one last time, a silent vow passing from me to her. One underlined in possessive instincts. "I'll be right back," I told her. "Be a good girl and relax for me, okay?"

"Yes, Sir," she whispered, her shoulders slumping as she leaned back against the headboard.

"Thank you for your obedience, Adalyn." I meant it in reference to both our scene and now. "You're perfect and strong and very much *mine*."

CHAPTER TWENTY-NINE
ADALYN

EVERYTHING SMELLED LIKE FRESH EUCALYPTUS.

I inhaled deeply, allowing the scent to cleanse me entirely as Asher ran his fingers through my hair. He'd bathed me thoroughly, washed my hair in the shower, soaped me up, and rinsed me off. Then he'd wrapped me up in a towel.

Now he combed my hair with his hands, unknotting the strands with a gentleness that made me warm all over. He'd set me up on the counter, parted my legs, and stepped between my thighs. Then he'd reached around me to begin this process while studying the back of my head in the mirror behind me.

I'd seen Doms do things like this at Ecstasy. But I'd never experienced it. Most of my Masters just wanted to fuck and leave afterward.

Not Asher.

He'd seen to my pleasure. He'd given me an odd sense of control even while demonstrating his strength and power.

And now he was making me feel *whole*.

My eyes misted with tears, my heart suddenly in my throat.

I didn't know how to handle this kindness. I didn't know how to understand or accept it. This... this wasn't my life.

Yet he made me want to live this existence. He made me crave something I shouldn't. He made me desire *forever*.

"Shh," he hushed softly, his lips grazing my forehead. "You're safe, Adalyn. I have you."

But for how long? I longed to ask. *How long will you treat me like this?*

I wasn't sure what was worse anymore—the notion of this being a fucked-up game or the idea that this might be real.

Because if it was real, it could be taken away from me.

At least with a game, I would have expected it.

However, to grow used to this treatment only to have it ripped away from me? *That* would hurt me more than anyone ever had.

"Adalyn," he whispered, his hands coming around to my face, his thumbs wiping away the tears beneath my eyes. "You're safe, sweetheart. I'm right here."

"I know." My voice was no longer hoarse, but it still sounded like a rasp to my ears. "I know you're here. I just... I just don't know how long..." I trailed off, my shoulders slumping. I felt so weak. So young. So *naïve.*

The confidence I often faked at the clubs didn't exist here.

I was just me. Broken Adalyn. Terrified of the future.

What happened to the woman who killed Nathan? I wondered.

God, that felt like a lifetime ago.

I... I wasn't her anymore.

I was someone new. But I wasn't sure if I liked this new version or not. She seemed to *feel*. And *feeling* sucked.

"How long what?" Asher asked me, one of his palms falling to my thigh. "How long I'll be here?"

I almost denied it because I didn't want to face the fear. However, I was too exhausted to hide anymore. This man had pulled out my heart and forced me to face everything it had to offer.

Part of me hated him for it.

The other part of me... the other part of me hoped he could *heal* it.

Which was why I nodded, confirming his question. *How long will you be here? Will you be around long enough to make me whole? Will you really protect me? Will you keep me?*

So many hard-to-voice questions.

But he seemed to hear them all because his dark gaze radiated understanding. Maybe I'd actually spoken all those inquiries out loud.

Because his expression exhibited an intensity that stole the breath from my lungs.

"I'll be here for as long as you want me," he told me, his words resembling a vow. They reminded me of what he'd claimed in bed about wanting me. I'd questioned him about it, but I couldn't fully remember everything we'd said.

However, it seemed he still felt the same way about keeping me.

"I want to be with you forever," I admitted in a whisper. "I never want to leave this place." It was the first time I'd ever felt *safe*, ever been taken care of, ever been *cherished*.

"Then you'll stay here with me forever," he answered simply, his palm hot against my cheek. "You're mine, Adalyn. And I'll ensure those Sin Cave assholes know it, too."

"Sin Cave assholes?" I repeated, blinking. Something about that phrase struck me as... as humorous. I actually felt my lips twitching, something I hadn't experienced in... how long? I couldn't remember. The last however many hours had felt like a century to me.

Everything was foggy.

My body felt renewed yet exhausted at the same time.

My mind longed for an escape, some place to stop functioning, just for a little while.

And my heart... my heart beat a little faster than it should, my soul warming the organ with knowledge of our potential future.

Here. With Asher.

He pressed his mouth to mine. "Yes. Sin Cave assholes." He skimmed his lips across my cheek to my ear, his palm going to my hip. "But I don't want to think about them right now, Adalyn. I want to think about removing this towel instead."

I shivered. "And then what?" I asked.

But a knock sounded against the door before he could reply. "Yeah?" His tone was just loud enough to be heard without qualifying as a yell.

"You decent?" a deep voice asked. "Oh, who the hell am I kidding? You're *never* decent."

"Shit," Asher cursed, reaching for a towel to wrap around his waist. My legs instantly closed, my heart skipping a beat at the sudden intrusion into our comforting bubble.

Someone new was here.

Someone with a masculine tone.

Someone Asher seemed to fear.

What's happening? Who is this? Is it time for the dream to end?

"Adalyn." Asher's dominance wrapped around me in a tight noose, forcing my gaze to his. "What's your safeword?"

"Dreams," I breathed.

"Good girl." He studied me for a moment, his dark irises swirling with knowledge. "Do you want to use that safeword right now?"

I swallowed. "I... I don't know," I admitted.

"Kane, give me five minutes," he said to the door, his words a command, not a request.

The other man didn't reply, but he didn't barge through the threshold either.

My chest rose and fell, my heart still skittering against my rib cage.

Asher approached me slowly, his hands loose at his sides. "The man out there is my half brother, Adalyn. He's not going to touch you. But he is going to protect us."

My brow furrowed. "Wh-what?"

"I told you I have a lot of siblings, sweetheart. Kane is one of my older brothers." He took another step toward me, the heat of his body brushing mine despite the gap between us. "He won't hurt you."

My heartbeat gradually returned to normal as I processed his words. "Okay."

"Okay?" he repeated.

I nodded. "Okay." If he said Kane wouldn't hurt me or touch me, then I believed him. But I did want to know what he meant by "protect us."

Asher's palm touched my cheek, his opposite hand going to my hip. I automatically parted my thighs for him, allowing him entry and kissing him as he pressed his lips to mine.

It felt so natural.

So... so... *expected.*

Like this was what life should be between us.

Which caused my pulse to soar for an entirely different reason as I wrapped my arms around his neck. His tongue entered my mouth, engaging me in a sensual dance that left me quivering against him.

More, please, I thought, my nipples beading beneath my towel.

The hand on my hip slid to my lower back. His touch branded me through the cotton as he pulled me to the edge of the counter, placing my hot center against his groin. He was hard and solid, even through the fabric wrapped around his waist.

I arched into him and he pressed back, his fingers sliding into my hair again to knot with my damp strands.

"Asher," I breathed, suddenly so hot that I couldn't think straight. "*Sir.*"

"Asher," he replied. "We're not scening right now, sweetheart. This is just you and me."

"But you asked for my safeword."

"To remind you that you always have an escape card," he replied. "No matter what. You say *dreams,* I stop."

"I don't think I'll ever really want you to stop," I admitted softly. "I... I think I just want *more.*"

He grinned, his hips pressing against mine. "Me, too, sweetheart. However, I need to talk to Kane. And I'm guessing he's up here because he wants to meet you." He pulled back a little to study my expression. "Do you want to meet him? Or should I tell him to fuck off?"

My eyebrows rose. "You would say that to him?"

"If you tell me you're not ready to meet him? Absolutely, I will. And he won't fault me for it, either. He's just as much of a Dom as I am. He understands the importance of protecting a woman. Hell, he values protection more than anyone I know. He even made a job of it."

"A job?" I echoed.

"He works in private security." His fingers loosened in my hair, his touch going to the back of my neck to tenderly massage the tight muscles there. "That's why he's here, Adalyn. He's going to ensure you're protected, no matter what."

I gaped at him. "What? What do you mean?"

"He knows how to help people disappear, Adalyn." Asher's palm squeezed the back of my neck, providing some much-needed assurance. "If something goes wrong, he'll get you to safety. And he will make it so no one can find you."

"You think something might go wrong?" I asked, searching his eyes. "Asher, if you... I can't let you put yourself at risk for me. That can't be an option. If you think it's going to go wrong, then just give me back to them."

I... I could never live with myself if something happened to him because of me.

Just thinking about it caused my heart to beat wildly all over again as the room began to shrink around us. "I... I can't, Asher. I can't—"

"*Adalyn.*" The harshness in his tone drew me back to him immediately, his dark irises swirling with command. "It's a secondary precaution. And after my discussions with Julian today, I have them right where we need them to be. It's going to be fine."

"Right where...?" I started, mimicking his phrasing without understanding him.

"They're in my debt, Adalyn. They've insulted me twice. And I've demanded that they let me keep you for recompense, just like we discussed." His palm slid from my nape to my face, his thumb tracing my cheekbone. "It's going to be all right, sweetheart. And Kane has flown in to guarantee it. He's the backup plan because I don't believe in relying on one single strategy. All right?"

Backup plan.

Debt.

Recompense.

Strategy.

My head was spinning with his words, but most of them registered as sensible. At least on a high level, anyway. But that didn't stop my brain from spiraling with *what-ifs.*

I knew this organization better than Asher.

I knew how they operated, what they demanded of their Elite, and how they preferred to play their games. I'd spent enough time in the clubs sucking their cocks to know how they spoke to and about each other.

It provided me with an inside edge.

One I should use.

Because it might help Asher. It might help us. It might ensure my ability to remain here.

"There's nowhere your brother could send me," I whispered. "They own security firms around the world. They're tapped into all the governments, too. That's not a viable backup plan."

"How about we meet with Kane and let him tell us what he thinks, then you can let us know where you see faults?" Asher suggested. And it wasn't worded in a condescending way like Nathan would have done it.

Instead, he sounded actually interested in what I had to say.

Like he would treat me as a partner in this.

Something about that had me sitting up a little

straighter. It made me feel... important. *Human*. And not so lost.

"I... I would like that," I admitted.

Asher nodded. "Good. Then maybe you'll be interested in hearing my plan, too."

"Yes," I replied. "Yes, I would."

His lips curled, his palm warm against my cheek. "That's my girl," he murmured, pride in his voice. "I trust you to help us survive, Adalyn. Because that's who you are —a survivor. And I need you to trust me to see everything through, too. Okay?"

I studied him for a beat before saying, "Okay." That appeared to be our *word* for this conversation. Yet it seemed to mean so much more.

"Good girl," he whispered, kissing me. "Then let's go find Kane. I'm sure he'll have a comment to give us about time."

"Time?"

"Mmm," he hummed. "You'll see."

CHAPTER THIRTY
ASHER

"Seventeen minutes, Ash," my brother said from the bottom of the stairs. He'd obviously decided to take himself on a tour of my house while waiting for me and Adalyn.

Or perhaps he'd just been doing a security sweep.

Hell, he'd probably done one before he'd even come into my house. Which left me wondering... "Who let you in?" I asked, eyeing the empty foyer around him.

His lips curled. "I let myself in." He cocked his head. "You need better locks. Maybe a working security system, too."

I rolled my eyes. "I live on a fucking island, Kane. That is my security."

Adalyn shivered beside me as I led her down the stairs. I'd gone over to her room to find a dress and some undergarments for her.

She'd thrown on the dress and nothing else, leaving her hair wet down her back.

I loved it. So natural and her. I'd pulled on a pair of sweats and opted against a shirt. It would be less to take off later.

Besides, it was the middle of the night. And Kane was early.

I guided Adalyn along beside me at the bottom of the stairs and walked right past my brother to head toward the kitchen.

Her stomach had growled when I'd handed her the dress, reminding me that she probably needed to eat something. Doctor Zansky had given her some fluids after sedating her earlier, but that wasn't food, just standard hydration and electrolytes.

Kane followed, causing Adalyn to try to glance back at him.

"Kitchen, sweetheart," I told her. "You need food."

She could meet my brother there.

I found her a seat at the island counter and lifted her onto the stool. Then I pressed my chest to her back as I reached around her to grip the marbled countertop in front of her. It effectively caged her in with my body, ensuring she felt safe as my brother entered the kitchen behind us.

Kane clearly picked up on my protective vibe, as he selected a seat two stools away from Adalyn, thus providing her with ample space.

I thanked him with a glance before focusing on Adalyn.

"What do you want to eat, darling?" I asked against her ear. "Breakfast or dinner?"

"Um." She shivered. "Surprise me?"

"Stuffed French toast with some fresh strawberries, please," my brother requested.

"That question wasn't for you," I told him.

"But it's your specialty," Kane supplied helpfully, his dark brows waggling in encouragement.

"I made her French toast this morning." Which was

technically yesterday now. But I doubted she wanted it again.

"But it wasn't stuffed," Adalyn murmured. "It was just French toast."

My eyebrows lifted as I pulled away to study her profile. "Was that a taunt, darling?"

"No. Just commenting that it was plain French toast, not *stuffed* French toast." The way her lips curled a little told me she was playing. And I rather liked that she felt comfortable enough to tease, even if slightly.

"I think you should make us stuffed French toast," Kane put in. "With fresh strawberries."

"And some bananas," Adalyn added, her eyes flicking up to me before focusing on the island again. Then her lips curled just a little more, confirming she was indeed playing.

"I see." I wrapped my arms around her to hug her from behind and pressed my lips to her temple. "Stuffed French toast with strawberries and bananas. Anything else?"

"Orange juice?" she asked softly.

"Of course," I replied, kissing her cheek as I tightened my hold around her in a gentle squeeze. "By the way, the pain in the ass at the end of the island is my brother, Kane Sinner." I looked at him. "This beautiful woman is Adalyn Rose. And she's mine."

I kissed her cheek again as I held his gaze, then released her to go about finding ingredients to make us all a late-night breakfast.

"I've never heard my brother claim a woman before," Kane said conversationally. "You must be special indeed."

"I don't know about special," she hedged. "Just..."

I waited for her to finish, but she didn't. I glanced over the fridge to find her frowning.

"You're very special," I told her. "Especially to me."

She blinked at me. "Yeah. But... but I don't know what I am."

"I just said what you are, Adalyn." I shut the door and walked over to her. "You're special."

"No, that's not what I mean. I normally say I'm a mistress or a visiting friend. But... but that doesn't feel right with you." She studied me. "I... I don't know how to reply."

"With the truth," I told her. "That you're *mine*. Not a mistress. Not a visiting friend. Just... mine."

"Yours."

"Yes." I brushed my knuckles across her cheek. "My Adalyn. And I'm your Asher."

"For as long as I want you," she clarified.

"Yes, sweetheart."

"So, for always," she said. "Because I never want to leave this place." She looked at my brother then, her expression suddenly clear. "You can't help me disappear, Mr. Sinner. I won't leave Asher."

His eyebrows lifted. "I see we're arriving straight at the point, then."

"I may have mentioned your work to her," I said. "And that you're here to ensure she gets out of here safely if things go south."

"Is that why I'm here?" He gave me a look, one I recognized because I often made the same expression when I was about to offer a blunt correction. "You think I would leave you on this island with those assholes?"

"I think I'm not going to give you a choice," I countered before returning to the fridge. "Adalyn matters most."

"I do not," she argued, causing me to glance sharply over my shoulder—and give her the same look my brother had just given me.

"Yes. You do," I told her, my tone brooking no argument.

It was my Dom voice. The one I knew would make her crawl.

Except she didn't crawl at all. She stood and marched over to me on her dainty, bare feet to poke me in the chest with her finger. "No. You will not sacrifice yourself for me."

"It's my job to protect you."

"Not at the expense of your own life," she bit back, her fierce expression and tone unlike anything I'd seen from her thus far. It was making me fucking hard. "I won't allow it."

My eyebrows shot up. "You won't *allow* it?" I finished grabbing what I needed from the fridge so I could shut the door, and set the items on the counter. Then I grasped her hips and walked her backward into the island. "You're not the boss here, little one."

She narrowed her eyes. "I could never live with myself if something happened to you because of me. Do you understand that?"

"Yes, because I feel the same way about you."

"But you're not the reason we're in this mess. *I* am."

"No, darling. *Nathan* is the reason we're in this mess. And you know what?"

"What?" she retorted, the fire in her gaze absolutely breathtaking.

"I'm glad we're in this mess."

"Well, I..." She blinked. "Wait, what?"

"You heard me. I'm *glad* we're in this mess." I lifted my hands away from her hips to grab her face. "Because this mess is how I met you. And all the trouble I'm about to go through is worth it. Because of how I feel about you."

"B-but... you... we..." She swallowed and shook her head. "Asher, we just met."

"Under incredibly intense circumstances, yes," I agreed. "However, I've chosen to keep you. And you just told me that you choose me, too. So what more is there to discuss, Adalyn? This is happening." I pressed my lips to hers before she could argue.

Fortunately, she kissed me back instead. Not aggressively, just sweetly.

Her eyes held mine as she did it, that fire flickering in her irises. It was such a beautiful sight. So much better than her tears and her fear.

This was Adalyn Rose.

My future.

The woman I desired as mine.

"Embrace it, darling," I murmured, my forehead touching hers. "We're in this together now. For better or for worse."

"This is crazy."

"Life is crazy," I returned. "But fate delivered you to this island. And I'm not about to turn my back on our destiny. Now go sit down on that stool and let me make you breakfast."

She stared up at me, her cheeks flushing a little. "Yes, Sir." She brushed a final kiss to my mouth before slipping out of my hold to go find her seat.

I palmed her ass as she moved, playfully tapping it as I said, "Good girl."

She jumped a little, then grinned, her flush spreading down toward her chest.

It hadn't been a punishing pat, just a loving one. And it seemed she liked it.

Because of course she did.

She enjoyed a little pain with her pleasure.

Which just made her that much more perfect for me.

Kane caught my gaze as she sat down, his expression

giving nothing away. But I knew he approved. If he didn't, he'd tell me with his eyes.

Instead, he seemed to be considering the situation.

He was always analyzing every angle, his teasing demeanor with me something he reserved only for those close to him. Outside of the family and away from friends, he was all business.

I supposed he had to be because of his chosen career path.

"So you met our baby sister, hmm?" Kane mused as I returned to my task. "I hope you didn't let that experience define the whole Sinner family. Darby's a bit of a brat."

I snorted in agreement.

"She seemed nice to me," Adalyn said diplomatically.

"She's going to tell the entire family that you two are together," Kane warned her.

"I don't mind." I could feel her eyes on me. "Assuming Asher doesn't mind."

"I don't mind," I echoed. "Darby can tell them whatever she wants. Makes no difference to me."

"What's Darby saying now?" a new voice asked as Clive entered the kitchen. "Is she making trouble?"

"Always," Kane replied.

I turned to find Clive and Bryant standing in my dining area. "Is my doorbell broken?" I asked.

"I told you to get that lock fixed," Kane said conversationally. "It's a hazard."

I shot him a look before checking on Adalyn. She was staring at Bryant and Clive with wide eyes, but she didn't appear to be scared. Just curious.

"How are you feeling, Ms. Rose?" Bryant asked her.

"Better," she replied, her dark irises flickering toward me. "Mr. Sinner is an excellent caretaker."

Bryant grunted. "Yeah, he has the healing touch."

"I do," I confirmed, walking toward the island to stand opposite Adalyn. "You okay with Clive and Bryant being here, sweetheart?"

She glanced at them again. "Um."

"You've met Bryant—he's the head of my security personnel. Clive is my other security manager, but he handles technology. They're safe and they won't touch you," I promised her.

Those beautiful dark orbs refocused on me. After a beat, she nodded and said, "Okay. I trust you."

Her words rendered me speechless for a breath, then my feet started moving without my guidance, taking me around the island and right up to her stool. I wrapped my palm around her nape and pulled her into a kiss, not giving a damn that we had an audience again.

Her hands went to my abdomen, her nails biting just a little into my skin as though she was trying to anchor me to her.

I licked her lower lip in response, then smiled. "Thank you, Adalyn."

She hummed something incoherent back at me, her pupils blown wide from our embrace. This whole experience in the kitchen was turning into a fun bout of foreplay.

The audience only added to the effect.

Especially since they were all staring at Adalyn with admiration in their eyes.

She was a beautiful woman and a natural submissive. They could all see the allure. But they would respect my claim.

I brushed my lips against her temple before going back to my preparations—which were taking a lot longer than they normally would because of all the distractions in the kitchen.

Clive and Bryant took over the stools closest to Kane, giving Adalyn room, but they engaged her in conversation by explaining how we all knew each other.

Clive told her how he used to work with Kane, which was how he met me.

Kane told her how I stole Clive to come work on my island—something that made me scoff and say, "Yeah, I'm sure his decision had nothing to do with trading Baltimore for Fiji."

They all laughed, including Adalyn. Although, hers was more of a soft sound of amusement. Still, I considered it an improvement after everything she'd been through.

She seemed genuinely pleased to be here, her smile sincere when I finally finished making breakfast.

I ended up with five plates, as I assumed Bryant and Clive intended to eat with us. But I served Adalyn first because she mattered most. "Freshly squeezed orange juice," I said, setting it beside her plate.

Her eyes shimmered with excitement. "Thank you."

I winked at her and went about serving the others. We all ate at the kitchen island rather than in the dining room. Which was fine. I often ate here instead of at the table. I had six stools. So it worked.

"This is really good," Adalyn told me about halfway through her plate. "I see why Kane insisted on it."

"My brother should have been a chef," Kane said.

"Shh," Bryant hushed. "Don't let Chef Caylin hear you, or she may worry about her job."

"Her job is very secure here," I assured him.

"I would think you'd like the idea of her leaving Asher's

private staff so that you could hire her to be on *yours*," Clive mused.

Bryant grinned. "I don't need to hire her to put her on my staff."

I rolled my eyes at his crude joke. Mostly because it was cheesy as fuck. And also because he really just needed to fuck her—*and Clive*—to get both of them out of his system.

Maybe the three of them could play.

I really didn't care. They just clearly wanted each other, and while I enjoyed a good bout of delayed gratification, these three were taking it to the extreme.

Adalyn finished every bite on her plate, her cheeks flushed from the effort. But her smile at the end warmed my heart. "Thank you," she said, taking her dishes to the sink.

I followed her with my own and stopped her when she started to clean up. "I've got it."

"But—"

"You agreed to let me take care of you," I said against her ear. "Now go sit down, and I'll bring you some more juice in a second."

She glanced back at me. "If I obey, can I taste you later?"

I grinned down at her. "Yeah, sweetheart. Be a good girl and you can taste me later." The fact that she saw that as a reward just made her all the more amazing.

Excitement shone brightly in her gaze as she wiggled away from me and let me work. The others all did their own dishes, then we ventured into the living area.

It was nearing four o'clock in the morning now.

But that didn't matter.

We had important items to discuss.

I'd save Adalyn's reward for later.

Kane looked at me expectantly as he hovered near an

armchair, and I knew what he wanted to know. *Can we begin talking, or do you want to say good night to her first?*

I pulled Adalyn onto the loveseat beside me. "She's staying for the conversation." Because this was just as much about Adalyn as it was about me. And hiding our plans from her would be wrong. "You can speak openly in front of her."

My brother nodded as he took a chair for himself. Clive and Bryant took over the sofa, their expressions void of their easy amusement over our middle-of-the-night breakfast.

"Let's start from the beginning," my brother suggested. "Tell me how a beautiful jewel like Adalyn Rose became a bride-in-training for an asshole like Taylor Huntington."

CHAPTER THIRTY-ONE
ASHER

I HADN'T TOLD Kane everything, but I'd told him enough.

Mostly because I didn't want to drag him into the heart of this Sin Cave fuckery, something he'd seemed to understand as we'd gone through all the parameters for the meeting.

We'd spent the last two days preparing, with Adalyn providing key details regarding how the Elite functioned and Bryant corroborating her facts with experiences of his own.

Some of the things she'd told us had caused my stomach to churn with rage. I wanted to murder every fucking man who had ever touched her and taught her how to master a slave-like status beneath them.

But I understood that was the role she had to play today.

Which was the only reason I allowed her to stand beside me in a gauzy white dress. It'd come from her own lingerie collection. It was meant to be worn with nothing beneath it, but I'd forced her to wear a white lace thong.

Something I regretted now because it just made her that much sexier beneath the sunlight.

I could see her rosy nipples through the thin fabric, the visual enticing and maddening at the same time. "I hate this," I muttered. "I hate doing this to you."

She glanced up at me questioningly. "Doing what?"

"Putting you on display like this." I wrapped my palm around the back of her neck and pulled her to me. "I don't want to share you, Adalyn."

"This isn't about sharing, Sir. This is about a scene. You're showing me off but also saying they can't touch me." Her lips curled a little. "And I don't mind being on display. You can touch me, if you like. The proof of it is between my thighs."

I arched a brow. "Are you playing with me, little one?" Because it certainly felt like she'd taken on the role of seductress, and she'd done it flawlessly.

"Playing or not, this feels real between us," she told me honestly. "And..." She stole a deep breath, her midnight irises glittering in the sunlight. "And I trust you, Asher."

There were those words again, the ones that made me feel like the biggest man in the room yet layered weights on my shoulders at the same time.

But I didn't mind the weights. I would carry the world on my back if it meant protecting her.

I tugged her toward me into a kiss, my mouth claiming hers openly as the passengers of the jet on the tarmac began disembarking. Bryant stood beside me, and Clive flanked Adalyn's right. Which left us cocooned by people I trusted and allowed me to devour her openly in front of our guests.

Let them see how much I adored her.

Let them see how serious I was about keeping her.

I didn't give a fuck. This woman was mine whether they wanted to agree or not.

When I finished, I pressed my lips to her ear. "Remember your safeword, Adalyn," I whispered, giving her nape a squeeze.

This wouldn't be a traditional scene by any stretch of the imagination. But I wanted her to feel safe. If she said *dreams*, I would do whatever I had to do to help her.

"Yes, Sir," she breathed, arching into me in clear invitation.

I chuckled and pulled away. "Such a little tease," I accused her, loud enough for the others to hear.

"Sounds familiar," a deep voice replied dryly.

Julian Jovanni.

He moved toward us with the grace of his birthright, his suit perfectly pressed despite the long flight here. The woman beside him appeared just as elegant in a black summer dress and strappy heels. She carried herself with a confidence that reminded me a bit of Adalyn, as did the subtle bow of her head.

Definitely a trained submissive.

And the hand at her back marked Julian as her Dom.

However, I knew he was more than that. They were married, and according to Bryant, they had a healthy relationship.

Of course, it hadn't started out that way.

I didn't know the details, but I suspected her being an arranged bride had something to do with it.

"Brianna, you're as beautiful as ever," Bryant greeted, using her full name rather than the nickname I'd learned during one of our calls. "You're welcome to tease me anytime, love."

Julian shook his head, his cheekbones even more

pronounced as he clenched his jaw. "Here all of five seconds and I already want to kill you. That has to be some sort of record, Bryant."

The head of my security grinned. "I aim to please." He followed that up with a waggle of eyebrows toward Brianna.

Adalyn slid a little closer to me in response, perhaps uncomfortable with the concept of sharing. However, Brianna merely smiled. Her eyes were hidden beneath a pair of dark shades, making it hard to read her emotions. But her grin seemed genuine.

Julian ignored Bryant and focused on me, extending his free hand to clasp mine. I moved away from Adalyn, purely to put myself between them, and accepted the gesture. "Mr. Jovanni."

"Mr. Sinner," he returned. "However, I think we can dispense with the formalities. The others are not far behind, and it would be best to provide a friendly front when they land."

I released his hand and nodded. "Julian, then," I said, using his first name as my form of agreement.

"Asher," he replied, glancing around me. "And this must be the beautiful Adalyn Rose."

I took a step back, allowing him to see her.

"Mr. Jovanni." She curtsied, going low to the ground in a manner that had me both aroused and irritated again. She was practically supplicating on the tarmac. Which should *not* be turning me on.

And yet, I couldn't help the stirring of interest in my groin at seeing her lowered before us so beautifully.

I held out my palm for her. She slid her hand into mine almost instinctively, allowing me to help her up into a standing position again. I kissed her wrist, rewarding her for her acceptance, and wrapped my arm around her waist.

"I can see why you want to keep her," Julian said softly, his gaze on her face. He didn't appear to mean it in a sexual manner, more of a possessive one. Something he confirmed as he glanced at his wife with a hint of claim in his dark gaze.

She looked back at him, raising a brow.

"You don't curtsy for me like that anymore," he told her.

Her lips curled. "Would you like me to, *Mr. Jovanni*?" There was some underlying meaning there when she spoke his name. Something that seemed to amuse him.

He considered her for a moment. "Perhaps later." His dark eyes met mine once more, his expression instantly all business. "As per our agreement, I have three security personnel on board. Bryant is familiar with all of them."

I nodded. I didn't typically allow private security on my island, but this wasn't a normal situation. And Bryant had convinced me it would be a show of good faith to allow Julian his usual bodyguards.

However, I'd ensured Julian understood that this was a concession on my part.

I'd also stated that Bryant would be in charge of their briefing upon arrival.

So I looked at my head of security now and asked, "Want to go greet your old friends?"

"I'd much rather play with Brianna," he murmured, eliciting another look from Julian. "But yeah, I'll go greet them."

"One of these days, I'm going to let them shoot you," Julian informed him softly.

"No, you won't," Bryant returned. "That would piss off Brianna."

"It would," she agreed. "Very much so."

"See?" Bryant winked at her again and slapped Julian on the back as he moved to his side. "You would also shoot me yourself rather than delegate the kill."

Julian smirked. "True." Then he grabbed Brianna and kissed her in a manner similar to how I'd kissed Adalyn several times this week—all passionate possession and clear claim.

Bryant chuckled at the display and shook his head. "We all know she's yours, Jules." Rather than wait around for a reply, he strolled toward the jet to handle the security team.

Clive didn't join him. He was in constant communication with Kane via an earpiece, thus allowing my brother to keep tabs on this conversation and the two arrivals.

We were only expecting two jets—Julian's and the Roses'.

"Stop flirting," Julian said, his voice underlined with a threat.

"I wouldn't dream of it," Brianna replied, her tone all bratty sub.

He narrowed his gaze.

And she stared back at him, her expression giving nothing away. Her glasses also made it impossible to see her eyes, but I suspected Julian knew exactly what look she was giving him.

He gripped her chin, the gesture one I recognized. Just as I recognized the subtle hint of defiance in her posture.

At least their playing appeared to be consensual, unlike the display between Nathan and Adalyn.

I allowed them their little game while I drew a line down Adalyn's spine with my index finger. She shivered in response, her hands flexing at her sides. I continued my path down to her ass, then across to her hip, before pressing my palm to hers.

She leaned into me, an action I rewarded by kissing the top of her head. Julian glanced at me, his expression knowing.

"We're expecting ten members to attend today's conference call," he informed me, his formal facade at the forefront again even while continuing to grasp Brianna's chin. "As you know, I wouldn't typically handle something like this personally. The fact that I am has several of the Elite intrigued and interested. This is also a unique situation. There will be a vote."

"And if it goes negatively?" I asked.

"It won't," Julian promised. "However, if it does, you'll still have my support. Which means a great deal in our world."

While I should be grateful for that information, I couldn't help inquiring, "How can I rely on your support? I realize you are friends with Bryant, and while I appreciate all you've done in my favor, I still hardly know you."

"Yes, that's true. However, I've been showing my value and support for nearly two weeks. That should award me some favor."

"It does. That's why Bryant is currently briefing your security detail," I said, gesturing to the four men at the bottom of the jet stairs. "I don't allow private protection on this island, as it belittles my own security. I made an exception for you."

"As you've said," he replied. "It's an exception I appreciate. I imagine you did not make that exception for Mr. Rose?"

"I did not provide him with the same courtesy, no." I'd barely even allowed his jet clearance to land. But I sort of needed him here to finish all this bullshit. “Mr. Rose hasn’t gained my respect. You have.”

“Then that should answer your question in regard to relying on my support. I’m not in the business of making friendships just to end them without cause, Asher.” He released Brianna’s chin as the security team approached. “Bryant, I’m trusting you to handle my female with care. Just remember that she’s mine.”

“She’s a diamond, Julian. So don’t worry. I know how to handle precious stones.” Bryant held out a hand.

Brianna gave him a humored look as she accepted the gesture, and she disappeared into the building with him and Julian’s security detail.

The moment the door closed, Julian’s shoulders tensed. It was a small tell, but one that confirmed my instincts about him and Brianna—he cared a great deal about her. And he did not like being separated from her.

Which confirmed that not all brides in the program were treated as harshly as Adalyn had been—something she’d told me, but it was nice to see proof of it.

My wrist buzzed with an incoming notice from my traffic controller. “Looks like the Rose jet will be landing within the next three minutes,” I said, hearing the confirmation of that arrival in the air.

Julian nodded. “I assume you have security on standby?”

“The airport is well staffed,” I confirmed. But as usual, my team was doing a good job of not being seen. My brother included.

He’d called in a few of his own employees as well, stationing them throughout key points on the island and near the airfield.

We were prepared for a multitude of scenarios.

Fortunately, the largest threat—the arrival of the infamous Red Prince—had gone without issue.

We hadn't known if Julian would actually bring Brianna with him. The fact that he did served as a show of friendship because it meant he trusted me and my island enough for her to visit with him.

Given what I'd just observed of his possessiveness, that display of trust was actually quite substantial.

I really did need to ask Bryant to share his history with Julian and Brianna because clearly they were closer than he'd implied. A lot closer than just a former working relationship, anyway.

Julian moved to my side and pulled a pair of sunglasses from his pocket to cover his eyes as he watched the incoming jet. "This should be interesting," he murmured.

"Indeed," I agreed, releasing Adalyn's hand to wrap my arm around her lower back. Clive still stood on her opposite side, placing all four of us in a line only ten or so feet away from the building behind us.

The wind picked up as the jet landed, causing Adalyn to shiver against me. It wasn't a cool day—those really didn't exist here—but we were in the shade of the building, which created a bit of a chill with the incoming arrival.

And her clothes didn't provide her with much protection.

So I pulled her closer into my side, lending her some of my heat. Similar to Julian, I wore a suit, which wasn't the most comfortable island attire, but it was needed today.

Because certain suit brands—like the one I wore now—represented wealth. And in this game, wealth was power.

The jet parked in an open slot on the tarmac. There were several guests on the island right now who kept their jets here in case they needed to leave without much notice.

Others arranged drop-off times and pick-up times. It all varied. But my scheduler kept everything well organized, allowing for the best use of space.

I slid one hand into my pocket as the airport personnel did their jobs.

The paperwork exchange went by quickly, my airport authorities sending me notices on the incoming arrival and other details.

I checked through each message, noting that there was nothing out of the ordinary.

"I'll handle introductions," Julian said as the doors opened.

My chin dipped in agreement. I hadn't actually spoken to Albert Rose yet on the phone. He'd emailed a few demands, but everything else had gone through Julian. So it made sense for him to manage the formalities here.

I ran my thumb along Adalyn's side, offering her what little comfort I could as her parents appeared in the doorway.

She didn't outwardly react, her posture confident while remaining submissive at the same time. It was an intoxicating presence that left me even more in awe of her.

Her father looked her over, completely unfazed by her attire.

I'd already hated him.

And now I hated him more.

Because a good father protected his child. But this man merely saw her as a commodity to be traded.

"Albert," Julian greeted. "Thank you for flying all this way."

"It wasn't like I had a choice," the dark-haired male replied flatly.

He was a decently good-looking man who had

obviously aged well with his full head of hair and fit physique. But his wife was the spitting image of Adalyn, just an older version.

And far more broken.

I could see it in the way she carried herself. She wasn't confident like her daughter. She was just... sad. No, not even that. She appeared to be lifeless, like a pretty doll without a soul.

The stark visual of what Adalyn's future would have been had Nathan Spencer not chosen my island for her graduation from training.

"Yes, well, I believe we all have Mr. Spencer to thank for that," Julian replied with an edge in his tone. "Mr. Sinner was not only kind enough to see to your daughter's welfare, but he's also offered us accommodations for this trip. We should be grateful to him for his hospitality after everything that's happened."

Such diplomatic words.

Yet they didn't faze Albert at all. He merely stared at Julian for a beat before looking at me. "We won't be needing accommodations. After all, my daughter has been taking advantage of your hospitality for long enough. We can be in the air in thirty minutes, and this problem will be solved."

My eyebrows lifted, surprised by his audacity.

"We'll be in a meeting in thirty minutes, Mr. Rose. A meeting that requires your presence," Julian said before I could reply.

"There is no need for a meeting," he replied, glancing back at his jet as a male stepped out onto the stair platform. "Mr. Huntington is here to personally thank Mr. Sinner for training Adalyn this week in Nathan's absence."

My body tensed.

However, Julian didn't react at all. He merely stood beside me, his expression giving nothing away.

"Once the formality is over with, Mr. Huntington will be collecting his bride and taking her home with him for a private engagement party," Albert continued. "And with that, this entire exercise will be finished."

CHAPTER THIRTY-TWO
ADALYN

My heart skipped a beat, my father's words replaying through my mind as I tried to process what they meant.

Taylor is here.

To take me home.

To an engagement party.

Because this exercise is complete.

Everything's a lie.

But what part? My father's words or Asher's promises?

Asher's arm tightened around my waist as Taylor descended the stairs. "You've clearly misunderstood the situation, Mr. Rose. Adalyn won't be going anywhere. And I won't be accepting a display of gratitude as a form of recompense. Especially after the insult of bringing an unwanted guest to my island after everything else that has already happened."

"Mr. Sinner," Julian interjected. "If you'll allow me to facilitate the call with our organization's Elite, I am confident this slight will be rectified immediately."

"Immediately would be having him walk back up those stairs and leaving right fucking now."

Taylor's eyebrows lifted in response as he walked toward us, Asher's stern words loud enough for him to hear. "Wow. That's certainly not the warm introduction I anticipated from the man who's been playing games with my fiancée for the last two weeks."

I frowned. *Playing games?*

"Unless this is all part of your training?" Taylor pressed, making my blood run cold. "Nathan's methods were quite conventional. Perhaps yours are less so?"

Asher ignored him, his focus on Julian as he said, "This is yet another insult against me and my island, Mr. Jovanni. If your organization isn't interested in taking me seriously, then that's their mistake."

"I assure you, we take you very seriously, Mr. Sinner."

"By directly disobeying my clear directions?" Asher countered.

"That is an issue for our discussion, which is why I strongly suggest that we meet with the Elite as planned. I believe that will solve several of our issues here." Julian's voice held a note of unadulterated dominance in it, the lethality and authority underlining his words making me dizzy.

This was the kind of man who walked into a club, picked a sub, and dominated her on the spot.

A dictator.

The biggest predator in the room.

And he was conveying that with just a few sternly worded sentences.

This is the Red Prince, I thought, shivering. His infamous reputation for violence painted him as an imposing figure who wasn't afraid to draw a little blood. But he tried to choose diplomacy first.

Or that was my understanding of the current situation, anyway.

He was warning them not to test him. And something told me he wouldn't be repeating that warning.

Which meant that my father's words were a lie.

This wasn't a game at all. Asher meant every word he'd said to me.

He wants me to be his.

Now we just needed the Sin Cave Elite to agree to it.

If I was understanding and reading Julian correctly, then he intended to help us. But only if we played by his rules.

My father had broken the agreement by bringing Taylor here.

In theory, that should result in Asher having the upper hand.

But only if he attended the meeting Julian had organized.

We need to play the game. I leaned into Asher's side. It was subtle, but just enough to remind him of where I stood. He glanced down at me, temporarily taking his eyes away from Julian.

Because he wanted to ensure that I was all right.

This was a good Dom. He cared about me. He read my cues, he ensured my pleasure, and he put my comfort first. Even in a situation brimming with violence, he still focused entirely on me and ignored the others, just because of my leaning into his side.

I want to be yours, I told him with my eyes. *But we need to play this game.*

I wasn't sure he would understand. But I hoped he could see my faith in him, in *us*, and would make the right decision.

He studied me for a long moment before glancing back at Julian. "Yes. We'll proceed to the meeting."

"Good decision," Julian replied.

My father sighed. "Fine. I was merely trying to expedite the inevitable."

"Is that what you were doing?" Julian asked. "Fascinating."

Asher drew a circle against my side with his thumb, the gesture one of reassurance. Or perhaps because he felt like subtly staking his claim. Regardless, it made me feel safe. At least until I caught Taylor's predatory gaze.

Soon, his blue eyes said as he traced over every inch of my exposed form.

I was used to walking around in less clothing than this, and it usually didn't faze me. But something about the way he looked at me made me wonder if we'd been wrong about everything.

I'd known from the beginning that Sin Cave was dangerous. I'd grown up in that world. Asher had not. He thought he knew what he was up against, but what if he didn't? What if our planning wasn't good enough? What if they hurt him?

He'd only allowed a few people on his island, including a handful of Julian's men. However, it only took one of them to take him down.

And then what?

Would I be the cause of his death?

My stomach churned with the thought. I couldn't allow that to happen. But what could I do to stop it?

If only Nathan hadn't brought me here.

However, then I wouldn't have met Asher.

And I... I couldn't regret that. He'd changed everything

for me. He'd taught me what life could be. I just hoped it wouldn't be at the expense of his own life.

His brother is here. Kane won't let anything happen to Asher.

But another look from Taylor had my blood going cold. *He knows something. He's too confident.*

Which meant we'd underestimated the situation.

What are they up to? How can I warn Asher?

"Where are we meeting?" Taylor asked, his tone cordial.

"In a conference villa." Asher sounded perfectly at ease, yet his arm felt tense around me. *Does he sense that something is wrong? Does he know they're up to something?*

"Lead the way, Mr. Sinner," Julian said, the command in his tone unmistakable.

Asher didn't argue. He merely turned toward the building, his arm pulling me with him. Clive walked behind us, putting all three of us at the front of the party.

It left our backsides exposed, something that stirred unease inside me.

Now would be a good time for Julian or one of the others to act.

Something Asher's men must have realized because two of them opened the door before we reached it, their eyes on the men at our backs.

I breathed a small sigh of relief as we entered the airport building.

At least until Taylor fell into step beside me. "You look lovely, Adalyn," he said, leaning closer to me. "A perfect little tease." His breath touched my shoulder, his proximity unnerving.

Taylor Huntington wasn't a bad-looking man. Actually, he was quite handsome.

But thanks to Nathan, I knew all about Taylor's

proclivities. He was a dark man with even darker tastes. He liked power. And he achieved that goal by belittling those he considered to be beneath him.

Probably to compensate for the fact that he was a spare heir. He wanted to feel important somewhere, so he asserted his authority in any situation where he could.

"I can't wait to remove—"

"Finish that sentence and we're going to have a problem," Asher interjected, coming to a stop and pulling me even closer to his side.

"Excuse me?" Taylor's light eyebrows hit his hairline. "She's my future wife. I can speak to her however I want to."

Asher's hand fell to my hip, his grip possessive. "That might have been true three weeks ago. But you made an egregious error in allowing Nathan Spencer to bring her to my island. Because he left behind a jewel, one I intend to keep."

Taylor released a shocked laugh. "You can't be serious."

"Deadly," Asher returned.

"Gentlemen, I believe we're getting ahead of ourselves," Julian said, stepping between Taylor and Asher. "I know she's a beautiful woman, but we have a schedule to keep and important negotiations to tend to."

Asher gave him a tight nod, then shared a meaningful look with Clive. After a beat, Asher used his hand on my hip to guide me forward again. This time Clive flanked my opposite side, walking along with us all the way to the row of parked cars outside.

Clive opened the passenger-side door of what I now knew was Asher's car, as he'd driven us here in the little two-seater.

"Oscar will take the Roses and their guest to our

meeting venue," Asher announced. "Clive will escort Julian. Adalyn is with me."

Taylor appeared ready to protest, so I took away his argument by sliding into the bucket seat. I shivered as the cool leather touched my skin.

Clive shut the door, muting everyone and everything outside the car. Then he remained standing there beside me until Asher finally joined me.

The engine roared to life, and Asher floored it out of the parking lot, making me grab the armrest in response.

Asher shifted gears, the car smoothing out into a reasonable speed as soon as the airport disappeared behind us. I swallowed, his ire hot against my skin.

I wasn't sure if I needed to apologize or remain quiet. I opted for the latter, as I suspected the former would set him off.

This was my fault. But it also wasn't. I was the cause without being the instigator.

"Adalyn." Asher's palm went to my thigh, his gentle touch at odds with the anger rolling off of him. "Are you all right?"

"Yes." I was currently in his car and with him, which made me feel safe.

"Taylor shouldn't be here."

I considered that for a moment. "Perhaps. But I understand why he's here."

My father had brought him here as a playing card, one he'd likely hoped would trump the game. Because he'd underestimated Asher. He'd assumed having Taylor here to rub some elbows would work magic into fixing this "issue."

Or maybe he'd thought it would come off as intimidating.

But Asher hadn't caved at all.

And now we were going to enter a new phase of the game.

I voiced a more concise summary of those thoughts out loud to Asher, causing him to fall quiet for a long moment.

"I'm worried he knows something or has some sort of plan," I added at the end. "He's too confident."

Asher still didn't reply, but his palm remained on my thigh.

He eventually gave my leg a squeeze before shifting again and pulling into another parking area near a villa that rivaled the size of his home. He'd pointed this one out to me the other day, telling me this was where he intended to host negotiations with Julian and my parents.

We were the first to arrive since he'd navigated the streets like a race car driver.

And he slipped out without saying a word.

I frowned and unbuckled my seat belt to follow. He met me at my side to pull me from the bucket seat, then pushed me up against his car after shutting the door.

"What's your safeword, Adalyn?"

I swallowed. "Dreams."

"Good girl." He ran his fingers through my hair and gathered the strands at the back of my head in a fist. "Now let's see if we can penetrate that confident shield of your former fiancé's, hmm?"

"Wh—"

Asher's mouth captured mine in a mind-bending kiss, his tongue dominating mine before I even had a chance to catch up to him.

This wasn't a gentle embrace.

This was a claiming.

His lips were possessive and commanding, leaving me with only one choice—submit.

And submit I did.

I gave in to him, allowing him to enchant me for this one small moment. I forgot everyone and everything and solely focused on him. My Sir. My Asher. My… my new existence.

Until the clearing of a throat interrupted the fantasy and yanked me back to reality.

But Asher didn't stop kissing me, his tongue whispering benedictions against mine that I hoped would come true.

I want this life. I want him.

At some point, I'd wrapped my arms around his neck and pressed my breasts into his chest. It was wanton and needy, but I didn't care. I just wanted to exist in this bubble of sensuality with Asher and never talk to anyone else again.

Alas, this wasn't a dream but real life.

As a result, our embrace had to come to an end.

But Asher didn't just yank himself away from me; he kissed me tenderly first and pressed his forehead to mine for a beat. Then he slowly moved back, his gaze on mine. His intense orbs brimmed with warning, and I knew things were about to change.

"Treat this like a scene," he'd told me earlier. "Your safeword still applies."

I'd wanted to argue that it didn't, as safewords didn't exist within Sin Cave. However, I trusted Asher to ensure it would work here on his island. He didn't play by their rules.

But they also didn't respect his rules.

Leaving me conflicted about what would happen next.

All I had was my faith in Asher and my desire to make it through this unscathed.

Which was a lot more than what I'd possessed when I'd first arrived—which had merely been a will to survive. Now

I had an ally. Someone to... to love. Someone to believe in. Someone who understood me and respected me. Someone to face this world with as a partner.

That had to be enough.

Because if it wasn't, then I suspected Asher would burn this island to the ground before allowing Taylor to take me.

I could see it in his expression now as he met the other man's furious gaze. *Mine,* Asher's eyes said. *She's fucking mine.*

We'll see, appeared to be Taylor's reply, making my stomach churn.

That sense of dread, that something wasn't quite what it seemed, continued to prick at my nerves. Perhaps I was overthinking it. Or maybe I was a natural pessimist.

But Taylor still exuded too much confidence.

And it was a confidence that left me uneasy as we all entered the building.

Asher was relying on all this to come to a vote. What if that was exactly what Taylor wanted to happen? What if he'd already influenced the outcome somehow?

Unlike Asher, Taylor was on the inside. That put Asher at an obvious disadvantage. Which he already knew.

But what if he'd put too much faith in Julian to make this work?

What if Julian was playing both sides?

What if... what if Julian didn't plan to bring this to a vote at all?

I glanced at him now and noted his expressionless face and regal cheekbones. He was considered a king at Sin Cave because of his family's partial ownership of the illicit enterprise. There were four primary families at the head of the table, and he was one of those four.

He didn't have to help Asher at all.

Yet he'd come here to personally handle this.

The question became: Was he really here to assist Asher? Or was he here for his own nefarious purposes?

As we entered the conference room, all I could think was, *Well, we're about to find out...*

CHAPTER THIRTY-THREE
ASHER

"KNEEL."

Adalyn and I had already spoken about this requirement prior to today's conference call, making me acutely aware of what would be expected of her during this meeting.

What I hadn't anticipated was Taylor's arrival.

Or the fact that *he* would be the one to issue that command to *my* female.

As far as I was concerned, he didn't possess a single ounce of claim over Adalyn Rose. His engagement to her had terminated the moment she'd set foot on my island.

She'd become mine in a matter of seconds.

Which made his authority over her nonexistent.

I caught her elbow to lead her away from where he stood, forcing her to ignore him entirely.

It seemed my show of possession outside had provoked him into needing to stake his claim. Which he'd weakly done via a command, his demeanor suggesting he'd assumed that would be enough.

Imbecile, I thought as I took my seat at the head of the

table. A pillow waited on the floor for Adalyn—something she'd told me earlier wouldn't be necessary, but I'd insisted anyway.

"Kneel for me, Adalyn," I murmured, the words for her and not for the rest of the room. But I held Taylor's gaze as I voiced them, ensuring he understood that she obeyed me, not him.

His jaw clenched in response.

I didn't acknowledge the reaction. I merely ran my fingers through Adalyn's hair as she obeyed me. She clasped her hands in her lap and bowed her head, her submission resolute. I brushed my knuckles along her cheek, praising her without words, then steepled my fingers together on the table and observed as everyone took their seats.

Julian sat directly across from me at the foot of the rectangular table.

Albert took the chair beside him with Taylor on Julian's opposite side.

And Adalyn's mother knelt on the ground near the door.

I had an extra pillow, but I doubted Adalyn's father would accept it.

As there were going to be a lot of negotiations today, I opted not to argue this one point. Mrs. Rose also seemed content to be a few feet away from her husband, so I would give her that moment of solitude.

Clive entered the room as Julian pulled a laptop out of a messenger bag. I hadn't noticed that bag upon his arrival but suspected one of his personnel had given it to Bryant, as they'd been carrying a few bags with them off the plane. Bryant had probably dropped it off here on the way to the villa with Julian's wife and their security detail.

Julian and Clive set everything up for the conference

call, connecting the laptop to the internet and video equipment. Then Clive left with a polite "I'll be in my office if you need me."

We'd decided earlier this week to remove him from this scenario as much as possible, mostly to protect him.

But he would be nearby should something go wrong.

Meanwhile, Bryant was handling Julian's security staff.

And Kane was busy supervising from afar via the comms.

I'd ensured this room was bug-free and surveillance-free, just in case Julian or one of the others decided to scan it. I wanted to keep everything above board and demonstrate good faith.

The fact that Julian didn't ask about the room's technology suggested he trusted me. Or perhaps it was a result of him trusting Bryant—which again made me want to know more about their history, as Julian didn't strike me as the trusting sort.

"Julian Jovanni," he said as the conference line asked for voice authorization. Then he pressed his thumb to a pad on the computer and waited.

The two projectors in the room came to life, showcasing several men in suits as they sat in their respective offices.

I recognized all of them as powerful individuals throughout the world.

Including Mitchell Brevington.

Having Adalyn focus on the ground actually made this a bit easier because I didn't have to worry about any of these men triggering her.

Although, she seemed to have found her confidence today. She'd grounded me in a moment of need earlier when I'd nearly lost my shit with Taylor's arrival. I would have to thank her for that later.

I should have done it in the car when we'd had a few minutes alone.

However, the words Taylor had spoken to her in the airport had blinded me with rage. I couldn't think beyond my need to claim her.

"I'm worried he knows something or has some sort of plan. He's too confident."

Adalyn's words played through my mind as I looked at Taylor again. His expression gave nothing away as he studied the screens, but I found myself agreeing with her.

I just couldn't decide if he had somehow already altered the outcome of this impending conversation or if his confidence was based on his relationship with Albert Rose.

Albert clearly had no desire to leave Adalyn with me. Perhaps the two of them had an agreement that Taylor felt confident in.

But what about the other high-ranking members of Sin Cave?

Julian said we were expecting ten members. It seemed nine of them were here.

Mitchell Brevington, king of a finance empire.

Geoff Kensington, big player in the oil industry.

Lawrence Earls, well-known figure in the entertainment world.

The profiles continued to roll through my mind as I glanced at each man individually, noting their names and business associations.

Quinton Carpenter, auto industry.

Trenton Krain, owner of the world's leading technology enterprise.

The other four men were all masters in their own rights, their power resolute.

Carver Langston was the final player to join the call, his

easy grin marking his arrival as he said, "Sorry. I was tied up."

Julian smirked. "Again?"

Carver shrugged. "She likes what she likes, Jules."

Several of the men grunted in response, clearly catching the underlying context of the conversation. Taylor's nostrils flared, his disgust palpable.

I merely smiled. "You would probably enjoy a visit to my island, Mr. Langston." The commentary about his playmate *liking* her role of tying him up suggested consent existed between him and his wife.

Or I assumed he'd meant his wife, anyway. He'd married her about two months ago, stirring quite the media frenzy over the wealthy bachelor finally settling down.

Did he marry her for love, or was she an Elite Bride? I wondered.

Although, those two items might not be alternates. Julian seemed to be proof that loving an Elite Bride was possible. Assuming his display earlier had been real and not faked.

"Ah, Mr. Sinner. I have longed to make your acquaintance and find out how to procure an invite to play there. Perhaps we'll discuss more after the meeting is over?"

"We can arrange a call and maybe a tour as well," I told him.

"Brilliant," he replied, all smiles.

He seemed rather jovial and fun-natured. I'd be willing to get to know him better and test his consensual values.

Of course, it helped that I didn't recognize his name from the list Clive had made of Adalyn's previous *tutors*.

Unfortunately, three of the men on this call were on that list.

Quinton, Geoff, and, of course, Mitchell.

Which made all three of them key players to observe in this discussion.

"Well, now that Carver has handled today's icebreaker part of the agenda, shall we move into formal introductions?" Julian asked, his tone holding a bit of a taunt for Carver, suggesting they were old friends. "Or does everyone feel comfortable with the players on the call?" His dark gaze went to me with that final question.

"I'm familiar with everyone," I informed him. "But for those who don't know me, I'm Asher Sinner. My late father enjoyed BDSM and founded several clubs throughout the world. Sinners Isle was one of those properties, and it's now mine."

"I've been to one of the Sinner clubs," Trenton murmured. "The Baltimore location."

Kane's club, I thought. "What did you think?"

"It was on par with our Ecstasy circuit, but I've heard your location is the best," he replied. His matter-of-fact tone suggested he wasn't trying to butter me up or compliment me, just being direct.

I grinned. "Well, my island offers a bit of a unique experience since you stay and play here rather than just visit for an evening of fun."

"Perhaps you'll be interested in allowing more of us to visit," Julian said. "Assuming our negotiations here go well."

"Yes," I agreed. "It's certainly a topic we can discuss."

"Then I recommend we get to the point," Julian replied. "Nathan Spencer brought Adalyn Rose to Sinners Isle for the culmination of her training. This was not an authorized visit from my part of the Sin Cave organization, nor was it a situation conducted under Asher Sinner's approval. As you all know, Mr. Sinner chose to terminate Mr. Spencer for the insult to—"

A beep interrupted him, followed by the addition of an eleventh image.

My gaze narrowed at the arrival. *Larry Huntington.*

From the corner of my eye, I caught Taylor's smile, suggesting that this was the moment he'd been waiting for —his father's arrival.

That's your trump card? I wanted to ask. *Your daddy showing up to save the day?*

Jesus. I almost felt bad for Taylor if he thought that would be enough to "fix" this situation.

What did he plan to offer me? A television network?

Or was he going to try to threaten me?

Good luck, I thought, focusing on the newcomer. *Do your worst, Mr. Huntington.*

He cleared his throat. "Sorry I'm late. It seems my conference call invitation wasn't in my inbox, so I had to log in via other means."

"Oh?" Julian glanced at Albert before looking at Larry again. "Happy you could join us, Larry. We were just discussing the justification of Nathan Spencer's death."

Larry nodded. "Yes. Good. Then we're just in time." He leaned forward to widen his camera angle, allowing us to see who sat beside him in his conference room.

Charles Spencer.

Fuck.

Taylor's grin widened even more, his gaze meeting mine as he seemed to say, *Wishing you would have just let us leave yet?*

"Charles," Julian greeted. "This is a surprise."

"A surprise that I wanted to be present for a discussion with my son's murderer? How is that a surprise to you,

Julian?" He arched a dark brow. "Perhaps because you failed to invite me to this call?"

Julian relaxed into his chair, the picture of nonchalance. "Apologies, Charles. I assumed you would respect and understand our need for a cordial discussion and wouldn't want to risk adding emotional commentary to the mix. I see now that it was a mistake of judgment on my part."

Jesus. This man was a master of word games and barbed commentary. *Note to self: Don't get on his bad side.* Because this was a guy I wanted in my corner, not against me.

"Regardless, we were discussing your son's poor decision to conduct Sin Cave business in an off-site location. He failed to run that request up through the appropriate channels and—"

"He asked me," Charles interjected.

"And me," Larry added.

"As well as me," Albert confirmed.

Julian's eyebrows rose. "So all three of you were aware of his decision to take an Elite Bride to an off-site facility for training, and none of you thought it wise to suggest against it?"

"He was intending to offer Mr. Sinner an opportunity while there to enjoy the fruits of his labor. Given his proclivities, we expected him to accept," Larry explained.

I snorted. "Then you're clearly unfamiliar with my *proclivities.*" Because I would *never* indulge in something so crude. "When I claim a woman, I don't share her, Mr. Huntington." It was a phrase meant for Larry and his idiot of a son. "I also value open communication, something Mr. Spencer did not provide. Instead, he took advantage of my hospitality and broke one of my island's rules—*consent.*"

All three of them grunted in reply to my comment.

As did Quinton.

But everyone else remained silent.

Mitchell even appeared slightly contrite, which was an interesting development. Perhaps he felt bad for his behavior. Or maybe he was recalling how close he came to dying on my island as a result of his behavior.

"So you killed my son because he, what, *insulted* you?" Charles demanded.

"Yes." There was no point in elaborating. Nor would I be apologizing for his son's death.

Adalyn shifted just a little at my side. Fortunately, the table hid her from view. That was one of the reasons I'd placed her there—only the top of her head could be seen, as she'd sat back on her heels after kneeling on the pillow.

"This is fucking ridiculous," Charles snapped. "He *killed* my son. Why are we even talking to him? Fucking shoot him."

Julian arched a brow. "Our organization insulted this man's integrity by conducting business on his property without authority. That—"

"And why do we care so much about his opinion of us?" Charles demanded. "He's a BDSM island owner. That hardly gives him any power here."

"I disagree," Mitchell replied. "Mr. Sinner has friends in high places throughout the world, many of whom are also members of our organization. That's why he's been on the potential membership list, something I'm going to assume you knew when you *approved* your son's visit to his island."

Carver nodded. "That's why he invited Mr. Sinner to partake in the fun, yes? I mean, Larry said he expected Mr. Sinner to accept that invitation. Perhaps you intended to use it as a form of recruitment, too?"

"I wasn't recruiting him," Larry replied. "But yes, I was aware of his candidacy."

"He's not a fucking member," Charles bit out. "Unlike my son, who was in good standing. His death should matter."

"And it does," Julian assured him. "But the fact of the matter is Nathan should never have carried out Sin Cave business on this island without appropriate consent."

"I agree," Mitchell replied.

"Me, too," Carver echoed.

"He had consent from the three of us," Larry argued.

"Yes, which makes the three of you complicit in this situation," Julian remarked. "Mr. Sinner should have been approached and spoken to prior to the engagement. Doing otherwise was an insult to his business. And therefore, I move that his response to the matter is justified."

"He's not a fucking member!" Charles shouted. "How is this even a discussion?"

"And now you see why you were not invited to this meeting, Mr. Spencer," Julian replied coldly. "I understand you are grieving, so I'm willing to ignore your outburst. But you cannot expect the rest of us to rule based on your emotions." Julian reached forward to click a button, muting the screen as Charles started to yell. "To the rest of you, I would like your unbiased opinions on the matter."

"It was an overreaction," Albert immediately said. "He should have sent Nathan home for us to reprimand."

I grunted. "Given what I've seen so far, I doubt that would have happened."

"You're not part of our organization, Mr. Sinner. You don't know how we operate or how we handle our business. So I recommend that you not comment on things you don't understand." Taylor's tone held a note of formality to it, but the condescending edge underlining his words was clear.

"On the contrary, I've shared quite a bit with him over the last two weeks," Julian countered. "Asher has been on our recruitment list for five years. So I accepted this opportunity as a sign of fate and took advantage of our time together to educate him. Mr. Sinner is quite ready to join our organization."

He paused for a beat, giving everyone—including me—a moment for that to sink in.

I had never expressed my readiness to join.

But it was known from our initial call that I likely wouldn't have a choice.

Nathan Spencer brought his business here, thereby forcing me into this organization whether I liked it or not.

"So if the issue is Mr. Sinner not being a permanent member of Sin Cave—thereby marking him as 'less than equal' to Nathan Spencer, as Charles has suggested—then perhaps we should start with approving Mr. Sinner's membership. Then we can move into discussions on appropriate reprimand." Julian fell silent again, his dark eyes searching the various screens.

"That does seem like a reasonable fix," Mitchell said after a few seconds of contemplation. "Has he named his terms for membership?"

"He has," Julian replied.

"And they are?" Carver asked.

"Are we really considering this?" Taylor interrupted. "He killed one of our members, so we're going to reward him with membership?"

Julian blinked at him. "Mr. Sinner acted in the best interest of his company and protected not only his asset but also his reputation in doing so. But I suppose you wouldn't understand that sort of sacrifice, would you? Perhaps your older brother would have been better suited for this meeting."

Taylor balked at that. "How dare—"

"Quiet," Mitchell snapped from the video. "I'm a busy man with a schedule to keep today, and I want to hear what Mr. Sinner's demands are so we can make a decision."

"Likewise," Trenton agreed flatly.

Several others nodded in agreement, leaving Taylor properly chastised in a corner.

"Right," Julian said. "His demand is quite simple. He wishes to join our organization by marrying Adalyn Rose."

CHAPTER THIRTY-FOUR
ASHER

My jaw almost unhinged, but by some miracle of fate, I managed to hold myself together.

Because *what the fuck?*

I had never said that.

I'd expressed a desire to keep her. But I'd never mentioned *marrying* her.

And Julian knew it, too.

He was playing some sort of game, not just with the members of Sin Cave but with me, too.

"And in return, he's agreed to allow my part of the organization access to a handful of villas on his island for training and celebration purposes," Julian continued, making up terms we had never discussed before. "But all visiting requests will go through me for approval. And not all requests will be approved."

"What are the parameters for approval?" Quinton asked, speaking for the first time.

"The parameters will be mutually defined between me and Mr. Sinner," Julian said, his words giving me pause.

"Mutually defined parameters" meaning what exactly?

I required consent.

And nothing about his part of the organization was consensual. It was all arranged marriages and trained brides.

"Interesting," Mitchell said, scratching his jaw.

"There's just one problem," Albert said. "Adalyn is already engaged to Larry's son."

His words had me glancing at Larry's screen to see him furiously typing on his keyboard with a fuming Charles beside him.

It would have been humorous to watch if it weren't so fucking infuriating.

Julian ignored them, as did everyone else, it seemed.

"True," Julian said, replying to Albert's comment regarding Adalyn's betrothal. "So name your terms, Albert."

"My terms?"

"For allowing Mr. Sinner to marry your daughter."

His lips parted. "He can't *marry* her. As I said, she's already engaged."

"It's not a formally announced engagement." Julian glanced at Taylor Huntington. "You wanted it to appear as a lurid affair, yes? To maintain your playboy status for as long as society allowed?"

"That's not—"

Julian looked back at Mr. Rose, dismissing Taylor without a second thought. "You are capable of renegotiating, Albert. Given that Mr. Sinner has been on the desired recruitment list for the last five years, perhaps you could establish a new alliance with his family. And we can finally have an in with the elite line of Sinner clubs."

"I can't negotiate for my siblings," I interjected. "Only myself."

Julian dipped his chin in acknowledgment. "And it so

happens that it's your club, specifically, that many of our network members are intrigued by. Fortunate for you, yes?"

My jaw ticked, but I nodded, playing his game. "Very fortunate."

"This is a very lucrative offer," Mitchell pointed out. "I've visited Sinners Isle several times. His facilities are top of the line and highly recommended in our circles."

"It provides an exclusive location for training some of our Elite Brides as well," Julian added. "And many of our members will be eager to book a potential stay on the isle as well. I imagine Mr. Sinner will work out a Sin Cave rate for those who qualify for a visit."

An interesting choice of wording, I thought. *Potential. Qualify*. Meaning he was writing into my membership agreement a way to control who visited my island.

Just like his comment regarding the mutually defined parameters.

This man really is a genius with words.

"I mean, I'm in," Carver said. "Easiest decision I've ever made."

"I would be interested as well," Trenton echoed.

Four of the others chimed in, voicing their agreement.

"I approve and would be interested in discussing some investment strategies with you, Mr. Sinner," Mitchell said.

"I would be open to those discussions," I told him, playing along. Because we both knew I wouldn't be entertaining any business ventures with him. Not after how he'd treated Adalyn. But he was staying true to his word now in helping me with this discussion, making me begrudgingly grateful to him for his assistance today.

Fortunately, his voice didn't appear to be bothering Adalyn.

She'd remained mostly still throughout the

conversation, only shifting when Nathan's death was mentioned.

It took conscious control not to reach down and touch her. But I needed to focus on the conversation to save us both.

"Well, obviously, I don't approve," Taylor put in. "She's my fucking bride."

"There are other candidates," Julian offered with a shrug. "I'm sure we can find you someone." His gaze went to Albert. "Have you decided on your terms?"

"So that's it? You all tell me who I marry my daughter off to, and I have to oblige?" Albert demanded, looking at the screens.

"It would be a lucrative opportunity for you," Mitchell replied. "Consider the resort Asher has built and the potential impact his expertise could have for your organization as a whole. The two of you could create a whole new chain of like-minded resorts together."

The very thought of that made my stomach churn—not the idea of a chain of resorts similar to Sinners Isle, but the thought of working with Albert Rose.

However, his words appeared to be giving Albert cause for consideration.

"I think a chain of that nature would pique the interest of several financial organizations and create a wealth of investment opportunity," Mitchell added.

"That is a very good point," Julian replied. "It's almost as though your two families are meant to unite."

"Yes," Albert said slowly, looking at me with a new light in his eyes. "That is an interesting concept."

"I would not be opposed to expanding," I admitted. It wasn't something I thought I would be able to do for at least another decade, but I'd consider it under the right circumstances.

"Albert, you can't—"

"Taylor, you understand how this game is played," Albert interjected. "If the Sin Cave Elite wish for Mr. Sinner to join, then I'm not in a position to deny them. And if it's my daughter he wants as a price for entry, then I'm inclined to give him what he desires."

"Excellent," Julian replied. "I imagine you have a few details you'll want to work through?"

"Yes." Albert met my gaze. "There are business ventures I want to discuss with my future son-in-law. But I think we can iron out those details during my stay here. That will give me time to explore the island and see what Sinners Isle is truly about."

This would be an interesting arrangement, but as it allowed me to keep Adalyn, I nodded in agreement. "I look forward to it," I lied.

Because I absolutely did not look forward to our discussion.

However, I would go through the formalities required to be able to free Adalyn from this hell.

Or offer her a semblance of freedom, anyway.

Taylor chuckled, the sound one I didn't expect to hear from him. "Wow," he said. "He kills Nate and gets to marry my bride? That's... *wow*."

"It's typically considered unwise to allow a prized possession out of your sight," I told him conversationally. "You never know when someone else may claim it."

He nodded. "Fair. But I didn't let her out of my sight, Julian." He leaned forward. "In fact, she's been very much within my sight for years."

I nearly asked him to clarify, but then it occurred to me what he meant just half a second too late.

Because he was already saying, "Which is how I know that you didn't kill Nate. She did. And I have video footage that proves it." He looked at the screens and at the men around the table. "He's lying to all of you."

Julian frowned. "There's video footage of Nathan Spencer's death?"

Shit.

Clive had mentioned a repository for the videos, but he hadn't found proof of anyone else accessing it. However, he'd also said something about a strange sort of encryption that he couldn't seem to hack. He'd assumed it was a security measure to keep the files secure.

But perhaps it was related to another access point.

Or maybe Taylor just had access to Nathan's passwords.

Unless they were Taylor's passwords all along, I thought. *What if Taylor was the one who created the original shared drive for Nathan to house all the videos in?*

It could have been meant to ensure Nathan's training methods were acceptable by Taylor's standards—which just made him a sick fuck.

Or he'd been keeping those videos for other means.

"Yes, I also watched it happen," Taylor explained. "Nathan called me that night after seeing Adalyn stash a bunch of knives around the villa. He was quite excited to teach her a lesson, and he set up a camera for me to observe. One she obviously didn't know about because she killed him while I watched."

"And you didn't think to report this sooner?" Julian demanded before looking at me. "And you lied about it?"

Jesus. If Taylor had the video feed from that night, then

he also knew Bryant and Clive had been with me when we found the body.

And he would have heard our conversation afterward.

"I wasn't brought into the discussions regarding what to do with this situation," Taylor said tightly. "Had I been included, I would have mentioned it sooner."

I considered him for a moment, my mind working quickly to develop an alternate strategy.

Yes, I'd obviously covered up the murder, but only to protect Adalyn.

However, Julian had a good point regarding the information and video footage. Why hadn't Taylor told everyone? Because from the expressions on the screen, both Larry and Charles were shocked by this reveal.

As was everyone else in the room and on the other streaming videos.

Which meant he hadn't told anyone.

And *this* was his final trump card, the one he'd intended to play as a last resort if things didn't go his way.

Because he hadn't wanted to admit to having the videos.

"I can play the footage, if you'd like," Taylor added. "I have it on my phone."

"Yes," Julian said. "I want to see it."

I stayed quiet while Taylor slid over the phone, as I wanted to see how much this would reveal. Would he also show my men arriving at the scene?

Clive had said the video was still recording while we were there, but he'd stated the footage was only going to Nathan's phone.

Maybe he'd been livestreaming with Taylor, but after Nathan's death, he'd hung up as he'd tried to figure out what to do.

So the rest of it was just recorded to the phone and never actually transferred to the shared drive.

Because the murder itself was never transferred either; Clive had said that videos had to be manually pushed there, which it seemed Nathan had been doing every few days.

"She's been very much within my sight for years."

Taylor's words played through my head as Julian connected the video to the conference call for everyone to watch.

"She's been very much within my sight for years."

Because he kept checking the video repository to review her training.

And perhaps more.

I glanced at the screen, already familiar with the scene, and noted the timestamp scrolling along the top, counting the seconds.

That hadn't been in the videos we'd seen.

And this footage said we were only a minute in, which began with the scramble for knives...

Either he'd cropped the file, or he didn't have the full video.

He taped this while livestreaming, I realized. *He'd hit Record the moment she started to truly fight back.*

Which meant he didn't have any of the feed that led up to this moment because Nathan had never had a chance to upload the full file.

The video ended shortly after Nathan took his last breath and showed Adalyn walking toward the patio doors, covered in blood.

"Is there more?" Julian demanded.

Taylor shook his head. "I recorded that myself from our livestream. But the full video will be on Nathan's phone, assuming Asher hasn't destroyed the evidence."

All eyes moved to me, including a pair of fuming dark ones that belonged to Julian. "Where is his phone?"

"I have it," I told him slowly, still processing everything that had been said.

The fact that Taylor knew the full video would be there told me he was very aware of Nathan's penchant for taping Adalyn. That, coupled with his comment about always having an eye on her, confirmed my suspicions that he was in the know about all those videos.

So did he tape them for personal pleasure?

Or as potential blackmail?

Perhaps a hint of both.

"Good. I want it," Julian said through his teeth. "And why the fuck didn't you tell me that Adalyn killed him?"

I shrugged. "It happened on my isle, thereby making it my responsibility to handle the fallout. It also doesn't change the fact that I would have killed him regardless of Adalyn's behavior. She did us all a favor by taking him out."

Julian's eyebrows hit his hairline. "Oh? And how do you justify such a statement? Because as Taylor already pointed out, you're not a member of our organization, Mr. Sinner. And given that you lied, I don't think your candidacy is going to be approved."

Several grunts of agreement followed that statement via the conference line.

"We value honesty among each other, which is a trait you clearly lack," Julian continued. "So tell us why you feel her killing Nathan Spencer was a *favor* to our organization?"

"Well, I don't know about the rest of you, but I'm not necessarily keen on being videotaped without my consent," I said, taking a risk. Because if Taylor hadn't seen the whole video of that day, it suggested Nathan didn't have an auto-upload function—something that Clive had also confirmed with his digging. Which meant Taylor wouldn't know if I told the truth now or not.

Well, he might know that I was lying.

But he wouldn't have *proof* of it.

And when I finished, his word would be null and void.

CHAPTER THIRTY-FIVE
ASHER

I STARED AT JULIAN. "You say your organization is about honesty."

"It is," he replied, narrowing his gaze.

"Then tell me, why did Nathan Spencer videotape my playtime with Adalyn Rose?" I demanded. "Because it certainly felt like blackmail to me when I found evidence of it on his drive. Along with those hundreds of other videos he had of previous encounters." I glanced at Mitchell. "Including several of your dates with Adalyn." I looked at Quinton next. "Yours, too." Geoff was the final one I looked at, driving home my point that I knew all three of them had fucked Adalyn. "And yours."

Julian's eyebrows shot upward. "*What?*"

"Oh, you mean that's not normal? Because I was livid when I found it. Why do you think I've been so fucking offended, Julian?"

We could have heard a pin drop after that statement.

"So yeah, when I found the video of me strangling Adalyn earlier that day while I fucked her, I decided it was in my best interest to claim that I'd murdered him.

Because I definitely would have, had he shown me that shit."

From the screen, it appeared Geoff, Mitchell, and Quinton felt similarly.

Which meant none of them knew about the recordings.

So maybe they'd just been for personal enjoyment. But I doubted it.

Especially given the ghostlike expression on Taylor's face now.

He knew about those videos, something he'd already more or less admitted with his statement about keeping his eyes on Adalyn.

The organization would need more proof, of course. And they might be able to find it on the laptop. Especially if it turned out that Taylor had originally created the data repository. I didn't know enough about technology to be certain of that possibility, but someone would.

And even if Taylor ended up not being involved—which I strongly doubted—Nathan was still guilty of videotaping sessions without consent, thus justifying his murder.

"So rather than punish Adalyn, I took the fall and kept her as a consolation prize." I shrugged. "I happen to enjoy a little fight in the bedroom, and she obviously has fire in her."

I reached down to pet her like one would a dog, the gesture purposeful for the room, but also my way of checking on her.

Because fuck, this was intense.

And if Taylor could prove I was lying... Adalyn and I would be royally fucked here.

"I... I didn't realize you had a session with her," he said slowly.

"I would show you proof of it, but I deleted the fucking

video the moment I saw it," I lied. "It was only on his phone and not in the data repository. But I haven't touched anything else. I only removed the footage of his time on this isle, as it's my property and therefore my responsibility to protect it."

"What did you plan to do with the others?" Julian asked, still studying me.

"I believe you'll have that answer if you call your security team," I told him. "Bryant should have handed everything over to them by now. That was the plan, anyway." That part wasn't a lie—we had intended to give the computer and phone to Julian because we didn't want them on the island.

And the phone had been completely wiped clean of all the footage from the villa, just like I'd already admitted.

However, we'd done that to protect Clive and Adalyn more than my isle.

Regardless of the reason, it was done.

And while it might be duplicitous on my account, I didn't give a fuck.

I valued honesty. But there was nothing *honest* about any of this.

Julian pulled out his phone, his gaze holding mine as he put it to his ear. "Tobias. Has Bryant given you anything?" He paused while he listened, nodding along as the other man spoke. "I see. I'm going to put you on speakerphone. I need you to repeat that." He set his phone down on the table. "Go ahead."

Tobias cleared his throat. "He gave me Nathan Spencer's effects, including his laptop and phone. There are some videos that I think you need to see. But, uh, we're still reviewing. There's a lot on here."

"Videos of other Sin Cave members fucking Adalyn Rose?" Julian asked.

"Among other things," Tobias replied. "Nathan has quite the repository."

"I see." Julian looked at Taylor. "Were you aware of this, Taylor?"

"No," he replied, his voice hoarse. "No, I wasn't aware."

"And you, Charles? Did you know?" Julian demanded, looking at the screen.

Silence followed.

I glanced at their screen to see if they were trying to speak, but they both appeared too shocked to comment.

"Oh, right, you're muted," Julian murmured. "Apologies." He didn't sound contrite in the slightest, obviously having done this on purpose. "There, you can speak now. Did you know Nathan Spencer had all those videos on his hard drive?"

"No," Charles said through his teeth. "I didn't."

"Larry?" Julian prompted.

He simply shook his head, seeming to be too tongue-tied to speak.

"I see." Julian fell silent for a beat. "Tobias, can you verify who has access to that data repository, or put one of our techs on it?"

"Yeah, Fox is on it already," Tobias replied.

"Good. Keep me updated."

"Always."

The call ended, and Julian looked at me and then at Taylor. "Well, this is an interesting development. You should have told me about the videos and Adalyn's involvement in the murder," he informed me flatly.

I nodded, agreeing to an extent.

"I had intended to discuss the videos in private during

your stay, as I wasn't sure what to do with them." Not a lie, and something Tobias had proved for me with that call. "And while I may not have killed Nathan, I took responsibility for it. Because, as I said, I would have done it anyway. I value consent on this island, something he very clearly violated. His death is justified."

"That's a point I won't argue," Julian said. "I also admire you for not trying to use those videos for blackmail against our organization. I imagine releasing those to the media could have been detrimental to our reputations."

"Indeed," I agreed. "Which is why I deleted my own." I continued brushing my fingers through Adalyn's hair. She hadn't moved an inch, making me wonder if she'd fallen into a trance or had disappeared into a safe space within her mind.

"I do wonder why Nathan chose to videotape those sessions," Julian pressed. "You're certain you have no idea, Taylor?"

The male in question had lost all signs of confidence, his face as white as a sheet. "N-no, I don't."

"Larry? Charles? Do either of you know?" Julian asked.

Both men shook their heads.

"Well, hopefully Fox will find out more for us." Julian grabbed his phone and put it back in his pocket, then sighed as he relaxed into his chair.

No one else spoke, all waiting for the clear leader in the room to take this conversation forward.

"Well, I believe the matter of Asher Sinner's membership is still in question. While I feel he should have shared this information with me sooner"—he cast me a pointed look—"he did prove integrity through intention. He's also new to our ways, so I personally volunteer to help assist him with his induction into our society. Assuming everyone approves, I mean."

"I don't approve," Taylor muttered. "He covered up Nate's murder and lied to all of us."

"The same could be said about you," Trenton replied. "You had proof of his murder and chose not to disclose it until the middle of our call."

"He's right," Quinton echoed. "You should have shared that information."

"Yes," Larry agreed, his tone holding a note of censure in it. "You absolutely should have shared that detail."

Taylor clenched his jaw. "So I'm the bad guy now? Not the outsider who covered up Adalyn's handiwork?"

"I think you're just disappointed that you can't punish your toy, Taylor," Carver said from the screen. "But it seems Asher has that part under control already. And more, he wants to keep her for himself."

"Yes," I confirmed. "I do."

"Then I say we let you tame the girl and marry her, if that's your desire." His lips curled, some of his easygoing nature seeming to appear again. "Perhaps it's even a bit of a punishment, as it's clear you'll have a lot of work ahead of you."

Julian grinned in response to that. "Enjoyable work?"

"Of course," Carver replied. "Something I believe you know a thing or two about."

"Why do you think I'm offering to mentor him?" Julian asked.

Carver chuckled. "Don't worry, old friend. I caught that, too."

Julian's grin only widened in response, then he glanced at the other screens. "What about the rest of you? Are there any objections?"

He waited for a ten-second count.

I half expected Taylor or his father to explode, but they both remained silent.

Charles did as well.

"Mr. Rose?" Julian prompted. "Does the aspect of Asher covering up your daughter's involvement in Nathan Spencer's murder change your opinion regarding her nuptials?"

"No, if anything, I'm grateful to Asher for taking her on. She clearly needs a firmer hand than what Taylor and Nathan were giving her," Albert replied.

It took conscious effort on my part not to react to that statement.

But it was very clear that my future father-in-law and I would *not* be friends.

Which would make working together interesting.

However, I'd do whatever I had to do to keep Adalyn. And I wasn't opposed to expanding Sinners Isle either. So it wasn't a terrible situation. Just an uncomfortable partnership.

"Excellent. Anyone else?" Julian asked again.

"You'll be handling the removal of those videos personally, yes?" Geoff asked, his voice gruff.

"Of course," Julian promised. "They'll never leave this island. Assuming they're not being shared, I mean. But we'll get to the bottom of it, Geoff. You have my word."

The other man nodded. "Then I'm good with this. I trust you to mentor the boy, Julian."

Boy, I thought, nearly rolling my eyes.

"It'll be a mutually beneficial partnership," Julian confirmed.

More nods around the table followed, causing Julian to grin.

"Beautiful, then we're all in agreement. Which brings us to our final matter: Nathan's death. I personally feel Asher reacted in a way many of us would have, had our own integrity and character been tested by such deceit. Therefore, I move to accept his decision in regard to Nathan Spencer."

Fuck, Julian was proving to be every bit as deadly as his nickname, just not in a violent sort of way.

No.

This man killed people with his knowledge and words.

Somehow, that made him even more lethal.

Because the man had just orchestrated my membership acceptance into Sin Cave simply to use that as a way to put me on equal footing with the other members. Which thereby afforded me clemency for killing Nathan Spencer. Because now the argument that I wasn't a member became null and void.

Brilliant, I thought. *This man is brilliant.*

"Any objections?" Julian asked.

Charles disappeared from the camera, obviously removing himself from the conversation.

I almost felt bad.

But his son was a fucking monster.

If Adalyn hadn't killed him, I sure as fuck would have.

She seemed to be holding her breath on the ground beside me.

Soon, I told myself, my fingers itching to touch her, to reassure her, to ensure she was okay.

Marriage.

We're going to be married.

Fuck. What does she think about that? Will she be okay with it?

This certainly wasn't the way I had envisioned myself becoming engaged to a woman.

"Hearing no dissent, I feel this matter is now closed. Are there any other items we need to discuss?" Julian's tone indicated false interest while his eyes cautioned everyone to stay silent.

He was clearly done with this meeting.

And given how well he'd played every card today, I couldn't blame him for wanting to wrap it up.

"I'll be in touch, Asher," Carver said. "About a visit."

"I look forward to it," I told him.

"I'll be reaching out as well," Trenton informed me.

I nodded. "I'll look for your message."

Julian grinned. "And so it begins," he said. "Welcome to Sin Cave, Asher."

CHAPTER THIRTY-SIX
ADALYN

MARRIAGE.

Family merger.

Hotel chain.

Sin Cave membership.

The truth about Nate's murder.

Videos.

All the words spun in my mind in a revolving circle of insanity. Why hadn't Asher mentioned that he'd asked for me to marry him? Was that his version of keeping me?

I wasn't exactly disappointed or angry, just... *shocked.*

He wants to marry me?

And he intended to allow Sin Cave to use his island? Hadn't that been something he was adamantly against? He'd claimed to have killed Nathan for that very reason. And now he planned to allow the organization access to certain villas?

For training?

It all seemed so contradictory to the man I knew.

There was something else at play here.

I kept puzzling through every statement, trying to sort out the details in my mind as the call ended.

And I still couldn't believe no one had reacted to the fact that I'd killed Nathan Spencer.

Was that punishment still coming? Would Julian handle it himself?

Or... or were they just going to let Asher punish me?

I don't understand how any of this is possible, I thought. *How... how did this happen?*

Had Asher truly saved me? Was this finally over?

No. He still needs to negotiate the hotel with my father.

But it sounded like everything else was done. Which... which left me breathless with anticipation. And riddled with confusion.

I vaguely heard Asher commenting about someone driving Taylor to the airport to await a pickup. I also heard him say something to my father about Oscar driving him and my mother to their villa. "I'll be by later to discuss those details," he added at the end.

"I look forward to it, Asher," my father replied, sounding more pleased than I'd ever heard him.

Because he wants to go into business with Asher.

Is that what Asher wants?

Was that his plan all along?

No. He wouldn't do that. He wanted nothing to do with Sin Cave, right?

And he lied about Nate's murder, saying something about a video. But there wasn't a video. He's also never strangled me.

The thoughts continued to spiral, making me dizzy. I started to sway, only to find a palm against my cheek as Asher knelt before me. "Adalyn, sweetheart, are you all right?" he asked, his intense eyes finding mine in the dark.

I blinked. *Dark. When did it become that way?*

My vision seemed blackened at the edges.

"Breathe for me, darling," he whispered. "Inhale, Adalyn."

I did, my chest rising with the motion and helping some of my vision to clear.

"Good girl," he murmured. "Again."

I obeyed because it felt right. *Safe*. Easy. Comforting. I liked listening to him and following his commands. It helped me feel a little lighter and less chaotic.

My mind slowly returned to normal, the loudness of my thoughts settling beneath a cloud of calm.

Asher drew his thumb along my jaw, praising me without words. His lips brushed my forehead as he pulled me up from the ground. Then he wrapped his jacket around me and helped me into a chair before handing me a bottle of water.

"A panic attack," he told me.

I blinked at him. "Hmm?"

"You started to have a panic attack. Why didn't you use your safeword?"

I stared blankly at him. "Panic attack?"

"I don't think she realized it was happening," a deep voice said. *Julian*. I couldn't see him, but I felt him hovering nearby.

Asher squatted before me again, ignoring him. "Drink your water."

I unscrewed the cap and took several sips.

"What were you thinking about?" he asked me softly. "What set you down that path? Was it someone you heard on the phone? Something that was said?"

I swallowed another gulp of water while I considered his questions. "You told them your price for membership was marriage?"

He frowned. "The idea of marrying me gave you a panic attack?"

What? "No. I just... I was thinking about your price. And the merger. And... questioning things."

"Questioning me," he rephrased. "And my intentions with you." His gaze went to the side to where I assumed Julian was standing outside of my view. "Because you told everyone I wanted to marry her."

"You said you wanted to keep her. That's the same thing in our world, Sinner." Julian moved to stand in my line of sight behind Asher. "And I do believe you want to marry her. I mean, you're on your knees for her right now. What's the difference?"

He wasn't technically on his knees; he was squatting. However, I didn't comment because I was too busy processing their conversation.

So Asher hadn't said he wanted to marry me, just keep me. Which was what we'd agreed on in the beginning. Yet Julian had twisted it into a weird sort of proposal. "And your island?" I asked. "Are you really okay with Sin Cave being here?"

Asher again looked at Julian, this time standing to face him. "That depends on our *mutually defined parameters.*"

Julian smirked. "Consent will be one of them, as I hear you value that here. That's why I'll be making the final approvals. I know who is consenting and who is not."

Asher took a step back to stand beside my chair, his hand going to the back of my neck. His thumb brushed my pulse as he asked Julian, "And I'm supposed to trust your word on that?"

"After everything I've done for you today? Abso-fucking-lutely. Because we both know damn well there was no video of you strangling Adalyn Rose. You covered up the murder because you wanted to save her from this hell."

Asher's eyes widened.

"Don't even try to deny it, Sinner. Reading people is what I do. The only reason I didn't call you out on it is because I know you lied for a noble cause. But if you ever fucking lie to me again, I will end you faster than you can blink." He arched a dark brow. "Tell me you understand."

I shivered, his dominance a whip in the air that curled around my senses and froze the blood in my veins.

Asher was a Dom.

But Julian? Julian existed on another level entirely.

"Everything I've done is to protect her," Asher replied. "And if that requires lying again, I would do it in a heartbeat. But it'll always be for her and no one else."

Julian considered him for a beat. "Then I return to my earlier statement regarding marriage—take the vows and you can lie for a good cause. One I would understand." Julian's tone held a dangerous note to it.

"Noted," Asher replied.

"Next time Adalyn kills someone, be honest with me. I think you'll find I'm more understanding on that sort of thing than anyone else you'll ever meet," he said.

"There won't be a next time unless someone touches her without approval," Asher replied. "Which reminds me, anyone who has ever touched her previously will not be permitted on my island."

Julian nodded. "I fully expected that requirement already. Consider it memorized and guaranteed."

"Good." Asher studied him for a long moment and sighed. "I'm grateful for your help today, Julian. But I won't apologize for covering up the murder."

"I know. As I said, you did it for the right reason. And in

your situation, I would have done the same. However, I meant what I said about honesty. The organization takes it seriously. Which is why I suspect Taylor Huntington is about to earn his due soon because we both know he was aware of that drive."

"Clive tried to find evidence of sharing on the drive, but he said it was locked down tight," Asher replied. "However, I'm wondering if Taylor set up that folder initially. He wouldn't need an additional login if he already had access to the original."

Julian nodded. "I'll have Fox pursue it. We'll find out if anyone else has seen those videos."

"Clive can help as needed. And as a show of good faith, I'll tell you that he's more aware of things than I've let on."

"Yes, I know," Julian replied. "And don't worry. You're permitted a few insiders, just like Bryant was closer to me than most."

"Good to know. I would like to keep Clive healthy and alive."

"We don't kill people for learning our secrets, Asher. We leave that work to our wives." He glanced down at me as he said it, his lips curling. "I look forward to the wedding. Perhaps my Bria can give your Adalyn some tips for the wedding night."

"The only one providing instruction will be me," Asher said, his touch tightening just a bit around my nape.

"I would never dream of intruding," Julian replied, lifting his palms into the air in a gesture of innocence. "However, I would be honored to stand in as your best man at the wedding."

Asher grunted, but his thumb continued to gently stroke my neck. "Bryant and Clive are going to have some things to say about that. My brothers, too."

Julian shrugged. "Fine. Bryant, Clive, and Kane can be your groomsmen. But poor Adalyn won't have any bridesmaids, as I doubt we can fly Jenica here in time for the wedding." He looked at me. "I also don't recommend introducing her to your parents."

My lips parted. "You know about Jenica?" And wait, had he just said *Kane*?

Asher must have caught that part as well because his thumb stilled against my pulse point. "How do you know my brother is on the island?"

Julian just gave him a look. "Please. You're not the only one with resources, Asher. And before you go questioning Bryant, I'll save you the trouble and tell you he had nothing to do with it. He's loyal to you, which is the primary reason I'm even here. If you've won him over, then you must be a good guy. And I could use more of those in my court."

"And you typically recruit friends by spying on them?" Asher countered.

"In my line of work, it's impossible to trust people. So yes, that is typically how I determine my allies."

Asher considered him for a long moment before conceding with a slight dip of his chin, the circular motions of his thumb resuming once more against my neck. "All right. I can respect that."

"Good." He held out his hand for Asher's. "Then I suspect you and I will be good allies going forward."

Asher accepted the gesture. "Then I guess you're going to be my best man."

Julian grinned. "If you need me to help with Albert in any way, let me know. But I think you can handle him from here."

Asher released his hand. "Was the hotel merger your idea or Mitchell's?"

"Mitchell's," Julian confirmed. "I think he feels quite bad for what he did to your Adalyn. However, I suspect nothing he does will ever be enough to earn your forgiveness."

"You suspect correctly."

He nodded. "Then you understand how I feel about Taylor Huntington."

Asher arched a brow. "Is that the real reason you helped us today?"

"Let's just say I'm not disappointed in the outcome," he murmured.

"Good to know," Asher replied. "Regardless of your reasoning, I appreciate you helping us today. I'm glad Bryant called you. And I'm glad I listened to his advice about trusting you."

Julian grunted. "Bryant is full of shit. You shouldn't trust him."

"And fuck you, too," Bryant retorted from the doorway. "See if I ever take another bullet for you again."

Julian didn't react to his arrival, suggesting he'd somehow sensed his presence there when he'd voiced his insult. Perhaps he'd seen him out of the corner of his eye. "You didn't take it for me," he replied. "You took it for her."

"Which is why I phrased it that way—for you? Never again. For Bria? Always."

Julian grinned and finally faced him. "I assume she's back at my villa?"

"She is. Pretty sure she's stashed a knife in every room, too."

Julian's lips curled upward. "Good." He looked at Asher. "I imagine the two of you need a moment. Maybe you can propose properly? I hear women like that sort of thing. Of course, I wouldn't know, so perhaps I'm not the best one to offer that advice."

"I would love to see you propose to Bria," Bryant mused. "She'd probably stab you."

Julian's gaze took on a dreamy, faraway state. "Maybe." Then he glanced down at me, his dark orbs radiating an intensity that instantly left me breathless. "I'm sorry, Adalyn."

Asher tensed beside me.

I blinked. "For what, Sir?"

"You may call me Julian," he told me softly. "And my apology extends to everything. For what it's worth, I think Asher is a much better match than Taylor."

I couldn't argue with him there. "I'm very happy to stay here."

Julian smiled. "Yes. I can see that." He returned his focus to Asher. "Can you plan a wedding in seven days?"

"Assuming all goes to plan with Albert, then yes."

"Excellent. Then I'll go let my Bria know we're staying for an impromptu vacation."

"You mean that wasn't in the cards originally?" Bryant asked. "Because you brought enough bags for a month."

"You can never be too prepared," Julian drawled, causing Asher to stare at him curiously.

Julian studied him back, the two men engaging in a weird sort of staring contest.

"You're nothing like I expected," Asher finally admitted.

Same, I thought.

"That's only because we share a friend." Julian's attention shifted to the friend in question. "You'll tell him what I do to those who share my business, yes?"

"Yep," Bryant confirmed.

"Brilliant." Julian started toward the door, only to pause

and glance back at Asher. "Let's have dinner tomorrow. I think Adalyn would like my Bria."

With that, he disappeared out the door, leaving me alone with Asher.

I finished my water and set the empty bottle on the table while Asher watched. Then I pushed up off the chair to balance on my heels. They were the standard stilettos I usually wore in situations involving the men of Sin Cave, but despite the added height, he still had several inches on me.

"You're giving up a lot for me," I told him. "You're allowing Sin Cave access to your island. You're tying yourself to me and to my family. You're literally marrying into the organization. And my father is going to want to profit from all of this. Are you sure this is what you want?"

"No," he answered, making me flinch. But then he grasped my cheeks and pulled me closer to him. "However, I'm sure *you* are what I want. Everything else... it's just details, Adalyn. If marrying you is what gives us the freedom to be together, then it's worth it. And as for your father, I have some ideas there that may benefit both of us."

"Ideas?" I repeated.

He nodded. "Perhaps that new branch of Rose Royale could be managed by us, meaning you and me. Would you like that?"

I gaped at him. "You'd like me to work for you?"

"No, darling. I would ask you to work *with* me. As a partner."

"What? Why?"

"Because that's what healthy couples do, Adalyn." He pressed his lips to mine. "And I want to be healthy. I want to make you happy. I want to live this journey with you and enjoy every moment. So if expanding and managing more isles suits your interests, then it suits mine."

"My father will never allow it," I whispered.

"Your father won't have a choice," he countered. "You told me his agreement with the Huntingtons was for Taylor to take over as CEO. Well, if I strike a similar deal, then it'll be my company to manage. Or at least the branch we create will be mine to own, as I won't allow your father any say in those operations."

"They chose Taylor because they could manage him," I told him.

"Yes, and Sin Cave chose me... because they *can't* manage me," Asher returned. "Your father and I will come to terms, I'll add financial incentive to his empire, and in return, he'll give us freedom to exist." His forehead met mine. "I'll be the one managing your father in this situation, not the other way around."

I would warn him not to underestimate my father, but I suspected he already knew.

And it would be my father who would underestimate Asher.

"Then we'll marry," I whispered.

"Are you all right with that?" Asher asked, pulling back to study my expression. "It can be in name only, if you want it to be. I'll never take away your freedom, Adalyn. I've told you that it's your choice to decide who touches you."

I believed him. If I asked for a name-only marriage, he'd do it, then give me the freedom to choose.

But I didn't want a name-only marriage.

Because I'd already chosen who I desired. I already knew who I wanted to touch me every day for the rest of my life.

Asher Sinner.

My Sir.

“I choose you,” I promised him. “I choose this. I choose us.”

“Are you sure?” he asked. “Because I would understand if you need time—”

I leaned up on my toes to kiss him, tired of talking. Tired of today. Tired of the meetings and the planning and everything else.

I just... I just wanted to exist. To be with him. To chase away everything else.

“Take me back to your villa, Sir,” I said against his mouth. “I need you to remind me that I’m yours.”

And I needed to show him that I meant this, that I wanted to be his.

“Please, Sir,” I whispered. “Please let me choose us.”

CHAPTER THIRTY-SEVEN

ASHER

ADALYN KNELT before me in my bedroom, her silky white gown leaving nothing to the imagination. She'd been wearing that damn thing all day, yet somehow it felt like I was seeing her for the first time.

Perhaps because of the changing circumstances.

And her words.

"Please let me choose us."

That request swirled through my thoughts the whole drive back to my villa and chased me up the stairs to my room.

And it echoed now as she knelt on the rug beside my bed.

I hadn't told her to do that. She'd immediately fallen into the submissive pose with her palms on her thighs and her head slightly bowed while her posture remained mostly erect.

So regal and perfect.

My beautiful Adalyn.

My intended bride. Fuck, that thought should not be

making me hard. The circumstances were so wrong. And yet nothing in my life had ever felt so damn right.

Fate had put this beautiful goddess on my island for me to claim, something I intended to do fully now.

We'd played a little this week between our planning sessions. However, we hadn't played like this. Everything until this moment had been exploratory in nature as I'd tried to learn her limits. We still had a long way to go, which was fine because we now had time. Plenty of it. A lifetime of it.

Because she's going to be fully mine.

As my wife.

Electricity sizzled down my spine as I removed my tie. Adalyn had worn my jacket the whole way home, my need to cover her up dictating her attire.

But now she was exposed and on her knees for me.

She'd removed the thong beneath—also on my command—allowing me a full view of her beautiful outfit. While I didn't agree with this being the only thing she ever wore, I could see the appeal of keeping her in clothes like this.

Perhaps I would make it a rule for the bedroom.

"What's your safeword, Adalyn?" I asked as I stepped up behind her.

"Dreams, Sir." Her voice held a breathy quality to it that went straight to my groin. Because it confirmed that she wanted this as badly as I did.

Mmm, I bet her thighs are soaked...

"Are you wet for me, sweetheart?" I asked her, an idea coming to my mind.

"Yes, Mr. Sinner."

"Prove it," I said as I lowered my hand over her shoulder

and opened it for her. "Take my tie and run it between your legs. Make it nice and wet for me and I'll reward you."

She shivered visibly as she replied with her usual phrase of consent. Then she took the silk from my fingers and drew it down her body before running it up her thigh beneath her translucent gown.

A soft moan slid from her lips as she did as she was told, rubbing my tie between her legs and saturating it with her arousal.

I rolled the sleeves of my dress shirt while she worked, and unfastened the two buttons near my neck, as I suddenly felt a bit suffocated by the fabric.

Then I started unbuckling my belt.

There were toys in here that I could use, but I preferred playing with Adalyn in this manner. It would help us ease into our future, and we could escalate from there.

Besides, she'd experienced enough toys for a lifetime.

What she needed now was my touch.

My tongue.

My hands.

My teeth.

Every part of me to erase every memory she possessed and chase all the nightmares from her mind.

"Let me see how wet you've made my tie, sweetheart," I said.

Adalyn trembled violently as she removed the silk from between her thighs. And her hand continued to shake when she lifted the fabric up for my review.

I leaned down to inhale her sweet scent. My tongue traced a decadent line along her fabric-covered palm, causing my abdomen to tighten with need. "Such a good girl," I praised. "So wet for me."

"Always, Sir," she said, her nipples beading beautifully beneath the fabric.

"Lick that tie clean for me, darling," I told her. "I want it spotless when you're done. And if you do it right, I'll let you suck my cock for dessert."

She immediately brought my tie to her mouth, eager to obey.

Because Adalyn Rose loved *tasting* me—that was her word. She considered it a reward, and fuck if I was going to complain about that.

But to be fair, I enjoyed tasting her just as much.

"Stroke your clit for me with your other hand," I told her. "I want that little nub swollen by the time I lick it."

She visibly quivered again, then groaned as she complied.

"You're close already, aren't you?" I said, still standing behind her. But I moved close enough for her to feel the heat of my thighs against her back. I still wore my pants and socks, my shoes and tie the only items I'd removed since walking into this room.

However, I knew she could feel my need radiating off my skin like a hot beacon of lust.

Because I could sense hers as well.

I didn't touch her, just continued to stand close enough for her to feel me. She couldn't see me this way either, something I intended to exploit as soon as I had my tie back.

She groaned as she confirmed being close to climax.

"Don't stop stroking your clit," I told her. "I want it so swollen that you feel ready to explode from just one flick of my tongue. Understood?"

"Yes, Sir," she breathed, arching a little as she fought to obey my command.

"And don't you dare come," I added.

She whimpered but gave another consenting response before continuing to lick my tie. When she finally finished, she lifted it for my review.

"Very good, sweetheart," I told her, pleased with her work. "Now close your eyes for me, Adalyn."

Goose bumps pebbled down her arms at my request, her hand stilling between her thighs.

"You know your safeword," I reminded her. "Do you want to use it?"

"No," she whispered. "No, Sir, I don't."

I shifted so I could see her profile and watched as she closed her eyes.

We would be pushing a bit of a limit by doing this. I knew part of what grounded her was knowing it was me touching her. But I wanted her to know it was me regardless of whether or not she could see me. I wanted her to memorize the feel of my skin on hers and never once question who caressed her.

"Good girl, Adalyn." I slid the damp silk around her eyes and slowly brought the fabric to the back of her head to tie it against her hair. "Keep stroking your clit for me."

She trembled again, but this time it was more of an aroused tremble than a fearful one. She just needed to move past the initial moment to realize it was me behind her, tying this makeshift blindfold around her head. I ran my knuckles down her neck when I finished, admiring her pretty flush.

"You're beautiful," I told her. "And this dress is killing me, sweetheart. I'm torn between ripping it off of you and gently removing it so you can wear it again."

That fucker had thought he would be the one taking it off her.

Well, he didn't exist here. Nor would he ever travel here again.

Adalyn Rose was mine.

Forever.

And I wanted to make sure she knew what that meant.

"Thank you, Sir," she replied. "I will gladly wear it again for you. I'll wear whatever you want."

"Mmm," I hummed, loving the sound of her voice while she spoke. So sultry and aroused. "Are you swollen yet?"

"Yes."

"Show me," I told her. "Lift that skirt and spread your pussy for me."

I stepped away from her back to move to her front.

Her lips parted, her senses already heightening, thanks to the blindfold. She swallowed as she followed my command, her thighs widening a little more to ensure I could really see her as she parted her folds with her fingers.

Fuck, but she was perfect.

I wanted to devour every inch of her wet cunt.

But she wasn't quite where I wanted her yet.

"Keep stroking, darling. I want it to hurt." Just a little. Just enough to make her climax so damn hard she lost her sense of reality.

She bit her lip, likely to keep herself from complaining, and went back to stroking herself.

"Pinch it for me." She did. "Harder, sweetheart." I wanted to see her flinch. "*Harder*, Adalyn." She complied and winced so harshly that she released her bottom lip from her teeth, thus allowing a soft cry to escape. "Good girl. Now massage it with your thumb. Yes, just like that. Pretend it's me. Mmm, yes, beautiful. Now don't stop and don't come."

I suspected there were tears in her beautiful eyes.

Which meant she was almost where I wanted her.

"Use your free hand to expose your tits," I told her. "Pull the straps down." She reached up with her trembling fingers to obey. "Yes, like that. Drag them all the way down for me." *Fucking beautiful.* Her nipples were so hard that they caught on the fabric. She jolted at her touch below. "Don't come, Adalyn."

She quivered almost violently in response, clearly trying to hold back her climax.

I didn't give her a reprieve.

I pushed her.

Because I knew she could take it.

More than that, she *liked* it.

As was evidenced by the flush coloring her chest.

"Play with your tit, sweetheart. Pinch that pretty nipple for me and pretend it's my teeth."

I unbuttoned the top of my pants, my cock throbbing at the sight of this stunning woman playing with herself on her knees before me. Her mouth parted as she heard the sound of my zipper, her tongue dampening her lips in obvious invitation.

"Switch to your other breast," I demanded. "Make your nipple hurt and pinch your clit again."

She was practically panting from my words, her body tensing so significantly that I could tell she would come the instant I gave her permission.

But I didn't.

I prolonged her torment as I took off my shirt, the fabric rustling just loud enough for her to hear. Then I kicked off my socks and pants, leaving me more naked than her. But she couldn't see me. She could only hear me. And that was part of the fun.

"Open your mouth for me," I told her. "Wider." She complied. "Now stick out your tongue."

She was vibrating on her knees, her hands working her body even more, thanks to my commands.

I gave myself a stroke, drawing some of my precum to the tip, and moved forward to wipe it along her wet tongue. "Swallow, Adalyn."

She obeyed on a groan. "*Please*, Sir."

"Please what, Adalyn? Do you want more of my cum? Or do you want me to let you come?"

"Both," she whispered.

"Greedy girl," I accused. "No. You have to choose. My cum or your orgasm."

It was a cruel choice.

But I'd give her whichever one she wanted more.

She wanted to choose. So I gave her that option. This was about her, about giving in to her choice of *us*.

"Your cum," she said after a beat. "I want your cum, Sir."

Fuck. "All right, sweetheart. Open your mouth again."

She immediately complied, her tongue sliding out in welcome as well.

My thighs tensed, my lower abdomen pulsating with *need*.

"Don't stop stroking yourself," I told her.

"Y-yes, Sir," she breathed.

"Open," I said again because her reply had caused her mouth to close.

Her lips parted once more as I stepped forward to take a fistful of her hair. Then I fed her my cock one inch at a time, the glorious heat of her mouth a welcome kiss against my skin.

She moaned in response, her hand working herself below as she continued to pulse with desire.

"Take me deep, darling. Relax your throat." I pushed in as far as she would allow, my balls tightening with the need to explode down my shaft. But I worked myself over her tongue instead, delaying my own gratification while giving her ample precum to swallow.

Because fuck, this woman undid me.

And her little hums just made it that much harder to focus.

"Do you want my cum in your throat or in your cunt?" I asked as I pulled out enough for her to answer around my cock.

Even with the blindfold on, I could tell she was trying to maintain eye contact with me.

"Cunt or throat, sweetheart," I repeated when she didn't answer me.

"Cunt," she mouthed around me.

"Is that because you want to be allowed to come?" I asked. "Because I'm not ready for you to come yet."

She shuddered. "Th-throat," she decided, changing her mind.

"Good choice," I told her, because she would have struggled not to come if I fucked her.

Her throat contracted around me as she sucked me deep, her palm leaving her tit to cup my balls. I didn't reprimand her for it, instead allowing her that move of control.

And watched as she devoured my shaft like a starving woman.

"Jesus, Adalyn," I breathed. "You suck my cock better than I knew was even fucking possible."

My words seemed to embolden her, and she added a

tongue swirl to the motion that nearly made my knees buckle.

"Fuck, stop teasing me and make me come. Right fucking now," I demanded, using my grasp in her hair to drive her on.

She skimmed the underside of my dick with her teeth, that little hint of violence shoving me right to the edge.

Then she swallowed around my head, causing me to go off like a fucking firework.

I practically exploded down her throat, my orgasm so intense I lost my sight for a few blinks. My body *burned*.

And Adalyn... my darling, sweet girl... just kept swallowing.

Each time her throat worked, I swore I came just a little more.

She didn't gag or falter, taking every drop and continuing to suck long after I finished.

Fucking perfect, I thought for the thousandth time. "God, I'm so glad you're mine," I said with a shudder. "I'm never going to share you. That mouth is mine. And your cunt is mine, too. As is your ass."

Fuck, I needed to take her everywhere. *Claim* her entirely.

And from the eager way she continued sucking me off, I could tell she wanted that, too.

I pulled out of her mouth and bent to pick her up. Then I threw her onto the bed and ripped the gauzy fabric off of her. I'd buy her a new one.

I suddenly had the need to dominate every inch of her, my cock already jumping at the notion of fucking her.

"You make me feel young," I told her. "Like I could come for hours on end." And I probably could. But I wanted her to scream first.

I didn't give her a moment to settle on the mattress. I went straight for her clit with my teeth and nibbled the swollen nub until she was crying out for mercy. My tongue followed, refusing to give her an inch.

"Sir!" she screamed. "Please! Please, Asher. Oh *God...*"

"No, Adalyn," I told her, thrusting two fingers inside her and loving how fucking wet she was. I drew my fingers back toward her ass, using the dampness to insert a digit and judge her reaction to the sensation. She arched beneath me in clear approval.

"I... I... I need..." she panted, her body burning so hot I could tell she was on the brink of losing her mind.

I inserted a second finger, then pressed my thumb against her pussy entrance, and fucked her with my fingers and thumb, driving her that much closer to the edge while my teeth skimmed her sensitive flesh.

"*Sir.*"

I smiled. "Yes?"

"*Please...*"

"Hmm," I hummed, purposely vibrating her clit and knowing she was right on the edge of sobbing. "Okay, Adalyn. Come for me." I sealed my mouth around her, and all it took was one brush of my tongue for her to tumble over into an oblivion that had her entire body shaking as she screamed loud enough for the entire island to hear.

A sick part of me hoped it reached Taylor's ears.

Because *mine.*

I removed her fucking gown, not you, Huntington.

And now I was going to claim her ass.

I inserted a third finger while she was still lost to her orgasm, my mouth sending her over into a second climax that had her crying out my name even louder than before.

Hmm, maybe I want her cunt instead, I thought, enjoying how her sheath tightened around my thumb.

"I'm going to fuck you," I told her. "No condom." Because we'd had the conversation about birth control and diseases. I wanted her bare. "Tell me if you want me to take your pussy or your ass. Or both."

I could start in her pussy and end in her ass. But I needed her to choose.

Because that was the point of our session.

Choice.

"Both," she said on a pant, her beautiful body pink, aroused, and sweating.

So damn stunning.

"I need you on your knees," I told her. "Can you handle that?"

"Yes," she hissed, her palms meeting the mattress as she tried to start rolling.

"So eager," I mused, moving to allow her the flexibility to shift.

She went to her hands and knees, her body shaking with the effort.

"Fuck me," she demanded, making me chuckle.

"Was that a command, little one?" I taunted.

"Please fuck me, Sir," she immediately amended.

I went to my knees behind her and leaned over her to kiss her shoulder blade. "Good girl," I whispered against her damp skin.

Then I grabbed her hips and thrust into her pussy without warning.

She cried out in response, her walls clamping down around me as residual pulses of her orgasm massaged my cock.

Jesus Christ, I was not going to last long. But I needed

her to come one more time. I reached around her to stroke her between her thighs while my opposite hand remained on her hip, allowing me to set a rhythm.

"Tell me who is fucking you, Adalyn," I demanded.

"My Sir."

"And who is your Sir?"

"Asher Sinner," she replied automatically.

"And what else is he going to be?" I asked her.

"My... my Master."

"No." I stopped fucking her. "What else will I be to you?"

"My..." She trailed off and pressed back against me, trying to make me resume my pace.

I pinched her clit in response.

"Whose cock is inside you, sweetheart?"

"My Sir's cock, Mr. Sinner."

"And who is your Sir?" I repeated.

"Asher Sinner."

"What is he to you? What title?" I kissed her shoulder blade. "What are we, sweetheart? What did you choose?"

I wanted her to say this, to remember it, to *know* it.

"We're us. For always," she whispered.

"Why for always?"

"Because you're mine and I'm yours."

"And what are we going to do to make sure everyone knows that, Adalyn?"

"We're going to... to marry each other," she said softly, her body vibrating beneath mine. "You're... my future husband."

"Yes, sweet girl, I am," I replied, kissing her shoulder again and then the back of her neck. "So tell me again whose cock is inside you."

"My Sir's cock," she repeated. "The cock of my future husband."

"*Fuck,*" I breathed, alarmed by how much that statement turned me on. I slammed into her, my body needing to stake a claim, to make her mine, to ensure she understood that I wanted this just as much as she did.

I.

Choose.

You.

Too.

I told her with each thrust, my fingers playing with her swollen flesh, pinching and massaging and taking her to the point of no return.

But just as she was about to come, I pulled out of her and moved my cock to her ass.

She froze, right on the cusp of orgasm, and waited for me to work myself into her from behind. I didn't want to hurt her, so I went slower, which delayed her pleasure and heightened mine as a result.

"More," she begged. "*More.*"

"Shh," I hushed her. "You'll take what I give you as I give it to you."

"Yes, Sir," she whispered, sounding pained. "Future husband, Sir."

My hips shot forward at her words, making my jaw clench. *Brat.* She'd done that on purpose.

But I couldn't even be mad.

Nor could I punish her for it.

Not when she felt so fucking good around my shaft.

"Breathe for me," I said, pulling almost all the way out before driving back into her. "Good girl, Adalyn. Such a good girl for me."

Minus pushing me over the edge.

But damn if I could fault her for it.

"Harder, future husband, Sir."

I smacked her lightly on the ass. "Quiet."

"But I want more," she replied. "I want your claim. I want your choice. Please, Sir. Please."

God, she knew how to play this game better than I did.

Because I was a slave to her desires.

She was my sub, and she wanted pleasure from me. That made it my job to deliver.

So I gave her what she wanted. I allowed her that bit of control and fucked her so hard she screamed and clenched down around me.

It felt so damn good.

So fucking divine.

My goddess.

My Adalyn.

My sweet girl.

I wanted to own every inch of her, and I did, just as much as she owned me.

"Come for me," I demanded, my thumb against her clit. It wasn't the hand I'd used to penetrate her ass, but I couldn't focus enough to fuck her with my fingers. I was too lost to the sensations her exquisite form unleashed on mine.

Fortunately, all she needed was a few strokes.

And she went off into another wave of oblivion that yanked me right down with her into the depths of passionate bliss.

Every part of me shook, my legs quaking with the force of my orgasm as I emptied myself into her ass, claiming her thoroughly.

In an hour, I would do this again in her pussy.

Then I'd fuck her mouth.

Then I'd repeat this dance until our wedding day.

Because I wanted her so full of my claim that she couldn't even consider choosing a path other than the aisle that led to that fucking altar.

"Mine," I said, collapsing onto the bed and pulling her into my side. "You're mine for always, Adalyn Rose."

"And you're mine, too, Asher Sinner," she replied, her voice groggy with the need to sleep.

I'd hold her for a few minutes.

Afterward, I'd invite her into the bath. I'd take care of her. I'd show her again what a Dom should do.

Then I'd spend every day for the rest of our lives repeating these motions until she no longer remembered anyone or anything else before us.

She would be my island's goddess.

And I would be her faithful servant.

Worshipping her. Loving her. Cherishing her. And respecting her.

The way a man should be with a woman.

Especially one as beautiful and unique and as strong as my darling Adalyn Rose.

EPILOGUE: ASHER

"So. When are you going to tell our siblings that you had an impromptu wedding that you didn't invite any of them to?" Kane asked as I approached him on the beach.

"You mean you haven't sent out a group text yet?"

He snorted and took a swig of his beer. "I'm not Darby."

I grinned and tapped my bottle against his. "Cheers to that."

"Cheers to you," he countered. "A married man. And here I thought I came to Fiji to shoot some shit."

"I wouldn't say that too loudly, or my security detail may label you as a threat," Julian said, joining us.

Kane flashed him a look. "They already know I'm a threat."

Julian smirked. "Maybe."

"I'd still like to know how you knew he was here," I said conversationally.

"There are many secrets I'll never share, Sinner. That's one of them," Julian replied, a glass of blood-red wine in his hand. Because of course that was his alcohol of choice.

I glanced over to see my bride smiling at something Bria

had just said, the two women huddled together in a way that suggested they were sharing secrets.

"I'm not sure I like them being friends," I murmured, my eyes narrowing. I meant it as a joke. But I also didn't. Bria and Adalyn were going to cause trouble together. *Two bratty subs.*

Well.

At least I would have fun later.

Julian followed my gaze. "That's too bad, *mentee*. Because I plan to visit often. And Bria has already said that she'll be joining me when we return. While I enjoy declining some of her requests, that's not one I'll be saying no to."

Mentee was his new nickname for me since he was supposedly my Sin Cave mentor. Whatever the fuck that meant.

I'd handled all the negotiations with Albert regarding our family merger. All I had to do was pay him a percentage of the profit from our new brand of Sinner-Rose Isles, and he would leave all the management to me.

Adalyn had already said she would like to help.

So we would be co-leading that enterprise and paying her father a measly five percent to fuck right off.

When I'd shared the deal with Julian, he'd nodded in approval.

And that was the extent of his mentoring.

Yet now he claimed he would be returning.

As Adalyn grinned again, I decided that wouldn't be the end of the world. I rather liked her smile.

Her happiness had grown exponentially over the last week, only faltering slightly this morning when her father had walked her down the aisle.

But the moment he'd handed her to me, she'd beamed.

And she'd been smiling ever since.

I watched as the setting sun played over her dark waves. She'd tucked a Fijian hibiscus behind her ear, reminding me of our first stroll to breakfast. God, that felt like a year ago. But it'd really only been a few weeks.

Amazing how time moved in situations such as this.

Bryant approached Adalyn, saying something that had her tilting her head back on a laugh. Then her daring dark eyes slid over to mine, suggesting that whatever he'd said was about me.

And she liked it.

Hmm. I set my beer down. "You two have fun. I have a wife to woo."

"I'm going to tell Tru you said that," Kane called after me.

I waved him off, not caring at all.

He could tell all my siblings about this wedding. They'd probably demand another reception, and that was fine. This had been for me and Adalyn, to secure our futures together. Everything else failed to matter.

I prowled toward her and grabbed her by the hips to pull her away from Bria and Bryant. She giggled, clearly a bit tipsy from her champagne. I took her flute and placed it on a nearby table, then twirled her onto the sandy floor.

We'd decided on an outdoor reception.

Her parents hadn't bothered to attend, satisfied with the vows and signed paperwork from earlier. There'd been a photographer as well so that photos could be shared with the media when we were ready to announce our elopement. It seemed I'd stolen Taylor's plans of having a whirlwind affair that ended in matrimonial bliss.

The only difference was that Adalyn and I had actually found happiness together.

Something she proved as she smiled up at me now as though I were the brightest star in her universe. "You look beautiful in this dress, Mrs. Sinner," I told her. "I look forward to removing it later."

She smiled. "I have another gown to wear for you tonight," she informed me. "You'll be removing that instead."

I arched a brow. "Oh?"

She nodded. "Trust me."

"I do," I told her.

She giggled again. "We already said that today."

"Yes, because we're married now."

Her eyes widened, and then she laughed again.

"How much champagne have you had?"

"Too much," she admitted, hiccuping. "But I don't think that's why I feel so light right now."

"Oh? And what's making you feel *light* right now, Mrs. Sinner?"

She glanced around as though ensuring no one else could hear her. Then she very softly said, "My husband."

My lips curled. "Are you trying to seduce me, *wife*?"

She considered it for a moment and started to nod. "Yes. I think I will always be trying to seduce you."

"Was that part of the vows?"

She shrugged. "They were part of my mental vows."

"And what else do your versions of the vows say?" I asked, amused.

"I, Adalyn Rose, promise to always seduce Asher Sinner. Because I really like sucking his cock. And I'm hoping he'll let me do that on our wedding night and for all nights going forward."

I laughed outright even while growing hard for my devious little sub. "You want to hear my vow?"

She nodded eagerly, clearly in a playful mood. It lightened my heart to see her like this. I hoped this part of her would remain. I knew there would be dark days, but they would be worth it to experience the light.

I cleared my throat as I considered her. "I, Asher Sinner, promise to always care for Adalyn Rose. To erase all her nightmares. To always cherish her. And to ensure, that one day, she realizes that dreams do exist. Because we're living one. Right now. Forever and always."

Her eyes rounded, all signs of her laughter fleeing behind a mask of emotion. "Oh, Asher..."

I pressed my lips to hers. "I meant every word, Adalyn."

She swallowed, her hands going to my face as my palms secured her waist. She studied me for a long moment before saying, "I'm going to need a new safeword."

I arched a brow. "Are you?"

She nodded. "Because you're right. This is a dream. And it's one I want to keep living."

"Yeah?"

"Yeah," she whispered. "Now take me home and make me your wife."

"You're already my wife," I said against her mouth.

"Then fuck me, husband."

I grinned. "You'll have to tell me your new safeword first."

"Nightmare," she said. "Because those don't exist anymore. Not when I'm with you."

I threaded my fingers through her hair and tugged her away just enough to stare down into her beautiful eyes. "Nightmare," I repeated.

"Nightmare," she echoed.

I nodded. "I will endeavor to ensure you never say that word again."

"Unless you ask for my safeword."

"Only then," I said.

She smiled. "Only then. And I changed my mind."

I arched a brow. "About what?"

"Where I want you to fuck me."

"I'm listening."

She pulled away from me, her expression one that suggested we were about to play a game. "I want to fuck in the ocean."

"It's almost night, Adalyn."

"Then you'd better catch me quickly," she said with a giggle and took off down the beach with her white dress floating in the wind around her.

Running barefoot in the sand.

Like an enchantment in the moonlight.

Just like a goddess.

My goddess.

My forever.

My wife.

THE END

Thank you for reading!

S. Firecox is the SINful pseudonym for a USA Today and International Bestselling Erotica Author. She publishes secretly under this name and fully embraces her dark side with Sin Cave Publications.

https://www.sincaveromancebooks.com/

ALSO BY S. FIRECOX

Standalone Dark Romance

Colorful Temptations - An Older Brother's Best Friend Romance

Isle of Sin - Dark Romantic Suspense

Scarlet Mark - Dark Romantic Suspense

To Have & To Deceive: An Arranged Marriage Romance

Romantic/Erotic Shorts:

Always Second Best: An Arranged Marriage Novella

The Possession: : Captive Romance/Multiple Partners

Made in United States
Troutdale, OR
05/19/2024